Praise for *Copperhead*

"This is an outstanding exploration of the interplay between beauty, power, and female freedom. Connolly's a master at engaging with the theme that any power gained by physical beauty is neutralized by how easily it can be exploited. Jane's sister, Helen, is an unlikely yet deeply likable heroine whose struggle to overcome feelings of self-doubt and weakness will endear her to readers. No longer bound by the constraints of reformulating the gothic classic, Connolly expands her world of fey, dwarvven, and (sometimes monstrous) humans n a truly rich and satisfying way."

—*RT Book Reviews* (4½ stars)

loving from the gothic to the political, this feminist urban ntasy (sequel to 2012's *Jane Eyre* pastiche *Ironskin*) shifts he war with the fey from countryside to cityscape. . . . Conolly is more inventive than in her previous book. . . . More ccessful than the citywide threat are the domestic dilemas and a romantic triangle with Helen at its apex."

—*Publishers Weekly*

dom have I seen such elegant world-building. An amazg, exciting, imaginative, and empowering story."

—*Smart Bitches, Trashy Books*

gothic mystery that weaves fey menace into the glittering ade of high society. The alternate world Tina Connolly has created grows even more haunting and fascinating with this second installment. I can't wait to read more."

—Leah Cypess, author of *Mistwood*

Praise for *Ironskin*

"[An] entertaining and thought-provoking debut novel. . . . Connolly's novel masterfully illuminates our fascination with these bygone times, setting the story in a time and place reminiscent of early twentieth-century Britain—a time of great technological and social change."

—*Portland Monthly*

"Jane is ferocious and splendid; the hero is tormented and tragic. Tina Connolly has crafted a steampunk Beauty and the Beast tale, beautifully and cleverly reversed. Don't miss this debut."

—Ann Aguirre, national bestselling author of *Enclave*

"The plot owes much to Charlotte Bronte's *Jane Eyre,* along with a number of fairy tales (notably 'Bluebeard' and 'Beauty and the Beast'); more novel is the unusual world, where humans had come to depend on fey magics for power and technology and now must return to science for answers. An intriguing, often involving combination . . . a very promising first novel."

—*Locus*

"A lyrical, beautifully crafted debut. I was particularly taken with the beautifully conceived strangeness of Connolly's fey-touched, just-a-shade-away alternate magical England. A haunting exploration of the true price one must pay for magic, beauty, and love, *Ironskin* will stay with me for a long time to come."

—M. K. Hobson, author of *The Native Star*

"This is an astonishing book: an evocative re-imagination of *Jane Eyre* that concerns itself with beauty, love, and social upheaval. Jane Eliot is an unforgettable protagonist, and the setting is strange and familiar at the same time. Connolly's fey creatures manage to be both ethereal and menacing. This lyrical and utterly marvelous debut is one of the standout books of the year."

—*RT Book Reviews* (4½ stars, Top Pick!)

"Clever and romantic at the same time—no mean feat. A magical and entertaining waltz across the fairy forests and dark moors just a sideways step or two from Haworth Parsonage."

—Ian R. MacLeod, author of *Wake Up and Dream*

"Connolly has created a complex and well-drawn world here, and the story is indeed an original and imaginative take on the gothic-fiction tradition. An intriguing and ambitious fantasy tale."

—*Kirkus Reviews*

TOR BOOKS BY TINA CONNOLLY

Ironskin

Copperhead

*Silverblind**

*forthcoming

Copperhead

TINA CONNOLLY

A Tom Doherty Associates Book
New York

This is a work of fiction. All of the characters, organizations, and events portrayed in this novel are either products of the author's imagination or are used fictitiously.

COPPERHEAD

A Tor Book
Published by Tom Doherty Associates, LLC
175 Fifth Avenue
New York, NY 10010

www.tor-forge.com

The Library of Congress has cataloged the hardcover edition as follows:

Connolly, Tina.
Copperhead / Tina Connolly.—1st ed.
p. cm.
ISBN 978-0-7653-3060-4 (hardcover)
ISBN 978-1-4299-9305-0 (e-book)
1. Fantasy fiction. I. Title.
PS3603.O5473C66 2013
813'.6—dc23

2013018471

ISBN 978-0-7653-3062-8 (trade paperback)

Tor books may be purchased for educational, business, or promotional use. For information on bulk purchases, please contact Macmillan Corporate and Premium Sales Department at 1-800-221-7945, extension 5442, or write specialmarkets@macmillan.com.

First Edition: October 2013
First Trade Paperback Edition: September 2014

Printed in the United States of America

0 9 8 7 6 5 4 3 2 1

For the grandparents—

especially my grandmother

Chapter 1

A HOUSE OF HYDRA

The door was grey, ash and soot and smog grey, the grey of a city choked on its own failure. The full iron mask, padded though it was, was ice-cold in the frigid November night. Helen slipped one lilac-gloved finger under the chin of the mask and angled it so she could better see out of the eyeholes. Yes. Even here at the Grimsbys', the stoop and sidewalk and bushes were blanketed with misty shreds of blue.

The fey.

Bits of the fey.

With one hand Helen found her sister Jane, standing just behind her. With the other she reached for the copper door-knocker, then stopped as her fingers closed on the rapping bit—the coiled tail of a seven-headed copperhead hydra. The emblem of the Copperhead Society was spreading faster and faster these days, almost as fast as the blue bits of fey that lay quiescent throughout the city.

But Mr. Grimsby was the leader of Copperhead. It was his house, his meeting. And her husband, Alistair, would want to take the lead.

Helen's fingers fell away and she stood there in the frosty

air, ice crystals on her breath and Jane's cold fingers squeezed in the grip of her gloved hand. Two patient women. Protected. Waiting. Helen turned to Jane and with frost in her breath mouthed, "Soon."

Jane nodded. Unlike Helen, her face was bare—and yet not, for she had thin iron strips embedded in her skin that outlined her perfect, inhuman features. The strips ringed her eyes, followed the curve of her cheekbone, ran along her jawline—an eerie but not ugly effect, especially when contrasted with the perfection of her face. Those iron strips, Helen's iron mask—all to protect the two women from the deadly fey. Jane's green eyes glittered in the cold and Helen suddenly thought of all she could do, *would* do, to help the vulnerable women like herself, to help Jane. Helen would redeem herself yet.

"Hurry, hurry, girls," said a refined voice behind them. Alistair Huntingdon squeezed between the two sisters to bang imperiously on the doorknocker. "This is the most dangerous part of the trip, Helen. You must hurry inside."

I have my iron mask on, Helen thought rebelliously, but all she said was, "Of course, darling."

Alistair pointed one yellow-gloved finger at a patch of blue coiled on the front lawn, a handsbreadth from the iron railing that would be poison to it. "I say, is that one moving? I swear I saw it move."

Helen's nerves twitched as he pointed, but she willed herself to stay calm. The blue bits of fey coated the city these days, covered everything not iron. She had even seen a motorcar with blue mist clinging to its rubber tires. But the bits of fey were mostly silent, mostly still.

Mostly.

Luckily the door was opened then by a man who looked more brawn than butler, who muttered through the ritual "An' ye be human, enter," and then with a hefty white-gloved hand brought them forcefully over the iron threshold and inside.

The air was warm. It would be close before the night was out, Helen thought, stuck in that room full of hot tempers and single-minded men. Or was it that her nerves were busy jangling, now that they were here, now that she needed to convince Jane of what they were to do tonight . . . and under whose noses?

A homely maid took their wraps. With relief, Helen reached to unbuckle her iron mask, but her husband stopped her. "Could be dangerous."

"Security seems tight enough," said Helen. "Besides, do you really think this house—of all houses—isn't fully iron-barred at each door, every window? The fey can't cross that without invitation. Jane and I will be safe."

"I would trust Grimsby with my life," said Alistair immediately.

"Good," said Helen, reaching again for the buckles.

"But not yours. Consider, my pet. Remember that a fey almost took you over before. No, I'm not risking that again."

"Seems like if you paid for this face you ought to let people see it," said Helen, or rather, she didn't say it as she knew it would be just one teensy remark too far. No point in letting her wretched tongue ruin all of her evening's plans over the urge to get a dig in, especially when his face was already going white around the nostrils. She pulled back into delightful, chattering Helen, and said, "I understand you're looking out for me, Alistair dear! Very sensible of you and of course I shall obey. It did occur to me though—one teensy little thought—if I were to go unmasked, then I would be the most beautiful woman in the room. All the other women with fey faces like mine will be too afraid to go unmasked. But I could be so charming that I win everyone over—to your cause, of course. For your goals."

A covetous spark leapt to Alistair's eye. "Perhaps there is merit in what you say. As you say, Grimsby's house is surely the safest in town. He hates the blue scum even more than I do, if possible."

"Excellent," said Helen, and unbuckled her mask and handed it to the homely maid before her husband could rescind his permission. "Now, Jane, if you're finished, let's go to the powder room and smooth our hair after those mussing buckles, shall we?" She flashed her brilliant smile around the room.

Helen took Jane's arm and whisked them away into a small powder room. Helen had been to the Grimsbys' once before, in the short halcyon time between marrying Alistair Huntingdon seven months ago but before the blue fey appeared in the city, and Copperhead rose up along with it. Well, those days hadn't been entirely perfect, but they seemed so now. This house had been hung with tiny yellow lights—the new electricity coming into vogue. Before the Great War, relations had been amicable, if distant, with the rarely seen fey, and a steady trade of fey technology had kept humans supplied with clean energy—"bluepacks" that ran all the lights and cars and trolleys. But eight years ago the fey attacked. The Great War started between the two races, and trade stopped, leaving humans bereft of all their borrowed technology. Humans had struggled to pull society back from collapse, while fighting the forest-dwelling fey—an enemy of blue mist that could emulate humans—or worse, animate their dead bodies. The war dragged on for nearly four years, then abruptly the fey disappeared. Slowly people dared hope they were gone for good—slowly hope and laughter and silk stockings returned to the city. That dance seven months ago had been lovely and perfect, one of those few evenings when Helen had felt as though she fit in with her new, rarefied society. She had worn a slinky green velvet dress and coppery T-strap shoes, her red-gold hair all over curls. And she had been pretty. Plain pretty, not inhumanly perfect . . .

Helen came back to reality with a sigh and turned away from the mirror. "Now, Jane," she said. "Tell me who you need to meet tonight. The most important candidate is Millicent Grimsby, but so many women of The Hundred will be here with their husbands. You should be able to meet a fair number of them." Her tongue beat with the urge to say what Jane needed to do with Millicent, but she held it. Millicent's safety was riding on her. She could not tip their hand too soon, even to Jane. The less Jane knew till the last second, the less she could give away in a glance, a look, a misplaced word at the end of a sentence. Oh, when she thought of that horrible Mr. Grimsby . . . Helen told her racing heartbeat to still, but her heart never obeyed her.

Jane looked at her sister from under level black brows. "Does he always order you around like that?"

Helen blinked and with an effort brought her worries and plans back to the present, ran through the past few moments since disembarking from the motorcar and entering the Grimsbys'. She smiled, ordering it to reach her eyes. "Now, Jane, don't you concern yourself with darling Alistair." She turned back to the mirror for something to do, smoothed copper-blond curls around her inhumanly perfect face. "All of The Hundred of us are in danger. Isn't it good that he's concerned?"

"Well," said Jane.

"Besides, you saw how well I handled him. Everything is *tout à fait*."

"You did, and I'm impressed," said Jane. "You always were good at smoothing ruffled feathers. But about Alistair—"

Helen whirled back. "Tell me whom you need to meet," she cut in, because she could see Jane was gearing up for another of her dreary arguments about feminine inequality, and when stubborn Jane met stubborn Helen, the battle could last all night. Jane did not understand about necessary compromises. "Do you have a list of The Hundred or something?"

"I do," said Jane. "But I don't think that will be necessary."

She pointed over Helen's shoulder, and Helen turned and looked into the large room. Heartache throbbed, remembering it as she had last seen it, the ballroom, the music, dancing so light on her toes in time, in time, in time. . . .

Focus, Helen. It is a bare sober room now, with dark dresses and long hard benches. No rumbas, no foxtrots, and if the occasional sharp laugh escapes into the close air it is because these women will not be completely contained by fear. Focus, Helen—until she saw what Jane meant.

At least half of the seated women were wearing iron masks.

"All right then," said Helen.

"That's a third of them right there," breathed Jane. The two sisters stood, looking at the cold iron masks dotting the room.

Over the last several years, a hundred of the richest

women—and a few men—had secretly had their faces worked on by one Edward Rochart, an enigmatic artist who was now Jane's fiancé. Every woman had come back a dazzling version of herself—and in most cases the changes were even deniable, put down to a "restorative holiday" in the countryside.

But the idyll had turned sour—Jane had discovered six months ago that the "fey beauty" of The Hundred was exactly that. They had each had their old face replaced by a mask—a mask made of the dangerous fey themselves.

And anyone who had fey attached to their bodies was at risk of being taken over by the fey. That was the secret to how the fey had animated dead bodies during the war—they had killed humans with bombs that coated the victim with their own fey substance—little bits of themselves. Then they could move in. But dead bodies only lasted so long. The Fey Queen had figured out how to use Rochart to get these women to coat themselves in fey voluntarily—an unwitting accomplice to a plan to take over the city from the inside, fey slipping into highly placed women and erasing their personalities completely.

It had even happened to Helen. Only Jane's quick application of an iron spike into her arm had killed the fey and saved her. Helen shuddered, remembering the moment. The whole fey slipping into Helen through the bit of fey on her face, crackling through her thoughts, erasing. Telling Helen things would be so much better if she simply didn't exist, and Helen, feeling that that might be true . . .

"I just don't understand why I'm getting so much resistance," said Jane. Jane was on a mission to make each of The Hundred safer by returning their original human faces to them. But she was not making as much headway as she had hoped.

"Because once you have been the most beautiful woman in the room, it's impossible to give up," Helen said.

"It's pathetic to be so focused on appearance," said Jane sharply. Jane's face had been scarred for so long due to fey shrapnel from the Great War that she came at this from a different angle, Helen thought. Jane had just wanted to be normal. But everyone else had always been normal. And now they had a chance to be extraordinary.

"It's not pathetic at all," Helen said softly. "Just think about the power you hold. You have always been just another face. And now everyone turns to you, asks your opinion. Those men who run your lives—suddenly they will do anything for you, if you favor them with a look. There is a touch of fey glamour at your command, yes, but more, there is just the fact that suddenly everyone thinks you are somebody. You are *worth* something."

"And that's enough to set against cold hard facts?" said Jane. "The cold hard fact that if you go outside without your iron mask, a fey could take you over and you'd be gone like that?" She snapped her fingers.

"What cold hard facts?" returned Helen. "How many people were in that ballroom when it happened to me? Only a handful of people saw it actually happen—and look, here I am, right as rain and twice as sparkling. It's much easier to pretend that the danger isn't as real as you say it is. Especially when their option is their old face back." She took a breath before the slightly pointed jab, but she needed Jane to see how much she was in need of Helen's help. "Besides, you probably wave their old face around in front of them when you try to convince them. Hard to be thrilled by the idea when you're looking at your nasty old face, stretched and hideous from drying on the wall."

"Give me some credit," said Jane.

Helen raised her eyebrows.

"Well. Maybe once," said Jane. "But I've learned since then. And I've learned how to reverse the sags and stretch marks during the facelift procedure."

"But they'll never be beautiful again," said Helen.

"No," Jane admitted. "There is that."

It was almost time to tell Jane her plan. The first part of her plan. But how would Jane take it? Jane was so self-sufficient, and she was not used to thinking of her younger sister as helpful.

"So tell me which one is Millicent Grimsby," Jane said. "I can't tell one masked woman from the next."

Despite the worry in the air, Helen laughed, and pulled her sister out into the crowd of dark suits and gowns. You still saw women around town in the popular sherbet hues, but tonight they were in darker colors: navy, black. Yet the women had not sacrificed any more than color. Gowns were still bias-cut and clingy. Sheer stockings, still dear due to the factory problems since the Great War, clung sleekly to every calf. Heels were high, adorned with jeweled pins and rounded toes. Hair was curled or waved—earlier in the year it had been longer, but you were seeing bobs more and more, perhaps as a minor rebellion against the tension in the city, the curfews, the iron masks. Helen herself was in deep plum silk charmeuse—she looked washed-out in black—the jacket ornamented with large pearl buttons.

Men were less interesting, sartorially speaking, but tended

to be quite conservative still. Suits had become spare and close-fitting at the start of the Great War, and they still looked the same. Women would find ways to rebel against conservative dress, Helen thought, but men seemed fine to continue on indefinitely. Really, the only item of fashion for men that had changed in the last six months was the introduction of those copper lapel pins in the shape of a writhing hydra.

Copperhead.

Helen studied the dresses, the figures, and the hair before saying, "She's over there, by the fireplace." She did not know Millicent terribly well—Helen's marriage seven months ago had been followed a month later by the advent of the fey to the city, and the men of Alistair's set had grown more and more cautious in letting their women leave their houses. But Helen would recognize those mousy shoulders anywhere, that tilt and droop of the small figure. With her perfect face hidden behind iron, there was no fey glamour to offset her timidly curved form. Millicent always seemed to be making herself smaller.

"So, this Millicent," said Jane, as Helen pointed her out. "What did you want to tell me about her? You seem bursting with some news. I brought her face as you asked, but you just told me *not* to 'wave it around in front of her as I try to convince her.'" She eyed her younger sister. "I don't suppose you're finally going to let me do *you,* are you?"

"Not yet," said Helen, and she lit up inside, for now was the moment. "Because I need every ounce of fey charisma I can get. I have a plan, a great grand plan." A breath. "I'm going to help you."

Jane looked dubious. "Even with the bit of fey in your face, you wouldn't be able to do the facelifts right away. I barely have the ability to wield the fey power to do it, and that's after months of practice."

"No no no," said Helen. "I'm going to help you talk The Hundred into it."

Jane looked nonplussed. "Thank you for your offer, but I don't see how your presence will help. I'm the one with the experience with the facelifts and the history with the fey. Surely if I tell them the facts, they'll understand that it has to be done."

Helen raised her eyebrows at Jane. "Really?" she said. "How long have you been working at this task? Half a year?"

"Off and on," said Jane. "But I've been studying to do the facelifts, too. It hasn't been all talking to the women."

"And you've managed to convince how many of The Hundred?"

"Well. Six," said Jane.

Helen squeezed her sister's arm. "So don't be a goose, silly. This is exactly where I come in. Look, I might not be perfectly tactful always—"

Jane raised her eyebrows at this.

"—but your idea of tact is to force out the words 'in my opinion' as you tell someone exactly what you think of them."

"So what's part two of this grand plan?" Jane said dryly to this tactless comment.

"I've already talked to Millicent," Helen said, and the words she had told herself to keep in tumbled all out. Her face lit up, glowing with the joy of the surprise of it, with the good she was going to accomplish for Millicent, for Jane. "She's all ready for you. She wants you to replace her face. Tonight."

Jane turned a shocked face on Helen and shoved her

younger sister into the nearest alcove to whisper furiously at her. "Tonight? It's not a haircut, Helen. It's a serious operation. It's not something I can just do, just like that."

"You can," insisted Helen, heart rat-a-tat. "But you have to do it secretly, upstairs, while everyone is downstairs. It's her only chance." Jane couldn't say that she was wrong, that she was foolish. This was *new* Helen, determined to make things come out right. "You have all your supplies, don't you?" Helen pointed at the carpetbag that Jane carried everywhere.

"I suppose," said Jane. "But—"

"But nothing; you're just nervous, now that I've done it so quickly and gotten everything ready to go." The words tumbled headlong from her lips. The mad rush, the intrigue, the heady thrill of brink-of-success: it all made her feel so alive.

"True, but I have justification for nerves," said Jane. "It's a dangerous operation at the best of times. To do it with no warning, on a tight timeframe, no room for error?" She shook her head. "You just don't understand."

Helen felt the familiar pressure against her skull in response to people telling her she was wrong, that she didn't understand, that she *couldn't do something.* The pounding in her head thudded as her will rose up, flattening everything before her like the sound of a bell spreading across town. "No, *you* don't," she said, and it was with tremendous effort that she kept her voice low, whispering the words right into Jane's ear. "Mr. Grimsby won't let her go anywhere. Won't let her leave the house. Says it's unsafe—though with the iron mask it's perfectly safe—well, at least as safe as it is for anybody. She's a *prisoner,* Jane. And she wants this done—but he won't let her. Says he doesn't trust you. Something about *dwarvven* connections and rabid women's lib ideals."

That lit a spark in Jane's green eyes, as Helen had known it would. It was simple truth, but Helen knew how to deploy incendiary truth.

"Well," said Jane. "Well." She rocked back on her heels. "I will talk to her. Tell her about the procedure. My goal is to help them all, obviously. But tonight, with no warning? Perhaps she will be sensible and let us pick a day next week—do it with more preparation."

Millicent wouldn't, Helen was sure. Poor Millicent Grimsby had begged and begged for an outing, and finally Grimsby had brought her, iron-masked and heavily guarded, to a Copperhead meeting of the men at Helen and Alistair's house. Safely ensconced in Helen's bedroom, Millicent had poured her heart out and Helen's own heart had burst in response.

It was up to Helen to save her, and it had to be tonight. Jane would just have to understand.

Helen showed Jane how to slip around to the back stairs and wind her way to the garret. After a suitable interval, she caught Millicent's eye and gave her the nod. The small woman in the iron mask did not nod, did not move. But Helen knew she knew.

It was quite dark outside now. The room pressed together, quieting and erupting by turns as people found seats or decided to stand. The room was packed, for which Helen was immensely grateful. She found a spot that seemed perfect for sneaking away.

Men—leaders—came into the room in a clump. They had been off somewhere with Grimsby. Her husband, Alistair, was among the gang of men. They spilled into the room like a pack of hunting dogs, jostling each other as they moved to the front. Before Grimsby stirred them into a passion over

Copperhead, they had spent all their time drinking and gaming. When they moved, when they tumbled and rolled, she saw the puppy dog in them still. Helen was glad she did not have her mask on, obscuring her vision. The electricity was at half the brightness it had been for that dance in the spring. It was dim yellow, unlike the familiar blue light of her childhood. Before the Great War.

The men straightened as they drew closer to the front and the strange sheet-covered lump in the middle of the room. They no longer reminded her of anything tame, but something fiercer, colder, and they stood straight around each other as if they were one pack surveying their quarry. Everything drew still as their presence filled the room, all eyes turned to the front. Helen searched around, checking for her escape route, and in doing so caught a tiny flicker of movement by the window—a lithe man in closely fitted black leaned on the windowsill as if he had always been standing there. But what then would have drawn her attention?

Boarham and Morse—Grimsby's two particular right-hand men—moved to flank the machine. Morse was stoop-shouldered and pinch-faced, the meanest of them all. Boarham was heavy, lumpy, toadying. "We will begin," said Boarham, "by updating you on the preparations that have been made as we remain under siege by the fey. Later in the evening will be the event you are most anxious for: Grimsby will reveal his new weapon that—we hope—will eventually annihilate the fey for good."

Breath caught at the word, at the hope. *Annihilate.*

"We move ever closer to our goal," Boarham said. "*One People. One Race.*" All around her, fingers flicked out to touch their hydra lapel pins in solidarity. "But first a moment to remember James Morrow, who since our last meeting was a casualty of the fey blight, when the blue carpeting his front garden turned out not to be powerless bits of many different fey, but one whole fey, lurking in wait with a concealed fey bomb. . . ."

Now.

It was not Helen's style to move quietly. She moved by chatter and misdirection. But for this moment she needed to slink, and she did, moving like a bit of sunlight falling noiselessly through canopy leaves.

Her blood pounded as she climbed the garret stairs, slipped through the door.

The garret was irregular and pocked with gables. A cluster of candelabra lit the area with the most headroom; the rest of the garret fell away into dark piles of unwanted things as it sloped to the black wooden floor. It smelled of mildewing wood; of the sour poison of mothballs; of beeswax. Millicent lay in the center of the light, a small dark figure on a daybed draped with a white sheet. Jane worked efficiently around her, setting out her tools on a heavy scarred chest. No matter what nerves Jane had professed, as always, her sister seemed as cold as ice.

It was going to be done. Her plan would work. Helen wanted to clap her hands and burst into speech, tell the two women a million things, but she restrained herself, moving noiselessly over to the white daybed, still like falling sun.

Helen remembered the day Mr. Rochart had worked on her—the small white room, the deep sleep as he etched around the skin of her face to replace it. She had had such peculiar dreams. Strange to think that her sister had learned to carry out the same fey-powered operation.

Millicent had been staring out the slanted skylight at the fog that obscured the stars, but now she turned her face to see Helen, and pressed her hand. "It will be all right," she said softly. "I have told your sister everything. She will help."

"Excellent," said Helen, wondering what "everything" was.

Jane turned from her preparations. "You did a good thing by setting this up," she told Helen.

Helen warmed at the praise. She felt almost holy in that moment, filled with *doing things right.*

"We're going to get her out of here tonight. And then deal with you-know-who." Jane and Millicent exchanged a significant glance.

"Good," said Helen. "Wait, what?"

"Millicent has to get away from this house for good," said Jane. "As soon as I make her safe from the fey."

Helen did not like Mr. Grimsby one bit—the Copperhead leader seemed the coldest of any of Alistair's friends—and heaven knows none of them were worth much; but still, she was shocked. "Leave her husband?"

A small tap on the door, and before the women could react, it opened and a little boy sidled around the splintering doorframe, a jar clutched in his hand.

"Oh dear, Tam," said Millicent Grimsby, and she sat up and hurried to the small figure at the door. She bent down so he could whisper in her ear, his hand clenched on her dark skirts. In the flicker of candlelight, the contents of the other jar appeared to be moving.

"I'm sorry," Millicent said, standing up again. "Tam is supposed to be asleep, but he saw Miss Eliot from the staircase and wanted to ask her about her iron. He's really a sweet child—I'm so sorry, I know it's quite inappropriate, but you have no idea how stubborn he gets."

"I can imagine something of it," said Jane with a rueful smile, and she knelt by the boy, one flickering taper in hand. "My face has iron in it," she said. "Do you want to touch it?"

Tam put his free hand to Jane's face, considering. "What does it do?" he said.

Helen saw Jane search for an explanation, not because she was flustered—Jane was much better with small children than Helen was—but because it was complicated to explain. Jane had been an "ironskin," one of those hit with fey shrapnel during the war who wore iron to cover the grotesque, poisonous scars. Rochart had made her a new, fey-perfect face to replace her disfigurement. Now Jane had thin iron strips set right on top of the fey skin in her face to keep the fey from taking her over. At least Helen could remove her iron mask when she was indoors, but poor Jane would never look normal again.

"The iron helps keep me safe from the fey," Jane said at last. "Like the iron strips around your door and windows."

Tam looked up at Mrs. Grimsby, puzzled.

"This house was built post-war," Millicent said to the boy. "It's too new to have iron. Your father is working on the problem, but with the fey suddenly everywhere, iron's gone short again."

Helen saw Jane roll her eyes at that and she hastened to intervene before Jane could go off on one of her rants about how the city folk didn't have any sense, building without iron in the first place. "I just realized that's a bug jar," said Helen to the small boy. "Are you collecting bugs?"

"For my snake," he said. "I found a little garden snake. He's green."

Helen shuddered in delight. "And you collect live bugs for him? My goodness."

Tam offered her a shy smile, possibly uncertain whether she was teasing him. "Do you want to feed him one?"

"Not now, Tam." Millicent Grimsby shook her perfect face and Helen saw again how very young she was, younger than Helen herself, who was barely eighteen and a half. (Though she felt she had aged a lifetime in the last six months; it was a mercy her fey face didn't show eye bags and wrinkles or she was sure she would have them.)

"After we visit with your mother," promised Helen.

"Tam is not mine," Millicent Grimsby said quietly in response. "His mother died in a motorcar accident, poor thing. I'm the second Mrs. Grimsby, you see. Married last winter. My mother thought he was such a catch. . . ." Her voice trailed off, lost, and Helen overflowed with sympathy again. What kind of mother would tell this poor girl to accept frightening, fanatic Mr. Grimsby, wealthy though he might be?

"Can I stay and play with the birdcages?" said Tam.

"Oh, sweetheart," said Millicent. She led the boy to the door and whispered something in his ear. He nodded and squeezed her fingers before plodding back down the staircase. Millicent Grimsby stared after the small disappearing form, her fingers knotted together. She wheeled and turned on Jane, her mousy form straightening, filling with iron. "You need to make them all safe, Jane," said Millicent. She moved into the light. "Make them listen to you."

Jane pressed Millicent's small hands. "That's where Helen comes in," she said. "She's going to help win all of The Hundred over to our cause. And soon."

Warmth flooded a tight knot in her chest. Jane did want

her to help. Jane trusted her. Jane saw that Helen was worth something. And deeper, inside—*don't screw up this time.*

Millicent turned her big brown eyes on Helen, and even Helen, with her own fey charm, felt the fey allure. "I'm so glad you're on our side," Millicent said. "You know what it's really like to be attacked by the fey. You can be a real leader of the cause."

Jane was the real leader, thank goodness, but Helen was not about to rile up Millicent before the dangerous surgery. "Of course I will," she said easily. "But did you say you're going to run away?" She could see it now, little Millicent and her small frightened boy, in flight, on the run. A dangerous mission, fleeing through the cold winter winds . . .

"Not *run* away," said Jane. "She is her own person and Mr. Grimsby does not own her. We are leaving for her own good."

Helen waved semantics aside. "And it *must* be tonight," she added, seizing onto the new plan. "Mr. Grimsby won't let Millicent have her iron mask, so she can't leave on her own. She needs your help."

Jane nodded. "I must make her safe and then we need to go, now, while we still can. We'll take Tam with us. You will go downstairs and pretend not to know a thing."

"I am excellent at that," said Helen. She turned back and said, "Wait, though. What's this about convincing The Hundred *soon*? These things take time, you know."

Millicent and Jane exchanged a significant glance as Millicent got back into position on the daybed. "There's movement afoot," Jane said. "Things are about to come to a head."

"Things?"

Jane whispered over Millicent's body. "The fey, Helen. The fey are rising again. Some follower of the dead Fey Queen, we think, has riled up the fey—is planning to infiltrate the city just as the Fey Queen had planned, by taking over the women. We can't allow this opening for a foothold. We need every one of The Hundred safe as soon as possible." Jane looked at Millicent for confirmation, who nodded. Jane stretched out a hand and laid it on Helen's, a reverse of when Helen used to comfort her during times of ironskin stress. "But the walls have ears . . . and we must hurry to get Millicent and her son out of here. Come to my flat tonight after the meeting and I'll tell you the rest. You promise?"

Helen was not at all sure how her plan to give Millicent back her face had snowballed into Helen going down to the wharf to find Jane's flat in the frostbitten November night, but she nodded to quick skip over the part where people wanted her to promise things. Promises were such cold, hard-hearted, rigid things.

Millicent Grimsby lay down. Then she sat up, took Helen's hands, and squeezed them. "You won't let him find out you helped me escape, will you?"

"Who, Mr. Huntingdon?" said Helen, startled by the woman's concern. "Don't worry about me. I'll be fine."

Millicent set her lips and nodded.

"Now just relax," said Helen.

Millicent Grimsby lay back down, closing her eyes. Her thin hands clenched the sheets, the knuckles white.

Jane carefully took some of the precious fey-infused clay from the water bag inside the carpetbag and smeared a thin layer on her hands, adding to the power she could control. Jane placed one hand on Millicent's forehead and one hand on her heart, till the woman's eyes fluttered, and finally stopped. Her breathing and heartbeat slowed.

Then she was as still as marble.

"One hundred of them," Helen said softly.

"And you're key to this," said Jane. "You have one purpose for the next week. Convince every last one of them. Be single-minded. I'll do the rest."

Helen swallowed. "But what if—?"

"No buts," said Jane. "I've got my own plans that have to happen. Scalpel, please, and then you'd better go. You'll need an alibi—isn't that what the detectives call it?"

Helen wiped the scalpel with carbolic disinfectant and passed the handle to Jane. In her fey trance, the woman seemed like a lifeless doll, as if there had never been a mind activating that beautiful, silent face.

The crowd downstairs was on recess as Grimsby and stoop-shouldered Morse fiddled with the machine under the sheet. It might be a meeting, but it was still society. The earthy smell of liver pâté trickled by as more of the homely maids passed canapés and drinks. What was this fashion for unpleasant-faced girls? thought Helen. But she supposed it was Grimsby's grim fanaticism again. Fey had always been drawn to beauty in humans—the faces that The Hundred wore were fey-beautiful. The ugliness of the serving girls was proof. No fey here. Grimsby himself was perhaps the perfect Copperhead leader in that regard. He had a hard, unfriendly look, and his features were too sharp and jutting to be at all pleasant.

No fey here.

Nervous energy coursed through her as she wended her way through the crowd, smiling and nodding. As she had told Alistair, going without the mask made her the prettiest woman there, and it was obvious in the way heads turned to track her passage. Normally she would have basked in the attention—the pleasure of it hadn't completely worn off, when among these people who hadn't been quick to welcome her after her marriage. But tonight she did not want attention. Tonight her heart beat a steady thrum at what her sister was doing upstairs.

Helen was determined to help Jane. She remembered full well the moment of fey takeover. Only Jane's quick action plunging an iron spike into Helen's arm had killed the fey inside her, saved her life. Helen had roused from her fey trance a day later to find a team of the best doctors in the city hovering over her bed, waiting for any movement.

But were things really as dire as Jane had said just now? Why the sudden haste? The earliest of The Hundred had received their fey faces several years ago. They were all being very careful these days, going out with their iron masks. But all the blue bits of fey did was sit there—well, mostly. Still, surely they weren't gearing up for some takeover of The Hundred like Jane said, like Alistair and Copperhead thought. Frankly, it would be ridiculous. What no one seemed to remember was that the Fey Queen's plan had been to have fey *secretly* infiltrate those women and men and land themselves in influential positions, ready to take over from the inside. You couldn't secretly infiltrate if everyone knew you were coming, could you?

And Helen was determined to help Jane, to convince the women Jane couldn't. But quickly? She thought through some of the women she knew off the top of her head—the self-absorbed wife of the prime minister, there in grey. (She had not sacrificed her apricot-hued shoes, though.) Stubborn Alice Pennyfeather. Close-minded Lady Dalrymple. All transformed from their workaday selves into ethereally beautiful women, and their social status similarly elevated. Even with the iron masks, The Hundred ran the social scene. No, as much as Helen liked a good intrigue, even she was sensible enough to know that she would need more time than a few days.

The men straightened up, the crowd herded back to their seats. They squashed onto the long benches, stood in the makeshift aisles, ranged long legs along the windowsill. There was silence, and in it Grimsby said quietly, "This is what you have come to see."

The cloth was whisked away to reveal a strange device. The center was a large copper ball, full of ridges and rivets. It looked like claws clasping each other, or perhaps snakes that writhed over the copper ball. It was held firmly in an open cube of iron, crisscrossed with wrought iron that curlicued in a curious pattern. In the front of the box was a child-sized door.

"In this box," said Grimsby, "I have trapped a fey."

Murmurs, tremors. Men who would shout if it weren't improper.

With a great creaking and grinding, the copper ball slowly opened its interlocking layers. Inside hovered a blue ball of light. When the copper was completely opened, the light burst out of the ball and flung itself at the open door of the iron box.

The guests shrieked and ducked.

But the blue light did not seem to be able to pass beyond the threshold. It thudded to a stop right at the boundary of the open door. Then it launched itself at the side wall, coming to a stop a hairsbreadth from the wrought iron. Back, forth, up and down, till it was spinning around and around the cage with savage ferocity.

"There, you see?" said Alistair. "Completely trapped."

"And well-deserved," shouted someone from a bench, someone who had had too much wine.

"It's beautiful," whispered Helen, so quietly that no one could hear her. No one must, or could have, and yet next to her was a slight man in black, and he gave one short sharp nod, not looking at her. But that could be about anything.

Her fingers twisted her handkerchief as if to tear it. How far along were Jane and Millicent? So long to carefully take off the current face, so long to press down the old face and bind it in place, so long to return Millicent from that still-as-death sleep. Helen's fingers wanted to burst out of her hands, fly like birds to check on the women, flutter at Mr. Grimsby, claw his eyes out for being so hateful to poor Millicent. . . .

"I captured this fey by using one piece of a fey as a seed," said Grimsby. "The machine finds all the other pieces of that particular fey and draws them in, restoring the whole fey to itself." He grinned cruelly. "Ironically enough, it runs on fey power."

"And then that fey you captured can be destroyed forever," put in Alistair, his face sharp and blue in the glow. "Show them, Grimsby."

A hint of malice crept across Grimsby's face at Alistair's words. Now he bent his tall bony frame to the machine. If he had made it, why didn't he make it to measure, thought Helen, for Grimsby seemed like some kind of strange praying mantis folded around too-small prey.

A switch—a thrum as the machine turned on. The blue light keened with pain. It mutated wildly, turning itself into all manner of things—a frog, a tree, a sparrow. A face, shining out of the light—low gasps as it formed the face of a small child, tears running down its face. "Help me," it said, and the words thrummed inside Helen's skull. She felt a tremendous compulsion to run over and let that child free—and by the looks of it, many of the others felt that, too.

The thrumming grew louder. The face splintered and reformed, struggling to keep its shape. "He's caught me, he's caught me. Help—"

A small boom like an implosion, and it was gone.

Grimsby turned off the machine and straightened up with a smile. "No mess, no fuss," he said. "We have never been able to destroy a fey before, unless it was trapped in a human. But this? Very tidy. One People. One Race."

Silence in the room as men and women grappled with what they had just seen. Helen felt as if she would be violently ill. She twisted her fingers together, focused on that sliver of pain to distract her.

Finally a female voice said, "Forgive the impertinence, but how do you get the piece of fey into the machine to begin with? Who bells the cat?"

Helen looked, but she could not see who had spoken. Grimsby smiled, as if this question was on cue, as if he had waited for just this opportunity. Helen did not like that smile. She put a hand to her seat, starting to turn, wondering if she could slip away. But one of the homely maids was standing there, Helen's iron mask in her hands.

"When I turn on the general setting it pulls in the first piece of fey it can find," Grimsby said. "A dangerous setting, you can see, to have fey come rushing at you." A calm, meaningful voice. "More dangerous still for those who have fey lurking in their skin. I need every endangered woman to be thoroughly shielded, please." Heads swiveled as he nodded at Helen.

With shaky fingers Helen buckled her mask in place. She needed to get upstairs to warn Jane. But the maid was there and all eyes upon her.

"Windows open," Grimsby said, and Helen saw that Millicent was right, that there was no iron bolted into the wooden frames. The cold November air rushed in. Grimsby folded himself around his device again, long fingers sliding over the copper curves till they found the heavy lever. He pulled it down.

The masked women gasped and Helen knew they felt it, too.

A strange, almost hypnotic pull, tickling around the edges of the iron mask. Eerie, but faint, a fingernail-on-chalkboard sensation that she did not like but could withstand. She wondered how strong the compulsion would be without the iron mask. Would it suck the bit of fey right out of her face, or would it make Helen herself get up and throw herself inside that machine?

"Nothing's happening," grumbled one of the men, and several iron-masked faces turned his way, staring.

"Increasing power," said Grimsby.

He cranked the copper wheel, and suddenly there was blue in the small room, blue out in the middle of the benches. In the middle of the guests—right through the guests, who screamed. A masked woman fainted, and several men stood, angry and red-faced.

"The piece of fey is resisting," said Grimsby, eyes gleaming. "It must be a bigger piece than I expected. More massed intelligence. It's attempting to form a shape." His eyes narrowed. "Except . . ."

Except this figure had a familiar face.

This figure held a scalpel.

"Jane," said Helen, and it did not seem to matter how loud the room was, she was heard. The name carried around the room in waves as Helen pushed her way to the space that had formed in the center of the room.

It was a wavy blue picture of Jane, Jane who had been bending over a still form on a white bed. But Jane wore iron, Helen thought—and then she saw that the blue light was most sharply focused on her hands, the hands that she had smeared with the fey-infused clay.

Jane looked up and through Helen. Her eyes were glassy with concentration, filmed over with white fatigue. Her mouth seemed to be shouting something Helen could not hear. Millicent's fey mask was off, the face underneath red and horrifying. Helen could not look away, even though it felt as though she was being sucked back a great distance. The blue air whirled around her, and her ears popped as the pressure in her head grew tighter and tighter, and Jane seemed to be farther and farther away.

"Jane!" Helen shouted. "Jane!"

Jane looked directly at her then. Her dark hair was wild and blowing about her head. The attic furniture loomed behind her like a crouching beast. Jane held Millicent's old face in her hands, clutching it in front of her.

<<Impressive>> Helen heard, and it seemed to be a voice in her head alone, or not even a voice, but the memory of a voice, a thought of one. <<Not what we expected, is it?>>

Now Jane was straight, the scalpel was gone. She was arching, shrieking. The strips of iron on her face glowed, brighter than the rest of the blue that made up the strange picture of her. Voices screamed. Jane turned and Helen thought Jane was facing her, thought Jane saw her. Jane's lips faintly moved and Helen read, "Stop it . . . stop it . . . stop it. . . ." Jane seemed to bend in the direction of the copper machine. Stooping, still shouting, "Stop it, stop it."

Behind the copper ball Grimsby's face was backlit from the blue glow, and she could not tell if it was cruelty or fear she read there.

"Turn it off, turn it off," Helen yelled at Alistair, but he shouted back, "Do you want the fey to be freed? I'm not going near it!"

Helen was not conscious of thought in that moment, but if she had stopped to examine the impulse that made her feet pick up and run forward, not away, it would have been something like: If it destroys me, it destroys me—but it will not hurt Jane.

There were those whose lives were worth something. Those who were trying to do good. Those who were determined as all hell to set things right in the world, and didn't waste their days spouting off nonsense about "one race" or the cut of their hemline.

Those people needed to be around to save the rest of them from themselves.

Helen threw herself onto the lever and shoved it down with all her might.

And then everything went dark.

Chapter 2

THE IRONSKIN

The pressure slowly faded out and vanished, and then the room was the plain dark of a burned-out light. A hundred burned-out lights—all the electricity had winked out, and now the guests milled frantically about, crashing into one another, voices piling on top of the next, fluttering for explanations. Shouts rang out; orders coldly given by Grimsby: "Round the women up. Make them safe." *Don't let them leave.*

Helen felt her way toward the wall, tugging her iron mask off so she could not be detected by some man feeling it and attempting to make her safe. She had to get up the stairs and make sure Jane was all right. But the crowd was frantic and just as Helen's fingers touched solid wall a heavy man crashed into her and she thudded to the ground. She felt as if she would have enjoyed a good panic right about then, but instead she kept her head down and reached once more for the wall. This time someone tripped over her, catching their sharp-toed shoe in her belly.

As she rolled away from that she lost the wall, and ended up trying to stand in the melee and protect her head from more high heels. She was jostled and bumped and then suddenly there was a hand on her shoulder, guiding her back to safety. Alistair.

She clung to the hand and gasped out, "Help me," as the man in blackness steered her along the wall and toward the hall that led to the back stairs to the garret. She found the stairwell railing with one hand and pressed her husband's with the other.

But the hand did not have a ring. It was not her husband's hand. It disentangled itself, and the man it belonged to said in her ear, "Trust none of them," pressed something small into her hand, and was gone. From the other room came commotion still, and blinks of light as the servant girls brought in oil lamps.

Helen held on to the railing and went up the stairs.

It was pitch-black, but her hand found the worn door at the top and opened it, and there was a faint bit of light from the fog-shrouded moonlight. Enough to see that what was in her hand looked like an old-fashioned flashlight, the sort that ran on the mini-bluepacks of fey technology and had not been seen since. But when she slid the button it came on with the yellow of the modern electric lights, not fey blue.

She might have wondered more about it, but her thoughts were filled with Jane, Jane, Jane, and she ran the flashlight around the slanted room, fast at first, then slower and slower as the sweeps revealed no Jane, and her shaking nerves told her to fear the worst.

A body lay on the daybed, one arm flung down, white in the moonlight. All the candles were snuffed out. Helen crossed to the daybed. Played her flashlight slowly from feet to head. The woman's face was white and pale.

Millicent.

She wore her beautiful face, as Helen had last seen her, though in the vision just now she thought she had seen Millicent with no face at all. Helen peered closer and saw the red line running around the outline of her face, saw it was slightly crooked, as if it had been hastily shoved back into place so she would not be lying here with no face at all.

But Millicent was not breathing, did not move. She lay in her fine black dress, sunk in the bone-stillness of fey sleep.

And there was no Jane, still there was no Jane. A cold wind swept through the garret and Helen shivered.

Small footstep noise behind her, and Helen whirled. It was Jane, it was the mystery man with the flashlight—no.

It was the small boy. Tam. He blinked in the flashlight's glare. He had a jar with a tiny creature in it and Helen's heart burst into a million pieces.

"Everyone was shouting and it woke up Sam," he said.

"Oh, Tam," said Helen. She hurried over to him, keeping the flashlight away from Millicent and blocking her from his view. "Your stepmamma's . . . resting now. Perhaps you can show her your pet later."

She knelt beside him at the top of the stairs. From below the lanterns had turned back to light—they had got the power working again. She heard the heavy pounding steps of men, moving closer.

Tam wriggled the small jar of bugs out of his pocket. "Do you want to feed Sam now?" he said. He pressed the small jar into Helen's hand as Helen crouched, listening, waiting. She pulled Tam to the side in the garret room as they came up the steps, all those men, thundering up and into the small attic room. Alistair and Hattersley and Morse, and more she did not know, for Copperhead seemed bigger every day. Grimsby was at the head of them and he went straight to Millicent, lantern swinging, a hunting dog to its prey. The yellow light gleamed upward onto his chin, casting cruel black shadows across his face. A white candle fell to the floor.

Helen thought how awful she would feel if that were Jane, if that were Mother, if that were someone she loved so devotedly that her heart would shatter to see them like that, trapped in the fey sleep, all unknowing if they could ever come out. She tried to transfer that sympathy to Mr. Grimsby, but she watched the black shadows curl across his face and could not do it.

"Millicent . . . ," Grimsby said, and then he turned, and his lamplight fell on Helen, holding on to his son. "What do you know about this?"

All the men crowded in, and Alistair turned on her, his face sharp with the surety of her betrayal. Which was not fair, she thought. "I don't know anything," she said, which was at least partly true. She had known that Jane and Millicent were up here. But Jane knew how to do the operation. Helen did not know what had happened to bring them to this disaster, and if anything, she thought it likely to be the men's fault, the fault of that dreadful machine Grimsby called their salvation. "You all saw me downstairs. I thought I heard noises from up here. I came up to try to find Jane." Her arm tightened on Tam, who, surprisingly for a small boy, did not immediately squirm away.

The movement seemed to call attention to the boy. "Come here, son," Grimsby said in a thin, cold voice. Tam obediently wriggled free and crossed the room in silent steps that seemed to shake the floor.

"It is good you are here, Thomas," said Grimsby, looking

down at the boy. Tam seemed very small next to that tall thin man. He was a mannequin, frozen, his fingers tight on his glass jar. "I have very sad news to tell you, so you must be brave."

The constriction inside Helen's chest loosened an inch. Mr. Grimsby would make it okay. He and his son would become closer while they waited and worried about Millicent. He was not as frightening as she had always thought.

"Your stepmother is dead." Grimsby stared down at Tam and Helen saw that little form suppress a flinch. Tam did not speak.

"I say, Grims—," said one of the other men and then was silent.

Helen found her voice. "But she's *not* dead," she said, moving impulsively to Millicent. "She's in the fey sleep. She might wake up." Helen smoothed Millicent's hair, pressed her wrist, willing the pulse to suddenly start.

Mr. Grimsby cut her off. "As good as dead, for what fey would be willing to revive her? Do not count on a children's tale, a sleeping beauty revived. We have to prepare ourselves for the worst." Now he knelt beside his son at last, but apparently only to pick up something he saw on the floor. Helen could not think what it might be, but the movement called her attention to another find—Jane's carpetbag, humped in a bit of shadow by the door.

Grimsby rose, his hand clenched around his prize. "And I know what will be the most important to you, son. Justice. Vengeance. We will make the murderer suffer." Pause. Beat. "And we know who the murderer is." Grimsby pointed at Helen, a tactile placeholder for his accused. "The fiend who did this is Jane Eliot. The ironskin."

Grimsby opened his hand and in the yellow lantern light she saw it.

A tangle of iron strips, the iron that had crisscrossed Jane's perfect, fey-infused face.

The iron that had protected Jane from the fey.

The men looked curiously at Helen. Alistair's face was lit with a wild mixture of worry and glee.

This must be problematic with his social standing, she thought, and it was as if from a long way away, just as she had felt downstairs when Grimsby's machine had been running. He's so pleased to have the news—he's grown to loathe Jane—and yet no one sensible would want an accused murderer in the family.

If you had put a dagger to her throat and said how would Alistair react to something like this . . . well, deep inside she might have predicted it, every word. But she would have told that small voice it was wrong, that Alistair would never rejoice at such a thing. That she would never stand here seeing it now, in the flesh, Alistair—her husband, Alistair—rubbing his hands together and pondering over how Copperhead would trap her sister. The unholy glee at having an excuse to bring Jane down was written from ear to ear.

Helen had thought Alistair handsome when she met him, charming. The fact that he was wealthy was an added inducement—she was grateful for his wealth in a way she dared not remember, even now, without doubling up in shame. She had loved him once; she had been grateful. She had thought he would be kind to her. Was he not kind? She stared at the restless energy burning behind those reddened, soft cheeks, and wondered what she had done wrong to make him into who he was now.

"Well, Helen," said Alistair. "Do you know where your sister might have run to?"

"No . . . no," she said, and the part of her that was social, that carried on despite whatever true Helen felt deep inside, did a pretty little gasp for the men to see. Raised the pitch of her voice and said in a silly way, "Goodness, you don't really think my sister did anything wrong, do you? If anything, it seemed as though that machine did something to *her*."

"The machine did nothing to her except reveal her despicable behavior," said Grimsby. "Meddling in things she didn't understand. Shouldn't be dealing with. If she crossed into those forbidden boundaries, she was as good as working with *them*."

"Jane? No. She hates the fey as much as any of you."

"It's not a question of hating the fey," Grimsby said. His blue eyes were intense; they burned into Helen as if they could see every little thought flicker across her brain. "This is what Copperhead is here for, Mrs. Huntingdon, don't you understand? One People. One Race. Nothing good can come of mixing with the *other,* even with the best intentions. Humans will only be safe once the fey and dwarves are eradicated. Your sister was working with things she could not control, and when the machine revealed her actions to us, she ran." With a sweep of his long arm he pointed to the skylight in the slanted roof, now open—the source of the cold wind Helen had felt moments ago.

Stoop-shouldered Morse crossed to the skylight and looked down. "She could have gotten onto the neighbor's fire escape from here," he said. A twisted smile played across his face. "Unless she fell and broke her legs."

"She was frightened by the disaster she had caused, and she ran," cut in Grimsby.

"I'm sure she meant well," said one of the other men. Hattersley, the drunkest and most good-natured of the bunch.

Grimsby rounded on Hattersley, blue eyes flaming. "You dare say that with my wife right there?" He flicked his fingers in the direction of Millicent, a cold gesture somehow more dramatic than a sweep of arms. "'Meant' doesn't enter into it." Those keen blue eyes bored into Helen as he swiftly crossed the room and seized her shoulders. Suddenly she wondered how she could have ever written this man off as one of Alistair's drunk friends. He was something else, something more. His iron grey hair was close-cropped; it lay flat across a sleek snaky skull. "You must tell us where she is. Where she would have gone."

His eyes were penetrating her, sweeping back and forth. She was hiding in her own mind from him, darting between black bushes while the searchlight of his eyes swept the grounds. He would find her in another minute; everything she knew would come tumbling out. With an effort she gasped again, let a tear or two rise to the surface of her eyes. "Oh, Mr. Grimsby, you're hurting me!" which was in point of fact true, but mostly it gave her a chance to duck her head away from his gaze, blink obscuring tears into place.

"Come, Grimsby, don't manhandle my little one," said Alistair. "She doesn't know anything. You see her face—could someone with a face like that even leave the house? Let alone plot things."

Helen turned her perfect face on the men, tears standing in her eyes. Her fey allure seemed to soften them all, even Grimsby, who dropped her arms and stepped back a pace. "Can we go home now?" she said meekly. "This is all so . . .

so disturbing. That such a thing could happen to poor Millicent. And with Jane involved . . ."

"I must stay," Alistair told her, "but I will have you driven home. I will come later."

"Be safe," Hattersley said kindly, and Helen nodded, picked up the carpetbag ever so casually, and fled down the stairs in careful slow meek steps, heart racing, brain burning clear.

Away from them in the hallways she walked faster and faster, grabbing her coat, her lilac gloves, her iron mask, kicked under a chair by the attic stairs. Her passage was slowed by the glut of couples hurrying home, away from the disastrous meeting. She nodded to them politely, trying to control the energy that burned within. Carefully tied the iron mask in place and told the massive butler to have their driver bring the motorcar around. There would not be any word to report to Alistair that she had done anything wrong.

At last inside the car, she curled her fingers around the door handle and slammed it closed, heart racing.

Jane was gone.

Millicent might die.

And then Grimsby was going to blame Jane for his wife's death.

It was too clear. The men of Copperhead hated Jane already, hated that she was trying to help their wives regain some measure of freedom. The cowards like Morse and Boarham made fun of her when she wasn't there (they were scared to do it to her face). Helen had tried to help Jane; Jane had tried to help Millicent, and now everything was a mess.

Worse, Jane would not have left Millicent in the fey sleep

without a very good reason. Jane was too responsible, too duty-bound to run just because something spooked her. Perhaps Mr. Grimsby's machine had caused her so much pain that she had had to flee. No, Helen did not like that idea. But perhaps the machine had messed up the operation to the point where Jane could not rouse Millicent. And then, the only thing Jane could do was press the old face in place in case Millicent *did* wake up, and run before the men caught her and hauled her off for their own brand of questioning.

And in that case, where would Jane have run?

"Mrs. Huntingdon?" the chauffeur said patiently again.

"Yes, please take me home, Adam," Helen said. She found she was sitting in the middle of the backseat in a huddle, and she forced her legs to straighten to the floor. "How's your mother doing? Are her legs still troubling her?"

"It comes and goes," Adam said, "but she said to tell you thanks for the oranges." The car started moving and then abruptly jerked to a halt. Alistair was banging on the rear window.

Helen swallowed and straightened as he pulled open the door and got in, slamming it behind him. "I thought you were staying here," she said, her words muffled and hollow.

"I am. I am!" Alistair waved his hands in frustration. "You don't know what it's like up there."

"With poor Millicent?"

"They're all ranting at me, Helen. What do I do about you?"

"About me?"

"Boarham said if I'd cast Jane out this never would have happened, and Grimsby said I needed to have a tighter grip on you. He said you and Jane are working against us. That you aren't following the party line. But I trust you, Helen."

"I'm glad to hear it," she said.

Alistair looked up at her, indecision written on his face. "I'm going to need your mask."

"What?"

He nodded more firmly, as if trying to convince them both. "I need it, Helen. Grimsby said so, and he's right. You need to be protected. I need to make you safe."

"The mask makes me safe."

"But you love your sister," said Alistair. "I understand that, even if she's not worth it. I do understand."

"Yes? . . ."

"And I know you. You're about to charge off to find her, or rescue her, or some sort of harebrained goose chase. I need to make you safe." He reached up to Helen, and before she could think of any clever way to talk him out of it, before she could jump from the motorcar and run so fast, so fast, he unbuckled the straps and lifted it from her face, leaving her skin exposed to the warmed air of the vehicle.

She blinked at him, and she thought then that perhaps her face would calm him, that he would turn and see how lovely she was, and give in. Maybe smile and call her his pet, like he used to do.

But he thrust his fingers through the eyehole of the mask he held and said, "Yes, this is much better, isn't it? Much better for us both." He patted her silk-skirted leg and then hurried from the car, her iron mask dangling from his canary-gloved fingertips as he hurried back into the house.

Silence passed, and at length Adam said, "Home, miss?"

As if she had a choice.

"Yes," Helen managed, and turned her trembling lips away from his sightline, looked out the window into the icy night.

Adam turned out of the drive. She could feel his worry like a palpable presence. That was the way it was since Rochart replaced her old face with the fey version—she seemed to have a sixth sense of what people wanted, what they felt. Now Adam was trying to help her make things better, help her show a stiff upper lip. "Those oranges cheered my mum right up, I'll tell you."

"Good," said Helen. The gaslights cast strange shadows through the mists of fey. "I'll send over some more."

Her eyes closed against the fey, against the night, thinking about poor Millicent. Without Jane's fey power keeping Millicent protected and under thrall, no one could survive a process like the facelift. How long would Millicent stay in the fey sleep? Jane herself was no fey—her power was not that vast. If Helen did not find Jane soon . . . she was very afraid Millicent would waste away and die, as Mr. Grimsby seemed to want to believe already. Millicent was on death's door because of what Jane had done, but it wasn't Jane's fault, it was that horrid Mr. Grimsby and his machine. How would she make those men believe that?

And what would they do to Jane once they found her? It would be Jane against Copperhead, and Helen didn't give a fig for those chances. She had to find her sister before they did. She closed her eyes, in that moment hating herself for the blithe way she had seen Millicent's escape, for the casual way she had set up Jane to help Millicent. As if it were all a game. "I didn't mean it," she whispered fiercely. "Jane, come home."

"What's that, ma'am?"

"Stop here," she said, before she knew what she was saying.

Adam pulled to the side, looking dubiously at the strip of storefronts lining the wide thoroughfare. "Probably all closed, ma'am." She heard in the cautious sentence all the things he couldn't say, both: *Don't get yourself into trouble,* and, equally, *Don't make me lose my position.*

She seized Jane's carpetbag. "I've got to find my sister," she said. "She's my *family.*"

He nodded slowly, thinking this over.

"Please don't tell my husband when you pick him up," she said. "I'll—I don't know. Take a cab or the trolley or something. If he finds out . . . I'll swear to him I left from home and you know nothing about it."

"Do you have money?"

Of course she didn't. "Oh, Adam, why am I such a wreck?"

"You're not a wreck, ma'am," he said in his stoic way, and handed her some coins from his pocket. "I'd watch out for the trolley, though. Full of malcontent *dwarvven* causing trouble, they say."

"I'll be careful," Helen said, and promised, "I'll pay you back tomorrow morning."

"I know you will, ma'am." He opened the door for her and looked dubiously down at her unprotected face.

No mask. No iron.

She almost flung herself back in the safety of his car. But she had to find Jane. She had to save Millicent.

Adam's grey-black eyebrows knitted. "You're *sure* you'll be fine?"

He couldn't order her to stay home and be safe the way Alistair could. It was as close as he could come to asking if she was certain she wasn't mad. She supposed she was mad.

She pressed his arm and said, "Not a word to Alistair. Not a word!"

He nodded solemnly, and she turned and set off as if she was full of purpose, hurrying off before she could change her mind.

It was pitch dark now, except for the faint glow of the eerie blue mist. Helen strode down the cold empty street, intensely aware of her bare face. She started every time she thought she saw a quiver from the mist.

Where was Jane living now?

Jane had lived with them for a couple months earlier in the year, helping Helen to convalesce from the fey attack. Jane had often taken the train down to the country to see her fiancé, Edward Rochart, and his daughter, Dorie. But as the grey summer continued, the blue bits of fey started appearing—little by little, settling over the city. Alistair's gang turned from horses and dice to secret meetings where they plotted to rid the world of anything inhuman—*dwarvven* and fey.

Helen had not paid it much attention at first, assuming there was more drinking than politicking going on. But Jane did, and Jane was becoming more and more visible, agitating to fix the faces of the beautiful women. Beautiful women who refused to give up their dangerous beauty. Husbands who, though supposedly anti-fey, were not quite as quick to sign off on their wives returning to their old faces. It sometimes reminded Helen of that old fey story about the knight told to choose whether his wife should be beautiful at day and ugly at night, or vice versa. It was clear what these men were choosing.

To be fair, it wasn't just the men. Helen had actually heard that fake masks were popping up at dances around the city. Not at the very best houses, mind you, but down a rung or two. For the price of some iron, you could pretend that you were a dazzling beauty underneath. Tempt some bachelor with the promise of what he might find, safe inside his home, once he carried you over that iron threshold . . .

Oh, Jane would never believe that one. Helen could just imagine her vitriol now. She sighed. Stubborn Jane did not see that you simply had to let these men, men like Alistair and Grimsby, have their own way. There was no arguing with obstinate fools. Not to mention that Jane's temper (never good in the old days) had gotten on edge after her fiancé had gone into the woods with his fey-touched daughter—Helen didn't know exactly why, as Jane called the decision foolish and pigheaded and refused to discuss it. Jane stopped returning to the country, and therefore spent more and more time at Helen and Alistair's house. Which resulted in a violent quarrel between Jane and Alistair that ended with Jane stalking out to find some terrible shack to live in and Alistair threatening to hurl her ironskin self from the door if she came through it again.

Helen realized she was paused on the street corner close to the trolley stop, staring at a shop completely covered in blue. Early on, the city had tried paying poor folks to scrape blue off of walls and streets. But the fey had seemed to organize and retaliate—targeting only the cleaners, until at last the mounting number of deaths had caused the city to abandon that plan. Her fingers clenched around the handles of Jane's carpetbag as she stood there in the biting cold. There had been a bakery there, before. But the bits of fey kept coming and coming, like ivy climbing the walls, choking the windows and doors. The owners had tried everything. Finally they moved out. She thought she had heard they decamped to some relatives in the country—ironic, when all the fey once came from there.

After the owners left, the mists of fey just got worse and worse, till no one would walk up to that shop for love or money. The mist thickened. Bulged.

But she had never realized that it sort of thrummed before.

Or that the tendrils coming off the house came so close to the sidewalk.

Helen's heart jolted, beat a wild rhythm, flooded her body with the command to run.

No, the house had not been like that before.

The mists were moving. Toward her.

The interwoven bits of fey flowed from the store, creeping toward her across the front walk, all of that thick deadly blue coming at her like a slow-building wave.

Helen ran.

She pelted down the street, breath white in the cold, eyes watering from the November wind. The carpetbag beat a lumpy rhythm against her side and still she ran, not looking back, down and around the corner until she got to the trolley station where, wonder of wonders, a trolley was just preparing to depart. She flung herself through the closing doors and it pulled away.

She moved to the window, looked out between the pasted-up notices and garish advertisements to see if she saw a blue wave tearing down the street after them. But she saw nothing more than the familiar thin scarves of blue that dotted the houses and shops and streets.

Her breath fogged the glass and her face came back into focus, white and strained, mouth dark and breathing fast.

Good night, she looked a mess.

Helen sat down in an empty seat with the carpetbag firmly on her knees, still breathing hard, and attempted to smooth her hair. Slowly she adjusted her skirts, straightened the silk jacket of her dress where it had twisted around her waist, felt her heartbeat slow. A weary ticket-taker moved down the aisle, stuck a hand out for her pence without inquiring into her distress.

She had only rarely been on the trolley, and never this late at night before. It had been down for most of the war—all the fey trade had ceased at the beginning of the war, and everyone had quickly run out of those fey bluepacks that used to power everything so cleanly. Tech had come lurching back in a number of different directions at once, as humans tried to make up for the missing energy. The electric trolley had been one of the big civic pushes to get going again—but that did not mean that everyone rode it equally. Men outnumbered women, but a few women did ride it. The working poor, in old-fashioned layers of skirts, headed home to the factory slums from some slightly better position elsewhere. Reformers like Jane, in trim suits or even slacks, working for their pet causes: women's votes or *dwarvven* accessibility or some equally tedious thing. Women in silk dresses, no matter how civic-minded they were, did not ride the trolley. Helen wrapped her dark coat more tightly around the plum silk, as if that would help her blend in.

The passengers were the one thing Helen liked about the trolley. Despite the fact that they made it cramped and smelly, they were also interesting, because people were interesting. She had always liked people—but now with the fey mask her interest in people seemed even more pronounced.

People . . .

Helen realized with a jolt that all the men in the trolley were staring at her, whether openly or surreptitiously.

She had no iron mask.

She suddenly felt naked. The iron mask was not just protection from the fey. It was protection from herself. It was protection from her own fey charm affecting everyone around her. She had gotten used to the mask turning it off, but now it was on in full force.

Now she was vulnerable.

"Do you have the time, miss?" It was a young man, fishing for an opportunity to speak to her. You should never engage any of them, she knew, but she always felt a sort of kinship for the young ones. She knew what it was to *want.*

"I'm sorry, no," said Helen. In the old days it had taken more than a smile to make a man blush, but now with the fey glamour every moment of charisma was magnified, and he went bright red to the ears, though he pretended not to.

"Does she look like she'd carry a watch?" said another man, rougher. "No place to keep it in that getup."

Her coat was hardly revealing, unless he meant her legs. She was not going to inquire what he meant.

With effort she pulled the carpetbag onto her lap and started to go through it for something to do, some way to pointedly ignore the riders around her.

Surely among everything else the ever-alert Jane had some iron in here, something Helen could use to defend herself from fey. She opened the clasp and peered into the bag's dark contents.

The trolley was dim and the inside of the carpetbag grey-black. Helen poked around the rough interior, trying to feel things out without exposing them to the gaze of the other passengers. That tied-up roll of felt, there—those were the tools Jane used for the facelift. Helen did not remember putting them in the bag, but she must have done it in her shock.

In a pocket compartment was a sloshy bag of clay in water. A larger compartment held a rough wooden box, secured in place. She would have to pull it out to discover what was inside. She rummaged around the main compartment, found a scarf and hairpins. A small leather-bound book. Train-ticket stubs.

Apparently not everything in here pertained to Jane's secret work.

At the very bottom Helen found some of that ironcloth that Jane used to help her focus the fey power. Helen had tried it, but so far she had not gotten the hang of it. Jane used the combination of the iron plus the fey to direct the bit of fey she still wore on her face—give her the power to put Millicent into the fey trance, for example. Late one night Jane had confided to Helen that she had actually used the fey power to make someone do her bidding once—but that it had scared her enough that she never intended to do it again.

Perhaps the cloth would substitute for the iron mask that Alistair had taken; perhaps Helen could use it as protection. She pulled the cloth out to examine it, and her hand knocked against a small glass jar. Tam's bugs. She must have put them in the carpetbag as she left the house.

Helen did not particularly like bugs, but her hand closed on the jar and she smiled wistfully, remembering Tam. The poor boy—mother gone, now stepmamma, left alone with that horrible man and his horrible friends. Should she have tried to take him with her? But how could she, when his father was right there? She did not know what you could do for a case like that.

Just then the trolley came to a jerking stop, throwing folks who were standing off balance. A very short elderly woman stumbled near Helen, her bag tumbling to the ground. Helen jumped to retrieve it and helped the woman to sit on the bench next to her, half-listening to the litany of complaints rising from all sides.

"How can I keep my night shift when—"

"Boss makes me punch in—"

"Docked pay—"

"Fey on the tracks," one said knowledgeably, though that didn't seem likely. The blue mist shied away from iron.

"Are you all right?" said Helen. The old woman had not quite let go of her arm, though it was likely she was finding the bench difficult as her feet did not touch the floor.

The woman's fingers tightened and Helen looked up to find the bored ticket-taker staring down at them, his face now purple with indignation.

"Your kind isn't to be here," he spat at the old woman. "Back of the trolley."

Helen looked to the very back of the trolley. She saw a cluster of very short men and women there, bracing themselves against the wall for balance. The trolley straps dangled high over their heads.

The *dwarvven*.

The woman's wrinkled chin jutted out. No one from the back was running to her aid—though the *dwarvven* were said to be stubborn, fighting folk, these men and women looked tired and worn-out. Ready to be home.

"C'mon, dwarf," the ticket-taker said. *Dwarf* had not been a slur once, but it was quickly becoming one under Copperhead's influence. It was the way they said it. The way they refused to attempt the word the *dwarvven* themselves used.

Helen placed her hand on top of the woman's wrinkled one. "This is my grandmother," she said pleasantly to the ticket-taker. Confidentially, leaning forward, "Poor nutrition in her youth, poor thing, combined with a bad case of scoliosis. Oh, I expect by the time I'm her age I'll be no higher than my knees are now." She ran her fingers up her stockings to her knees, pushing aside the plum silk, and gave him a nice view of her legs in their bronze heels. "Can't you just imagine?"

The ticket-taker looked a little glazed by the flow of words and by the legs.

Helen dropped her skirt and said, "Thank you so kindly for checking up on us. I feel so much safer now. We won't take up any more of your time."

With a lurch the trolley started again. Dazed, the ticket-taker stumbled on, and the *dwarvven* woman's fingers relaxed on Helen's arm. She pulled her knitting from her bag and began to focus on the flying needles. But under her breath the woman said softly, "I owe you," to Helen.

Helen patted the woman's arm, watching the wicked points of the needles fly. "Don't be silly, Grandmother."

Helen turned back to Jane's carpetbag, grinning inwardly. She rather thought the *dwarvven* woman would be just fine on her own, now that she had those weapons in her hand again.

But the flash of legs had attracted the attention she'd been trying to avoid.

The boor nudged the young man who had asked about the time. "Ask her to the dance hall with ya. Pretty silky thing like that, even if she is stuck up."

Helen flicked a glance over at the two men, assessing the need to be wary. She had encountered rough characters at the tenpence dance hall back in the day. But she had always had a knack for finding protectors. Their loose, dark button-shirts and slacks said working men—the young man, at least, was well-groomed and nicely buttoned, which spoke better for his intentions. She smiled kindly at the young man and had the satisfaction of watching him scoot away from the drunkard, trying to stay in her good graces.

"Too good for us, she thinks," said the boor. "I could tell her a thing or two about that."

Several seats down she caught an amused expression. A man had carved out a spot for himself on the crowded trolley by crouching lightly on the back of one of the seats, hovering over rougher, sturdier looking fellows. A fresh notice pasted behind him read: YOUR EYES ARE OUR EYES! ALERT THE CONDUCTOR TO SUSPICIOUS PERSONS. His face looked familiar, but she could not think why at first. He had a lean, graceful look, like the dancers she and Alistair had seen at the theatre last spring, before he started spending all his evenings with those terrible friends of his. Helen thought she had seen this man recently, exchanged a smile with him—that was it, wasn't it? He looked like—or was—the man from the meeting tonight, who had perched on the windowsill during the demonstration. Everything prior to the disaster seemed to have vanished from her head. She looked more closely. The man was on the slight side, but all slim muscle and amused mouth. Amused at *her* expense—watching her try to cope with the boor. Helen was perfectly capable of defending herself through wit at a party—but what good would wit do you with a sloshed village idiot like this?

Well, she'd have to say something, or be on edge for the rest of the trip. Helen turned to face the boor, who was still making comments under his breath. Her mind raced through what she could say to tactfully make him stop. *Was* there anything?

"Like the story a sweet Moll Abalone," said the boor, "who thought she was a lady fine, but when she found she could make her way by not being a lady . . . whoo boy! Just think on that, girlie. Oh cockles and mussels alive, alive-o . . ."

The lithe man raised amused eyebrows at Helen and Helen's temper lit like a match touched to dry kindling. She unscrewed the bug jar she held and dumped the entire contents on the drunken boor's head. Bugs and grass rained down around him, and his jaw fell slack in shock.

So did Helen's, for she had not entirely meant to do that. What on earth came over her sometimes? It was as if she had no willpower at all.

The young man opposite laughed delightedly. "You show him, miss," he said. "More than a pretty face, aren't you?" and several others clapped.

Helen's grin faded as quickly as it had come, as the drunken boor lurched from his seat, more quickly than she would have guessed. Crickets fell from his shoulders and suddenly the hot blast of whiskey was in her face, the rough red-pored face close and hot. In his hand was a knife.

Chapter 3

BAREFACED

She had no time to do more than register the danger and suddenly the man was gone, shoved away. The lithe man stood between them, his back to her. He was wearing some sort of dark leather jacket over slim trousers, made from a tough woven material. It was all very close-fitting, and free of loops and pockets and things that would catch. It was an outfit made for getting away from something. "Here now," he said softly, dangerously, and then his voice dropped even lower, and despite the absolute stillness of the fascinated trolley car Helen could not hear what he said into the man's ear. It was something, though, for Helen could see one of the boor's outstretched hands, and it shook, and then he drunkenly backed up a pace, then another, then another, then turned and pushed his way through protesting bodies toward the other end of the trolley.

Despite her relief, she had had experience with rescuers. Rescuing a woman was helpful, kind—but generally also an excuse on the rescuer's part to talk to her. She appreciated his audacity, but that sort of fellow was always harder to tactfully get rid of. Telling them you were married didn't always stop them.

And she worried that this one had followed her. How could they have coincidentally ended up on the same trolley? Was he interested in her, or did he have another, more dangerous motive for turning up twice in her life tonight?

Helen turned back from watching the boor go, pasting a pleasant smile of thanks on her face, ready to parse the man's motives, feel him out.

But he was gone. The folks around her were watching the drunkard leave. The *dwarvven* grandmother had her knitting needles thrust outward, watching the boor leave with a fierce expression on her face. The mysterious man must have taken the opportunity to vanish in the other direction, into the crush of bodies. Helen felt oddly put out.

Attention started to shift back her way, and Helen quickly turned her gaze back to the bag, shutting out the curious stares. Focus, she told herself. Be smart for Jane. She needs you now. There's something in here that will tell you exactly where she lives, more than vaguely *by the wharf.* There must be something in here that will help. The ironcloth, perhaps. Make a veil out of that, like Jane used to wear. That would give you some protection.

No, not you. Focus. What would help *Jane*?

The leather book had a ribbon bookmark in it. Helen opened it to that page and saw a list of names. Then suddenly, thinking, she turned the leather-bound book upside down and flapped its pages, wanting something to fall out. But there was nothing. She looked on the outside of the carpetbag to see if she could find an address, but she was not surprised not to. Jane had always been secretive. She had vanished to the city after their little brother, Charlie, died, and Helen hadn't known where she'd gone till much later, till long after Mother died, long after Helen had given up standing by the door every night, wishing her last remaining family member would walk in.

Vanished. To the city.

To a place where she had gone for sanctuary.

Abruptly Helen stood. There was one person who might be able to direct her to her sister's whereabouts.

The night was cold and Helen was tired of walking by the time she neared the foundry on the river. The factories were more here—the smell and smoke greater. But the bits of fey were fewer. Helen saw hardly any as she picked her way down the river-splashed streets, across cobblestoned patches of street as well as rutted packed dirt, hard and frosted with ice crystals. Slush patterned her stockinged legs, the tops of her feet, slid into her bronze heels. Even in the frozen air there was a thin smell of river and sewage and fish.

A form lurched up to her in the dark. Helen gasped and jumped away as its arms swung toward her like a dead thing. In a moment of stark memory she saw a battlefield long ago, saw a familiar farmer fall to the fey, then rise up just like this as a fey took over his dead body. Lurching with stiff arms, trying to make the limbs obey the new mind.

"What's going, pretty?" said the man drunkenly. "How much then?"

Helen's heart kept up its mad pounding rush. She did not have a jar of bugs, she did not have a rescuer, but she was not going to be helpless. In the moonlight she turned square to the man and said with all her will, "Go home. Go home."

He wavered. "Don't wanna go home. Wanna drink and a pretty."

"Drink yourself into oblivion for all I care," Helen told him. "But not with me." She glared at him until he finally backed down, staggered away.

She breathed carefully, making her heart slow. Her silk dress and stockings were too thin for the cold air. She wrapped her wool coat more tightly, tucked her gloved fingers under her arms. She should be wearing her furs, as ridiculous as that would be in this part of town. Where was that damn foundry?

The square, redbrick building opposite looked vaguely familiar. It had certainly not been papered with that line of identical posters five years ago, though. Yellow posters with a red seven-headed snake, and the words ONE PEOPLE! ONE RACE! repeated twenty times on the wall in case you missed the first one.

She touched the curling edges of the very last poster and closed her eyes, trying to visualize the twists and turns she had taken. She had visited Jane once at the foundry, five years ago now. If she thought about it the right way she could almost see it; she was so close. . . . Eyes half-shut, she moved quickly and with purpose, down another block, around some stairs, and suddenly there it was, the iron fence sharp and forbidding. Her eyes opened against the black night and she stared at it, uncertain now how she had gotten there.

Or was it simply that she didn't know what to do now that she had arrived?

There was an iron hydra coiled on the gate. That was a new feature.

Helen shuddered as she touched it, the iron cold and firm through her lilac gloves. What was she getting herself into here? She had thought of this as a safe place, because Jane had always spoken of it as her haven. But zealotry could override logic.

She waited, shivering. Then behind the gate, as if he had always been standing in the shadows, she saw him. The man who ran the foundry; what was his name? Niklas. Tall and broad, wrapped in warm leathers against the night.

"What's a fey groupie want here?" he said. "Couldn't wait till morning to get a new mask?"

Of course. The iron masks came from here. She had forgotten. Oh, wouldn't Jane have had a biting remark for her about that? The careless rich, who don't even know where their salvation comes from. "No," Helen said. "I mean, yes, I need one badly. I can pay. . . ."

"Of course you can. And extra for interrupting my dinner. Wait." He melted away into the night, leaving Helen straining her eyes to see into the tangle of iron and machinery behind the bars. The yard was more crowded than she had remembered it, more filled with hulking boxes with gears and spokes and arms, machines that seemed half-alive under the blue moonlight. She remembered it as a yard of dirt and seagulls and rusting scrap metal, but now it was thick and dense. An enormous metal tower built in front of the old shop building blocked out part of the sky. It was chained with long loops of thick iron links. Everything smelled of soot and hot metal.

"Here it is," he said, for he was back again. Niklas held the mask up for her inspection. A plain solid iron mask with mesh wires over the airholes. Identical to the one she had had, to the one all the women had. As if they were anonymous, all these wives, a mass of interchangeable women. A funereal army. "Now pay up." He named a price and Helen fumbled through her coat pockets as if she would have money inside, but she didn't, she never did, because you didn't do that, you simply received credit at all the shops. The change the chauffeur had given her was gone for the trolley; there was nothing that would approach the cost of a full mask.

"Bother," she said. Lying, said, "I'm sure I have something here," because you did that sort of thing to stall for time, and she didn't want him to disappear with her mask and leave her there in the cold on the street at the gate of a foundry she wasn't sure how she found or if she could find again. She pulled up Jane's carpetbag and rifled through it. Nothing . . . nothing . . .

"Why do you have that?" Niklas said in a low voice.

"Oh!" said Helen. "You recognize it? I'm trying to find her. I'm her sister. And she—I'm trying to find her flat, but I don't know the address. That's actually why I came here. To see if you knew." She smiled up at him, trying to be her winsomest self, but she sensed it was going to have little effect on this big barrel of a man.

"Why should I give her address to you if she doesn't want to be found?" said Niklas.

Helen stopped short. "That's not the question I was hoping you'd ask," she admitted.

"Which is?"

"How can you prove you're her sister? Because that I've thought over and I came up with three different ways on the trolley here. One. We're exactly the same size. Two—"

He grunted, interrupting her. "How's the trolley running these days?"

"Slow," she said. "It stopped twice tonight, and everyone was complaining that they're always late to work." It seemed as though she went up in his estimation for riding the trolley.

Perhaps Niklas had an affinity for all that machinery; perhaps he liked its populist nature.

Perhaps he understood that it meant she was serious about finding Jane.

Silence, during which Helen felt the cold sinking further, creeping into her marrow. "There are an incredible number of boors on the trolley," she added, knowing as she said it that his estimation of her would go back down. But she hated silence; it made her mouth say things. She stamped her feet in place, wishing he'd invite her inside if he was going to stand here and interrogate her. She opened her mouth to say so when the giant spoke again.

"Again," said Niklas. "Why should I help you find her if she doesn't want to be found?"

"Because she's in trouble," Helen said gently. "She was doing a facelift. It was going fine and then I went downstairs and Mr. Grimsby—of Copperhead, you know—turned on this machine and then everything went to pieces. The air went blue and roaring and the lights went out. And when I went upstairs Jane was gone. She must have run. . . ." She shook her head helplessly. "I just don't know. And now—"

"And now? . . ." There was a dangerous rumble in his voice. "There's worse?"

"Jane said Millicent said the fey are rising up," she said in a hushed voice, watching his fingers tighten on the mask. "Led by . . . well, no, they didn't know. Some follower of the Fey Queen, they thought."

"The Fey King," he breathed. Helen turned big eyes on him. "Trumped-up, self-proclaimed, of course. Ordinary fey are indolent and leaderless. But every so often, one comes along with the willpower to bring them all to heel. That one is here in the city now."

Helen swallowed. "How do you know?"

"Been studying how to capture the blue demons," he said calmly. "But then you've seen that, you said. Since I turned one of the machines over to our leader for further use and investigation."

"To . . . to Mr. Grimsby?" She could hardly hear him say "*our* leader" without shuddering.

"He's continuing to make improvements to best capture and destroy the blue demons. For my part, I have found interrogation with cold iron to be useful."

Helen's eyes traveled to the iron building by his forge. Her heart thumped in her chest. How could Jane have such a fondness for this man? He chilled her marrow. "So I have to find Jane," she said faintly, "before it's too late."

There was more silence, which she barely stopped herself from filling with a variety of pleas.

At last he spoke. "Three blocks north, two blocks east. Over the pawnshop there."

"Thank you," said Helen. "Thank—"

"There's something broken in this city," he said. "Blue scum all over it. Something's broken and it started with Jane and that *havlen* woman and whatever happened six months ago. Jane told me she'd received a nasty letter this summer. A death threat."

Havlen was a derogatory *dwarvven* term for mixed-race human and *dwarvven*—Helen vaguely knew the woman Niklas referred to, someone who worked for Edward Rochart. But a death threat? "Oh no," said Helen.

He steamrollered through her worry. "Jane didn't say more. And she shouldn't be mixing herself up with these facelifts—she was getting herself in over her head, I told her. Messing with power she couldn't control. They should all just be shot, the lot of them. That would take care of that nonsense. We fought." He exhaled. "Well. I guess I was right. Don't take any pride in that." Suddenly a hand was squeezing her shoulder—he had pushed it through a gap in the gate, and was standing right there, huge and frightening. "You find her," he said. "You find her and make her stop."

Helen hurried down the route Niklas had instructed. The night air was bitter on her bare face. She felt around in the carpetbag, pulled out the ironcloth, pressed it to her skin. Perhaps it made her feel safer, but it made it impossible to see in the black night. There weren't as many gaslights down here, but there were orange-yellow rectangles where taverns let out patrons, spilling into the cold night. And bits of blue. She put the ironcloth away and hurried faster.

Niklas's words rang through her head. "They should all just be shot, the lot of them." The Hundred, he meant. And yet Niklas himself was ironskin, cursed just as Jane had been with fey that scarred his skin and emitted a slow stream of poisonous emotion. Helen felt nothing but compassion for The Hundred, the women who had only wanted to be prettier. But perhaps she was alone in that.

Helen had to circle the block before she found the grungy brick building with the three iron balls denoting pawnshop. There was an iron staircase on the outside. Yes, this was the sort of nasty place Jane would run to, something surrounded by iron. Wearily Helen climbed the stairs—and found a locked and no doubt iron-chained door. She banged on it, calling "Jane, Jane." But no one came.

Helen jiggled the door handle helplessly, thinking of the long, hopeless walk home. She did not realize how thoroughly she had longed to find Jane here until she wasn't. The frigid iron of the staircase seeped up through the soles of her shoes to her already numb toes; her fingers were curled stiff against the cold.

And then the door was opened from the inside.

Helen looked up, startled, at a figure wearing an iron mask. A lump of disappointment formed in her belly. This person was too tall.

"Oh, hurry in out of that nasty cold stuff," the person said, quite heedless of the safety protocol that dictated one should spout clever greetings to make sure the fey were not invited over the threshold, lines ranging from the formal "An' ye be human, enter," to the cheeky lower-class admonition: "Stay out." Helen realized after she spoke that it was a woman, despite the fact that she was wearing slacks. Her heavy, dark brown hair was cut in an asymmetric bob that fell across one of the mask's eyeholes, and the thick scent of jasmine perfume lingered around her. "You must be looking for Jane," the woman said as Helen entered, stripping off her lilac gloves and blowing on her hands.

"Yes," said Helen. "I'm her sister. But—"

"Helen!" she said. "How delightful. And so fashionably brave, too." Her finger inscribed a circle around her own mask, indicating Helen's lack of one. "I think someone beat us here. Do you know if Jane's safe?"

"I don't know where she is," said Helen, swallowing the crushing disaster down, willing herself to find hope. "But she probably wasn't here when this happened. I hope." Her sister was tidy; Helen could not imagine the room being the way it was on Jane's account. It was unheated and tiny; cot and table and woodstove all in one room, with a single door leading to what she supposed might be the rest of the house, possibly a shared bath. The woman had turned on an oil lamp, and it cast an orange glow around the wreckage of the room.

The room had been ransacked.

"Perhaps she's out being brave and bold and doing good works," said the woman.

"Maybe," temporized Helen. She could not think. If Jane had not gone here, then where would she have gone? Helen and Alistair's home? It seemed unlikely. What had she said? *I have my own plans. . . .*

Helen sent tentative feelers out, wondering what the woman's purpose was—and if anything could be deduced from her about Jane's whereabouts. "I suppose you were here to see Jane? She's trying to explain to you her—*our* noble goals? Talk you into letting her . . . you know. Work on your face?" she said. It was as tactful as she could manage around the frostbitten fingers and the tangled knots of worry.

"You've got it all wrong," the woman said. "I'm dying to have my old face back. Let's rip it off."

"Really?" said Helen. "Most women have been very resistant. So far only—," but she thought belatedly that perhaps she shouldn't mention poor Mrs. Grimsby.

"Well, I don't care what anyone else thinks," the woman said decidedly. "I wouldn't have done it except it seemed good for my career. But then the visions!"

"Did you have nightmares, too?" said Helen.

"Oh, my goodness. Did you have dreams where a bunch of

beautifully creepy men and women stood around you in a circle and then it turned out they were all wearing your face?"

"Um. No," said Helen.

The woman paced around the overturned chairs, setting them up straight for something to do. Her face went in and out of the shadows flung by the oil lamp. "I'm an actor, you see. But I always got the odd roles. The wacky maiden aunt. The cryptic fortune-teller. And then I heard about this man who would make you beautiful, and I thought, wouldn't it be nice to be the ingénue for once?" Her brusque voice momentarily went wistful. "You see what I mean, don't you?" She pulled off her iron mask to reveal an exquisitely strong, purposeful face. Striking and glamorous with the fey, and yet Helen could imagine the face as it must have been before—the sort of woman you might call handsome if you wanted a way to describe how her face made you feel—a woman with purpose and character in spades, but not a beauty.

"But it turned out you were the same inside as you were before," Helen murmured.

The woman heard her and laughed, a strong laugh like a ship breaking through the sea. It displayed a nice white set of teeth, even except for a gap in front. "Well, I expected that, you know. I'm no fool. But I didn't expect the voices in my head. The wallpaper swimming in. And that is not worth it in the slightest, and I'm ready to take my old face back and enjoy being the wacky maiden aunt again. Besides, between you and me, being the ingénue isn't all it's cracked up to be. Drippy girls pining over young men who aren't worth it. I had my fun—my rabid fans, my scandalous love affairs. Sat as an artist's model for the bronze outside the ballet, you know the one—?"

"Intimately," said Helen dryly.

The woman laughed again and put out a hand, strong and bold like a man's. "I like you," she said. "There's more in you than one would suspect."

Helen thought that might be sort of an insult, but it was said so forthrightly she couldn't possibly take offense. She shook the woman's hand heartily in her own. "Helen Huntingdon," she said.

"Eglantine Frye," the woman said. "But please, call me Frye."

"All right," said Helen. She had never met someone like this; she knew how to make bright and brittle small talk with men and women of all sorts but not hold a real conversation with this strong-willed woman in slacks who stood in her sister's destroyed flat, joking about ripping off her face. "Frye it is."

"Great," said Frye. "So tell me. How soon can you replace my face?"

Helen looked at the woman in shock.

"I'm serious," said Frye. "Jane's not here but you are. She wanted to do me last week. I shouldn't have beat around the metaphorical bush, but I wanted one last good carouse before going back to my old life. So here I am, high on courage and gin and no Jane."

"You don't want me to do that," said Helen.

"I don't want this face anymore," Frye said adamantly. "I'm in danger with it."

"You're in danger if I try," said Helen. "Beyond the fact that I don't know how—that's how Jane disappeared tonight. She was doing a facelift and something went wrong. Besides, you wouldn't want me even if I thought I could do it. I'm . . ."

I'm silly, she wanted to say. I'm not sensible. And when I make big decisions, like marrying Alistair, I think maybe I ruin everything. How could you trust me to do something big like this, something important? "I'm not Jane," she finished lamely.

"Hold everything," Frye said. "You're saying Jane actually disappeared?" She whistled like a boy as she surveyed the wrecked flat. "This is looking grimmer by the moment." Frye seemed to do nothing by economy. She swung back around to look at Helen and her whole frame followed the motion of her glance. "But that's why you're here, isn't it? To find Jane. No! To find clues—to track her down. She must have gone underground, gone into hiding. Say no more. I'll help you search."

Frye fell to with a will, sorting the small room to rights. Helen fell in beside her, sorting through the shadows. Gone into hiding, she thought. Yes. That's all. Jane has gone into hiding—*I have my own plans*—and Helen would find a clue here to where that hiding place was. She was not sure exactly what that clue would be, but surely something would turn up if she just kept standing up chairs and hanging up clothes. Not that there were many clothes to hang up. Two dresses, both dark—and probably only that many so Jane wouldn't have to stand in her slip and wash her only change of clothes in the communal sink. None of the pretty things she had given Jane. No, this was sensible Jane from head to toe, and Helen thought again how useful she could have been—would still be—to Jane in her quest. Those women didn't want their savior to be sensible and plain. Nobody trusted sensible and plain. They trusted smart. Turned out. Fashionable.

"Whoever wrecked this was looking for something,"

mused Frye, her penciled eyebrows knitting together. "But what could you hide in a room this small?"

"Or maybe they wanted to disguise whatever it was they were doing," said Helen.

"Mmm, like in *The Ruby Dagger of Deidre,*" said Frye. "You come back after the second act to find the heroine's place ransacked—but it was all so the bad guy could *plant* the murder weapon on her."

"And if the murder weapon's a face?" Helen said. There were lots of meanings to that, and Frye didn't even know about Millicent, but she laughed anyway.

"Yes, I like your style," Frye said. "You can work on my face. I'll be your first victim."

"You don't know a thing about me," protested Helen as she tried to wedge a broken chair leg back in place.

Frye shrugged. "I'm a good judge of character. And my mind's made up. Even Jane had to start somewhere. You have all her stuff, don't you?" She pointed dramatically at the carpetbag. "I always saw her carrying that."

Helen nodded. "But I couldn't possibly make the fey power work. Jane studied all summer to learn how to do it. And . . . she's just good at that kind of thing."

Frye swung around and stood there casually studying her, hands slouched in pockets as if they were discussing where to eat lunch and not how to replace her face. "Jane said you were cleverer than you knew," she said.

Helen felt suddenly, strangely, lighter. Buoyed up. "I . . . I could try," she said at last. "I make no promises. But I could put the clay on my hands and see how it feels. If I think I could do what she could."

"Excellent," said Frye. "Shall we find a bed then?" She gestured at Jane's slashed cot.

"Gah, no!" said Helen. More calmly: "I mean, no. Not tonight. I have to rest." And the memory of that botched operation was so fresh, so cutting. What was this woman thinking, trying to entrust this to her?

"Tomorrow, then. You can come to my place."

"I can't," said Helen. "I'm not supposed to—"

Frye looked at her curiously.

"I mean. It's dangerous on the streets for us without the masks. And I've . . . misplaced mine. You'll have to come to me. Some early morning would be the best time to sneak in."

"Fine," said Frye, who was apparently willing to let Helen win some of the arguments, as long as she got the main point she wanted. "Next Monday, perhaps—no shows on Monday. Can I wear slacks? Or is your neighborhood too stuffy?"

"Well . . . ," said Helen.

"Your face says it all," said Frye. "I have a dress, don't worry. I'm an actor, darling. I'll blend in so I can sneak in." She paused, studying Helen curiously. "Why are we sneaking me in?"

"Well," said Helen, *again,* but this woman threw her off balance. "That is. My husband doesn't know I'm carrying on Jane's work." The words, slipping out, startled her. *She was carrying on Jane's work.* She was going to convince The Hundred. She *was.*

"Say no more," said Frye. "Your marital affairs are absolutely your business and I am not going to pry. You find a good time next week and I will sneak in wearing a perfectly acceptable dress to see you."

"And I will only *try* the clay," put in Helen. "I'm not promising anything beyond that."

"Yes, yes. Agreed?"

"Agreed," said Helen, and for the first time that day a genuine smile broke through the worries and fears.

"You're much prettier when you smile," said Frye.

"I thought I was pretty already," said Helen cynically.

"It's not about the face, you know? I *have* learned that. Should've learned it sooner, but we all have our upbringings to contend with. When you entered the door you looked grim, but just now you look as though you could move mountains."

"Maybe I can," said Helen. This woman thought she could do things. And she didn't even have the excuse of being family, who maybe only thought it was good for you if they said they believed in you. Maybe she *could* move mountains. Maybe she could try.

"So tell me," said Frye. "What can I do for you in return?"

Helen looked down at the piece of furniture she had been trying vainly to lift. "Help me move this trunk," she said.

With Frye's help the trunk slid scratchily over the dusty floor to reveal a small trapdoor. "This is it," crowed Frye. She brought the oil lamp closer, wafting the cloud of oil stink along with it.

Helen levered the trapdoor up to reveal several rafters' worth of storage space under the floor.

Empty.

Helen tugged the corner of her coat under her stockinged knees and carefully knelt there, feeling around under the floorboards. Dust. Grit. Things she didn't want to touch, but Tam would probably appreciate. Her fingers closed on a bit of splintery wood and she pulled it out, examining it. It was roughly made and yet lined with velvet.

"What's down there?" said Frye, kneeling next to her with the oil lamp, heedless of her slacks. "The murder weapon? The face?"

"The face," Helen repeated in slow realization. "Yes. That's what this held. A face. One of our old faces." There had been one just like it in the carpetbag—it must have held Millicent's old face—perhaps it still did.

Carefully Frye took the box from Helen and held it up to her own face, checking the measure. "It would fit," she agreed, cradling the box in long fingers. "Do you think they were all here?"

"I do," said Helen. "All the ones she hadn't done yet. All of *us*." She looked at Frye, her stomach clenching in knots. "Who would want our old faces?"

Frye shook her head. "Looks as though I'll be waiting a while longer for my facelift then. I suppose you're off the hook, unless you want me to sneak in for the sheer fun of it." She exhaled, rocking back on her heels. "Oh, Jane, Jane, Jane. I *told* you I had a spare bedroom."

Helen's fingers swept the interior one last time. There was paper or something lodged into that crack in the board, tucked there for safekeeping. She teased it from the board, pulled it forth and into the glow of the lamp.

A message. A note.

Cold sliced up Helen's spine as she studied the words cut and pieced together, letter by letter.

LEAVE THE CITY NOW BEFORE YOU GET HURT.

Chapter 4

THE HUNDRED

Helen held the threat out with nerveless fingers for Frye, who read it and then put a comforting hand on her shoulder. "Them as talk big don't do nuthin'," Frye declaimed, no doubt quoting some line in a play. "You'll find her." She peered at the note. "That *L* looks like the *L* on the Lovage's Gin bottle."

"Great!" Helen said cynically. "We can narrow it down to everyone who drinks gin." She wavered to her feet, folded the note, and tucked it inside Jane's carpetbag where she wouldn't have to see it anymore. She rubbed the backs of her hands against her eyes, which were stinging from the stirred-up dust. "Did you find anything else?"

"A photo," said Frye. "Jane and some man with rumpled hair."

"That's her fiancé," said Helen, studying the small blue-and-white fey tech photo that Frye held out. "She looks . . . happy there," she said, and the world came crashing down on her silk shoulders again. She had to make everything right. She had to let Jane's fiancé know what had happened. No, he was gone himself, into the dangerous forests with his daughter. But she should wire the housekeeper at Silver Birch Hall.

Helen stumbled to her feet, away from Frye's kind touch. Numbly she wrapped her coat more tightly, hunched her shoulders against the cold. So much to do, and no assurance that anything she did would make it right. It seemed just as likely that she would get herself in over her head again, and need rescuing herself, when there was no one left to rescue her. . . .

"Why are you leaving me?" said Frye, as Helen put her hand to the doorknob.

"The trolley," said Helen, and Frye laughed a loud bellow.

"Doesn't run much past dark, what do you think? You probably caught the last one getting here."

Helen's eyes were wide with despair at this last blow. All sense fled and silly words tumbled from the depths of her heart. "You mean—so I'll never get home and I've already walked miles and the calluses are blisters, why didn't I break the heels in, of course I never wear the sensible shoes because sensible means hideous, and he'll be so angry if he happened to check on me and I'm tired, so very tired. . . ."

Frye handed Helen a handkerchief. "I drive a car, love. I'll take you home."

Helen drifted under a pile of lap robes, semi-awake. Frye hummed some mournful-sounding musical number to herself, but otherwise kept quiet. The grey mist smeared with blue drifted by and Helen thought how it seemed that you jumped ship from person to person, always seeking a new one to be your rock. But they sank. She could leap into this spot where she was in Frye's motorcar; a protected island, just drive on till morning. But it would sink, too. They all did, in the end.

Frye turned into the street Helen had told her, and Helen pointed out their house. The square windows in the games room—Alistair's room—were golden. He was home. He was awake.

She was so very, very tired.

"She's just lying low, out of danger," said Frye as she pulled to a stop. "It's what anyone would do. She'll come home."

"Thank you," Helen said, stumbling out of the motorcar. Her blistered feet landed in a puddle, splashing ice up her legs. She fumbled in her inner coat pocket for a card. "Look, here's my address. Send me word if anything turns up."

Frye's face held concern as she took the card. "You're all right?"

Weak grin, game face. "Nothing two olives and a little Lovage's Gin won't cure," Helen said jauntily to Frye, and waited for the woman's answering grin before turning away and striding into the house as if she had every right to return to it at two in the morning.

Helen closed the front door softly behind her, running through excuses in her head, ones that didn't involve getting Adam in trouble. None of them were very good, or believable.

The thin electric light spilled out of the games room into a triangle in the hallway. She had never thought much of the idea that one should face the music. In fact she thought she'd rather go hide in bed now, and let him yell at her in the morning, if he must. Maybe Jane would be home by then and everything would be fine, fine.

But she heard a scratchy melody drifting out, and she

stepped out of her ruined shoes and crept down the hall on stocking feet to see.

The gramophone was on. Even the rich had long ago run out of the fey bluepacks that used to power everything, but Alistair's circle were trying out the newest inventions as soon as they were relatively safe, and Alistair had recently had the house wired for electricity. He had purchased an electric gramophone five times the size of the old one that ran on bluepacks. It was a massive cabinet, and it smelled funny when it ran. But it did run, and right now it was playing through an old waltz that made Helen want to lift her arms to a partner and turn around the floor.

The music fell to a quiet moment, and under that she heard snoring.

Helen dared to peek around the door, then. Alistair was stretched out in the armchair in front of the fireplace, emptied whiskey glass on the table next to him, fast asleep. The contents of his pockets were on the end table, wallet among them, and Helen remembered that she had to pay back Adam. On noiseless feet she went in, heady with the up and down of the night, feeling in a strange way that surely he couldn't wake up right this second if he hadn't already.

Helen extracted the notes from the leather wallet, watching him, thinking, I loved you once. She had gone into the marriage expecting to make it work. To be good to him. To *repay* him. To care for him and run his household and generally do all the things a wife should—wasn't that enough to make a partnership last? Love didn't have to be thrilling, fascinating, throw-yourself-off-a-cliff sort of love. They could care for each other in a friendly fashion, bring their charm and her beauty and his wealth to the table, bounty to share.

They *had* cared for each other. And yet, everything had become so unequal.

No options, she thought to herself.

That was where she had been a year ago, why she had signed up with Alistair. It seemed the best way out of the abysmal hole she'd gotten herself into, and he had been so kind, she thought then. So charming. They had danced every night at the tenpence dance hall, the wildest, gayest dances, him in black and she all in white with a grass green sash. . . . Marrying him had been a sensible, calculated decision.

Perhaps she wasn't a very skilled mathematician.

She turned to leave the room, and he stirred, and she stopped, one hand on the wood corner of the gramophone, heart in throat.

"Another round," he murmured. "Another."

She wondered if the men had been over, after that terrible meeting at the Grimsbys'. She had loved his parties at first—she loved parties, after all. But more and more they just seemed an excuse for drunken behavior, not chat and wit and dancing. And then afterward those men would all stay over, for days on end, wheeling about the parlor and the library and everywhere else, sucking down port.

And that horrid Mr. Grimsby with them. Oh, he was abstemious enough. His method of entertaining himself was worse—all that "One People One Race" business that Alistair had at first scoffed at, but now seemed more and more fervent about. Alistair had avoided the Great War—paid a young factory worker to take his place. Most of the wealthy men left had done the same. The ones that hadn't . . . well. They weren't here. In some strange way, the men of Alistair's set seemed to be making up for their dereliction then by cleaving to Grimsby's racial purity fanaticism now. Alistair had had a *dwarvven* chambermaid when she married him seven months ago. Boarham had had a *dwarvven* groundskeeper, Morse a *dwarvven* cook. All since dismissed.

Helen stared at her sleeping husband for a long time. But all she really saw was an image in her head, stark like the old blue-and-white fey-tech cameras: Millicent Grimsby, stone-still on the cold white daybed, a red line tracing the outline of her perfect face.

She dreams that she is ten again, playing on the field that will one day be a battlefield, that will one day kill her little brother, Charlie. But that is still three years away. The war rages on, but it has not touched Harbrook, and the only foretelling of the battlefield is the yellow cowslips that carpet the field. They will be there on the day that Charlie dies and Jane marches in with him and Helen stays behind with Mother, who would dissolve without them.

It is hard to stay behind. It is hard to be the one who says, Mother, I will not leave you, and watch your brother and sister march into war without you. To tell yourself, you are a coward for staying, and to yet feel you would be a coward to go. It is hard to watch the wounded come home, and the dead never, and to *be there.* Just be there.

But that is not yet, Helen says fiercely, and the dream pulls back and she is ten, still ten, and she is playing with Charlie in a field of cowslips. She has plaited them into her hair, and Charlie, who is nine, is whacking their heads off with a stick. It is a rare holiday from school and work and Jane has promised to help her paint a picture but instead, restless Jane is at the edge of the forest, poking the undergrowth as if to uncover a lurking fey.

She can't remember how it happened on that day, but here in the dream she calls to Jane and Jane does not answer. Helen runs to the edge of the forest, calling her name, but Jane goes in, away from her, deeper and deeper, well past the first ray of light, till she is dissolved, vanished in the black woods. Helen whirls around, but Charlie is vanished. Jane is gone. And all there is is Helen, clutching the last tree at the edge of the forest, shouting Jane, Jane, Jane. . . .

The next morning Helen woke curled in her bed, sore in every limb. She, Helen, whose idea of a long walk was meandering beautifully twice around the garden, had walked more than she'd walked in a month of Sundays, and in the freezing cold to boot. Her thighs ached and when she dared to stand they felt like jelly.

She tugged off her sleeping mask, hobbled to her wardrobe, and pulled out her softest, most shapeless wool dress to wear; wriggled into a big cardigan over that. Her head was groggy and her bare legs still cold and sore under the dress. She hobbled to her vanity and dabbed a touch of lilac scent behind her earlobes, then just stood there, trying to think about springtime and sunshine, and not about missing Jane or the confrontation with Alistair last night in the car.

Then she got back in bed.

The maid brought chocolate and toast and a vivid orange envelope. Helen opened it while Mary chattered through recent gossip. Helen was awfully fond of Mary for just this reason, yet this morning she could not concentrate on anything the maid said. Helen's head was a brick wall, and Mary's gossip dashed itself into it and fell back, exhausted. After Mary had repeated the choice bit about Lord Meriwether and his naughty ice statuary for the third time, looking progressively more downcast with each telling, Helen finally said, "I'm sorry, Mary, my head's a muddle. You'll have to tell me later."

"Yes'm," Mary said dubiously. Helen could almost hear her thoughts: The mistress must be sick.

The orange envelope was from Frye, Helen found, when she finally got her focus on it. A short, equally orange note inside said, in strong slashing handwriting:

> DIVINE *to meet you.* MUST *have just one last carouse with this face. Having a few friends over tonight after the show gets out. Stop by Will Call for* Painted Ladies Ahoy! *if you want tix. Tell them I sent you and* NOT *to fob you off with restricted viewing, otherwise you'll miss my number with the lampshade.*
>
> *FRYE.*
>
> *PS: You* MUST *come to the party as I will have Alberta, Betty, and Desirée there.*
> *PS 2: Don't worry. We will find Jane.*

Helen turned the orange note over, seeking further explanation of the three cryptic ladies, but found nothing but a scribbled black address.

She leaned against her tufted pink headboard and closed her eyes. It would be so comforting to just go back to sleep. To stay in bed all day. Surely Alistair would be over his anger by now. She needn't talk about it, or even talk to him at all. She could just curl under the covers and no one would expect anything of her. The house would run itself—Alistair had never seen fit to let her take on any responsibilities from the efficient housekeeper. Jane would turn up when she was good and ready, would laugh at Helen for worrying about her. Yes, it would be smart of all of them to not expect anything of her. She, Helen, was not a bit dependable.

She burrowed into her pillow and pulled the covers over her head.

Yet she could not return to sleep. She tossed and turned, wriggled and squirmed—and then found herself sitting back up and dragging the carpetbag over to the bed, all the while admonishing herself that she was undependable, unreliable, and was going back to bed right now.

There was a clue in the carpetbag, the back of her mind told her. There was something she had seen and overlooked, distracted. No, not the train stubs.

The leather book—it was a journal. That handwritten list of names.

Helen pulled the journal out of the rough carpetbag and studied it. It was a faded maroon leather sleeve, soft with long use, that fit over bound paper. The red ribbon bookmark had fallen out when she shook it, but she turned the pages until she found the list of names that she remembered.

She skimmed the list, certain now that she knew what they were. It was The Hundred, as Jane called them. The list of women who were in danger. The Prime Minister's wife. Lady Dalrymple. Monica Preston-Smythe—ooh, Helen hadn't known that. A few men were sprinkled through, and a few people were known only by a first name. Other than that, it read like a society page, a who's who of the most influential women in the city.

The names were written in ink, in Jane's tiny precise hand. Helen flipped to the end of the names and saw that at the top of a clean page writing followed, a name followed by copious notes. Henrietta Lindcombe. She recognized that as the first facelift Jane had done. "Mrs. Lindcombe is nervous but I think I have talked her into it," wrote Jane. "After she had that close encounter with a fey in the park she was a much easier catch. Before that it was all 'I don't believe the danger is what you say it is.' I am reminded time and again that the war was fought in the country, and the city folk were never exposed to it. So many of the wealthy men paid others to go in their place. The war is a hundred miles away and five years gone, and the blue in the city are just another obstacle you learn to live with, like pickpockets. You avoid the waterfront for pickpockets; you wear an iron mask for the fey. You pretend that's enough, and yet . . . If only all of them could be nearly attacked, they might be more willing to accede to what I know to be true and necessary!"

Helen skimmed the description until she saw the part that said "At last." And then, a long description of how it had felt to perform her first facelift, on Mrs. Lindcombe. Helen shuddered and turned the page. The next page was also labeled with a name, the second one on the list, but it was blank beneath. Same with the next page, and the next. Helen flipped through several blank pages until she found the next page with writing on it. Millicent Grimsby.

But poor Millicent was not Jane's second facelift. There were no dates on these, and Jane's organizational system was meant to keep track of all the interactions Jane had had while trying to convince a particular woman to do the facelift—it wasn't meant for someone trying to sort out a timeline to find Jane after she had vanished.

Helen flipped through the book. The pages were ordered by

the list of women, which was the same list as at the beginning. Each one was numbered. She did not know if that was the order that Mr. Rochart had done their faces, but whatever it was, it was certainly not the order in which Jane was removing them.

Helen sighed. This was why she had married Alistair, among other reasons. She just wasn't any use at focused concentration like this, sorting through the details. This was a matter for the police—if the police weren't firmly in Copperhead's pocket, that was. She didn't dare expose her sister to the charges of murder. No, it was all up to Helen, but how could she possibly hope to solve this mystery?

She shook her head. That was a ridiculous way to think. She might be a fool and a coward, but she was a stubborn one, and Jane needed her. *I have my own plans,* Jane had said. *You convince The Hundred.*

Helen would.

So what did she know? She knew Jane had completed some facelifts. Six, she thought Jane had said. Helen was not sure—but surely this journal knew.

Helen pulled out a pad and pencil, flipped to the beginning of the book, and began writing down every name that had notes under it. The ones that had the additional notes about the facelift she crossed back out.

It turned out that Jane had indeed done a half-dozen facelifts. Helen spent a few minutes trying to decide whether to strike through poor Millicent Grimsby's name or not and in the end drew a soft wiggly line through it with the lead, whispering an apology under her breath.

That left her with eighteen women with notes underneath.

Eighteen women that Jane had tried and failed to impress upon the need for changing their face.

Jane had definitely needed her help.

Helen found the first of those attempted women in the book and glanced at the end of the entry.

"Terrible afternoon," read the journal. "Agatha Flintwhistle threw me out on my ear and threatened to sic the police upon me if I so much as walked on the other side of the sidewalk from her. I am not entirely certain what I said, but she seems to be convinced that allowing me to help her would lead down 'the slippery path of sin into suffrage and other such nonsense.' At that point I flat-out said that I would be very glad to see women get the vote, if for no other reason than that they could think about something other than the cut of their hair for once. (Her bob was set with so much of that smelly fixative nonsense that when she shook her head, not one single piece moved.) That was when the police and the sidewalk, &c, were mentioned. I think I will not be going back for a time."

Helen laughed an oh dear sort of laugh. Jane had really, *really* needed her.

She went through all the women who had notes but no record of finishing with facelifts. Many of the entries ended in disaster like the first one. Helen knew most of these women socially—some even more so. When she read about Louisa Mayfew being standoffish to Jane, she muttered under her breath, no, no, Jane! That's not how you manage *her*. First you tell her how much you like the piano. Then the parlor. Then that snot rag of a child. *Then* she'll be eating out of your hand. You don't barge in like a schoolteacher and try to tell a Mayfew what to do.

If Jane—no, *when* Jane made it back safely, Helen was going straight around to all these folks with her and mending fences. They were all ripe for the picking and didn't even know it.

It seemed as though there were only two entries left that didn't end in success or disaster. They were Rosemary Higgins and Calendula Smith. Rosemary was noted as "abroad but promised to speak with me upon return," but what really caught Helen's eye was at the end of Calendula Smith's entry, where Jane mentioned "after this encounter, the next woman will be a piece of cake."

That is, if Helen was reading that right, Calendula Smith was the last woman (except for Millicent) that Jane had tried to convince before her untimely disappearance. And while Frye thought Jane had just gone to ground, Helen couldn't help but feel that Jane would have tried to contact her by now. Besides, there was that ransacked flat and death threat.

She couldn't bear to think that something had happened to Jane, so she firmly told herself that Jane was in hiding, exactly as Frye thought. And therefore, she was to follow Jane's words: *You have one purpose for the next week. Convince every last one of them.*

All the same, why not kill two birds with one stone? If Helen was going to convince The Hundred for Jane, she had to start somewhere. It didn't seem too likely that pillar-of-society Calendula Smith would have threatened Jane with a torn-paper note and then had her abducted, merely for the insult of asking Calendula to take her old face back. But Calendula might know something. Jane hadn't even told *Helen* about the death threat, but maybe she had let something slip to someone.

Calendula was the perfect place to start.

By now Helen had finished the chocolate and toast, and she felt much less muddled. She felt alive and engaged again, the way she had last night when Frye had told her she could move mountains. She was going to find Jane—going to have The Hundred primed and ready for her—and then everything, surely everything, would be right as rain.

The door opened and Alistair poked his head in.

Helen did not jump, but her fingers on the journal did, tensing up into little mountains. Had he checked in on her bedroom? Did he know she had been out? She slid the journal under the covers as he crept around the door, looking woebegone.

"I'm sorry," he said immediately, coming up to the foot of the bed and twining his fingers around the iron rails. A cloud of lavender soap and ambergris drifted in with him. "I was in shock last night from that horrible disaster. And then I had some whiskey to soften the blow. I believe I yelled at you in the motorcar?" He looked up at her under his lashes and she softened. She was safe after all. And it was so hard to be mad at him when he put on his penitent little-boy face. Because it wasn't just a face, she knew. He really did mean it. He truly was sorry.

"You took the one thing that makes me safe," she said. "As if you didn't trust me." Perhaps not the wisest thing to say, but Helen had never been good at holding her tongue. She would never be the sort to charm folks through shy silence. And if you liked using words, well . . . sometimes you used too many of them.

Alistair rubbed tired eyes in a rather ill-looking face. She didn't envy him that hangover. "Look, I was upset from being with Grimsby," he said.

"The man would rile up a saint," Helen agreed. "Oh, you meant . . . the other thing." Millicent.

"And to make it up to you," Alistair said, cutting across her sentence. His sometimes haughty face broke into a charming grin. "A little gift for my little pet." He tossed a paper-wrapped packet into her outstretched hands. "Go on. Open it."

The pink paper was warm and slightly rough in her palms. Helen teased the edge free with her fingernail and tore open the paper to reveal an intricate copper necklace. She hooked one finger under the chain and lifted it, breathing in as it caught the light. "Oh, Alistair," she said. "How pretty." The twisted coils of copper spun delicately on the chain.

Alistair did love her. He was sorry. She remembered another fight they had had a few weeks ago—something silly that ended with him throwing her three-legged footstool down the stairs, breaking off a leg. He had brought her a new stool the next day, with a dozen roses on it, crimson-hearted and perfect.

"Put it on," he said. "I want to see how you look in it."

Laughing, she started to obey. Curiously, the clasp was worked into the pendant part of the necklace—one of the copper coils curved over as if biting the copper chain. She looked closer. No, not *as if* biting. "It's a hydra," she said flatly.

"A more feminine version," Alistair said. "Grimsby had them made up specially for all the wives. I was going to wait to give it to you, but then I decided you needed it today." He took the clasp from her hands and fastened it around her neck, letting it hang down over the high crew-neck of the wool dress. "There you are; a perfect doll," he declared.

Helen's fingers ran over the little snake heads. She was not certain she cared to be marked so publicly as the wife of a

Copperhead party member. Yet she pasted a smile to her face, reminding herself that Alistair was trying to be kind. He seemed in so much a better humor this morning that she dared press for details about last night.

"Oh, we didn't stay at Grimsby's long after I sent you home," he said, with a dismissive wave. "Frightfully gruesome, what? He dragged some private sleuth out of bed to poke around the place and then set the maids to cleaning. The rest of us dragged him out of there to roulette. We've all been through it before when he lost his first wife—gotta keep moving. Continuing the meeting's all very well but you can't do that sort of thing when your buddy's got an eyeful of his girl lying stiff as a plank, can you?" Alistair slouched over to the window and pushed aside her curtains so he could stare out into the grey November morning. "Loses wife one to the dwarves, wife two to the fey—man's got a rotten string of luck." He whistled softly and turned back to her. "Made me glad I haven't let you do anything so foolish, especially after that night in May. No, you're safe and sound right here, and I'm glad to know that when I'm out with the boys."

Helen hurried past that before he could directly order her to stay in. "Alistair," she said to his back. "Why don't you stay in tonight? Give up the boys for one night. We'll . . . I don't know, have our own dance, right here in the house. Remember when we used to dance?" Things could be like they were, she thought, without the night after night of drinking, the drinking that led to the shouting and the stool-throwing and the glass-smashing. . . .

He took a step away, making closed-off, disentangling gestures. "Now, lambkin, you know that I can't very well look as though my wife has me on a string, can I? I have plans with the boys. We need to take Grimsby out and get him rip-roaring drunk."

"You get that every night, with less excuse," Helen said before she thought. It was the sort of thing you couldn't say to Alistair without having him get all cold and ragey and she instantly regretted it. She knew that, goodness knows she knew that; why did she keep doing it?

"I merely do what's necessary to keep our image up," Alistair said icily. "One has to be seen socially doing the sort of things a man does. And since only one of us is fit to go out and keep our name active in the minds of our social peers . . ."

Argh, thought Helen, I *want* to go out, but she knew like anything that if she went down that road there would be no escape and she would end up in a confrontation about her staying home. She fell back on her usual trick of distraction. "Well, I think it's just divine the way you all rally around poor Mr. Grimsby. And his darling son, too; poor Tam would be miserable else."

"Who?" said Alistair. "Oh, Grimsby's boy. His second time on the roller-coaster, too. Don't worry, we brought him out to roulette, too. Gave him a drink."

"Alistair!" she said, and now she really was shocked.

He held up his hands. "Just beer, just beer. Well, I'd better be off." He closed the curtains, blocking out the thin grey light. "We have a full day planned."

His eyes roved the room and she leaned to one side, shifting to hide the lump of journal under the covers. The carpetbag, thankfully, was hidden by the hanging folds of the quilt. He smiled at her, thin and tight under his cap of glossy fixed curls. "Don't wait up, my pet," he said, and then he was gone.

Helen slumped against the tufted headboard, feeling as if

she'd been through a battle. Poor Tam, alone with those terrible men. There had to be something she could do to help him. She was not overly fond of children, no. She was glad to be through with governessing. And yet . . . roulette and beer? Her fingers rubbed the snake heads of the necklace as she tugged the journal out from under the covers. With one hand she flipped through it one last time to make sure that really nothing was going to fall out of it—no train tickets or death threats.

Her eye fell at the end of the list, at the last two names that she had skimmed over, the last two pages in Jane's writing, blank except for the name at the top of each page. The women were not a perfect One Hundred after all, despite Jane's referring to them as such; the last numbered person was 99.

But what gave Helen the shock, despite knowing it must be there, was to see those names etched out in those precise letters, one after the other, just two more women on the fey hit list, their names a record of their mistakes.

98—Helen Huntingdon.

99—Jane Eliot.

Chapter 5

PLAYING THE GAME

There was another good reason to start with Calendula Smith, and that's that Helen knew where she lived—over by the Grimsbys. Helen had not spent any real time in the woman's company, but she had been to a dance there once. It was in the last six months—well, nearly all of her social engagements dated from after she received her fey face—so she had not seen the woman's new face. The iron masks were just coming into use for The Hundred, and this woman had one. Helen had watched them all whirling around the ballroom in their bright gowns and hard masks and felt more alone in a crowd than she had ever done in her life.

Helen had changed from the comfortable dress into something suitable for going out—a crisp wool suit in chartreuse. An unusual color, but one that brought out the glints in her copper blond hair. She had bowed to her blisters and put on her most comfortable shoes, and had tied a string of seed pearls around her neck. Went back and forth on Alistair's new necklace, but in the end decided to leave it on. He was trying to make it up to her, wasn't he? And it was pretty, even if it was Copperhead's symbol. It wouldn't hurt her to stay in their good graces while she slunk about town. She smoothed the chain down under the seed pearls, feeling the copper snake warm against her skin.

Helen knocked on Calendula Smith's doorknocker (a plain hoop, thankfully), and waited for the butler to formally forbid her to cross the iron threshold. Soon she and Mrs. Smith were seated in the parlor, drinking bergamot tea and eying each other with mutually concealed dislike.

"Dear Helen," said the woman. "It's so good to see you."

"And you, Calendula," said Helen, not meaning a word of it. This woman had shunned her at first, for the ridiculous and tangled reason of being the best friend of a woman who had wanted Alistair for herself. Helen never could understand being so tied up over a man that you (and all your friends) would hate another woman for his sake. Surely the first woman could have thought of a more interesting reason to hate Helen. Hate her for her copper blond curls, hate her for her blue eyes. But really. A man? And now Calendula Smith, hating Helen merely to stay in her friend's good graces.

Well, you played the game or it played you.

"Won't you have another piece of cake?" purred Mrs. Smith. "You're practically skin and bones."

"I know, it's a shame, isn't it?" returned Helen. "And yet Alistair was just saying how glad he was I hadn't let my figure go after marriage like some women."

"Men! Who can predict their bizarre tastes."

"I was just thinking the same."

The initial pleasantries exchanged, Helen looked around the room under pretense of admiring it. It was all over roses. A pink rose sofa perched daintily on a red rose rug, and two tasseled rose chairs faced each other. Rose-pink curtains in a gauze that was the very height of fashion draped the windows. It was completely hideous, Helen decided with satisfaction. But she smiled and made nice about the roses (not to mention Calendula's matching perfume) while deciding exactly how to play her hand.

"Now, Mrs. Huntingdon, come to the point. What can I do for you?"

Concern, Helen decided. Lead in with concern and goose it with gossip. "Well," she said dramatically. "I was just talking to my sister, Jane, and she said she'd seen you the other day."

Calendula tensed. Sort of around the shoulders, but Helen caught it. "I wasn't very interested in her conversation," Calendula said sharply. "Seems to me she should keep her nose in her own affairs."

"I'm so glad you feel that way," said Helen. "I told her it was unthinkable for a woman of your stature to go back to her old face."

Those perfect eyes narrowed. "I have no idea to what you refer. More tea?"

"Certainly," said Helen, and leaned back, studying the woman.

Calendula Smith's fey-brilliant face seemed incongruous on that broad-shouldered, wide-waisted body. But when Helen looked again—no, the woman was stunning after all. Helen had seen it time and again, but that was the brilliance of what Mr. Rochart had done. He had made each person not into some cookie-cutter girl, but into the most dazzling version of themselves. It was why you couldn't have said for sure with so many of them. You thought they were more beautiful—but was it that they were just more alive, more real?

This woman was not meant to be pretty. She was perhaps not meant to be a dainty little *girl,* although that was the sort of comment Jane was always chiding her for. But what else was Helen supposed to think? Mrs. Smith was built like a man, with a wide frame that strained against the panels of her mauve silk dress. A silk rose dangled incongruously from a waist that even the draped bias cut could not slim. "You should wear slacks," Helen said, and then put a hand to her mouth, far too late.

"Excuse me?" said Calendula Smith.

Helen valiantly tried to save the situation. "They're chic, I mean. I've been seeing them more frequently. I just thought you could carry them off."

"Thank you, I suppose," said Calendula, not sounding terribly mollified. "I'm not sure that slacks would be appropriate for a pillar of society. One has to set an example, you know."

"One does," agreed Helen. And then more gently she added, "And sometimes one has to do it by admitting mistakes have been made." She carefully did not say by whom. "Sometimes only the pillars can lead the way."

Calendula looked at her for a long time. At last, choosing her words with the air of someone stepping through a minefield, she said, "It's not just that people are drawn to beauty—though they are. The new face comes with its own glamour—a charisma I never had. And . . . you don't know it yet, Mrs. Huntingdon, but you get older and you become invisible. I work for the Children's Mercy Hospital. I raise funds for them. When I started volunteering, I thought I could really do something. I had all these connections. And yet . . . people listened to me politely and then went about their business.

"But then I got the new face."

Helen nodded, feeling the moment like a living thing between them, warm and growing. "And they listened."

"They all listened. I raised so much money the first year." Her words spilled out warm and impassioned. "Money we desperately needed. All those families who were barely getting by *before* their fathers died in the war. Mothers who had never had to ask for help before were bringing us children whose illnesses could have been prevented with better nutrition. . . ." Calendula suddenly recalled herself, and her face shuttered closed. "So you see that things are not as black-and-white as your sister would like to believe."

Calendula thought she was set against Helen, but the connection between them was there. Helen could find it again. Helen set down her empty teacup and began to unbutton one of the sleeves of her chartreuse jacket. "Do you remember the May Day celebration at my house?" she said.

"I fear my invitation must have gone astray," Calendula said tartly.

"I am glad to hear that, because it means you were safe," said Helen, not batting an eyelash. "But surely you heard the rumors."

"I did," admitted Calendula. "Bosh, I thought at the time. But then the fey started coming into the city . . . and I wasn't sure anymore."

Helen seized on this moment of genuine connection. "It's all true," she said, and then there was only simple truth, as she tried to make this woman hear it. "Shortly after Mr. Rochart gave me the new face. It really happened to me. I was invaded by the fey."

Calendula swallowed at hearing the tale confirmed. "My

brother went to one of those Copperhead meetings," she said. "He told me of this story. But to hear it from you . . ."

"I suppose Alistair must have spoken of it," said Helen. Most of their meetings were men only. She did not like the thought that she was being talked about, but perhaps the confirmation was helping to sway this woman.

Calendula looked away, at the rose-papered walls. "I'm not entirely sure about them," she said in a low voice. "My brother was filled with such a strange fervor after meeting with them. He said they had such great plans to clean the city of the *dwarvven*. I had thought we were allies—the *dwarvven* hate the fey, too. I do not trust blood heat. But I suppose you must know more what they are about, since your husband is among their leaders."

Helen bit her lip. "I do not," she said. She closed her eyes and dared say it. "I am not entirely sure I trust them either."

Calendula looked back at her. Genuine concern for their future was in her eyes. The connection between them was back again; she was listening to Helen. "What was it like?" she said. "Would I know if I was taken over? I have had such strange dreams."

"You would know," Helen assured her. "It was as if I was being erased. I had felt nervous anyway from the shock of the face—from the fey substance being attached. Have you—do you feel it, too?"

Calendula barely nodded.

"But then an actual fey, a whole fey—you know that your new face contains a little piece of fey, right?—came at me to take me over. When we have iron around the doorways we can forbid the entry. But when there's substance right on your face there's nothing you can do. It came in and I couldn't stop it."

A glint of hope rose in Calendula's eyes; she could refute Helen's dire warnings. "But you're here now," she said.

"Because Jane was standing a foot away and she drove sharp iron into my arm a few seconds after it happened," Helen said. "Imagine you're choking on a grape. That's the amount of time you have for someone else to save you." She had finished rolling back her sleeve during the conversation. Now she held out her arm to show the ugly puckered scar marking the flesh above her elbow.

Calendula looked at the scar. Helen saw wavering in her expression. Helen was so close she could taste it. Her fingers closed around the copper hydra and she squeezed it like a talisman. "The fey rips clean through you like the windstorm that tore the cupola off of the Queen's country house. You're blown out of your own body. You can't resist it. Within seconds it's replaced you and you're gone for good. And then you can't help the hospital at all, and what would they do without you?" Helen stared into Mrs. Smith's eyes, willing her to understand the truth of her words.

Slowly Calendula nodded, her face ashen. "And . . . there is no other option?"

"Not to be safe," said Helen. "You've seen them outside your door. When is the last time you stepped outside without your mask?"

A wistful look crossed the woman's handsome face. "I used to love sitting in Chester Park in the summer," she said. "Not good for the complexion, you know, but how lovely it was to just sit there with your face toward the sun. And we get so little sun . . . it seemed as though you could soak up enough on those few days to tide you over for the ten months of rain." She touched her cheek, unconsciously feeling the warmth. "I couldn't go outside this summer. Had to hurry straight from my car into a building. The mask was so hot in the sun I thought I might blister."

Helen knew what it was to love something and not be able to do it. She took Calendula's hands. "I don't believe your new face had anything to do with the fund-raising at all," she said. "I think you have the tenacity to do exactly what you did before all on your own. Raise twice as much money for the hospital as any year so far." Helen meant every word and she willed Calendula to see it. "Will you let us help you? Will you lead the way for the others?"

A beat—breath held, world waiting. Calendula squeezed Helen's hands in return, her lips set and resolute. "Yes," she said. "I will."

Helen left Calendula Smith's house full of triumph. One down. One promised. One woman, swung to the side of victory for Jane. She thought about writing it down in Jane's journal, but it seemed as though it would muddy Jane's notes, and besides, it wasn't Helen's style. Writing things down meant someone could find out what you really thought.

Helen hurried along the sidewalk, thinking about that curious thing Calendula had said about Copperhead planning to clean the city of *dwarvven.* Calendula Smith herself did not seem entirely in favor of Copperhead—and she was someone who tried to be at the forefront of society, so that was interesting. Helen had also questioned Calendula about Jane's visit. But Calendula seemed as stymied by Jane's disappearance as Helen.

Still, Calendula had been convinced. Helen would get another woman's name from the journal and go after her next. She was sticking to the plan. Jane would be proud.

The swathes of blue were thick outside Calendula's house. Helen put her hands in her pockets—found nothing. No iron. She closed her hand on her copper necklace, wishing it were iron.

There was a leaf pile in front of her—orange and red and gold—innocuous except for the blue underneath, oozing out from underneath the leaves. It was as if the blue was eating the leaf pile from the underside, sucking it up like mold. Helen went around, eyes on the pile.

By the time Helen made it to the post office, it was lunch and the place was busy, mostly with men wrapped in thick overcoats and mufflers. The heavily postered walls held the usual mix of advertisements for stamps and bonds, instructions about sending telegrams and what you could not put through the mail. Except there, that mustard-colored poster with the red hydra snake on it—that was certainly new. ONE PEOPLE. ONE RACE. Posters on a random warehouse by the wharf had been one thing, but to see them in a government building . . .

Helen shuddered and turned resolutely away from those thoughts. She charmed her way through the overcoats to a spot near the front of the line. (The *very* front was held by a coat-hanger-thin woman of the strict governess type, and Helen didn't think her eyelashes would work very well on that.) She still needed to work out what to say in a telegram, a stilted form of communication that squeezed all shades of meaning from your correspondence by making you be so wretchedly *brief*.

"Dear Mr. Rochart, please do not throw yourself out of any windows, but you must brace yourself for a shock of terrible proportions. . . ."

No, that was not it at all.

In the end she settled for "BAD NEWS SISTER VANISHED COME IF POSSIBLE SUSPECT BLUE." She hoped "blue" would communicate fey to Mr. Rochart; she did not at all trust the skinny rumpled clerk, who looked as if he would immediately sell the penciled pink notecard to the highest bidder if she so much as mentioned MURDER or FEY.

She felt a momentary uplift of pleasure as she exited the post office. She was solving things, and this time it would all come out right.

It was perhaps the combination of winning over Mrs. Smith plus the telegram that made her suddenly turn right and swing down a side street, march across big yellow and blue piles of leaves to do something she would never in a hundred years have thought she would do.

Ask to take charge of a small boy.

Her heart rattled as she knocked on the hydra knocker that hung on the front door.

It was not the same muscular butler as at the meeting the night before. It was a wizened old woman, who said, "An' ye be human, enter."

Helen stepped inside to an abruptly dark and empty house. "Where are all the things?" she said.

"Getting cleaned out," said the woman, who seemed quite happy to talk about it. "He can't abide anything of hers to be left, he says. First he took *her* out—and all still and quiet cold she was. Then fired all the servants round about midnight, them as been with the family for years. One shock on another,

I'll tell you, and then the constables crawling over it all this morning and so on, and him going out with those ruffian friends of his last night after such a tragedy." She lingered over her gossip with relish. "And then without a by-your-leave comes back from roulette and starts flinging everybody out around two A.M., brings in three young bucks with broad backs and they ferry furniture out all night and morning, nice electric lights blazing like they'd burn the house down. Dunno where they took all the things. Nothing left but his and Thomas's beds and some plates. Now me and my daughter come over from next door to help box things and mop. We've been with that family for years you see, know the history of the whole street. I daresay he wanted us as we don't talk too much."

"I daresay," murmured Helen. She peeked into the large drawing room. The tidy room she'd sat in only yesterday for the meeting was dismantled—the big items gone, the small items being packed into trunks and crates. It was oddly disorienting.

"You'll have heard about the lady then?"

"Yes," said Helen. "Terrible. And with that small boy, too."

"None of hers, but for all that she was better for him than that cold father of his," said the woman, lowering her voice. "Poor thing is just sitting in the attic where *she* was, and his father in and out and who-knows-where."

"That's actually why I've come," said Helen, leaping into it. "I wanted to stop by and chat with Tam. I thought he could use a friendly face." Stop by and get him out of here was more like it, but she managed not to say that. She added, "Millicent Grimsby and I were friends," which was stretching the point, but still, she thought they might have been, if they had had the opportunity to really know each other.

The woman shrugged. "You can go up in the attic for all of me. I've got no instructions to the contrary."

Helen went slowly up the stairs. Her heart went all tight again. Tam had had time to think about what happened to his stepmamma. Perhaps he knew she was responsible, she and Jane. He was not so young that he could not put things together.

Almost she fled, but the thought of Millicent lying still on the table steeled her spine and she went up.

Carefully she opened the door to the stairs that led to the garret, and went up and up. Her mind was full of poor Mrs. Grimsby.

The slanted room was empty—no furniture, no birdcages, no people. No daybed. No Millicent.

She turned, looking at where the daybed had been. She could see it still, Millicent Grimsby, pale as death, staring into nothing. . . .

"Come to gloat?"

Helen's heart leapt from her chest as she turned to see Mr. Grimsby.

He was so tall. Had he always been so tall? And he wore a finely cut suit of grey-black, and his eyes glittered.

She could not think what to say, but then he took a step toward her, out of the shadows, and the glitter in his eyes resolved to a stony black. "No, you have always been kind and asked after Millicent," he said. "I know you are not responsible for your sister's actions." He stretched his hands over where the daybed had been, and Helen saw that they were old, scarred hands, with thin ropes of scar tissue that ran up and disappeared into his sleeves.

"I am so sorry for what happened," Helen said, the words tumbling out, as they might to someone less frightening, to someone who was simply dealing with loss and was not, perhaps, the most powerful man in the city, with the ear of the Prime Minister. "Is she . . . is she still the same?"

A nod. "My Millicent," he said, and the words slipped out as if he was, after all, just a man. He ran a hand through his closely cropped black-and-grey hair, and she saw another of those ropy scars. It etched a white line in his hair, stopping just above his ear. It almost humanized him, that he could have an accident like anyone else.

Gently Helen persisted. "But where is she?"

Grimsby's eyes sharpened, glittering again. He swung on her like a hawk, and he seemed seven feet tall once more, and not a bit human. "Someplace safe. What are you doing here?"

Steel, and the right, bright words. "I was so worried about you, dear Mr. Grimsby," Helen said, and she made the pretty faces that she made to Alistair and his cronies when she wanted to be on their good side, to be petted and admired and not told to go to bed. "It must be so hard to deal with this situation! I can't think what I would do if something happened to Alistair. I should have so much to manage, the iron doctors to call, remedies to try, and hardly time for anything or anyone else."

"It has been busy," he admitted.

"Therefore I thought I would just pop in and see what I could do. I know Alistair will have thought of everything to help and my little help could hardly be that useful. Still, I thought if there was something you or Tam needed—"

"Who? Oh, young Thomas. No, no." He waved her off, but she pressed on.

"—perhaps just to take Tam on an outing, so you would have more time to deal with the situation. . . ."

He stopped and looked at her. Really looked at her, and she had the same sense as before that he was capable of penetrating her motives with one searching glance. But all he said was, "I'm so pleased you decided to wear our necklace. To join our glorious cause."

It was very odd to hear Mr. Grimsby say things like "glorious cause" in his cold dry voice, she reflected. Someone so fanatical should slaver and gleam. But she was not going to allow him to distract her. "Now Mr. Grimsby, you see it might be helpful if someone took your son to find more of his snakes and bugs and slimy et ceteras. Surely you have so much to do, if you are shutting up the house in addition to tending to Millicent."

"Perhaps I am too hasty," he mused. "Yes, you may take him for an—outing, as you say. When?"

"Anytime," said Helen, dismissing everything else she had to do from her mind. "Right now, even."

"No, tomorrow," he said. "I will send him to you tomorrow. Then we will be ready."

Ready? thought Helen, but all she said was, "How lovely; I shall look forward to helping out."

He said nothing, only stared at her, so she expected she was dismissed. Which probably made her dig her heels in, for she said, "Can I see him?"

He looked at her as if this were the strangest request anyone had ever had. She reflected crossly that that seemed to be a trait of his. "Young Thomas?"

"I would like to tell him how sorry I am," she said. If Mr. Grimsby thought he could shut his son up in the bedroom or cellar or wherever he had him, he had another think coming.

Silently Mr. Grimsby motioned her back down the garret, and led the way through the house to the back door, where he propped open the door with hand in a gesture that clearly meant: You can go through this door, but I am going back to lurking in garrets or whatever else it is I do. It was very rude, but as she would rather be out of his company posthaste, she didn't particularly mind the rudeness.

Tam was sitting on the damp ground in the cool morning, wrapped in coat and scarf and gloves. A little patch of sun had burned off some of the fog where he sat, but it was still chilly. He was busy tracking something on the ground.

Helen went down the steps into the back garden. She got all the way to Tam before she turned and saw Mr. Grimsby still standing, looking at them with covetous, glittering eyes. Did he know she was trying to get Tam away from his influence? She knelt, and Tam flicked his eyes sideways at her. Up close she could see that his face was unwashed; his cheeks streaked with the tracks of old tears.

"Tam," she said gently. "I am so sorry about your stepmamma."

He looked up at her, and when she saw his bright, wounded eyes, she knew the next question. "Did you make it happen?"

"I don't know," she said quietly, keeping her face turned away from the door. "We were helping your stepmamma so she would always be safe. But something went wrong." Helen did not know if there was a better way to talk to small children; all she could do was treat Tam the way she wished someone would have treated her—tell him the truth, as much as she could. To the side she saw the door swing shut; Mr. Grimsby was gone. "The fey are dangerous," she said. "But I'm trying to find my sister, and I hope my sister can fix your stepmamma."

He looked down at his jar, which had two june bugs thudding around in it. Slowly he opened the jar and watched them crawl out. "I didn't tell about you being up there with her," he said. "I'm a good liar."

"Er. Thank you," said Helen. She squeezed his shoulder. "Your father says I can take you for an outing tomorrow. Where would you like to go?"

A bit of interest played around his features. "The Natural History Museum? Stepmamma said they have a big reptile exhibit with basilisks and copperhead hydras." The big words flowed out with the ease of much use, though Helen was quite sure she had not heard of any of those creatures at his age, and even now could not tell you if a basilisk was a reptile or amphibian.

"Done," said Helen. "It'll be fun. I like snakes."

"I know," he said, and pointed at her necklace. "My dad gave me a pin like that. See?" He tugged on his coat lapel to show her.

Marking them. Owning them. Helen's fingers closed on the copper. She wanted to rip their emblem off, snap the chain. And yet she did not. So it was a hydra—Grimsby's hydra. Wasn't it proof that Alistair cared about her? Some days she needed that proof. She let the necklace fall, smiling down at Tam. "Till tomorrow, then. And we'll find you some more bugs. I'm afraid I lost yours."

Tam watched one of the june bugs crawl around the lip of the jar, uncertain what to do with its freedom. He picked up the lid and held it over the jar, trapping the bug inside. Raised it, lowered it. "Do they have *dwarvven* in the museum?" he said.

"Um," said Helen. "I don't think so. You mean like pictures of them?"

"Father said they should be rounded up and shot, and then the potato-faced man said they should be put on display as a lesson, and then Father said someday the last dwarf will be like the stuffed bear in the museum. I like the stuffed bear. I can see his claws up close. I would like to see the stuffed dwarf."

Helen recognized the "potato-faced man" as an accurate if unflattering description of Boarham. "I'm afraid there aren't any stuffed *dwarvven,*" she said. It disturbed her to hear the ugly slur "dwarf" fall as easily as "basilisk" from the boy's lips, but she supposed it was inevitable with that father of his. She stopped over the next bit and decided to say it anyway. "Whatever they say while drinking, take it with a grain of salt. I mean, it isn't all true . . . or *right.*"

He nodded as if he understood, although she wasn't sure he did. But the door was being opened by the cleaning woman, and clearly Helen's time was up. "Tomorrow," she promised, and left.

Back down the street toward the trolley. Helen was getting awfully sick of the trolley. She reached the stop in time to see one pulling away, and then she regretted saying she was sick of the trolley, for it was even more annoying to want to get on one and not be able.

Because it was a nice neighborhood, there was a small shelter, empty except for a *dwarvven* man just walking into it. She went in after him and stood there, stamping her feet against the cold. The brick wall around the Grimsbys' back garden had dampened the gale, but here it whisked through the street in full force, blowing dead leaves before it, covering and uncovering the swathes of blue that lined the sidewalks. Tomorrow she would not take the trolley, that's all. She would take

Tam in the car to the Natural History Museum . . . and oh goodness, Helen, how foolish were you? Supposedly you were doing such a clever job of sneaking out, and now you went and saw your husband's good friend and made arrangements to take his son out the next day? This is where rash decisions led you. The motive was good but the execution was abysmal.

Relax, she told herself. Alistair has never *expressly* forbidden you to leave. You are a grown woman, capable of leaving the house on your own. And yet she shook her head, despairing, running through increasingly ridiculous options in her head. She could get Mary to pretend to be Helen. She could ask Mr. Grimsby to lie about her visit.

People trickled into the shelter, waiting for the next trolley to pull up. Gentlemen, mostly, in worn but decent overcoats, copper lapel pins winking in buttonholes. A fellow in a soft cap eyed her and she tugged her own copper necklace out where it was more plainly visible. If she was marked as the wife of a top party member she might as well enjoy its benefits of implied protection. She moved away from him, closer to the *dwarvven* man, studying the inevitable lineup of posters. Trolley times and fares. A curling one for *Painted Ladies Ahoy!* that she smoothed out. She realized she had seen it before, and not known till now that the darling ink caricature of the central painted lady was clearly Frye.

"This shelter's becoming crowded, isn't it? Perhaps someone should know his place a little better," said the man in the cap. He was staring at the young *dwarvven.*

The *dwarvven* folded his arms and did not budge. He appeared to be in his early twenties—a dangerous age for getting into trouble. "Know it as well as you do."

"Not really right for your kind to be here with a lady present."

"By lady I suppose you mean yourself?"

The man in the cap went red and the mood in the shelter suddenly turned much uglier. Helen could feel the overcoated men slowly shifting, moving into a circle to enclose the *dwarvven.*

The man in the cap bent down as though he were lecturing a child, tapped the *dwarvven* on the nose. "One people," he said. "*One race.*"

The dwarvven was dying to take the first swing, she could tell. He settled for spitting: "You've learned your lesson well."

Just then the trolley pulled up and Helen saw her cue. She tapped on the man with the cap's sleeve and slid into the circle. "Thank you so kindly for protecting me," she said to the man in the cap, "and I feel much safer now. We were just going." She tugged on the *dwarvven*'s arm and pulled him through the openmouthed circle of men. Everyone was momentarily too stunned to resist, and Helen stepped onto the open trolley, motioning the *dwarvven* man to follow her.

But what had worked so beautifully with the *dwarvven* grandmother did not work with this young man.

He growled at her, "Don't plan to owe a debt to a *Copperhead,*" and turned away, back into the crowd. The air seemed to crackle with electricity. A knife flicked into his hand, and he crouched, motioning at the men to dare step forward. The overcoated men surrounded him, ringing him, a circle of leering hydras. He was so small compared to them, and yet as he gestured with his knife they backed up a step. "I'm tired of bending over to you lot," he shouted. "Don't think you can tell us what to do. Don't think it's not going to come back to bite you." A pile of maple leaves whisked furiously past, uncovering more and more blue on the sidewalk.

"Oh, just go on home to the slums," shouted one, and then suddenly he caught sight of something over the *dwarvven*'s shoulder and fell silent. Helen could not see what he saw, but one by one they all went agape, and backed up.

"That's right," jeered the *dwarvven.* "Cold metal will scare you, won't it? Not so brave now—"

The trolley doors closed in front of her as a sea of blue rose from the surrounding plants and maple tree and sidewalk. The air tingled as the blue surrounded the young *dwarvven.* He dropped his knife, trying frantically to extricate himself from the tangle of slithery blue.

And then there was a noise she hadn't heard in five years, a sharp metallic noise.

The explosion of a fey bomb.

Chapter 6

DANCING BACKWARDS

Helen tugged at the trolley doors, certain she should get back out and do *something,* although she did not know what. But the steel would not budge, and the conductor hurried over and said firmly, "Miss, stop, stop."

Through the greasy trolley windows she could see that the blue had died away, leaving only a small figure, still and silent upon the ground. The overcoated men were picking themselves up, dusting themselves off, hurriedly backing away from the scene of the accident. The explosion seemed to have been contained by the whirlwind of blue fey that brought it. No one else was hurt. But oh, that poor young man . . .

"Please sit down, miss. The trolley is starting."

From a distance she saw someone running. The trolley jerked under her feet, and through the tears standing in her eyes she saw a slight black-clad figure leap over a fence, running toward the man.

Him. The man she had seen twice now—at the Grimsbys' and on the trolley.

What was he doing here?

As he reached the crumpled form of the *dwarvven,* he looked at the trolley, and their eyes met. She was sure of it. Just for a second, and then they were pulling away, and she could no longer see anything clearly through the trolley window.

Helen opted for a long bath instead of *Painted Ladies Ahoy!* She washed her hair thoroughly, trying to scrub out the imaginary scent of blood and smoke and fey. There was no return telegram from Mr. Rochart yet. And Alistair had not come back—he was probably out with Grimsby, hearing that his wife had been gallivanting around town today. She sank under the water, eyes closed, and wished she could just stay there.

But she couldn't hold her breath forever. She climbed out and got into her mint green bathrobe and snuggled into her pink chair in front of the fireplace in her rooms. Mary had gotten it well and thoroughly going, and set out more chocolate, and some buttered toast, and a little vase with a red-leafed maple twig. Helen tossed the twig into the fireplace without a second thought.

There was a fashion magazine on the table (SKIRTS! FROM VAREE! it exclaimed) and Helen reached for it to complete her evening of sitting and drinking chocolate and forgetting about everything else (she was going to help Tam tomorrow, surely that was enough?) but instead her treacherous fingers picked up the faded leather journal, and her notepad and pencil, and then there she was, settling in for an evening of work.

"Bah," muttered Helen. Apparently she was going to see whom she could win over next, now that she had convinced Mrs. Smith. Her mind leapt back to Jane, and, sidetracked, she thought perhaps she should investigate what Mrs. Smith had said about the *dwarvven*. If Copperhead was anti-*dwarvven,* then perhaps *dwarvven* were anti-Copperhead? They had infiltrated a meeting, unbeknownst to anyone. Sure, okay. And then ransacked Jane's flat . . . why?

She tapped the pencil against her chin. Start over. Millicent was stuck in fey sleep and Jane was gone, but what if both things were an accident? What if someone had been trying to stop Millicent from running away, and ended up kidnapping Jane so she wouldn't tell anyone? But no, Millicent hadn't decided to run until Jane talked her into it. Scratch that. She rolled the pencil back and forth. What if it was an accident in a different way? Grimsby had surely not expected that showing off his toy would end in a disaster of that magnitude—surging the lights and so on. Perhaps his machine had been sabotaged. By the *dwarvven*? Again, why? And if whoever sabotaged the machine knew what effects it would have . . . well, Jane was anti-fey, but not anti-*dwarvven.* Jane was notoriously not aligned with Copperhead. And who knew that Jane was going to be in the garret doing a facelift that night? Only Helen, and though she was flaky and flighty, she knew she had not told.

Helen sighed and dropped the pencil into her lap. She could not make it make sense.

She went back to the notes she had made earlier, looking through the list of eighteen women Jane had tried and failed to convince. She had reread about half of them when a niggling thought in the back of her mind forced its way out. "Alberta," she said out loud, and peered at the short list again. Yes. Alberta was on it, right at the top, and halfway down there was a Betty.

Helen flipped back to the journal, to the long list of 99 women that started the book. Down at number 73 she saw Desirée.

"Bah," Helen said again, and pulled out Frye's bright orange missive from that morning to check. Those were the names in her PS: Alberta, Betty, and Desirée.

Helen stood, putting down her chocolate and kicking off her slippers. "Oh, bother, here we go," she muttered, and found herself dressing for a party and heading out the front door.

Frye's house was not at all like any of the other society houses she'd been to. And of course not; Frye was not exactly high society. Yet she was clearly educated and well-spoken, she had some money—oh, artists were hard to classify. She lived in a medium-sized brick house on a row of other brick houses. But inside, every square inch was covered with artwork and memorabilia. Helen moved down the hallway, looking at the framed sheets of music, signed by their composers; lush oils, charcoal sketches, dashed-off nudes. She thought that Jane should be the one to be here; she would appreciate it. But then, this woman knew Jane, didn't she? Perhaps Jane had already seen this bounty of art.

The hall began to curve around a central staircase, and the wall decor turned from art to theatre memorabilia. Posters from shows, some framed, some not, some torn, some signed, all the way from cheap printings to elaborate productions with color painted onto them. Some of the newest ones had STARRING MISS EGLANTINE FRYE in bold letters on them. Interspersed were curio shelves with gloves and cups and beads and a wide variety of oddities that Helen could only assume were props, mementos. Behind it all was intricate wallpaper, the pattern of which changed every time it had the slightest excuse of a corner or chair rail.

The wood floors were covered with long runners of carpets in exotic patterns. Flowers bloomed in profusion; birds darted in between them. Helen got so caught up in trying to decide whether there was a pattern to the birds that she only belatedly realized she was still hanging around the hallway, and piano music was banging away at a distance, somewhere else in the house.

Her spirits began to rise with the prospect of dancing. It was emphatically not what she was here for. She was here to talk to Frye, to find those other three women that Frye had lured her here for, to convince them all to see the light, to come to Jane. To find out if they knew anything about Jane. She had done it this afternoon; she could do it again.

But, oh, the dance. Oh, how she missed the dance.

Helen followed the curve in the hallway and there in a burst of light was the party. It was a small room, too small for the number of laughing bodies that filled it. But it was gold and warm and glittering with strings of that yellow electric light. The heady smell of burning clove cigarettes drifted out, and from somewhere else, almonds. The music came from a battered upright piano in the back corner—a long-legged man in fitted sweater and wide slacks thumped out a riotous tune, and three young women in variously scarlet red, bright orange, and deep purple dresses sang with him. The one in bright orange was perched on top of the piano and was dark-skinned, slim, and so lovely that even Helen did a double take.

Well, she'd found one of the women, she thought dryly.

Chairs and stools were pushed back against the wall and in the middle, a messy glut of couples and singles danced the very latest dances, wild affairs with kicks and elbows and enthusiasm. A smile began to curve up Helen's face. She had not seen these dances since the days at the tenpence music hall. Heaven knows they did not do them in Alistair's house, or any of the other places she went.

A hand grabbed hers and suddenly she was in the dance, despite all her good intentions to stay on task. A good-looking chap with a riot of curls swung her in and out, and she dredged up old memories from seven months ago to keep pace with him, glad that seven months ago was not hopelessly out of date, that she was somewhat still au courant.

The piano thumped to a stop, and the curly-haired chap beckoned an invitation for the next, eyes sparkling, but she demurred, smiling at him, and threaded her way through the dancers to the doorway. The party spilled out into the next small room, and then to the balcony after that, where French doors stood ajar and brought in welcome relief. She was pleased to see that the time she had spent at her wardrobe attempting to figure out exactly what you wore to an actor's aftershow party was not in vain; many of the girls were wearing the more up-to-the-minute higher waists and wide shoulders of her own seafoam silk. Some outfits were more daring, and some simply fit no scene that she knew at all, and she particularly studied those girls, watching to see where creativity had hit on something new and desirable.

She fetched up against a trio of giggling girls whose combination of baby fat and gangle marked them as probably too young to be here. She wondered if they were actors, too; she wondered if she had ever been that young. Behind them, a woman in an atrocious purple dress made of scraps of silk and what looked like faux fur looked out an open window into the night. She turned at Helen's approach, and the perfection of her heart-shaped face made Helen instantly sure she had found a comrade.

You didn't just *ask,* though.

"Breath of air?" she said to the wistful-looking girl.

"Bit stuffy, ain't it?" the girl said. "It was hot in the theatre tonight, too." She fanned herself with a discarded playbill and wafted over a cloud of rose perfume. It was the same expensive scent as Calendula Smith's, which was both amusing and informational. This girl must have a benefactor.

"Are you an actor?" said Helen. She wondered if the girl had chosen the face for the same reason as Frye, to advance her career. But the girl's dreadful accent would probably hold her back, she thought. Frye could switch in and out of beautiful diction at will, apparently, and Helen had paid attention to her own when she first started working as a governess, trying to eradicate any country from it. This girl sounded as though she had marbles in her mouth.

"No," the girl said wistfully. "I'm just a dresser for Ruth." The way she said *Ruth* made it sound like it was someone Helen should know. "It's a good job and I've met a nice man from it but it ain't exactly like being onstage now is it?" She crossed her long legs and it seemed to Helen that the "nice man" must be the someone who had paid for her face and scent, for surely this girl with the terrible accent had no connections or money of her own.

"I'm Helen," she said.

"Betty," the girl said, confirming Helen's hunch that she was one of the three she was supposed to meet. "You been in a show with Frye?" Dull envy flashed in her eyes.

"No, we just met last night," Helen said.

"Oh," said Betty. "Seems like you could be. I thought this

would do it," and she gestured at the perfect face, "but seems not. Do you think the producers want something else besides face and body? 'Cause I don't know what else I got." Her forehead furrowed prettily. "You are like me, ain't you?"

"Yes," said Helen. "We are alike." Betty nodded, and Helen followed up that line of persuasion, adding, "I often feel it didn't really change anything inside. Do you feel that?"

This philosophical statement seemed to go over Betty's head. "Inside? I still have the same body, I suppose. I was asleep for the part where the man did it. I was so scared when he knocked me out."

Helen seized on this admission. "I was scared, too," she said. "And now when I go outside, because of the fey."

That was it. Betty's eyes grew wide and she said, "I didn't know there was gonna be all this fey everywhere. I have to wear my iron mask every time I leave the theatre or Richard's flat, and Richard, that's my man you know, he says what did he do it for if I can't be seen, but he don't know what it's like to know there's blue devils waiting to get into your bones. I don't think a man really can know, do you?"

"No," said Helen fervently. "Look, my sister, Jane, is helping people change back. I think you should let her help you."

Wide eyes again, looking to Helen for help. "Do you really think I should? She scared me a bit, she was so determined I should do what she said. I don't like being afraid, it's just the worst feeling, worse than auditioning where your throat dries up and so on."

"I think you should change back," Helen said gently. "I think we all should. What about Ruth? Is she nice?"

Betty nodded emphatically. "For all she's *Ruth,* she's nicer to me even than me mum."

"Stay with Ruth and be her dresser always. You don't want to be onstage anyway, because it's frightening up there. If you want to move on from dressing you should try to work up to being—" and Helen seized on what she could intuit from Betty's dress— "a costumer. You'd be an important part of the theatre without having to be afraid."

"Do you really think so?" said Betty. It was amazing what a smile could do for even a phenomenally pretty face. "I designed this dress even, did you have any idea?"

"Not at all," lied Helen, "and it's stunning. Look, I have to say hello to Frye, but as soon as my sister gets back into town we'll set you up and she'll get you fixed back. Is it a deal?"

Betty put out her hand, then withdrew. "Does it cost? I hate to ask Richard for yet more."

"No, it doesn't," said Helen.

Betty grinned, and you could suddenly see the down-home city girl inside the fey beauty. "I'll make you a dress of your own to thank you. You and your sister."

Helen tried not to look startled. "That's very kind of you, Betty. Thank you."

"I'm gonna go tell Ruth I'll be her dresser always," Betty said. "Excuse me." She slipped off her stool, her slit skirt displaying her long legs as she crossed the room.

Helen turned away from the window, pleased. One down, and sneaking out for the evening was already proving worthwhile.

Through the doorway to the piano room she saw Frye, and she decided to brave the crowd again, circling around the crush of dancers, around the outskirts of the packed room. The current dance was a complicated and lively one that Helen did not know. She watched the patterns as she threaded her way through a waft of clove-drenched smoke, filing it away in the hope that someday she would get to dance it. She watched everyone's feet so carefully that she almost got whacked three separate times by elbows.

The piano finished with a flourish, the singers laughed and bowed to applause, and someone shouted, "Too easy! Try harder!"

"The Shadow?" shouted back the pianist. "Change partners, everyone!" Shouts and cheers, and he plunged into the prelude of a familiar and intricate melody that went with a dance that was a mind-bending cross between a formal waltz and a risqué tango.

All around her men and women released hands and found new ones, and Helen got pushed inside the dance floor. She pushed down the *want* and tried to slither away, eluding eyebrow-raised offers, outstretched hands.

The dance proper started and the music all came back to her now, filled her from head to toe like a plucked violin string and she hummed along, remembering a night she had danced it with Alistair in the tenpence ballroom. Why did he not dance these dances in high society? He knew them. She kept going, avoiding the glides of the couples as they spun around for the back-to-front portion of the dance, where you did not look at your partner but let him guide you. If your partner was good, it was tremendous. Alistair had never been good.

She was nearly out of the crowd when a hand slid behind her at a precise turn in the music, memory made flesh. One hand at her waist, one at the hand, its fingers firmly wrapping around her palm, and then her feet were moving through the familiar steps before she was fully aware of it. It had happened so like a dream that she had given in to that ache without realizing; she was dancing in reality before she knew it.

She laughed with a moment of pure joy at the audacity of the young man who held her. "Who is this?" she said.

"We have never been formally introduced," he said, his breath warm on her ear, "yet I have seen you more than once."

If that was true then it was a puzzle; for Helen could not think who of her set might have overlap with Frye's acquaintance. They turned and turned, and her feet moved with the joy of the music as she pondered. His hands were neither rough nor soft—lean and callused, hands that did things. A hint of something musky, like sandalwood, lingered in the air as they turned. Someone artsy, someone bohemian, someone not stuffy. That ruled out nearly everyone, she thought cynically.

But be fair, Helen. Not everyone was bland and insipid, just because Alistair was so obsessed with status. She could figure this man out. She could tell from the way he held her that he was not tall—perhaps just her height. That ought to narrow it down and yet she still could not think who it might be. He held her waist lightly; she could turn at any time, and yet she did not. It amused her to play his guessing game.

"Lionel Winterstock," Helen said, naming a wealthy young man who wrote a lot of bad poetry and might think it exciting to know a bohemian slacks-wearing actress. "No—Georgie Pennyfeather." True, Pennyweather's rebellion had only extended so far as once upon a time thinking about running away to the Faraway East, but then deciding better of it—but he was short.

"Nothing so grand. Close your eyes."

She did, and he spun her out, and in, somehow avoiding the other spinning couples that clustered the floor. Helen was a good dancer, but he, perhaps, was better. Or perhaps just exceptionally good at partnering. The subtle cues from his fingertips directed her safely away from him and back, even with her eyes closed.

"There. We're safe now. Continue your guessing game."

"Let's see," said Helen. She watched the eyes of the other couples as they danced for a clue. How did they look at her, at her partner? Smiles, grins, perhaps a touch of envy from a young woman or two. No surprise at seeing him, though, so he was part of this set, and known. "Are you an actor? No, wait. How did you meet Frye?" That would cover more information.

"Not onstage," he said, "though she did a remarkable Vera Velda on the Feathertoad stage last season. I may have been in the audience, just passing through. I may even have rushed up to her afterwards with an armful of roses gathered from every twopenny flowergirl in the street, laid them at her feet like some demented thing." His touch was so delicate, so fine, she fancied she could feel the amused, rueful twinge slide along his bones. "She let me down easy."

"Kind of her," said Helen.

"My turn," he said. "What kind of game are you playing?"

It was said lightly, yet she tensed under his fingers.

"Easy, easy," he said. "A simple question."

"I have no game," she said tightly.

"A woman of mystery, then," he said. "Who turns up in surprising places. I expect next I'll see you in the *dwarvven* slums, dancing around the statue of Queen Maud."

Dwarvven, not dwarf. Not a member of Copperhead,

though that was unlikely from the mere fact that he was here. His hands were on hers and he was silent. She said brightly back, "All right then, why do you come? Clearly not to show off your limited dancing prowess." A weak jab for such a clever dancer, but damned if she was going to let him sail by on that charm alone.

"And I thought I was making such headway, too," he complained. "Eyes."

"This is the last time," she warned, but she obeyed and felt him guide her through the spin. "And you haven't answered my question."

"Professional curiosity," he said lightly. "Final pattern. Want to try it?"

Laughing, she extended her arm for the last bit. If he thought he could do it backwards she wouldn't be the one to fail. They spun in, out, feet tripped the fast bit at the end, and finished in the lift. Except there he finally did stumble against another couple, and they landed with a thud. Helen was grinning as she straightened up. "Now I know it's Lionel," she said. "No one else would dare."

"It is not," he said, laughter in his voice.

Helen wheeled to find herself in the arms of the young man she had seen three times before—at the Grimsbys', on the trolley, and near the fey attack.

Chapter 7

SECRETS IN THE NIGHT

"You," she said, and stared, agape.

"You," he agreed, studying her in return.

He was indeed just her height—and she was not tall—but lithe, as if he were a professional dancer or acrobat. His clothes were similar to yesterday's—fitted, trim, nondescript—the sort of clothes she had identified as being for a quick getaway. His hair was ruddy-brown and his eyes flashed with light. Even in the gay room of actors and singers in bright colors he seemed like something wilder, something more real and alive. "Who on earth are you?"

"Who wants to know?"

A bit of temper flashed at his evasions. "After that uninvited dance, I think I have the right to know."

"You didn't seem to mind the dance while dancing."

"My *husband* might mind," she said, trying to squash him.

"There's always a husband," he said, unsquashable.

She glared at him, but his grin was unrepentant.

"There's someone looking for you," he said, and pointed over her shoulder.

"I'm not falling for that—," said Helen, but then Frye

swooped in and enveloped her in a one-armed embrace that knocked her off balance.

"Helen, darling!" shouted Frye over the clamor of the party. "You made it. Have you met the girls?"

"Alberta, Betty, and Desirée?" guessed Helen.

"The same."

"No," said Helen, "but I did meet—"

But of course he was gone.

"Bah," Helen said, and turned back to Frye, who looped a companionable arm around her shoulders and led her off to the open bar.

"Now I will tell you all about them so you can bring them over to the side of good and light." Frye gestured to the bartender, who seemed as though he might be a fellow actor she'd roped in for the night. "Two martinis, very dirty." She turned back to Helen. "Desirée is divine. She has the most glorious voice. And this rubbish little old husband, but we don't talk about him."

The bartender had a striped shirt rolled up over olive-skinned muscles and a lopsided, winsome grin that he employed to great effect on the pair of them. "Very dirty," he repeated.

"None of your lip, and put in more olives," said Frye. She had a long purple caftan embroidered with a dragon that billowed around filmy green slacks, and dark red heels that made her even taller. "Now, it turns out Desirée is allergic to iron. Can't wear one of the face masks without going a funny shade of green. So she'll be no problem at all. Just scheduling conflicts with her; she's got engagements all over the place, and next week she's going to—"

"Is she here?" cut in Helen.

"Yes, and she's wearing the most atrocious peppermint-striped dress; you can't miss it. She lets that ancient husband pick out her clothing. I can't imagine why."

"Maybe she actually likes him," said Helen.

Frye dismissed this with a wave. "Oh, what glorious martinis, Cosmo. Helen, yours," and she passed it across.

Cosmo grinned his lopsided grin at her and went to the next order. Helen rather liked that he seemed to be immune to her fey charm, perhaps through so much saturation in association with the charming actors around them, including the three enhanced women. That man she had danced with had seemed to be immune, too, although that hadn't left her with exactly the same positive feeling.

"What about the other two?" Helen said to Frye, who had gone into an explanation of a perfectly terrible martini she had had last week while Helen hadn't been listening.

"Oh, yes," said Frye. "Just keep me focused. And Cosmo, one for the road if you would—?"—this while tapping the martini glass. "So little Betty's here somewhere, in this dreadful purple fur thing she made herself, but she is an absolute lamb, you will love her."

Helen noted for future reference that Frye didn't seem to think much of anyone else's personal taste. Of course, if that peppermint dress over there by the punch bowl was Desirée . . . perhaps Frye was just speaking truth. "I think I found Betty," she said. "Did Jane mention talking with her?"

"Oh, Jane," said Frye. "Now of course we both love Jane, but between you and me and the hall tree she went about it all wrong. Betty just needs to be told what to do, but not in a schoolmistressy way, you know? She's an utter lamb, and you need to sit her down and hold her hand and tell her it will be all right and she can stop being afraid once she changes back. She's going to get fired if she's too afraid to get to performances, which she currently is, so you sit her down and explain that very nicely to her and she'll come along."

"Like a little lamb," agreed Helen, satisfied that Frye's estimate dovetailed so nicely with Helen's accomplishment. She saw the mysterious fellow over by the window and turned to Frye. "Say, do you know who that man is—?" she started to say, but just then a tall lady in yellow ran up and air-kissed Frye and started talking a mile a minute about some performance that had been *disastrous,* didn't Frye know. Helen waited patiently a few moments, as Frye turned half back to Helen and said "oh dear" and "just a minute," but Helen perfectly well knew the signs of a busy hostess with three hundred people who wanted to talk to her, so she slipped away and tried to find the girl in the orange dress who had been singing at the piano.

The pianist was still banging away, and had been joined by a plump brown man in disheveled tie and specs. They were having too good a time at their duet to be interrupted.

You would think it wouldn't be that hard to spot someone in orange, Helen thought, but here it was. The whole room was alive with color and fashion, and she was rather amused to note that everything she knew about fashion (and she knew rather a lot; on a good day she could pin you to an income and street just by the cut of the coat you wore) went out the window here, where it was apparently not only acceptable, but celebrated, to cross-dress in slacks or a bow tie, or to make a dress out of a slip with feathers stitched on, or to combine pink and orange, crimson and aqua, silver and gold.

The whole gaiety and life of the small house made her

quite happy and giddy, as though she'd finally found a place to relax and just be. It was strange how sometimes you could feel that in a crowd, particularly as sometimes you couldn't.

"Frye said you wanted to see me?"

Helen turned to see the perfect face of the dark-skinned girl in orange who'd been sitting on top of the piano. Hard to judge age with The Hundred, but Helen would guess mid-twenties. "Alberta?" she said.

The young woman nodded, eyeing her warily. Helen wished Frye had prepped her so she knew what this one was about. Jane's only notes had been: Met. Dismal.

"I'm Helen," she said. "I just met Frye last night and she dragged me over here. Are you in the show with her?" She began feeling out what the girl did for a living. It seemed as though most of the women at the party had jobs, even if they were exciting artistic ones.

Alberta shook her head. "Nightclubs," she said.

"Oh, a singer," said Helen. She was realizing that for the women she had met through Frye, a more beautiful face was not just vanity—it was part of their livelihood. Where did that fall on Jane's line of who should and shouldn't make themselves more beautiful? People would always rather go hear a beautiful *chanteuse* than a plain one, even if they had the exact same voice.

But Alberta shook her head. "Saxophone," she said.

Helen's face crinkled in puzzlement.

A tiny smile broke through on Alberta's sullen beautiful face. "I know. There aren't too many of us. I can sing well enough, but . . . no. I play sax in a cabaret band called *Sturm und Drang*. You might have heard of us."

"I have," said Helen, though admittedly the "heard of"

amounted to Alistair grinching about the terrible modern music that was becoming popular for no discernible reason that he, Alistair, could see. She looked at Alberta with new respect. "But then why. . . ."

Alberta looked wary. "Frye mentioned you. You're Jane's sister, aren't you? You're wasting your time."

"To convince you to do the facelift? It really is safer."

Alberta rolled her eyes. "Spare me. I'm not like all of you rich ladies who just wanted to be prettier."

Helen tried not to be offended by the venom in her tone. Or at least, reminded herself that it didn't matter if she was offended. "Why then?" she said, as neutrally as she could manage.

Alberta looked at her coldly. "Abusive husband," she said. The words were sharp and blunt. "Wouldn't grant me a divorce. Thought he could beat me and I wouldn't mind." She showed teeth. "Turns out I did." At Helen's horrified expression her face relaxed and she laughed again. "I didn't smash his face in with a frying pan or anything, don't worry. Just ran away. A . . . friend . . . helped me scrape up the money to change my face."

Helen could tell from her pursed lips she was not going to say any more about the friend, so instead she asked, "So you're not just a more beautiful version of before?"

"No," said Alberta. "It's nice to be beautiful; I don't mind that. As long as I was getting it done, why not go all the way, you know? But the point is that I'm not the same. And he can't recognize me."

Helen thought of all the folks she'd met, that this woman was the hardest to want to convince. Who was she to tell this woman to go back in living in fear for her life?

And yet, Alberta was in danger now, too, and the facelifts needed to be done. The wistfulness in Alberta's voice when she said "I'm not the same" was Helen's necessary clue. "You miss your old face?" she said.

"Sure, who wouldn't?" said Alberta, but her tone was brash over loss.

Helen touched her arm. "I won't try to convince you to change back," she said, "because honestly, I'm not sure you should."

"Oh. Good," said Alberta with surprise.

"I miss my old face, and it was pretty much the same," Helen said. "Although it had freckles, and this one doesn't. Turns out for all my time spent trying to get rid of freckles . . . I miss them once they're gone. Silly, I suppose. Well, Alistair never liked them."

Alberta nodded. "So you changed for your husband, too."

It was true, though Helen hadn't thought about it in those terms. Alistair had said it would erase the freckles—fix the imperceptible bump on her nose—et cetera. That she needed to be as beautiful as the Prime Minister's wife to make all those people who laughed at her when she used the wrong fork respect her.

"And it's not right, is it?" Helen said. "It's as if they took something that was yours. You can leave . . . but you're still changed by them. They still have power over that piece of you. You're never really free."

"True," said Alberta. She looked thoughtful and Helen judged the moment right to excuse herself for another martini. She had started out just exercising her wits to find arguments to work, but the conversation had dredged up things she hadn't really thought about, and wasn't sure she wanted to. A little shaken, she looked at herself for a long time in the window into the night, running pale fingers over the missing freckles, and thinking.

After Alberta, the third one was a piece of cake. Fortified with another gin from the winsome bartender, Helen met with Desirée, and armed with Frye's information about the iron allergy, had no trouble extracting a promise to meet with Jane as soon as she was found. Indeed, Desirée sounded eager, and she pulled back the locks of her hair to show Helen where her cheek was blistered around the edge of the iron mask. It reminded Helen of the bloodred line around Millicent's face, and she shuddered.

At last some rather languid-looking actors vacated one of Frye's striped divans, and Helen seized it gladly. Her legs were protesting yesterday's exercise, and she was starting to get tired. Also, it had just occurred to her that she had come here on the trolley, and just like last night, the trolley was certainly done running for the day. Zero foresight. Zip. She drained the last of her gin, postponing the problem of getting home for a bit longer. She could flag down a cab . . . if she had her purse . . . if she begged Frye for a loan. . . . Of course, Frye might try to get Helen to stay, and attempt that facelift all by herself. . . .

Helen crossed her ankles on a carved elephant that was doubling as a coffee table and tried to imagine following through on Frye's demand that she take over Jane's line of work. Perhaps Frye thought through consequences even less than she, Helen did. She wondered how that worked out for Frye. It seemed to, but then Frye seemed to be all alone in the world. Maybe if your muddles only muddled you, you could make your way better. You wouldn't be always trying to atone for past muddles, and muddling more.

As if summoned by Helen's thoughts, the purple caftan ballooned into her sight and Frye stood in front of her and the carved elephant. "I don't want this face," Frye said. She had a martini in each hand and a peculiarly desperate expression on her face.

"I know," said Helen, with a twinge of exasperation and a good deal of sympathy. "But even if I *could* do it I couldn't do it tonight. One, we don't know where your real face is, and two, I've had three gins."

Frye's fingers tensed on the martini glasses. Up close Helen could see that her fingernails were jade green. "You don't know, do you?" said Frye. "You can do things with it."

Helen's heart beat faster. Jane had hinted at something like this. Something more than the natural fey glamour that simply made people want to please her. "What things?"

Frye slumped next to Helen on the striped divan in a cloud of jasmine. Her eyes were feverish and Helen thought that although Frye seemed to hold her liquor quite well, she was also possibly at the point where she was not going to remember any of this tomorrow.

"You have to be focused," Frye said. "Remember that."

"I will," said Helen, humoring her.

"Did you have a good time? Did you take the trolley again and need a ride? I bet you did, since it sounds like you have to sneak away from some dreary old husband."

"Focused," pointed out Helen, for Frye seemed to be evading her own story.

"I met this . . . artist," said Frye at last. She cradled the two martini glasses in one hand so she could gesture with the other. "I was desperately in love. It didn't matter how many other folks brought me flowers, you know? There was only one person I wanted. But even with all my fey glamour . . . No. Just not interested in someone like me. Heart of stone."

"It's the worst," agreed Helen.

Frye looked up and into Helen's face. "I changed all that," she whispered. "I changed it. With the fey power in the mask." Misery glittered in her eyes. "Where there was indifference I made love. I *made* someone love me." Haltingly, the words slipped out: "And you see I didn't deserve it. Anyone who could do what I did doesn't deserve to be loved."

Helen didn't know what to say, and Frye seemed to interpret her silence as disgust, for she looked away, shoulders crumpling. "Don't worry, I undid the changes. We've stopped speaking—they think it was a temporary lapse in judgment, I'm sure." Her free hand traced the stripes on the divan. "So you see I can't be trusted. I need the mask gone before I do it again."

Compassion riddled Helen's heart in response. "Love is not the worst thing in the world," she said gently, and put a warm hand on Frye's own.

Frye pressed Helen's fingers, then let them go. "Love is perhaps the best thing," she said, and she laced her fingers tightly around her martini glasses. "But forcing someone into it is perhaps the worst. Those Copperhead people have a term for it, what the fey did to the ones they took over. Brainwiping."

The party was thinning out at this hour of the night as actors slumped to divans or left for home. Frye's confession thinned out and died away, and Helen thought what a slippery slope this fey power was. Even before the power, she had employed her beauty and charm as tools; how could you not? They were her own, and she had sharpened them like razors. It seemed like all one could do, in this world where others had wealth and status at their disposal, and all she had were a couple of pretty little knives that would crack with age.

Across the room Helen saw her mysterious dance partner, chatting animatedly to a brunette woman with a curvy figure. If I were her I would not wear that horizontal panel at my waist, Helen mused.

Frye followed Helen's gaze. "Did you meet Roxanne?"

"That man," said Helen. It suddenly occurred to her that he could be a spy for Copperhead, here for some sinister purpose. "Do you know him?"

"Oh, you," said Frye. "Of course." She stood up, mussing Helen's perch on the cushions, and gestured imperiously, the two glasses she held clinking together. "Rook!" she said. "Rook!" He grinned impudently at Frye, excused himself from the brunette, and came loping over, sliding through the tangle of sitting-down bodies.

"You. Meet this young woman named Helen," said Frye. "Now, if I understand the situation correctly, she's going to need an escort home tonight." To Helen she said, "I would invite you to stay, but you're going to tell me no, and I don't do well when people tell me no." She turned back to Rook. "Now I know you're ridiculously charming and everything, but she has a husband so no funny business."

"No funny business," said Rook, shaking Helen's hand as soberly as if they were now meeting for the first time. That warm sandalwood scent lingered around her fingertips.

"Does everyone just do what she says?" said Helen, and

then immediately bit her tongue, for she hadn't meant it like that, not like she was betraying the confidence Frye had just shared.

Frye just laughed at her discomfort. "If they're smart they do," she said. She waved a pair of now-empty martini glasses at Helen. "I'll see you later this week."

Frye left and then they were alone in the crowd. All sorts of things to say whirled through her mind as she studied him, this man. Rook. He had no hydra pin—but if he were a spy, he wouldn't, would he? What did he want from her?

A hint of a smile played over Rook's features as he watched her studying him. Languidly he offered an arm and said, "Shall we?"

Helen settled on saying airily: "Kind of you to offer. But I'm afraid I find your suspicious ways suspicious. I don't need an escort who's going to trail ten feet behind me like a sneak."

"No, that's too far," he agreed. "I plan to be within . . . oh, about six inches."

His grin was irresistible, but she tried valiantly to be firm, to not let his charm trump her sensible suspicions. He had been at the Grimsbys', after all. For all she knew he was a spy for Copperhead, sent to keep an eye on her. "Really, you needn't," said Helen. "You have a whole party to amuse you. I'll be fine."

"As fine as when you dumped the bugs on that idiot on the trolley? And he turned into a raving lunatic?"

Helen couldn't think of a response to this. She tried, but by the time she'd come up with anything barely usable, she seemed to have her coat on and be at the door with him.

"Some people need to have bugs dumped on them," she

said brightly as she put on her lilac gloves. She tried to make it sound as though it was just good common sense.

"I quite agree," Rook said. "In fact, I found it quite admirable."

"Thank you," said Helen.

"And yet, if you can't promise me that you will incite no more men by throwing bugs on them, I think you'd better have an escort. You know. For their safety."

"There is that," said Helen. She muffled her scarf tightly around her chin and neck. It was no iron mask, but it made her feel better.

They stepped out into the cold.

Rook moved silently along beside her as they passed through the theatre district, crossed the empty trolley tracks, headed through the neighborhoods that would eventually take them up to Helen's own. If he stopped talking he could blend into the night and she would not see him again. It was odd—he was neither as tall nor as stout as Alistair, and yet Helen felt safer walking beside him in the night than she would have with her husband. It was a peculiar feeling to have in her gut about someone that her intellect told her to mistrust. Perhaps it was the way she had seen him interact with the drunkard on the trolley—sleek and swift, perfectly calm—and yet the man had immediately backed down. Yet even if she had not witnessed that moment she thought she would feel just as safe. Safe from others—but safe from him, too—despite his joke about staying close, if she told him to keep five feet away the whole journey home, she rather thought he would do that.

But how smart was it to trust him?

"You followed me last night, didn't you?" she said suddenly. "After the Copperhead meeting."

"I saw him take your iron mask," he said. Alistair, he meant. *Your husband,* he meant, but did not say it. "You were in danger."

"I was in a car," she said dryly. "You, what, ran along beside us because of a mask?"

"Stole a bike," Rook said cheerfully. "Borrowed if you're feeling generous. I did return it."

"It's certainly very flattering," said Helen, "I'll give you that." She looked sideways at him, trying to puzzle him out. Even if she believed that he had just followed her due to concern for her welfare, there was still the point that he was at a Copperhead meeting last night, and here in what might as well be the enemy camp tonight. Somehow she had ended up with a foot in both worlds—but how had he? "Where's your lapel pin?" she said. "Don't you walk the party line?"

His grin faded. "I had other business there last night. I am not a member of Copperhead."

"Other business," repeated Helen. "So now it really gets interesting. I doubt you were in charge of the catering." She stopped on the sidewalk. "And come to that, why were you near the trolley stop today? Did you know that was going to happen to that poor man?"

Rook looked sober at the reminder of the trolley stop incident. "Did you see what happened? Did he provoke those Copperhead men?"

"They started it," Helen protested, then admitted, "but he wouldn't back down."

"Moug always was a hothead."

"You knew him. I'm sorry."

He nodded, and added, "Look, I wasn't near you; we were

simply both near the Grimsbys'. Now can you take that suspicious look off your face? My intentions toward you are entirely honorable, I swear."

Helen noticed that he did not claim that *all* his intentions were honorable, but she let her shoulders loosen. Perhaps she *had* been too blunt. Normally she was better at keeping her conversation partner soothed, flattered, well bantered. But apart from not entirely trusting this man, the storm of worries in her chest swirled round and round, leaving her adrift. What on earth would she do without Jane? The lights from the theatre district faded behind them as they walked on, leaving them in a darker neighborhood of old row houses and shaggy bits of garden. They cut through a stretch of park, winding their way up into the hills.

"Things on your mind?" Rook said softly.

Helen laughed and tossed her hair, building up her wall again. "Just thinking how divine your Miss Frye looked in her dragon and slacks. I'm positive I could never pull off such a thing. Yet I think I should try to go to her little musicale, what's it called again? You tell me, do you think it would be worth seeing?"

The flow of chatter seemed to break and crash over him, leaving him unaffected. "I think it is likely ridiculous. Frye is better than her material."

It was so easy to pretend there was nothing more on her mind than flirting with a handsome stranger. So easy to fall into the role of frivolous, laughing Helen. "Ah, the sort of thing where you grab your date and waltz out at intermission for cocktails. Then you sneak back in, half-sloshed, and afterward . . ." But there her imagination failed her, never having known anyone in a play. "And what do you do then?"

"The curtain falls. Rises. The actors come out and the audience breaks into a completely unwarranted sea of applause, mostly based on the number of cocktails they have had. When they are done, we slip through the pass door and find Frye's dressing room. The biggest one, with the star. Which is probably the size of a shoebox and tucked under some stairs. We bring her flowers—"

"—oh, dear, I would have forgotten that—"

"—and she kisses our cheeks and we tell her how wonderful she was."

"We lie?"

"Like rugs," Rook said cheerfully. "Or, if you like, you tell her that the scenery was very beautiful, and you could hear all of the actors surprisingly well."

"Ohhh," she said, and then, "Oh," with the bump of reality.

He raised eyebrows at her.

"You make it sound so lovely, I can practically see it," Helen said. "It makes me wish we could go."

"Your Mr. Huntingdon could take you."

"No, he won't let me go out for the danger, and I owe him not to go for something frivolous."

Rook stopped then, and looked at her. "Helen," he said.

"What?" She was startled to hear her name on his lips.

He turned and walked faster. "You're cold, we should hurry."

She was confused. "What did I say?"

Rook wheeled back again, took her elbow. "Now look," he said. "What do you mean you can't go out? You're here now."

"I snuck," Helen said. "Or is it sneaked?" She thought she

could lighten the sudden tension, for she could not understand why he seemed to be angry.

"For Frye's party?"

"To talk to those women. Alberta and Betty and Desirée. To convince them to let Jane restore their old faces."

"Ah," Rook said, but the thing that looked fierce in him did not go, and he said, "Now look, Helen. What do you mean, you *owe* him?"

"Oh," said Helen. She did not know why, but she suddenly wanted to tell him, tell him more than she had ever told Jane, more than: *I'm so desperately tired of being poor.*

That was maybe half of the story. Maybe a tenth.

She turned away from his fierce gaze and started walking into the wind, opening her mouth before she lost her nerve. "My mother fell sick before she died," Helen said. It was strange how hard the words were to get out, even as something inside said *you can trust him with this.* She had never told the story, not to anyone. She was very good at changing the subject. "We tried a lot of doctors. A lot of medicine."

"Your family?" Rook said. He kept pace with her as they walked up the street, letting her manage the words in her own way. The houses were bigger here on the other side of the park, more porches and columns and windows . . . but still that blue, all that blue.

"Me," Helen said. "My father died several years before the war. My brother, Charlie . . . near the end of it. Jane was in the city, trying to heal herself. I wasn't very nice to her at the time, I'm afraid. It felt as though she'd abandoned me." Helen hadn't thought through this in years. At least, not while awake—sometimes the dreams slipped her back through time and she woke aching with regret for a vanished past. It didn't matter if she thought about it or consciously didn't think about it, it was all still there. That lost feeling of being thirteen and alone in the house with Mother, who was slipping further away each day despite all of Helen's efforts to bring her back.

"By the end, there was nothing left. Everything was mortgaged to the hilt or sold off. But I heard about a new doctor in the city. I went to him and begged. Well, he agreed to payment in installments. . . ." Helen trailed off. The night was cold and wet. The cloud cover blocked out the stars. Perhaps it was not clouds but smoke from the factories at the river, she thought, choking the sky. . . .

And these few sentences were more than she had said in years. She could not do any more, not just yet. "I don't want to talk about this," she said.

There was silence for a time. Then Rook said, "I grew up not knowing my father. Of course I was taller than everyone else. But *havlen* is an insult. Half-thing."

Helen looked at him, shocked. How had she seen him and not known? She had to recalibrate. This man was only half-human. And half-*dwarvven*. Alistair would never approve. *Copperhead* would never approve. He couldn't possibly be a member, then, unless he was a *dwarvven* spy, and in that case he had just carelessly handed a big secret to the wife of one of the top party members.

"I started out by punching everyone who called my mother a vile name. After a while I got a name for it."

"I would have figured you for the class clown type."

"When they finally threatened to throw me out of school for good I became the class clown instead. At least it's a time-honored position, in *dwarvven* society. Like being a writer. Being a joker. It gave me a tenuous place."

"It's so much easier to talk of fun things," Helen said. The way was getting steeper and it was hard to laugh. "If you talk silly then no one asks prying questions."

"So let's talk of terrible theatre some more," Rook said, but Helen heard a bite in his voice that made her ask, "You didn't stay the class clown?"

"Who does," he said, "when war comes?" There was a moment when the moon caught his eyes and she looked right into him and saw that there was a *thing,* a some-thing, a black dark thing. But then his eyes glinted with a grin once more and he said, "Now, you may talk of cabbages and sealing wax and everything else Dodgson wrote of, but we are done with secrets." He suddenly seized her arm and pointed to the footbridge they were nearing. "Have you ever climbed on a bridge rail in the middle of the night in November?"

"No!" Helen said, suddenly laughing, and Rook seized her arm, calling, "Race you," and pulled her up the street, as if the race were the two of them together, against some other, unknown opponent. The cold night was sharp in her throat and her heels skidded on the wet pavement, but she laughed, fast and fierce, giddy with the run.

The bridge railings turned out to be stone ledges, and there was a fair amount of blue fey draped over them.

"Mm," said Rook. "Perhaps we won't climb *these* railings." He looked at the blue. "No, I wanted to climb something." He reached down and peeled away a large swath of blue with his gloved hands.

"Rook!" she cried, hurrying toward him—then stopped, for her face was still bare.

He let the blue fall over the edge of the bridge. "Go home, little fey," he said. "Shoo." The blue glow slid down into the black night and vanished.

"Rook," she said again, shocked. "Do you have iron in your gloves?"

"No," he said, and peeled another piece away. "It'll be safe for you in a minute. Hang on."

"But . . . you're touching them. You saw what happened today, to that man. . . ."

"Yes," he said. "And yet the odds are very much against that. Or perhaps I like to live dangerously." He saw her expression and said, "Look, as much as I dislike the fey, a little piece isn't going to harm me. You do know what the old fey tech that you humans used to trade for was made from, don't you?"

Helen shook her head.

"Pieces of fey," he said. "All your bluepacks that used to power things. Bits of split-apart fey. It was a punishment for them. They don't like being torn apart like this." He gestured around the city at the swathes of blue. "Whoever their new leader is, they're strong enough to make it stick." He dropped another piece over the edge. "Anyway, the small bits aren't aware of much. It's not till you have a whole fey that you have problems."

"Well, I do know that much," Helen said. "But aren't you afraid there could be a big one hiding among these little bits?"

"I know," Rook said, peeling off another piece. "But I am watching, and I am quick on my feet." He dropped the bit of fey over the edge. She could see that they did not fall all the way into the water, but lazily drifted along just over it, looking for a new spot to rest. He looked over the edge, watching it go. "It doesn't matter what I saw today. They are still not the race I fear."

Helen did not say anything to that, because she knew which race he meant.

Humans.

Rook was *havlen,* so he was part-*dwarvven.* And Copperhead hated the *dwarvven* nearly as much as the fey, though she never could figure out why. Humans and *dwarvven* had been allies, once. The *dwarvven* did not like the fey, either.

"Well," said Rook. "If they knew what we've planned for them . . ."

"Humans?" Helen said sharply.

But Rook just waggled his eyebrows and grinned. "Gallows humor, that's all," he said. "If we knew what *they've* planned for us . . . we'd be in just as much trouble and misery." He pointed to a yellow poster, curled around the nearest streetlamp and visible in its golden glow. "Your Copperhead is getting higher in the capital's ear every day."

"They're not my Copperhead."

"Just married in, eh?"

She looked coldly at him.

He put up his hands. "My tongue always takes me too far," he said.

"Or not as far as you'd like?" she said, which made him laugh and pulled the moment back into something funnier than perhaps it should be. After all, what did he mean by *plans*?

They started walking again, off the bridge and into Alistair's neighborhood proper. There were more streetlamps here, and everything was more neatly maintained, making the bits of blue fey particularly jarring, like mold on bread. Her fingers were quite cold in her gloves.

"So you're half-*dwarvven,* and the *dwarvven* hate you, but you're working with them," Helen said, seeing if she could tease any more information out of him.

Rook looked at the night sky. "I'm always making up," he told it.

Helen did not know what for, but she knew what sort of a voice that was. That voice of always making up for leaving Charlie, leaving Jane, leaving Mother. Did Jane ever use that voice for leaving her? "To whom?"

"To myself." He closed those laughing hazel eyes and suddenly no part of him looked lighthearted and fun. With his eyes closed she suddenly saw the worry lines around his eyebrows. Saw the tight way his jaw set, as if it could do hard things. "When you have been willing to kill once, you see," he said, "it is assumed you will be willing to again."

She could not say something lighthearted to that, so she said nothing. It was a peculiar moment, to go from a man you had talked to about dancing and theatre to thinking: This man has killed. Is he a different man now? He is the same man, but I know something about his past that casts a long shadow over his future. He will always be a man who has killed.

They were walking up the gaslit street and at the cloud-shrouded moon she said: "The payment to the doctor was so huge, the day so far off . . . I simply couldn't ever meet it. I became more and more desperate. More skilled at dividing my life into two pieces. No one must know. I had taken it on to be responsible and important and clever, like Mother and Father and Jane, who were all gone, you see, and I was going to solve it in the same way. By myself. Of course I never was going to be able to meet the payment, and I suppose the doctor must have known that all along. As it drew nearer, he sought me out. Dropped hints of other methods of repayment. . . .

"I had hoped I could make the payments. But at some point you miss one and then the payments start escalating. I would come up with grand plans—there are always grand plans—for paying it off. I would make dresses for wealthy ladies and sell them. Things I could never accomplish because I would have to have money to buy the fabric in the first place. Or somehow—never quite satisfactorily explained how—I would get a second position, filling in for other nannies and governesses on their days off. But the thought of spending even more time with intolerable, spoilt children was . . . intolerable.

"For all my grand plans, what ended up happening was I would go down to the tenpence dance hall to drown my misery. Women no charge, you know. And the more you promise and flirt, the more men buy you coffee and pastries and bring you little tokens like scarves and so on. I became very good at promising and flirting. I mean, it's my natural bent anyway, I suppose. We can't all have high-minded skills.

"And there I was in a white dress with a green sash and I met Alistair." She smoothed her lilac gloves over each finger, feeling the outline of the manicured nails below. "I'm always making up for not going into battle," she said. "For not helping to kill the fey before they killed Charlie, and through him Mother, and nearly destroyed Jane."

Rook stopped there on the sidewalk. They were half a block from the house, Alistair's house. The gaslight flickered in the wind. She was watching the unreadable words on his face, so she didn't notice his hand move until it was there, brushing one copper curl off of her cheek. Then it was gone, leaving her stomach with a funny bottomed-out feeling and the thought that perhaps she had just imagined his hand moving and it was only the wind.

"Never be sorry that you could not kill," Rook said.

Ice formed on her breath as she stood there, until gold light came on in the windows of her house, and panic rose up. Helen turned from him then, and walked, faster and faster till she was racing up the stairs to her door, wind pulling water from her eyes. She tugged open the front door and hurried in but she had to look back. Rook was still there, a slim black outline in the cold.

Rook. Rook.

And she turned.

Alistair. Alistair.

The foyer was faintly lit with the light from the open door to the games room; the smell of a wood fire drifted down the hall. She closed the front door silently behind her. The air in the tiled foyer was chill and damp. She could try to make it to her room. She could confront him now and get the lecture over with.

Or perhaps she could brazen it out, though her cheeks were red-pink with cold, though the cold rose off her in waves. Still. Why not? She stripped off her coat and outer things, shoved them under the hall table, and glided on stockinged feet down the cherrywood floors of the hall to peek inside his games room.

Alistair was drunk.

He was by the fire, which glinted off his curls. His long

legs were propped on the table on a pile of newspapers; his hand hung loose over the leather club chair with a partial glass of whiskey in it.

Just as quietly, Helen began to tiptoe away. But not quietly enough.

"That you, doll?" said Alistair.

Helen crept back in. She was going to brazen it out, wasn't she? Be a good liar, like Tam had said he was. A lump caught in her throat as she thought of the boy stuck with Grimsby and the men tonight. Was his father even now filling that small head with tales of rage and revenge?

"I wondered if you were still up," Helen said.

He stared moodily over his glass into the fire. "All white she was. Is. Still," he said. Yes, very drunk. "But we dragged Grimsby away from there."

"To get drunk?" she said. The words just slipped out.

Alistair sloshed to his feet, arm over the top of the chair to look at her. "Yes, to get drunk," he said, making his point with a waving finger. "You wouldn't deny him that, would you? Course you would, coldhearted witch, no fun at all . . ."

Helen was stung by this sudden attack. "Don't I go to all the parties with you?"

Alistair waved this away. "Not what I mean. Your sister, always looking at me as though I weren't fit to black your shoes. As if I hadn't rescued you." He cupped his hands and opened them in an expansive gesture, spilling the rest of the whiskey onto the shining floor. Bitter alcohol scented the fire-warmed air.

Helen did not care to talk about this, and particularly not with this version of Alistair. "You should go to bed," she said. "I'll send George in to clean."

"Bed?" he said. "You don't tell me when to go to bed. Unless you're coming."

"No, thank you," said Helen. She prepared to make her escape, but his voice rose a level and stopped her.

"You don't tell me what to clean," he said, and opened his hand, letting the whiskey glass smash to the floor.

Now Helen did back up a step.

"You should have heard them all last night," hissed Alistair. "Talking about your sister. My fault for taking her in. My fault for not throwing her on the street immediately. Your connections. Dragging us down." He advanced. "Insinuating I can't run my own household."

Helen's heart beat wildly. Social drinking she could understand; everyone did it. Sometimes you accidentally drank too much and regretted it the next day. But not these frightening rages—and they had been coming more and more frequently. Her hand felt along the doorframe for something to shield herself, but there was nothing, and she was exposed in his glare as he advanced.

"Stop it," she said, but Alistair reeled on her, flush with drink.

"Where have you been?" he said, and there was a keen edge to his words.

"Out," Helen said. Her hands trembled as she turned, but she would not cower in front of him. She had made her choice. He had been charming and handsome and sure and she had thought she must very probably love him. And it had made so much sense . . . hadn't it? Jane had her career, her plans, but Helen had nothing except her face, and that face was supposed to land her her fortune. Which was Alistair Huntingdon, her charming white knight coming to save her.

His face reddened further as she turned away. "Out with that man on the street? That . . . *dwarf*?"

Helen froze, the ugly slur ringing in her ears. He had seen them.

Alistair's smile was cruel. He had her. "Yes, I saw you. Barefaced and brazen, out walking with Grimsby's pet dwarf," he said. "Did he tell you he's an informant for us? Where'd you find him—when you sneaked off to find Jane? Or were you slumming with the dwarves? Mixing, mingling, rutting? . . ."

"Don't suppose it's any of your business," she said, and felt the country drawl that irritated him slip out.

She was cold and he was hot. He grabbed her wrist and sleeve, stumbled as she jerked. A button tore off as she pulled away, as she slipped and fell on the polished floor. Her hand skidded on the broken whiskey glass.

"I paid for you," Alistair spat. "Paid for your face."

Helen closed her eyes, clutching her injured hand to her chest, wishing she could close her ears against the torrent of abuse that flowed from his lips. Accusations, true and fair, she knew like a knifepoint in the ribs. Her eyes opened on that thought, that even if they were true and fair it hurt, it hurt, and she could not stand it. She clutched the copper necklace he had given her so tightly, her cut palm painful against the cold snake heads.

He was ranting and everything Frye had confessed to poured into her thoughts. Helen stared at Alistair and thought, You will apologize now. You will tell me you still love me. That things will be all right.

She did it more on a miserable whim than anything. More on a fragile wish that things could be as they were. As she had seen him when she first met him, that shining white knight. Wielding the fey power to change someone was hard; Jane had said so frequently. Frye had said she studied for a long time.

She did not expect Alistair's eyes to go glassy as she clutched her necklace, willing him to change. For him to turn and say, "Forgive me, Helen."

Chapter 8

THE HYDRA STRIKES

Helen backed up a pace as he moved closer, stumbled, sat down in the leather club chair.

"I am being too harsh," Alistair said, and again, "Forgive me."

"There is nothing to forgive," Helen said automatically, for wasn't this what she had wanted? Alistair leaned in, half-smiling, and yet . . . some hesitation, some lurch in his walk recalled that dead farmer, a mask for a fey.

"I love you," he said. He dropped to one knee beside her and took her hand, a simple, caring gesture. "I have been too busy to spend time with you recently. We should travel together. Get out of the city for a while. You always wanted to see Varee."

"I have," her voice said, but her head shook, *no no no.* His fingers closed around hers. Trembling, shaking, she said: "They have beautiful fashions."

"We will buy you mountains of dresses." But that was something Alistair *would* say. He was not ungenerous. He liked to see her beautiful, beautifully attired. She was being silly. Alistair was being thoughtful. It was what she had wanted. "We will pick out exactly the sorts of things you like."

"And send them back for alterations until they're perfect," Helen said. She recalled how they had sent back dress after dress from before the wedding and she wanted to smile back at him. She had dreamed up things she'd never known she wanted, and he had indulged all those dreams.

"You know what you should do," said Alistair, eyes shiny and bright. "You should learn to create your own patterns. You have such beautiful fashion sense. You could set up a little atelier right here among the shops, be a modern woman."

The idea was breathtaking. It was as if he had looked to the bottom of her soul and pulled out something she had never thought to want, and now that she saw it hanging there, shining, she felt her heart beating out of her chest with pure lust for the idea.

It was not his idea. It was not Alistair.

"No!" Helen cried.

He let go of her hand, confused.

"No," she said again, and with a great surge of will let everything relax and her mind wipe clean until the strange thread that bound them broke.

Alistair faltered, standing, and she thought his eyes swam clear, but he turned his head away from her, it was so hard to tell. . . . He turned back, saw her frightened face. "No what? No pretty dresses? Don't be silly, pet."

"Stay away," she said firmly, feet planted.

His temper rebounded. "You've been out. You and that double-crossing dwarf are plotting against us all. You're the reason Copperhead's turning against me, why they're keeping secrets from me. Do you deny it?"

"Deny what?" She was at sea.

"You know where she is, you useless doll. Where is she?"

His voice rose and rose. "Where is Jane Eliot? Where is Jane?"

"I don't know, I don't know," gasped Helen, and backing up, slammed the door to his room in his face. Then turned and ran, scooping up her things from the hall as she went. Her stockinged feet slid on the cold floor, slipped numbly on the stairs, till she threw herself into her bedroom and locked the door.

She did not know what she would do if he came—if it came to a direct confrontation like that. She was good at sliding away, at giving in. She did not know how to tell him "No," and take that. But she knew how to run, and he was drunk, and he might let her go, finding the game not worth the candle.

Helen pressed her ear to the door for a long time, staring at her bleeding palm, smelling the whiskey soaked into her seafoam silk. But nobody came.

In her dreams she sees the house, their old house. Except it is not theirs anymore. Charlie is gone, Jane is gone, Mother is gone. Helen lives on charity, on borrowed time and space in a bit of attic at the neighbors'. Like Helen's family, the neighbors straddle that uncomfortable line between gentility and poverty, except they are further down the ladder. The wife had money, once. The husband has a bit of land and he tries to make it pay. They had one cow and now they have two, for the Eliots' former cow is keeping Helen in skirts and schooling.

Helen is not given to moping. She is angry at being alone. She is heartbroken (at least, something feels broken inside) at being here in an attic without Charlie and Jane and Mother, or perhaps what she means is, without people who love her.

People who chose to leave her. That is not fair, and yet. She saw Mother waste away for *no Charlie,* even though Helen was there. She saw Jane run to the city to find someone else to love her, even though Helen was there.

And Charlie is gone because Helen was *not* there. Because Helen could not pick up a staff and kill.

That is what it comes around to, every time she runs through it, and then something in her head tells her that Jane and Mother were right to leave, because when it came down to it, Helen had proved she couldn't be there for someone who needed her.

It doesn't matter that she knows this is nonsense. Every time her heart breaks a little more. Her spine stiffens a little more. Her jokes become louder and shriller, as she covers herself up in a cloud of decorative nonsense.

They like her at the village school, when she lets them. She goes through several cycles in the time she is there, before she goes off to governess in the city. She lets them all like her and then she pushes them all away. The method varies. Once her best friend acts nasty to her. Polly. Calls her a charity case, right in front of Sam, whom Polly likes, too. Helen has no idea why on this day it is suddenly too much, but it is, and she runs away. It is late spring, and she lives on the land and stolen table scraps for a week, and when she comes back it is summer, and she doesn't see any of them for three months, is gone when they stop in, lets all those relationships heal around her, because she is better at being alone.

When school starts in the fall Polly is best friends with someone else, and Sam has moved away, and Helen comes in and dazzles them, and runs the school with an iron fist for a season. But then that pales and she drops all her friends, again, yet again, for they are not really friends, she knows inside, no matter what they claim, and turns to her studies for a few months.

At graduation she is invited to all the parties, and they give her mementos and write "remember me" in her memory book, but if you asked them, they would none of them say that she had truly been their friend, only perhaps that they would like her to be, or that she had been "a good deal of fun, when she wanted to be."

It's one of those dreams where you can know what others said about you, just as if you were dead and they talked around your coffin.

She's not dead, though. She's still not dead. They all might have left her, but she's still here.

If she woke right now she would find the eiderdown wrapped around her legs, clutched in her hands. She would find her lips pressed, her cheeks wet. But she does not.

At last Helen did wake, to a gentle tapping on the door. "Ma'am?" said the voice of Mary. Helen opened bleary eyes, stiff with salt and frustration. Why was Mary knocking? Why didn't she just leave the tray?

She had locked the door, she remembered now. She pulled on her robe and padded to the door, blinking her eyes to clear them. Her palm was stiff with dried blood. There was another stiff spot on her cheek and ear from touching her face with her palm. She shook her hair forward over her cheek and curled her hand closed as she opened the door.

Mary's face was apologetic. "I wouldn't have woken you this early, but a woman brought him by and said you wanted him. Is it so?"

Helen looked down to see the small face of Tam, his hands clutching the inevitable glass jar.

He smiled tentatively when he saw her. "Museum?" he said hopefully.

Helen knelt beside him, mint green robe billowing out around her. "Yes," she promised. "But I have to get permission. Are those caterpillars?"

He nodded and thrust the jar forward for her inspection.

"Nice," she said. "I like the one with the red spots."

"His name is Biter," said Tam.

Helen reached forward without thinking. Mary sucked in breath at the sight of her hand. "I saw the glass, ma'am," she murmured, and her worried eyes met Helen's.

Helen looked away. She stood up and took Tam's hand with her good one. "Do you want some breakfast? Mary, bring something nice, will you?"

Mary promptly produced a rolling cart. "We've had him down in the kitchen for ten minutes," she said. "I rustled up everything I could find." She laid buttered toast and cherry jam and sugared oranges on a tray, and tried not to wince when Helen's hair swung away from the blood on her cheek.

The two women installed Tam on a pink tufted seat and watched him go to town on the buttered toast. Helen stood, watching him, knowing she should just stay at home. Play dominoes with Tam and enjoy the luxury of not having to make any more decisions.

When you have knuckled under once, it is assumed you will knuckle under again.

Her stiff hand clenched into a fist.

"Is Alistair still asleep?" she said.

Mary nodded. Helen hesitated, uncertain how to ask in

front of Tam if Alistair was in the sort of post-drunken state that meant he would be passed out for several more hours. But Mary intuited her question and added in a low voice, "Probably till lunch, ma'am."

The plan, such as it was, solidified. Helen raised eyebrows at Mary. "Cover for us?"

"Always and forever."

Tam stopped in midchew of his toast, butter and crumbs on his cheeks. He looked from one defiant woman to the other.

"Finish up," Helen said, "and then museum."

They had Adam drive them to the Natural History Museum, and they were first in line for the museum's opening at ten. They did indeed see the unusual reptiles exhibit (*Reptomania!*), spent all morning learning about the way basilisks *opto-paralyze* their prey, and the nesting habits of the extinct parasitic minidodo. (They nested in the ears of an also-extinct species of crocodile, and therefore were deemed acceptable to sneak into *Reptomania!*)

But perhaps most interesting of all to Helen was the glass case with a mated pair of copperhead hydras. "That's your necklace!" Tam said when he saw them, and he was right. Even more than Copperhead's flat lapel pins, her twisted copper necklace caught the essence of the unusual snake. The hydras were a lovely shimmery copper color, the sort of thing you would go up to and pet, if you didn't know better.

"'The beautiful copperhead hydra never attacks unless provoked,'" Tam read slowly, sounding out the words. "'This much-maleeg—'"

"Maligned," supplied Helen.

"'—species is noteworthy for its regenerative powers. Through the process of duogeneration, if one head is damaged, two more grow in its place. However, the resulting heads are weaker than the original, so the process cannot continue indefinitely.' What's that mean?"

"It can't have a hundred heads, say," Helen explained. "At some point it gets too weak to support all its heads. Like the poor female there." She read from a different sign about the individual hydras in the glass tank, interpreting it to Tam. "She was in a circus sideshow. They kept cutting off her heads so she'd grow more, and people would pay more money. The museum rescued her."

Helen and Tam looked in at the two hydras. The male had nine heads, all shiny and glossy and snappy. But the female hydra's slim trunk blossomed into a thick tree of writhing heads. Many of the heads in the middle were stunted and limp, like shoots that couldn't reach the light. But the other heads were twice as ferocious to make up for it. "She wants to live," said Helen.

Tam looked again at his species placard. "'The copperhead hydra has one more trick up its sleeve. As it dies from cranial overgrowth, it begins to secrete a deadly poison through its pores.'"

Helen peered at her own card. "That's what happened to the circus keeper," she said.

"Good," said Tam with relish. They looked at the poisonous female hydra with its forest of heads and both of them shuddered with glee.

After the museum they went to the big downtown department store and had lunch, right out in the atrium where you could see everybody. Helen was in a chic herringbone suit and wide hat that had seemed very museumy to her, and although it was admittedly a little odd, she kept her gloves on through lunch to hide the bandage on her hand. Tam was decked out in acquired regalia—a canvas hat like all the explorer-scientists wore, and a pair of binoculars he was very taken with. (He had even agreed they were suitable recompense for Helen making off with his jar of bugs.) Between spoonfuls of bisque, Tam peered through the binoculars to discover what people on the other side of the restaurant were eating—a game that delighted both of them very much. After lunch and after ices Helen let Tam ride the elevator up and down for an hour—much to the amusement of the elevator operator. There was a Copperhead poster in the elevator and Helen peeled it off when the operator's back was turned, ground it under her heel. All in all, it was a lovely day and Helen didn't regret a bit of it till they arrived home in the late afternoon and she saw Alistair's lights on.

Then, despite all her brave intentions, her fingers trembled in the lilac gloves.

"And when I grow up, I'll see the pterodactlia go into a cocoon, and then wait a long time, and then they'll metamorphose and that means they'll become man-eating butterflies, but I won't be afraid. . . . ," Tam was explaining. He was more excited than she'd seen him yet.

Her spine crumbled. She bent down to Tam, her shoulders next to his. "Can you do me a big favor?" she said, her words weak and whispery.

"What?"

"I wasn't supposed to go out today," Helen said. "You know how it's dangerous out with the fey. We kind of snuck out."

Tam nodded.

"If Mr. Huntingdon asks, can you pretend we didn't go to the museum?" she said. "So I don't get in trouble? Say we just went to the next-door neighbor's to play with their son."

"Lie?" he said.

"Well." She was teaching him cowardice and lying. If Jane were here her sharp tongue would reduce Helen to coals in two seconds flat. "Yes," Helen said.

Tam thought about this. "Okay," he said, and reminded her, "I'm good at lying."

"I guess you said that," said Helen.

"You just watch," said Tam. "Will you find me some food for my snake though? Usually father gets me things when I lie."

"Certainly," said Helen.

"The copperhead hydras ate slugs. I think my garter snake would like slugs, don't you?"

Helen winced at the thought. "It's a deal," she said.

She took the boy in the back way and they crept up the staircase to her set of rooms. Mary was just starting a fire. As with Helen, Mary's defiance had wilted into worry and fear. She turned when she saw them and said in a rushed whisper, "Oh good; I just saw the master in the games room and he's in such a state. He'll be up here any minute. I put out your tea like it's been half-eaten, but I can always bring you more."

"Mary, that's brilliant," said Helen. She tried to smile and project reassurance. "What sort of state? Did he just wake, or did he go out and find trouble?" Drink, opium, horse didn't win? Tripped on a stick and fired a gardener? Drop of rain plashed his lovingly buffed windshield?

Mary shook her head. "Something to do with Copperhead,

I think." She lowered her voice. "That Grimsby could incite the angels to riot."

Tam looked up at the mention of his father's name. Helen hurriedly motioned him to sit down and eat from the leftover scraps Mary had artfully arranged. "Oh, that's a new hair ribbon, isn't it, Mary? I like that plum shade on you." Which was true, as well as turning the conversation away from the boy. "Did my telegram finally come? Tam, take off your explorer hat and try the cream cakes. If they don't vanish it'll definitely look fake." She whirled around, tugging off her coat and hat, shoving things to the back of the wardrobe.

"Something came," said Mary, passing her a sealed and folded slip of paper. "I got it away from the butler just in time. And the ribbon's from that new beau I was telling you about—"

Tam bounced. "Miss Helen, Miss Helen, I'm going to go into the forest and capture a copperhead hydra—"

"Ooh, Mary, the clerk? Yes, you and me both, Tam." Helen shoved the telegram into a pocket and plopped down on one of the pink tufted stools by the tea tray just as the door opened and Alistair burst in.

His face was red from his hangover, his movements stiff and painful. The lavender soap smell meant he had been up a little while, yet clearly not long enough to feel himself again. He looked like a schoolteacher who has finally found an excuse to whip a particularly disliked child. His glittering eyes roved the room until he found her, and then he pounced. "Have you been thinking about our discussion?"

Helen stood, brushing her skirt off, thinking what to say about the small boy sitting opposite, cream cake clutched in one grubby paw, eyes wide.

Alistair's eye fell on him. "Who's that? What's he doing here?"

"Tam—," she started, but he apparently didn't really care, because he continued headlong, brushing her response aside.

"I've been going through everything I can think of about where to find Jane. You can make it up to me if you find her. We can make it up to Grimsby if we turn her in. I know the only reason I'm on the outs is because of this Jane nonsense. Grimsby and Morse and Boarham were all together without me this morning, did you know?"

"Maybe they were having pancakes," Helen murmured.

Alistair paced. "Well, Hattersley's on my side. He was just here and he swears he saw Jane last night, near the statue of Queen Maud on the pier. Why would she be there? It's all just warehouses and the dwarfslum."

"I don't know," said Helen. "Why don't you ask your *dwarven* spy?"

Alistair waved this aside irritably. "Don't hold what a man says when drinking against him. You know I couldn't possibly suspect you of fraternizing with those half-size mongrels any more than you have to. Now look. We are going to go get Jane and trap her. And then she'll pay for what she did to Grimsby. And we will all be back in business."

Helen just looked at Alistair, at a loss for words. How had the man she thought she married turned into this man?

"Why is he here?" murmured Alistair, pointing at Tam. He ran fingers through his tight curls, hectic motions.

"His father said he could come for an outing," started Helen. "We've just been having tea—," but Alistair brushed that aside just as he had the boy's name. She saw then that sometimes lies were useless, if others didn't care enough to look under their noses. Alistair was filled with these new thoughts of capturing Jane. He probably didn't even realize who Tam was, though he had just seen him at the Grimsbys'. Alistair was really only focused on himself, his friends, his jockeying for position—he certainly did not care about children, who could supply him with neither gossip nor gambling. She stared at her husband, thinking: Be who you were. Be who I thought you were.

"Leave him," he said. "We're going to get Jane."

Helen set down her toast with trembling fingers. "I may have agreed to marry you, but I didn't agree to do everything you ordered," she said.

"I'm not ordering," Alistair said. "You're being irrational. It must be those horrid folks you're hanging around with—Jane and her bluestocking friends, those traitors. If she's in the dwarfslum, it's probably because she's in league with those disgusting creatures." He looked over her head, thoughtful. "Yes, she'd probably be just the sort to take up with one of them, now that she's no longer deformed. Miscegenation would be nothing to her. . . ."

That was the point that made her snap.

She turned on him and said softly, "You will apologize now."

She watched until his eyes went glassy, and then he said, "I'm sorry. I am."

The decorative nonsense was burned away. "Mary, take Tam from the room, please," Helen said softly. As the door shut behind them she said, "I hold to my end of the marriage contract. I see no reason for me or my family to be treated like this."

"Of course not," he said.

It was heady, saying these ridiculously domineering things. She could spout off anything she cared to and make him agree with her. It was as if someone had had a weight on her all this time and had just pulled it off. And she found that she was twice as tall as she thought.

"I can go where I want, and if there's danger I can damn well walk into it if I want," she said. "I am in charge of my own safety."

"You are," he agreed.

The things Jane and Frye and Rook had said all came bubbling up. She didn't even know they had come in and registered.

"We are married, but you don't own me," she said.

Alistair sank to one of her tufted chairs. His eyes looked concerned, and she wondered if the changes she was effecting would last while she was gone, or wear off when she turned her back. She found at the moment she didn't really care.

"I'm going down to a place that isn't safe for children," Helen said. "You will watch Tam. Send word to his father that he can stay over. You can"—she cast around—"play dominoes with him, look at maps, catch bugs. That sort of thing. You will not leave him alone. You will not, I don't know, take him out back and teach him to smoke cigars."

"Of course not," said Alistair, and he sounded shocked. She thought that was an interesting wrinkle she had introduced, that she could make Alistair sound shocked.

"Good," Helen said. "Ask Mary to help you. She has a bunch of little brothers. Now I am out the door."

"Helen?" said Alistair. He sounded almost . . . humble. "When are you coming back?"

"When I discover what's going on," said Helen. She looked at him, sitting meekly on the small chair. His face was Alistair's, but he wasn't anyone she knew. It was the opposite of a mask, as if the physical body of Alistair was a mask for something else, something Helen had created and put into animate Alistair.

She supposed it should give her the creeps. At the very least she should feel guilty, unconscionably guilty, so very guilty that she couldn't possibly leave the house.

Instead she gave him one more tweak. "Don't drink any of that whiskey," she said.

"No, Helen."

"Good," she said. She blew him a jaunty kiss. "Don't wait up."

There was a mess of factories and warehouses by the statue of Queen Maud on the pier, but only one was lit blue in the windows. The sharp lines of the factory contrasted against the misty evening as Helen crept closer through muck and stench to peer through a cracked dirty window. Inside she could see . . . cages? Yes, rows of iron-barred cages, she thought, and surrounding them a misty blue haze. Helen squinted through the greasy glass. The blue haze almost seemed to have forms in it—as if it were people dancing and talking and running. Helen stepped away from the warehouse and into the shadows of the building opposite, puzzled by the blue-lit windows. Did nobody care that the warehouse seemed to be fey-infested? Or were they just being cautious? People passing by the warehouse didn't give it a second glance, though they did seem to be giving it a wide berth.

The door was locked. She went around and around the

building until at last she found a window ajar. It was head-height, but over some piles of rubbish and cans she thought she could use. The old Helen would have gone home, but this Helen adjusted the skirt on her herringbone suit and climbed up, prised the window open, and slid on through. There was a table beneath the window and so that side was easy after all.

The warehouse was big and dim and crowded, as if it were concurrently being used both for shipping storage and illicit fey activity. The window that she had come through was about in the middle of the long rectangle, and it was right under a duct blowing hot air—surprising that the warehouse was heated. The half of the building on the right, toward the wide double doors, was crates and machinery and all manner of piles of things. On the left were the cages, and the thin blue fog.

They were big cages, big enough to hold a person, and they lined the back half of the heated warehouse, competing for space with more crates, machinery, and junk. There were no good angles from which to see everything at once; Helen crept carefully around teetering piles, expecting something to leap out at her at any minute. A mouse skittered in front of her, and she jumped back against a cage, heart hammering fast. The blue fog crept around the cages, avoiding the iron bars, curling around her fingers. She grimaced and fought down panic. Rook had reminded her that a little bit of fey would not hurt anyone—was itself hurt, in a manner of speaking. Come to that, what *was* the blue fog, exactly? It was not as solid as the shimmery pieces of fey that lined the city. No, it was more vaporous even than that, as if a fey had been blown to smithereens.

There was a square hole cut from the center door of the

cage—not quite big enough for a person to fit through. Over the hole hung a dented metal funnel mounted to a pale oval. A rubber hose snaked out of the funnel, and she followed it around piles of boxes, heart again hammering in her throat until she found where it ended.

Grimsby's machine.

There was the large cube of wrought iron she had seen at the meeting. In the center was the ball made of writhing curls of copper. Wired inside of the cube were the ends of dozens of these rubber hoses, all snaking through the bars and away into the warehouse. The blue fog drifted lazily around her, and she remembered Grimsby blasting that small fey to a million bits of blue, and she thought she might be sick.

She tried to wave the fog away—stop breathing it in—tried to move away from the box, but she stumbled against all those snaking tubes, and as she put her hand out for balance it went right between the wrought iron and into the cube, and she touched the coiled copper snakes.

A chaotic swirl of confusion, a whirlwind of colors. Helen felt pulled in a million directions at once. She was seeing things, so many things, and her eyes couldn't make sense of the torrent of images that attacked her.

She pulled back, stood up.

Slowly the warehouse resolved. Breathing heavily, she let the chaos of color die away. What had she seen? Flashes of the city, she thought. Lots of blue. Faces, voices. Stronger—a building, perhaps something like this warehouse?

Yes, she had a feeling that the warehouse itself had flashed through her mind. She narrowed her eyes, remembering the demonstration at the meeting. Grimsby had used the machine to capture a fey. Used it to destroy a fey. What else could it do? She remembered Niklas saying that he had made the machine and turned it over to Grimsby for further tinkering.

Steadying her nerve, Helen closed her eyes, reached through the iron railing, and grasped the copper box with both hands. Her fingers fit into and under the copper snakes disturbingly well. They seemed to mold their coils to her thin fingers. Perhaps they were hollow tubes, for patterns of warmth ran along her skin. The chaotic swirl started again, but this time she was expecting it. She tried to relax, tried to let her mind make sense of what she saw. Buildings, faces, voices . . . men, walking, talking. That face looked like the Prime Minister—was he nearby?

She thought she had seen the warehouse the first time. She tried to visualize it from the outside and the pictures of it increased in response to her focus. She felt bludgeoned by it, as if it were some strange dream where she could see the building from all sides at once, and even an image of the copper box, nearly from where she would be seeing it in real life, but a trifle lower. And then another image that seemed to be the back of the warehouse; a part she hadn't seen, but she recognized the tubes and cages.

It was too overwhelming. Helen let go, extricated her fingers from the copper.

But she looked at Grimsby's machine with respect. Is that what Grimsby had seen with it, when he was attempting to pull in a piece of fey? Certainly the machine did more than just destroy. Someone could see all over the city, if they learned how to cope with the barrage of sights and sounds. Someone with a more powerful brain—or perhaps, simply someone with more fey power, since Grimsby had said the machine ran on the fey energy. Maybe that's why she was able to see a little bit with it—the fey in her face. Perhaps with a lot of hard work she could figure out what it did and how it worked, and why she saw the back of the warehouse but not the front.

The back of the warehouse . . .

Helen turned around. But there was no one standing there, was there? Not right behind her. But maybe farther back, around the crates . . .

There was a dark shape. Not a shape. A figure, a person. In the back, half-hidden behind the row of cages, holding a funnel next to her face . . .

Helen's legs were running before her head completely knew what she had seen. "Jane!" she shouted, making all the blue fog swirl and unsettle. "Jane!"

Chapter 9

THE TROUBLE WITH JANE

Jane turned her perfect face to look at Helen. It was pale in the slanted light of the warehouse. Her green eyes were wide and vacant, and her dark brown hair all in a tumble.

"Oh, thank goodness," said Helen. "You won't believe everything I've been trying to do in your name. I swear I'm making a hash of things. I know I thought I could help you, but honestly I am so ready to give this whole ridiculous The Hundred project back to you, and sweep it under the rug, and take you out for tea and cakes. It's been a nightmare." Helen slowed as she approached her sister. Was Jane listening? Helen repeated her sister's name again, but now slower, wondering. "Jane?"

Jane blinked several times. "Helen?" she said finally.

"Yes, silly," said Helen. "I've found you and will get you home. But where have you been? Did you come here on your own? And aren't you cold?"

Jane looked down, holding the funnel with its attached hose in one hand like a bouquet. She was still wearing the dress she had worn to the meeting—it was silky and misty grey, and still she had no coat, for Helen had that. "Perhaps I am cold," Jane said, as if testing out the idea.

"Well, I'll get you your coat. Or—no, I'll get you a better coat. That ridiculous old thing you had; it's not even worth giving as a hand-me-down. I'd feel terrible if I saw Mary walking out in that coat. I have an allowance, and there are some new ones in fashion that would very much suit—wide shoulders, belted to a narrow waist; all these gorgeous slashing lines."

"Slashing lines . . . ," said Jane, fingering her cheek. Up close the filtered daylight revealed raw pink lines crossing the white face. The lines where the iron had been.

Helen's heart seized. Jane was so vulnerable. Jane had always been the strong one, when they had been together. And when Jane fled to the city she was defined by her absence. I cannot ask Jane about medicine for Mother, I cannot let Jane make the decision about the cow. Helen wanted Jane to be the strong one again. "What happened to you?" Helen said again, but gently.

"I was working with Millicent when the room went blue," Jane said slowly. "Everything felt strummed and tense, like when your hair stands on end. Like a lightning storm. And then . . . I felt I saw you standing up there in the attic. And there were people around you, but you were shouting to me. I felt as if I was being pulled in two. It hurt—not physically, exactly, but if you could be pulled in two without it hurting, then that's what it felt like. I saw you and a tangle of copper, and then I saw Millicent and the attic. Both on top of each other. It was too much. I couldn't take being pulled apart. I felt like there was someone behind me? Someone grabbed me? I think

I blacked out. And then . . ." Jane looked around at the warehouse as if seeing it for the first time. "I don't know exactly. I woke up here, and my iron was gone—it feels as though I skinned my knee, but on my face." She put a hand to the pink lines that traced around her features. "But I didn't really wake up, not all at once. I feel as though I've been sleepwalking while I try to put the two halves of me back together."

Helen did not like the sound of this. And the being pulled in two . . . "What are you doing with that funnel?" she said sharply. "Does it have chloroform coming out of it or something?" She took the funnel from Jane's hand and sniffed at it from a good distance, but smelled nothing. "Not that that proves anything," Helen muttered. She dropped the funnel on the ground and kicked it away. Took Jane's hand and tugged her sister around the boxes to the copper box with its snaking black tubes. "Does this look familiar to you? Have you touched it?"

"Perhaps I should," Jane said, reaching for it.

"No," Helen said sharply, and pulled her sister's arm away. "It might be dangerous to you." She was so overwhelmed. Grimsby's invention *had* done something to Jane two nights ago, and now here they were in this warehouse with the same device and a confused Jane. "Look, when I touched this I saw a whole bunch of things," Helen said. "Is that how it felt in the house, with Millicent? Or maybe, your problem is because you were actually in a fey trance at the time, working on Millicent? And then she—" She bit her tongue, sure it would be too much of a shock for Jane to tell her about Millicent. Jane seemed so fragile.

"Millicent?" said Jane. "I met a Millicent, long ago. She was all in white with a green sash, and she was dancing. . . ."

Helen's fingers clutched tightly on Jane's arm. "Jane—," she said, but then there was a rustle from the other end of the warehouse, a muffled thump, footsteps. . . .

Helen's fingers tightened all the way and pulled Jane through the tangle of crates and cages and machinery, back to the open window. Up on the rickety table, teetering, and now the lock on the front door was rattling.

"Out you go," Helen said, and locked her hands under Jane's heel, lifting her up. Jane might not have gone as quickly as Helen would have liked, but she did pull herself through the window, and out, and Helen heard her jump to the piles of slag below.

The lock clicked as Helen pulled herself up after Jane. It was hard without the heel boost she had given Jane. Helen had not climbed anything since she lived in the country. She felt the seams of her skirt start to go and she hoisted the material higher, painfully aware that Frye's slacks would be better for this sort of thing. Men had it so much easier—even unfit Alistair could have managed this window more efficiently, because he would have had better clothes for it. A most unusual idea occurred to her for the first time, which was that perhaps it was all too convenient for men like Alistair that women like Helen stayed in dresses that you couldn't run or climb in.

The door opened with an audible creak just as she got her elbows through the window and pushed herself through the last little bit. Helen desperately wanted to know who was coming in, but she even more desperately did not want to get caught. This was all Jane's problem. Jane could worry about who was doing what. Helen could step down and return to her original plan of merely running interference for Jane on

The Hundred, sending women her way. Away from danger and decisions.

Helen slid to the trash containers and then to the ground, tumbling onto the muddy cobblestones. She kept going till she was standing again, trying not to mind her poor ruined skirt. The cut on her palm felt as though it had opened up from the strain; she peeled that lilac glove carefully free of the bandage and stuffed it in her pocket before it could be ruined. Her good hand closed on Jane's arm, Jane who was staring up at the sky with a vaguely curious expression, completely ignoring the goose bumps raising all the hairs on her arm from the November wind.

Helen took off her coat and laid it over her sister's shoulders. "Let's get out of here," Helen said. "Frye will know what to do."

Frye's door was opened by the gorgeous woman in orange from the party, Alberta—though tonight she was wearing bright yellow, with a drift of poppies floating down from one shoulder. Her black hair was twisted up on her head and decorated with another gauzy poppy. Perhaps she had just come from a gig with *Sturm und Drang.* "Come for a nightcap?" Alberta said. "Frye's still at her show, but you can join the party."

"Wasn't there a party last night?" said Helen. She tugged at her split skirt seam, vainly pushing the edges back together.

"Oh, that party," said Alberta. "Sure. But a few folks dropped by tonight after early gigs finished. Some people never really go home. Frye's too kind to boot them out."

Alberta turned and led the way down the hall, gold T-straps clicking on the floor. Helen twisted back to point out the show posters and memorabilia to Jane, but Jane was drifting blankly along. "Do they just stay for weeks?" Helen said. The thought of jumping ship on her life came back again. She could crash on Frye's floor like the other bohemians. Perhaps she would have to learn how to go onstage. She rather liked the idea of having a hundred people watch her sing a torch song while twenty backup men danced in top hats behind her. Except she couldn't sing. Still, why should that matter in a daydream?

"Sometimes they're here awhile," agreed Alberta. "Folks between gigs, in the off-seasons. Waiting for that next big role. Course, sometimes she gets tired of us, all at once, and kicks everyone out for a week and hibernates. But right now we're in the other part of the cycle."

Alberta led them up the circular staircase to the second floor. It was not the wild party of the night before, but there were a handful of people crowded around a low table at the landing, playing some sort of game that involved much jumping up and reciting, or bursting into song. Rook was not among them.

Helen turned to Alberta. "Honestly I was wondering if we could stay over," she said. "Jane needs to sleep, and she can't go back to my house. But Frye's not here to ask, and also I wanted her advice. . . ."

Alberta shrugged, the organza poppies rippling on her dress. "Frye would tell you to stay if she were here," she said. "She always does. My sax and I have the spare room, but the attic has several cots, if you don't mind that some actor might stumble up and crash there, too."

"That's fine," said Helen, who was more concerned with getting Jane to rest than complete propriety. She looked back at Jane, who was watching the wallpaper with a good deal of interest. How could she hand her problems off, if no one was able to take them on? "Actually I will take that nightcap," Helen said.

"I believe there are martinis in the pitcher," said Alberta, pointing at the side table. "Door to the attic through there, lamp to the right at the top. Sheets and towels in the trunk." She folded her arms, watching Helen with her perfect face. Helen dearly wanted to ask if her words from the night before had had an effect, but she knew perfectly well that if she asked point-blank Alberta would tell her no, and retreat. So Helen merely nodded, and poured a martini for herself and a tumbler of water for Jane, and pushed Jane before her up the steep narrow stairs to the attic.

A chill crept up her spine as she went up the stairs, but she told herself firmly to stop it. This was not the Grimsbys' attic. She found the oil lamp where Alberta had indicated, turned the key, and then found with relief that this attic didn't remind her of the Grimsbys' in the slightest. It had a lot of stuff, true—didn't all attics?—but there the resemblance ended. This attic was a long rectangle with steeply sloped rafters—you could really only stand up in the middle. And the stuff here was more theatre things—costumes, mostly—hanging on loops of wire nailed to the rafters. Dresses, slacks, blouses, feathered hats and boas, all different styles and decades, separated one cot from the next and afforded a bit of privacy. Trunks and hat boxes were wedged between the cots, but a big black trunk nearest the door had LINENS painted on it in theatrical red and gold. Helen went quietly down the narrow aisle to make sure they were alone, then took Jane and sat her down on the very last cot, where Jane would have to pass her if she tried to go wandering in the night.

"First some water," Helen said, and handed the water glass to her sister, setting her own glass down on a trunk by the cot. Jane obediently downed the whole glass. "Now a swallow of this will help you sleep," Helen said, and handed Jane her martini. Jane began to drink it, too, as though it were water, and Helen cried, "Stop, stop," and snatched the glass away again. "That should knock you out," she said. "Maybe you'll sleep it off."

"Sleep it off," Jane said dreamily as Helen made up the cot and tucked her into it. She closed her eyes and rolled over.

Helen began making up her own cot, pondering what to do next. She had found Jane, but now what? Jane could not fix The Hundred in this state—nor could she restore poor Millicent Grimsby, even if they knew where to find her. Jane could not even simply be Jane. Helen would have to figure out how to restore her sister to herself, if a good night's sleep didn't do the trick. She peeked around the row of costumes. Jane appeared to be sound asleep.

Helen eased off her heels and sank to the cot. She carefully pried up the bandage on her palm to check the cut. It seemed to be doing well enough, though she thought she should see if Frye had some fresh gauze and tape. It was a shame that she'd done all that warehouse-climbing in that skirt—the seam was ripped open, her shirt was smudged, and mud had smeared across her side and rear. The seam she could fix, but the skirt would need careful soaking and reshaping. Yet that was all she had to wear tomorrow, unless Frye's generosity extended to letting Helen borrow one of the dresses up here. Curious despite the problems pressing on her shoulders, Helen looked through the clothes that separated her cot from Jane's, automatically cataloging what period each dress was, and what sort of person would wear it. Lavender sachets hung thickly between the dresses, perfuming the room whenever she touched them. There were plenty of regular Frye clothes in the mix as well—caftans and slacks, neither of which she was sure she wanted to try, even if they would fit. Frye was much taller and more broad-shouldered than Helen. Still, that peacock blue knit dress there could be cinched with the belt she had on and look rather nice. With a few more minutes and a needle she could put a couple of darts in, raise the hem, and have something rather chic. . . .

Thought became action, and Helen slid off her ruined clothes and slipped into the knit dress, adjusting it to get it to hang correctly. She crouched under the steep rafters to take the belt from her skirt on the floor, and stopped as something fell from her skirt pocket.

The telegram Mary had handed her that afternoon, just before Alistair walked in. Helen's heart raced as she ripped open the seal. What would Mr. Rochart say about what she had told him? And now, Jane was back, and she would need to inform him of the new situation. . . .

"PER FOREST, SELF-STYLED BLUE KING IN CITY. MOVING FAST," it read. "TAKING NEXT TRAIN FOR JANE. ROCHART."

Her face paled as she deciphered the cryptic sentences. Blue King—the Fey King, that meant. Confirmation of what Niklas had said—a fey who called himself the Fey King was here, in the city. Rochart had learned it from his strange, dangerous excursion into the forest with Dorie. They must have just returned.

Helen stood, in a frenzy of what to do. She paced—no, there was no room to pace here, and things everywhere she turned— Energy sent her down the attic steps. The small party had drifted downstairs—they could be heard at the piano. Frye was still not there, nor was she in any of the other public rooms. Helen went back up the stairs and paced the second-floor landing, wanting desperately to talk to someone, to unburden herself, when Alberta stuck her head out to see what the noise was. Her hairdo was still intact, but she was in a pair of men's blue-and-white-striped pyjamas, smelling of a clean citrusy soap.

"A telegram fell out of my pocket," Helen said incoherently. "And things are happening fast, and if Mr. Rochart's coming to find Jane, where is he going to go? Alistair's, and I'm not there. . . ."

"Did you have too much gin?" said Alberta.

"None yet," said Helen.

Alberta sighed. "Come to my room and tell me everything." She turned and padded to the guest room, Helen behind her. The small guest room had a double bed, layered with several quilts, a dresser shellacked in shiny black, and hooks randomly spaced around the walls, two of which held a bright yellow and a bright orange dress. Under the window stood a battered metal music stand and an open case with a silver sax in it. Alberta plonked down cross-legged on the bed and passed Helen a silver flask. "That's actually decent stuff," she said, "and if you drink it all you owe me a bottle."

Helen took a cautious sip and found that it was, indeed, a

decent scotch. "Two nights ago Jane and I almost killed someone," she said.

"That's an opening," said Alberta. She began taking down her hairdo with its silk poppy. "Go on."

Another sip to loosen the tongue and it all came out, all Helen's worries and fears and questions. "And I thought once Jane turned up I could go back to being her helper—let her make the big decisions. Except I don't know if she was drugged or what but she's definitely not deciding anything tonight. So now the question is should I go back to Alistair's right now and try to meet up with her fiancé or not," she finished up. "I mean, if he's there, he could take over. But even if I do go, I can't take Jane with me. This is really good scotch."

"Okay, back up," said Alberta. "Now firstly, this fiancé guy is a rich man. He's not going to go straight from the train to your husband's house, even if he is worried about Jane. He'll get a hotel. Secondly, if he has the sense given to little green apples, he'll know things might be touchy at your place. He'll send a message 'round to you for how to reach him."

"And Alistair will intercept that," said Helen. "No, wait, Alistair has changed." She took another drink.

"It'll be coded," put in Alberta. "Haven't you ever had to be dodgy before?"

"Ppffft. Only when I was trying to get away from that doctor. And the creditors. And those men who would follow me around the dance hall and just watch, you know?" Helen waved a hand dramatically. "Just *watch* . . ."

"I'll take that, thank you," said Alberta, and she plucked the silver flask back from Helen, peered inside. "You owe me."

Helen studied the pretty face sitting across from her on

the bed. It was in fact very pleasant to feel warmed all over, and as though you could just say anything you wanted, without running through all those damn machinations of *thought*. "So are you going to change back?" Helen said. And the calculating part of her brain thought, well, maybe now is in fact the only time you could get away with asking Alberta that question.

Alberta ran her fingers over the patterned silver flask. "I don't know," she said, and there was a connection, an honesty to the words. "It seems to me I'm completely justified in staying this way."

Helen nodded. "In fact that's true," she said. "Keep your iron and don't mind me."

"Why haven't *you* changed back yet?"

"So I can convince people against their will," Helen said. She suddenly grinned. "And so I can stay prettiest the longest."

It was the first real smile she'd gotten from Alberta. "Wait," she said, and she got off the bed, and padded in her blue-and-white pyjamas to the open saxophone case. From a velvet pocket she took out a cheap battered locket and passed it to Helen.

Even tipsy, Helen had a guess what was in it. "Is this you?" she said. Alberta said nothing, just waited while Helen teased open the locket to reveal two pictures inside. They were faded, the old blue-and-white photos of the pre-war fey tech. One was of an attractive, smiling, dark-skinned girl of about eighteen. The other was a woman a generation older.

"That one's me," said Alberta, and there was a lurching moment where Helen thought she meant the older woman, but then Alberta said, "and that's my mother."

"You look so much alike," Helen said, and immediately modified, "Looked." She glanced up into Alberta's beautiful face and realized then what was hard for her, what had been hard all along. "Is she gone?"

"It's an old story, isn't it?" said Alberta. Her hand closed on the locket, snapping it shut. "The war, you know."

"I know," said Helen, and she covered Alberta's hand with her own. "I know."

Helen woke to find Jane standing at the end of her bed, staring at her. It made her sit up straight, which made her crack her head on the steep rafters. "Goodness, Jane, what on earth?" It was morning, and light filtered in through porthole windows on each end of the attic.

"I know you like dresses and all," said Jane. "But what on earth are we doing in this giant wardrobe?"

"Jane!" crowed Helen. "You're feeling better!"

"If having one's head inside a vise is feeling better, then yes," Jane said dryly. "Honestly, where are we?"

"The garret at Frye's. You know Frye."

"Of course," said Jane, and turned to walk toward the door, then suddenly turned white and crumpled to the ground in a heap.

"Jane!" shrieked Helen, and ran to help her up.

"I'm sorry. . . . ," Jane said faintly. "Sort of . . . dizzy. . . ." Her face was dead white.

"When did you last eat?"

"I don't remember?" Jane looked even whiter, if possible. "I . . . don't remember much, actually. We were at the Grimsbys'?"

"Oh dear," said Helen. "That was three days ago. Do you think you've eaten anything since then?"

"It's all sort of a blur," Jane confessed. "I remember a warehouse . . . seeing you there. . . ." She grimaced. "I don't remember it having much in the way of eggs and toast."

"Let's go downstairs," said Helen. She smoothed out Frye's dress, which she apparently had slept in—well, she remembered doing so perfectly well, it wasn't as though she had drunk *that* much—it was more that it was odd in the morning to discover what had seemed like a good idea the night before. She shoved her feet into her heels and helped Jane down the stairs.

The landing was empty, but clinking sounds emanated from the kitchen, along with a low voice chanting, "Hangover cure, hangover cure . . . ," until a sharper voice made it stop.

The kitchen was one of those modern compact efficiency stations. It would be rather dreary, except that Frye had knocked out a wall to meet the small dining room, and painted the remaining studs deep plum. The long-legged piano player from the other night was cheerfully mixing drinks for a small clump of less-cheery-looking revelers. Helen did not think anyone had come up to the attic, so she could only assume they had collapsed in a heap on the parlor divans. Through the gap between the purple studs Helen could see the other piano player, the rumpled brownish one, still looking rumpled in loud plaid trousers and frying up slices of bacon.

"Morning," she said, and there was a muffled chorus of grunts in response.

Alberta looked up from the china cup she was cradling in her hands. Her face was friendly but wary, as if admitting they had had a moment last night, but not particularly sure she was ready to extend that into friendship. "Hangover cure?" she said. "The Professor's frying up greasy things and Stephen's making Dead Dwarves."

Jane raised her eyebrows.

"Tomato juice and vodka," explained Helen to her sister, glad to see a familiar disapproving look on Jane's face. "And an egg." Because the egg made it all right or something. Oh, whatever. Now everyone's looking at you. Hurry up and move past it. "I'd take tea if you have it," Helen said.

Alberta nodded at the brown stoneware teapot next to a pile of mismatched cups and mugs. "How's that bacon coming, Professor?"

"On in five," said the man frying bacon.

Helen found an empty seat. There was a scarlet blanket draped over one of the chairs and she tugged it off and wrapped it around Jane, who looked as though she might faint or be ill at any moment. She provided her sister with toast, and water, and toast again, and then Jane said, "I'd better lie down *right now,*" so Helen helped her to the nearest divan. After that she finally sat down herself, cradling a cup of precious hot tea in her hands.

"I'm pretty sure Frye's up," said Alberta, but just then Frye swept in in crimson silk pyjama pants, holding a newspaper, her color high.

Her gaze swept the room, taking in the two sisters. "You found Jane!" she said to Helen. Helen nodded and started to explain, but Frye held up a finger and forestalled her. "Tell me everything in just a minute. This is first." She brandished the newspaper and proclaimed to the room, "You are all staying here until further notice."

"I'm not," said Stephen, "I play rehearsal piano at the Pine Theatre at noon. Dead Dwarf?"

"*You* may go," said Frye, with a dramatic sweep of her arm, simultaneously taking the tumbler he offered, "because you are a *man*."

"Excuse me?" said Alberta.

Frye plonked down the newspaper on the table. "Curfew Announced," it read in big letters, and then below it, a raft of tiny details. "Curfew starts at sundown—which, I might add, is six o'clock this time of year—and it is for all women."

"What?"

"Let me see."

"Not just all women with fey faces," said Frye, indicating herself and Alberta. "All women."

Stephen vaulted the chair and looked more closely at the paper in front of Frye. "Not just all women," he said. "All *dwarvven,* too."

"And probably anyone even remotely different after that," Alberta said soberly. She exchanged a look with Stephen. The rumpled man frying eggs had come in to watch, and he stood over Stephen's shoulder, not noticing as grease dripped onto the table from his spatula.

"This is madness," said one of the other women, a blonde in wrinkled sea green silk. "How will the shows run? You can't have *The Lady Was Willing* without the lady." She patted her hair.

"I thought you were playing the best friend," said a trim, plain-faced brunette.

"I never said I wasn't. And the point is the same."

"There's a dozen of us in the Winter Wonderland panto chorus that opens Friday," said the brunette. "I mean, forget all the leads for a moment. We play the snowflakes and singing skiers and everything else. You take out the chorus and you'd have a pretty sorry-looking show."

"The stage will be all men again," rumbled the Professor. "I can finally play Lady MacDeath."

"If you're quite done thinking only of yourself," said Alberta.

"Let me see that," said Helen, cutting through the chorus of moans. She picked up the newspaper and saw that Frye had not been exaggerating. The notice was couched in a lot of doublespeak about *safety* and *welfare* that reminded her uncomfortably of Alistair's words upon taking her mask, as if he had been a mouthpiece parroting Grimsby. Perhaps even more disturbing was that at the very bottom it said, "By order of Parliament and Copperhead."

"Things must be bad if they're getting their name on official legislation," Stephen said soberly.

"Things as in the fey?" said Frye. "Or things as in the state of the men in this country trying to make us all frightened, using the fey as an excuse so they can run things?"

"Both," said Stephen.

"Whose side are you on?" put in the Professor. "Don't tar all men with this, it's a *class* problem. . . ."

The argument rose and the room blurred in her sights as Helen thought: Yes, Stephen is right that things are bad. It is like poor Millicent with the perfect face and the iron mask. It would be a real danger to go out, but that did not mean Grimsby had the right to make her a prisoner in her own house. Who is this Grimsby, that my indolent husband has turned to him? That this country gives him the right to tell half of us when we can leave our house, where we can and can't work? She spread her fingers on the tablecloth, smoothing linen wrinkles out to her saucer.

"Well, that's that," said the brunette. "I'm getting down to the theatre right now to get my cancellation pay before anyone else tries it."

"Surely there'll be exceptions for people who are working," said the blonde.

"No exceptions," said Alberta, pointing to the notice. "It's almost like they want us to be stuck at home, unable to earn a living."

"It's exactly like that," said Frye, her face flushed with frustration and anger.

"If *Sturm und Drang* think they can replace me with a man they have another think coming," said Alberta.

"*Saucy Solstice Spectacular!* won't need a rehearsal pianist if this news holds true," Stephen said glumly. "You can't have the story of three leggy dance-hall girls looking for love on the darkest day of the year without the girls."

"Men," said the Professor. "Recast it all with men."

"Ugh," said Alberta.

One by one they hurried out into the November air, till all that was left was Frye and Jane and Helen and the leftover scent of blackened bacon.

Frye sank to one of the vacated chairs, her lanky frame collapsing. "From one perspective it hardly matters," she said. "Ticket sales were down down down on *Ahoy!* This is just the death knell. Those silly actors aren't even realizing they've lost half their audience as well. And how many men would go see an all-male *Saucy Solstice Whatnot*? Just the Professor and his sort of friends, and you can't live off of that." Frye rubbed the heels of her hands over tired eyes, smearing the remnants of olive eyeshadow around. Then she rocked her chair back and gently nudged Jane, who was still flat on the divan. "But I guess it's finally a good time for me to do the facelift," she said. "I'm so glad you've come home safe."

"Urggh," said Jane, eyes still closed.

"She's not safe yet," Helen said in a low voice to Frye. It felt odd, speaking for her older sister when she was right there, but Jane was not exactly standing up and taking charge of things, either.

Frye took a closer look at the prone figure on the divan. "What happened?"

"Lack of food, for starters," said Helen. "I don't think she's eaten for three days." She lowered her voice. "Which begs the question, why doesn't she remember what happened during those three days." To her sister she said, "Jane, tell Frye how you felt during the facelift. When the copper machine started."

"Like I was split in two," Jane said hoarsely. "Torn right down the center like a paper doll. And no, I don't remember much about the warehouse, but I *can* hear you talking about me." She struggled to sit up. "I think I could try some water again."

Frye's penciled eyebrows arched high at the sight of Jane's bare face with the reddened lines where the iron strips had been. In the daylight the lines looked raised, scarred. Helen wondered if they would ever fade. Frye's jade-green nails gripped Helen's sleeve. "Do you think . . . could you have been taken over by a *fey*?"

Jane glared. "No."

Helen shook her head as she gave Jane the water. "I don't see how it could be. If a fey takes you over it's stuck there till either you or it dies. It can't go in and out. When a fey tried to take me over, it immediately started erasing me. In a matter of seconds I would have been gone for good."

Frye sighed. "It makes me wish I'd done that facelift when you asked," she said. "But there's always one more audition, one more show, one last party. . . ."

"Facelift?" said Jane. She looked sharply at Helen. "You've been helping me, haven't you?"

Helen suddenly beamed, for she *had*. "Yes," she said. "I've got you three convinced already. More to follow, I'm sure."

"Three in one day," said Jane, and there was respect in her voice. "Good." She clutched the water glass and her eyes grew fierce. "Yet not enough. We have to do all the facelifts. Immediately."

Helen and Frye looked at each other. "Jane, honey, you're not well enough," began Frye.

Jane shook her head. "I will be. I have to. I need the women to go to the warehouse, where their faces are. I need everyone."

"How are their faces in the warehouse?" said Helen. "It looked as though they were stolen from your apartment."

"Nonsense; they're not stolen. They've been taken to the warehouse," said Jane positively. "Rows and rows and rows of them, looking at you with their black blank eyes. Now *you* must bring *them* to their faces. All The Hundred women. I need all of them, to match them up."

"Okay," Helen soothed, for she had seen no such rows and rows as Jane described. "I know. They're not safe, are they?"

"You're not listening," said Jane, and she lurched to her

feet, steadying herself on Helen's chair. "They're not safe, Helen, listen to what I'm saying. They're not safe."

"I am listening," said Helen. "Please sit back down." She helped her sister back to the divan and said, "Oh, Jane, please be reasonable with yourself. You need food and rest. You don't even know what happened to Millicent. . . ." She trailed off, thinking again that the shock would be too much for Jane.

"Who, Mrs. Grimsby?" said Jane. "Oh, Mr. Grimsby has her. He's taking good care of her. She'll be right as rain."

"You mean . . . is she out of the fey sleep then? But she shouldn't be with Mr. Grimsby. She was trying to get *away* from him," Helen said. "We all were, and now there you were in a warehouse that he must know about, because it had his invention in it." She rather thought she might like to lie down on a divan herself. "Now look. You said Millicent told you something. About a Fey King, and a plot, yes?"

Jane looked sideways at her, rubbing her forehead. "How much did I tell you?"

"Just that," Helen said, thinking back. "That another fey might be following through on the dead queen's plot to infiltrate the city." Helen worried her fingers together. "Oh, but Jane, you don't even know. Niklas and Edward both confirmed it. Maybe this fey is planning to invade one of The Hundred. Or already has. We need to get them changed back. But we need their old faces."

"At the warehouse," said Jane. "Oh, my head."

"But why there? It doesn't sound safe," said Helen.

Jane sank down into her chair, fingers gouging into her temples. "Don't be silly, Helen. I know far more about this than you. The warehouse belongs to Mr. Grimsby alone. The rest of Copperhead doesn't know anything about it. And Mr. Grimsby's spending all of his days at Parliament now. So all you have to do is bring The Hundred to the warehouse tomorrow at noon. I'll do them all at once. Safety in numbers."

Helen looked at Frye. Frye said, "Well, I don't have a show to go to anymore. . . ."

"If we get The Hundred," said Helen to Jane, "will you stay here and sleep? You clearly haven't recovered from whatever that horrible machine did to you." She raised eyebrows at Frye in request.

"Of course you can and will stay here," said Frye. *"Fais comme chez toi."*

"Mmm, and I already did," said Helen, gesturing at the knit dress. "I hardly know you and here I am borrowing your clothes. But I split the seams of my skirt crawling in that warehouse."

"You should wear trousers," said Frye.

Helen laughed. "Well. Maybe." Frye still looked at her, and so she finally said, "I don't think yours would fit me, though, and even I know I shouldn't spend today altering slacks." It would be an interesting problem, she thought; she hadn't ever attempted to adapt slacks to fit and flatter hips.

Frye waved this aside. "Sometimes I think I'm storing half the theatrical wardrobes in the city," she said. "I'll see if I have something. Now Jane, I'm going to tuck you in the attic with toast and broth and a dirty book and then Helen and I will go find your women. I still have my fey face, so that extra charisma should help. I can be quite charming when I try."

Helen shook her head, slowly, resolutely. If this was going to work there was more to it than this. And sometimes, like fixing Alistair, maybe you just had to step in and start fixing situations, or at least sorting them out. "I can't," she said. "Frye, if you'll let me direct you—?"

"That's what actors are for."

"I'll give you Jane's journal and explain everything I know about it. Then you're in charge of getting all the women together. You and your charisma." Helen looked at her sister dubiously. Jane was staring off into space, fingers delicately tracing the raised pink line on her jaw where the iron had been. "Hopefully Jane can help if anything in the journal needs interpreting."

"And you?" said Frye.

"I'm going to the *dwarvven* slums," Helen said. "And find out what a certain *dwarvven* spy knows about all this."

Chapter 10

DWARFSLUM

Helen went straight to the statue of Queen Maud on the pier. She was sure now it wasn't coincidence that Rook had mentioned it at Frye's party. Not when Alistair mentioned Jane being spotted there, and then Jane turning up at the factory a half-block away. Besides, there was Alistair's insistence that Rook was a spy. That he was working for Grimsby all along—and more than the nebulous *other business* Rook had admitted to. Helen cringed, thinking of her frank admissions to Rook.

Helen didn't know if she could trust Rook—but him being a spy did not seem the sort of thing Alistair would lie about. Rook must be entangled with Copperhead somehow. He must know more than he was telling.

The area was rough. Even Frye, who had cheerfully gone down to the section of the waterfront where Jane's nasty flat was, had warned Helen not to go to the *dwarvven* slums. "It doesn't matter what he did or didn't know," Frye said. "Stay here and feed Jane chicken broth. I'll get those women for you."

Helen wished she could have taken Frye up on her offer. Yet something drove her on, so now she was here, walking through the rough alleys in a dress of peacock blue, carrying a little letter-opener of Frye's as though it would protect her from harm.

Dwarvven or human, the men mostly looked tired, she thought. Hopefully she wouldn't encounter trouble, especially since there was no slim black-clad man walking beside her tonight to save her from her own folly.

As if in response to that thought, a man sitting on a bench across the street looked over at her perfect face, caught her eye.

Look away, she thought fiercely. *Look away.* She had loved the attention at first; she had loved suddenly having that power over every single person she saw. But now, when she was tired and miserable and afraid . . . *look away.*

Perhaps her fierce expression warned the man off, for he went back to staring at his grimy hands, picking at them as if to worry some splinter free.

But he wasn't the only one.

She stared some men down, boldly, trusted in the power of her face and warded them away. It was not a skillful application of the power, as she had done with Alistair, changing his motives, changing his soul. It was merely the fey glamour she'd had for six months, with a little extra oomph behind it. *Let your gaze slide away.*

But she could feel the gazes pressing in from all sides, and finally she couldn't take the tension anymore. She picked one out, a man leaning against a crumbling brick building. He was perhaps the roughest-looking of all—bigger and wider than Alistair, who was a tall man. His gaze flicked across the street, idling time, just waiting for a mark to come into his vicinity.

Helen walked straight to him.

The man looked down at her, his face an interesting cross between leering and disbelief. "Well, look what dropped into my lap," he said in a soft rumble.

Helen's heart was a sledgehammer on her ribs. She had only tried something this complicated with Alistair, whom she knew intimately. What ridiculous thing was she doing now? Breathe. "I need protection from here to the *dwarvven* neighborhood," she said. "I'm told it isn't far. Here's something for your trouble." She took several coins from the inner pocket of her coat and dropped them into his palm. They disappeared inside his fist, but he made no further move.

The leer intensified. "And what makes you think—?"

Helen didn't have time for this. "You will take me now," she said, and put the full force of her will behind it. Her fingers closed around her copper hydra necklace, her talisman.

The man straightened up. "Yes'm," he said. "This way."

He strode stiffly down the block, as if his legs weren't completely under his control. Which they weren't, Helen reflected with satisfaction. Her knees shook with relief. She could get used to this. Fix anyone who threatened her or her friends. Fix Alistair to be the husband she had thought he would be. Perhaps after Jane restored Millicent to herself, Helen could even fix Grimsby, make him into a good husband for Millicent. Her power suffused her, overwhelmed her. Perhaps a great many of The Hundred could do with her help. Would she or Millicent have changed their faces without their husbands' insistence? And now she could solve that for them. She could fix all those husbands, every last one.

The man stopped at what looked like an entrance to a junk shop. "Right here, ma'am," he said.

"This is a store," Helen said, suddenly worried that she had messed him up with her power.

The big man actually grinned. "It is that." He pointed. "Through the back."

Helen went inside the dim store with some trepidation. Maybe she just thought she had changed him but she hadn't at all. Maybe there were men here ready to capture her and sell her off. Her mind created a million dramatic scenarios until she realized she was looking at a very small woman behind the dilapidated wooden counter.

"Er," said Helen. "I'm trying to find an acquaintance. He's *dwarvven*. Part."

The woman shrugged. "So?" She crossed her arms and Helen saw the chain mail glint at her wrists.

The store had no lighting, electric or otherwise—the only illumination came from the greasy windows. The back of the shop was curtained off in a patchwork of repurposed fabrics. As Helen watched, a line of ten short men came out from behind the curtain, stomped gruffly past, and vanished out the front door.

She was sure they couldn't have all been back there. The shop must indeed lead to where the *dwarvven* lived. But how . . .

Helen's eyes widened. "The compound's underground," she said.

The woman shrugged again.

"I need to speak with someone," persisted Helen. "How do I do that? Can't I go back there and find him?"

"No."

"Can I leave him a note?" Helen's gaze swept the shop.

She realized that it actually *was* a shop, not just items in the windows for pretend. In the dim light it appeared to be all secondhand stuff—a lot of metal implements. But fully one quarter of the store was piled high with used books of all shapes and sizes for the *dwarvven,* who notoriously loved to read. It was hard to be frightened of a pint-size woman who ran a bookstore, but Helen figured she'd better stay on guard nonetheless.

The woman finally came back with a full sentence. "What's your friend's name?"

"Rook," said Helen, aware that it might not do her any favors. The *dwarvven* weren't any kinder to mixed race than the humans were.

"I think you'd better leave," said the woman.

"He wants to see me," said Helen, and though it was not strictly true she thought it might as well be.

"I've no instructions on the matter," said the woman, and her arms stayed folded. Knowing the stubbornness of the *dwarvven,* Helen thought she might stay there till doomsday. She almost turned, and then she remembered.

She could fix this woman. She could make her change.

It was for a good cause, wasn't it? Helen bore down on the woman, saying with all her will, "You will let me in."

But the woman only snorted. "Think fey tactics will work on me? Now you're never getting in."

Helen stopped, embarrassed at being caught. She did not even have the nerve to apologize. She turned to go—and then a young man came through the curtain. A man who suddenly seemed tall in comparison to the others. "Rook!" she said.

"It's okay, Looth," he said. "She's with me."

The woman watched Helen the whole way back past the booth and through the curtain.

Rook led her around piles of junk, boxes and furniture and more stacks of books, until they reached a door that appeared to lead to an ordinary cellar. He motioned her in front of him and said under his breath, "I'm sorry for the way they act."

"You can't blame them," said Helen. She picked her way down the crumbling stone stairs. A few lights strung here and there lit patches of the tunnel with a faint yellow glow. They appeared to be getting into the remains of an old sewer system, long ago cut off from the new city plumbing. It was quite dank, but it did not smell any worse than mold. She put her wrist to her nose, breathing in the lavender scent of Frye's dress, and below that, her own citrusy smell from Frye's soap.

"Of course you can," said Rook. They reached the bottom of the stairs and he took her hand and pulled her along by the light of his electric flashlight. They were walking along a stone embankment; below them rainwater washed slowly along the old stone tunnels, heading out to sea. Marking the tunnels were painted symbols in different colors—they must form a map of sorts, but Helen could not see any pattern to them. "If they're justified in hating you simply for being human, then you're justified in hating them for being not," Rook said. "*Copperhead* is justified in their hatred. You can't legitimize hatred."

"Still," she said. "I guess I didn't expect a welcoming committee."

"Closed to outsiders," Rook said. He stopped and she looked up at him in the yellow flashlight glow. "I'm afraid you wouldn't fit in with the *dwarvven* any better than I would in your world." Helen looked at him wonderingly. "Not that they even accept me," he said, and there was a touch of bitter to his voice. "Except I'm useful."

"Rook," she said, for this was why she had come. "What is your role in this? Someone told me you're working for Grimsby as a spy. But you can't possibly be . . . can you?"

Quietly he said, "I only do what's necessary to get them to trust me."

So Alistair had been telling the truth. "A double agent," she said slowly. "You probably swear the same thing to Copperhead about your time here with the *dwarvven*."

His face was in shadow; she could not read it. "I wish I weren't working for either of them. But my history with the *dwarvven* is . . . complicated."

"Tell me," she said, remembering what he had said of his past two nights ago. "You know how I ended up on my path. Tell me how you went down yours." There was silence for a long time, and finally the things he hadn't said in the dark the other night came out now, in that cold quiet tunnel.

"It was almost six years ago," said Rook. "I was seventeen and it was almost the end of the war. You know what it's like when you're seventeen."

"Yes," murmured Helen.

"I thought I knew everything. And . . . I was angry. I was tired of being laughed at for being *havlen*. At the same time, being *havlen* meant I could go among the humans, and pass." He exhaled. "We were sick of the war dragging on, you know. The sensible ones hunkered down and figured it would be all over soon. But there are *dwarvven* who've hated humans for the last two hundred years, since Queen Maud's son threw us all out. They're not content to stay home and read books and invent things. They've had it in for humans. And after months and months of war . . . some of them started to believe they saw a way to make the humans pay. Chief among them was a girl named . . . Sorle." Rook suddenly stopped and looked sideways at her. "You don't really want to hear this, do you?"

"Tell me," she said, for although she was not sure that she wanted to hear that his life revolved around this Sorle person, she wanted to know his story. What was he capable of? What was he involved in? Why did she feel in her bones she could trust him completely, even when he'd admitted that he was playing the *dwarvven* and the humans off each other? The answer to that last was that she was a fool, of course. She was here in the *dwarvven* compound to prove it. Helen took a breath and wrapped her coat tighter. "Tell me."

Concern showed on his face. "You look tired," he said. "You didn't come here to hear this."

"What's that? It's easier not to tell embarrassing stories about yourself? You've already told me how you made a fool of yourself over Frye; now tell me how you fell for Sorle. It's the oldest story in the world, isn't it? You did everything she asked to win her heart."

Amusement flickered. "One usually does not tell the new lady about one's past affairs."

A delightful shudder danced along her bones, but she said lightly: "Not new, but old and married." Affairs was right. He was the sort of man who had a million. He talked to every girl the way he did her—which was delightful, make no mistake, but not exactly something you could take to the bank. She let the conversation flow away from him having to admit terrible secrets and into things that were amusing to talk about. "So spill. How many past girls have there been? A dozen? A hundred? A whole harem, as in the stories of famous lovers? But come to that, I couldn't possibly figure you for a famous lover, for we've already established that you have no idea of proper dancing nor etiquette."

"Oh, I have a clever way to refute that," he said.

"Which is?"

In the flashlight glow his hazel eyes looked into hers, light and laughing. His sandalwood scent curled around him. "Well," he said.

But then there was a noise behind them and twenty, fifty *dwarvven* poured down the main stairs and hurried through the tunnel, some bumping past them, some splashing in the few inches of rainwater on the concrete floor. They appeared not to mind the cold and dank. One of them hallooed cheerfully to Rook. "Bringing your latest girl to the dance?"

"Wouldn't miss it," said Rook. She watched his smile fade as he turned back to her.

For no reason she thought of Alistair. But things were going to be okay with Alistair now. She had the secret to making them okay. So it didn't matter how many girls Rook had, or what his past was. Not to *her*. "Tell me then," she said into the waiting silence. "What happened with Sorle?"

He walked a few more paces, pulled aside a curtain, and gestured her through. The new hallway seemed much the same in the cursory examination via flashlight, but the curtain dampened sound from the main tunnel. There was a stone ledge and they sat on it. The flashlight played around the puddles on the floor.

"Sorle," he said at last, "wanted to blow up Parliament."

Helen sucked air over teeth. "And?"

He stood the flashlight between them, where it caught the

edges of his expression. "We aren't quite as awful as you think," he said, "even if we were all seventeen and a pack of thickwits. We were going to do it when they were out of session. My job, of course, was to pass as human, be charming—get the keys from the night watchman to a certain back door we needed. They had other jobs like gathering the supplies for the explosive. Many of those were things that *dwarvven* have, you know—but of course most adults weren't going to be in favor of, or even informed of, this particular blow for justice till it was all safely over.

"I got the keys out safely. And then they all got caught on their end." His jaw went tight. "I went in to put the keys back, so the man wouldn't get into trouble. That's when he caught me. Ran after me down to the wharf—fought me. I hit him too hard—he fell into the water—it was nighttime and he was gone instantly. I waded in, holding on to the pier—but he was gone." He let out a long breath of air. "The problem with charming things out of people is that you have to understand them. And by the time you understand them, you care for them. . . ." He shook his head. "When his body washed up a couple weeks later, the human courts ruled it an accident."

"Oh, Rook . . . ," said Helen. "How did the *dwarvven* find out?"

"I told them," he said. "During the *dwarvven* trial. They censured the others and sent them home for community service for six months—by which time the war was over. But someone had actually died in my case—and then, I was *havlen*. I was officially told it was my bad blood showing. In public I was told off and sentenced to six years hard labor in the mines. I went there. It was . . . miserable. A month into it a man 'unofficially' came and told me I could better serve my people as a spy. . . ." He trailed off. "Sometimes I think it's worse than the mines."

She was silent and he said, "You see I've thoroughly managed to depress you. I propose all the secrets we share from now on be light and scandalous. Back in school, we did a production of *The Pirate Who Loved Queen Maud,* and I played the pirate—mostly because as the tallest I was best able to carry off our leading lady on my shoulder. All went well until I was required to leap from the set of the deck to the crocodile-infested waters. The boy playing the crocodile sat up and roared, and I tumbled end over end onto the deck, splitting my trousers in the process. Your turn."

The gap between the two stories was so large that it took her breath away, and she could not immediately find her clever response.

And so he picked up the flashlight and shone it elsewhere, away from them, and said lightly, "Well, keep your secrets then."

"I have no secrets," she said, finally picking up her cue. "I was just wondering how well the rest of the *dwarvven* danced."

"Come and find out," he said immediately. "Goodness knows we could use a lift around here. Times are hard and getting harder. So many *dwarvven* let go from their employment. Finding work never used to be a problem, until Copperhead gained a foothold in the city. Some *dwarvven* have already headed back to our own country, deep in the mountains. Given up on the city for a generation. But come back tonight and dance. We will have fun."

Helen sighed. "No, I was being silly. I have so much to do, now that I've found Jane. Frye's helping me convince The Hundred, but she can't do it all herself, even with her fey charisma. I should be doing that now, but I came down to ask you about your involvement with Copperhead. Which I guess if I believe you is nothing worse than I already knew. But after I found Jane at the warehouse I just didn't know what to think or whom to trust."

He stared at her. "What warehouse?"

"You mentioned the statue of Queen Maud," Helen said, "I thought as a joke. But Alistair mentioned it, too, and that led me to Jane, who was wandering around this strange warehouse full of cages, and Grimsby's invention; you know, from the meeting? Jane didn't exactly seem to be trapped there, but she was certainly there. And the warehouse must belong to Grimsby—Jane thought so, too. And if you're spying *on* them as well as *for* them, anyway . . . well. Tell me what you know."

"You found the warehouse? I wasn't sure there really was one. And you just, what, stumbled on it?"

"Well, it was kind of lit up blue," Helen said. "Not exactly hard."

"Lit up blue," Rook repeated. "To you, you mean?"

She stared at him. "To me only? Is that what you mean? But why me? Because of my face?"

Rook shook his head. "I don't know. Look, I need to find that place."

"So you guys can blow it up?" He looked wounded and Helen raised her lilac-gloved hands. "Look, I'm tired of pretending I'm a scatterbrain, even if it's generally true. If you're spying for the *dwarvven,* then clearly you have a reason. So even *if* I trust you—which might be a big if—then still still still. You guys are after Copperhead and Copperhead is after you and you can't just all go around acting tiresome and manly and declaring war."

Rook slumped down. "I'm not," he said. "But my history is against me." He gave her a rueful smile. "Even with you and you barely know it. Look, I won't make you show me the warehouse tonight. But I think you should bring Jane here, to me. If what you say is true, then Copperhead wants Jane for something she's able to do. They must have put her there in the warehouse, right?"

Helen's mind worked. "Or not all of Copperhead," she said slowly. "Alistair thought Jane was still missing. He thought that's why Grimsby and Morse and Boarham were mad at him. But this is Grimsby's warehouse, so he must have known Jane was there. Or even put her there, without telling Alistair and the other top party members. Which means . . . which means that Jane didn't run away after all. Jane said something about thinking there was a man in the attic. . . . Someone could have grabbed her."

Rook looked sober. "We were both right there, watching that machine like fools. If it hadn't gone haywire from interfering with Jane's process, you wouldn't have known she was missing for another hour." He puzzled it over. "But most of the key Copperhead players were by the machine."

Helen tried to focus, tried her damnedest to replay that scene in the attic, after the lights went out. Who was missing? "Boarham," she said slowly. Hefty thug Boarham. One of the two right-hand men. "Grimsby must have planned all along to kidnap Jane. He must have sent Boarham to grab her. Take her out the garret window and down the fire escape. Take her to the warehouse. Ransack her flat for those faces while I was busy taking the trolley . . ."

"With a motorcar he would have had plenty of time to beat the trolley," Rook agreed.

"But then, if Grimsby planned to take Jane, he must have known about my plan with Millicent to have Jane replace her face," Helen said. She clutched Rook's arm as her voice rose higher, connecting the dots. "He knew he was going to be leaving her in the fey sleep because of this. Where she might die. His own wife. His *own wife*." She realized what she had done and let go.

"Has Millicent recovered?" said Rook, tactfully not flinching away from her grasp.

Helen shook her head, trying to shake off the rising sensations of guilt and fear. "I don't know. I'm just now realizing that Jane was very vague on that point. And I don't even know where Grimsby's stashed her. He said someplace safe but . . . oh goodness. He could have just offed her and how would I know? She was trying to run away from him."

"Maybe he knew that part, too."

"And maybe she knew he knew. She told Jane something." Helen flung up her hands. "Ugh, that man is awful. I didn't know it was possible to hate him more." She paced, thinking. "All right. So why kidnap Jane? I knew Copperhead disliked Jane but they claimed it was because she was working against them. What if, for Grimsby at least, that's not entirely true? Jane did have extra powers before. She could actually use her fey substance in a way most women couldn't." Helen whirled, bits of gravel skidding off the walkway and down to the water below. "What if he took her to the warehouse to test his machine out on her? Three days of torture—that would make anyone lose it."

"Where is she now?"

"I left her at Frye's."

"Frye's trustworthy. No matter what you think of me."

"Trustworthy but not *there,*" returned Helen. "Frye was going to try to find some of those women and win them to the cause. Jane's all alone in the house. And she said—she said about the warehouse that things were patchy—going in and out. What if her mind's gone again? What if she was just temporarily sane this morning, and not all the way better? And then, with no one watching her . . . anyone could just waltz in and take her away."

Rook nodded, watching her come to the inevitable conclusion.

"I have to hide her where no one knows where she is," Helen said. "I have to bring her here."

"You can trust the *dwarvven,*" he said. "We might be grouchy, but we're forthright. We always pay our debts, and we'll always tell you when we hate you."

Helen managed a weak smile. "Good to know."

Heart in throat, Helen rang the bell at Frye's for ten minutes before Jane finally answered the door, apparently all alone. Frye must have lent her clothes, too, for Jane now wore a bulky royal purple cardigan over her grey evening dress. Helen's heart sank as she saw the vague expression on Jane's face, just as she had been in the warehouse.

"Oh, Jane," said Helen helplessly. "What took you so long to come to the door?"

"I was dancing," said Jane.

"With whom? Who's here?"

Jane shrugged. "I used to dance with Edward. And sometimes with Dorie. La, la . . ."

"Oh goodness, Mr. Rochart," said Helen. "What if he's finally arrived in the city and sent over a note?"

"Are we going somewhere?" said Jane.

"To safety," said Helen. "Before someone comes and takes you away and you just let them."

"My bag," said Jane. "I need my bag."

"Really?" said Helen. "You've managed just fine without it."

"My bag," repeated Jane. "My bag, my bag."

"Ugh," said Helen. She looked at the clock. "If we go all the way out to Alistair's, we're going to be late getting back to Rook. I told him an hour. And that new curfew's at dusk, you know."

Jane turned wide green eyes on Helen, stared at her as if this information had no possible meaning.

"On the other hand, maybe your fiancé *has* sent a note, and then maybe he'll have an idea of what's going on with you. He's had a lot more experience with fey problems than any of us."

"Fey problems?"

"Fine," said Helen. She dragged Jane out of Frye's and through the streets, eyes peeled for a cab. She swore several times. "This is no time to be taking the trolley," she said. "Where are those damn cabs?"

Jane merely followed, eyes wide and lost in some other world of her own. She looked ethereal, otherworldly, wafting along behind Helen. But at last they made it to the theatre district, which, even with the new curfew, was busy enough to have cabs. Helen hailed one of them and bustled Jane into it. Through the window she could see the glut of frantic actors milling around and commiserating with one another.

Helen gave the driver the address and they hurried through the cold night till they reached the ugly row house on the good street that belonged to Alistair. That was when it occurred to Helen that, even though she had "fixed" Alistair, it might not be enough to withstand the sight of seeing Jane, who apparently he thought should be held for murder.

"I am not going to waste time yelling at myself," muttered Helen.

"What's that, lady?" said the driver.

"Look, drive around the street a couple times. I'll be right back and we'll go somewhere else."

"It's your coin," he said.

"And don't let her out," said Helen, pointing to the pale figure in the back. Jane was pressed against the glass, long fingers moving slowly over it, tracing the lines of blue that covered the street.

"Look, lady, I don't go in for restraining loonies."

"If you lose my sister, I'm not paying you one penny," said Helen, and she slammed the door before he could argue one more word.

She hurried inside, dashed up the steps to her room. There was the carpetbag. Grabbed it. Dumped out a little jar of dried lavender on her vanity until she found the notes stashed at the bottom. Hopefully it would be enough for the fare. Helen turned to run and then thought, suddenly, *He said there would be a dance.*

It seemed ridiculous to go to a dance in the middle of a war. It was ridiculous.

And yet.

If she was going to be there anyway, keeping Jane safe, figuring out exactly what had happened to her, exactly what Rook knew . . .

Couldn't one as easily do that on the dance floor?

Just a waltz. Just a turn. Just . . .

Helen turned to her wardrobe and, knowing she only had a second, refused to let herself linger. She could try on outfits all day to find the perfect representation of what you wore to an unknown dance in a *dwarvven* slum when you didn't want to look as though you were impressing anybody but still wanted to slay all of them (all of them? Yes, all of them) with your beauty.

But there was no time. She had a go-to dress, an apple green ruffled voile that could withstand being shoved in a carpetbag, and she grabbed it and started for her bedroom door, colliding into a pale, troubled-looking Mary. "Mary," Helen said, seizing her hands. "Did any messages come for me? And am I in trouble for not coming home?"

Mary glanced behind her, down the open hallway. "I'm not sure he noticed exactly," she began, but Helen forestalled that.

"Wait, messages first."

"Yes," said Mary, "That fiancé of your sister. You only missed him by an hour. He said he'd be back and that you should tell me where to find you."

"Thank goodness he's in town," said Helen. Lowering her voice, she said, "Look, can you memorize the address to tell him? Copperhead mustn't know who's been helping us." Mary nodded, and came all the way into the bedroom, silently closing the door behind her. Helen gave her Frye's address, adding, "She'll know how to get ahold of us." She shook her head. "He must be terribly worried. Tell him we've found Jane if you see him first. Did he look all right?"

"A little wild-looking," Mary said. "Hair on end. But more despairing-like than spoiling for a fight. I don't think he wanted any trouble, but Mr. Morse came through the foyer just then and tried to pick a fight with Mr. Rochart, even with his crippled hand, and then he would have flattened him—flattened Mr. Rochart, I mean—but Mr. Hattersley came out and pulled them apart. The master didn't seem to notice."

"Oh no," said Helen. "Poor Edward."

In a hushed voice Mary added, "They were terrible, ma'am. They haven't been this bad since before you came."

"They used to be worse?"

"Well, after that terrible motorcar accident with Mr. Grimsby's wife, you know," said Mary. "They all got better for a little bit."

Helen shook her head. "I don't know," she said. Except Alistair saying . . . "A *dwarvven* was at fault for his first wife's death?"

Mary snorted. "Begging the master's pardon, ma'am, but, no. You know them. They had been drinking all night, of course—and Mr. Grimsby was quite wild in those days. And the first Mrs. Grimsby was here, pleading with him to come home. He told her he wouldn't be ordered about—of course they all cheered him on—and then he said he was fit to take them on a nice pleasure drive and they'd go where he wanted and so on. But of course he wasn't in any kind of state to do that. They hit another car—the other driver was a *dwarvven,* you see, that's where that comes in. Mrs. Grimsby was killed instantly. Mr. Grimsby went through the windshield. That's when he got into all the Copperhead stuff about *One People One Race* and started warping all of them to it, even though the *dwarvven* driver didn't do nothing. People go mad from guilt you know."

"Yes, they do," Helen said softly.

Mary shook her head. "I hate to say it, ma'am, but I don't know if I can stay in this position much longer. I hate to leave you with them, but . . ."

"I know," said Helen. "I'll write you a recommendation. I will."

She opened the door, and Mary added, "I really don't think you want to go down there, ma'am. It's not decent."

Voices drifted down the hall from the games room and Helen remembered, with a shocking start, that Tam must be down there with them. Of course, she had laid the *geis* on Alistair to behave, but . . . "You go to bed, Mary," she said. "Tell the housekeeper I said you could have the night off. George can go in if they need something."

Helen strode past Mary and went firmly down the hall. The male voices were louder, raucous. On top of them a female laugh drifted out and Helen felt her bones freeze. They had women over, too? She opened the door to the games room and took it in. Men, slouched in chairs, muddy feet on tables. Musky cologne, lavender soap, cheap floral perfume. A woman perched on the arm of Boarham's chair, another in Morse's lap. And a small figure in an explorer hat, sliding half-off a footstool, holding a tumbler of beer.

Alistair and his friends were getting Tam drunk.

Helen dropped Jane's bag and stormed into the room, a whirlwind of frustration at herself and them. "What are you doing? Absolutely not. What is this? What is . . . ?" she spluttered off in frustration. She could not even handle the topic of the women for the moment; all her focus was on that small boy she had tried to protect. She had given Alistair specific instructions. Not specific enough?

Alistair furrowed his brow. "You said to entertain him and have a good time."

"Not like this. I said—"

"Entertain him," finished Alistair.

"And we're doing that," said Boarham. He squeezed the waist of the girl perched on his chair and Helen saw with rapidly growing distaste that the girl was wearing a mask of iron. Not a real mask of iron. A lacy half mask meant to mimic Helen's own, but giving shape and allure to an ordinary set of features. Helen glanced at Morse, whose wife really did have a fey face. The girl in his lap was not his wife. She, too, wore a domino of grey silk.

Helen was left momentarily speechless.

"Look, Master Thomas, tell Miss Helen she can suck it," said Boarham.

"You can suck it," said Tam, sweet funny Tam.

Helen was a whirlwind of indecision. She couldn't leave Tam. And yet, how safe was it in the *dwarvven* underground? They wouldn't hurt a child, she was sure. That seemed a small hope to pin things on, and yet that small voice inside her told her she could still trust Rook.

She ran through her other options. Frye—gone. Jane—mentally gone. And she couldn't stay here at Alistair's house with Tam, because Jane was outside, circling in a cab, and if Jane came in these drunken louts would sober up and take her away for murder . . . or worse.

"You're coming with me," Helen said to Tam. At least he would be *with* her, and she could keep him safe, whatever happened.

"It was only one drink," said Hattersley, offering her a tipsy smile. "Young man has to learn to hold his beer."

"Get your coat," she told Tam. He crossed his arms, trying to imitate Boarham's pugnacious stance. "Now," she said, and he went.

Morse looked sharply at her from his spot in the armchair,

arm held firmly around the girl's waist. He had always been a nasty sort of drunk, she remembered. It struck her for the first time how sad it was that she could recite the exact sort of way all these men got drunk. Emotional, sleepy, quarrelsome . . . "What about that new curfew Grimsby got passed, hey? I expect you're supposed to be off the streets soon."

"To stop walking them," snorted Boarham, pleased with his wit. He tumbled the girl from the arm of the chair to his lap and she giggled.

Morse waved his glass of whiskey around with his free hand. "If she were my wife she'd know what's what," he told it.

"Some of us know how to sacrifice for the cause," said Boarham in a self-satisfied way to Morse. Helen imagined him slinging an unconscious Jane over his shoulder and she wanted to wipe that smirk off his face.

"She has an escort," Alistair said with a funny simpering smile. "That dwarf fellow of Grimsby's."

Morse barked laughter. "What, is she going to help him blow up the slums?" He smiled maliciously at Helen. "I didn't know you were into that sort of thing."

"I'm going," Helen said quietly, but firmly. She nodded at the quiet girl in Morse's lap, the giggling one in Boarham's. "You can come, too, if you want." But they both shook their heads no, and truth was Helen had no idea what she would do if the men rose up against her. They were so big, so wild, so unpredictable in their drunken whims. And she did not think she could change them the way she had changed Alistair. It had felt with Alistair as though she knew him so well she could move things, make new things lock, pull out the

Alistair she thought she knew. She had changed that man in the street through anger and fear. But a whole crowd of them, drunken and pressing in? No.

She looked at Alistair, relaxed in a chair with water in his hand. At least her power seemed to be holding. "You can go," he said dreamily.

"Really," said Morse.

Boarham snorted. "If he doesn't care about his reputation, why should you? Pass the whiskey."

"He cared about it the night we met those dancing girls from Varee," said Morse. He smirked at Helen and her heart beat faster. Surely he was not telling her to her face that Alistair was even worse than she had imagined. That it was only chance that he didn't have a girl captive in his chair, half-mask on her face.

Hattersley looked sideways at her. "Before your time," he muttered. He had always been the nicest of the bunch, though Helen did not know if that meant he was telling her the truth, or a lie to make her feel better.

"Has it really been that long?" said Morse. Ostentatiously he counted back months on his fingers. "November, October . . ." He shrugged, dropping the game. "What about your little theatre piece, Hattersley? Bitty or Betty or some such?" His free hand inscribed suggestive lines an inch away from the girl he held.

"She's fine," Hattersley said neutrally.

Morse dipped a finger in his whiskey and sucked it off. "Consolation prize after you-know-who?"

All of Alistair's friends suddenly stopped and looked at Helen, including Hattersley, who was frozen in shock. She felt her face flame bright red, and did not know exactly what had happened. She looked at Alistair, but he was staring off into nothing, a vacuous expression on his face.

Tam stumbled back in, his coat on upside down, laughing at himself. He had his jar of bugs in one hand and his binoculars strung around his neck. "Ready for an expodishon," he said.

Helen seized his free hand with relief. "Come on," she said gently. To the men she said, "Enjoy yourselves," and then she took Tam's hand and hurried out the door, eyes peeled for the circling cab. Had *Hattersley* been interested in her? She had never particularly thought about him. She hadn't even met him till the wedding, she thought, so what did he mean consolation prize? If Betty was the Betty Helen had met at Frye's party, they probably had been together longer than she had been married. Betty had mentioned a Richard, and she rather thought that might be Hattersley's first name.

Helen paused at the foot of the stairs, realizing the absence of what she sought.

The cab was not there.

She turned left, thinking the driver's circling might take him around that corner, and hurried Tam along down the street, watching. No moving cars; all was silent. It felt as though the city were preparing for the oncoming dusk and curfew. There was only a thin lone figure at the end of the road, walking slowly along and staring at the sky.

Jane.

Helen pulled Tam along until they caught up with Jane, and she seized her arm with her free hand. "What happened? Where's the cabbie?"

"I have bugs," said Tam. "They flyyyyy around."

"Do they?" said Jane.

"Jane," repeated Helen. "What happened?"

Jane turned those green eyes on her. "I was asking the driver if he'd ever touched one of the blue bits of fey and tried to see what it's thinking. Because I wonder how many bits have to join together to cross over into being full-fledged fey. A whole fey can lose some pieces, but they don't like it. When does it become just unthinking little bits, like we used to power our lights with? Do the small bits dream? One of the fey made me dream. And then the driver said any amount of money wasn't worth it and he stopped the car and opened the door and I got out and walked around the block just as we were doing in the car and now I'm here."

"Argh," said Helen. She did not know how she had gotten in a mess that involved standing on a street corner with an addled sister and a drunk child, late for an appointment in the *dwarvven* slums with a citywide curfew about to fall any moment. In that moment it seemed just more proof of her inability to make good decisions, for who else would find themselves like this? The one good thing was that surely there was nothing else to go wrong right now.

"It's snowing!" said Tam.

Really. *Snowing?*

"It's like cotton," Jane said dreamily.

"It's like bug guts. White floaty bug guts." Tam hiccuped. "I'm going to make snow pterodickle—pterodackle—snow man-eating butterflies."

"I am, too," said Jane.

"No, no, and no," said Helen firmly, and she got one hand on each of them before they plopped down on the as-yet-unsnowy-but-certainly-muddy ground. "We are going to find Rook. We are going on the trolley."

"Chugga chugga choo choo," said Tam.

"That's a train," said Helen, reflecting that it was hard to tell which part was drunk and which was small child. It was not something she'd ever expected to have to puzzle out. "Come on."

She tugged them both along through the falling snow. The wind was wet and the snow fell in big fat flakes that occupied both her charges, although her wrists grew sore from keeping a tight hold on them as they attempted to chase and eat snowflakes.

"The snow's like polka dots against the sky," said Jane.

"Doka pots," said Tam. "Pots pots pots."

"Your scarf is dragging," Helen told Jane. "Hold your bug jar with two hands, Tam."

"Then you'd be holding it," he said gleefully, because of course she was still holding one hand.

Grant me patience and a nice hot bath, thought Helen. "Just be careful. It's glass."

"Glass pots. Pots pots pots."

They rounded a corner and there was the trolley station. "Thank goodness," muttered Helen. There was a wait for the next trolley, in which time the sky got darker and darker and the snow got fiercer. By the time the trolley finally pulled up it was undeniably dusk, and here were two women with fey faces out against the rules. Not to mention a small drunk child, who, though he was male, still probably fell on the needs-curfew side of the curfew law. Helen hustled them onto the trolley, thinking that she had been without her iron mask all this time and hadn't even noticed. It was funny what a single-minded purpose and two lunatics would do for knocking worries right out of your head.

She hurried them on and sat them down on either side of her, knocking wet clumps of collecting snow from everybody's coats and cardigans and explorer hats. You could still look nice when you were on the run.

Jane clutched her carpetbag, and Tam hung on to Helen's coat pocket. He peered around, studying the passengers as if they were an unusual species of ant. Helen put a hand on both of theirs and tried to relax her shoulders and neck.

The trolley was wet from the snow and crowded from the bodies crammed into it. The crowds eased around Helen at every stop until she realized that there were very few people left in the spots designated for humans. But there were still people hurrying home. They spilled out from the back of the trolley—the *dwarvven*. Helen had not realized how many of them were in the city. She had not thought much of them at all until the last couple days. But now she saw them in the soot-coated greys and browns of the new factories and she thought they were surely too worn out to be a danger to anyone, regardless of what Copperhead relentlessly repeated about *dwarvven* unrest, *dwarvven* uprisings. She studied the notices around the trolley as if looking for clues to how far Copperhead had progressed. Again she saw: YOUR EYES ARE OUR EYES! And, over the door near the *dwarvven* end of the trolley: BE CIVIL, BE COURTEOUS, BE A CREDIT TO YOUR RACE.

Tam's attention was caught as well by the short people at the end of the car. He looked at them through his binoculars, then turned round eyes on Helen. "They're not even stuffed. They're *real* dwarves."

"The word is *dwarvven,*" said Helen in a low voice, "and hush."

"Father says dwarf," Tam said positively. "When he shot

one he gave me a whole terrarium for not telling. But that dwarf was dead. I never got to see a *live* one."

Helen felt a peculiar mixture of horror and mortification. "Tam, tell me later," she said. She was grateful that although the pitch of his small voice carried, the words were slurred and did not. He was looking green around the gills and she found herself hoping he would pass out rather than incite a riot on the trolley.

"No, I can't tell you," he said. "I promised not to tell, and Father always knows what I say and do. You can't lie to Father. Only for him. Like about the dead dwarf. Dead dead red dead head head dead . . ."

Thankfully, the trolley came to its final stop and Helen rose. "Here we are," she said, and pulled Jane and Tam along with her out of the trolley car onto the cold snowy street. The passengers slowly streamed off, parting around the three of them. "My bag," said Jane, and before Helen could stop her she turned and vanished back into the trolley.

"Jane," said Helen, and started after her, but then Tam, who apparently didn't feel so well after the trolley ride, turned and started emptying his stomach into the wet snow of a nearby bush.

Helen wanted to scream. She put a gentle hand on the boy's shoulders, waiting for him to finish.

She had rescued the boy, but now what? She was not cut out for this sort of responsibility. And what should she do with this new information from Tam? Would anyone take the word of a drunk child over a man with the ear of the Prime Minister? Well, get the boy to safety first. Push the rest of those thoughts aside for later.

Shouts rose and Helen raised her head, looking around for

Jane. As if in a dream everything seemed to quiet and slow, the open screaming faces, the shouts, the running. Men, women, *dwarvven,* running, running, running. The fire and smoke behind them, on the trolley, in a long slow build.

In slow motion Helen saw the trolley slide off the tracks and skid toward her.

Then nothing.

Chapter 11

SHRAPNEL

"Helen. Helen."

Jane was shaking her and she didn't want to get out of bed. No, she was dreaming. Jane hadn't lived with her in almost a year. But this was not that time, it was another time. This was at home, in the little shack of a home they shared after the war, after no Charlie. Mother was ill, had been ill for a while, and now here it was in the wee small hours and Jane was shaking Helen to say she was leaving. That fey blight on Jane's face writhed and curled as Jane's words tumbled from her lips and Helen thought like a lost thing inside, don't leave me here to watch Mother die. Don't leave me here. Don't leave me. . . .

"Helen!"

The sound of her name came through a great many layers of cotton. She opened eyes to find Rook bending over her. His lively hazel eyes were dark with concern as he worked over her arm.

"Thank goodness," he said, and she had to carefully sift through the ringing cotton to pick out the words. Their eyes met, and she had the funny thought that she was home again, as in that dream. Then the wicked light flashed in them, and he said, "On second thought, perhaps you don't want to know what I did to your dress."

Helen looked down to see a strip taken from the peacock blue hem. "Aaaand now it's the right length for me," she said dryly. A dress for Frye, a drink for Alberta, a jar of slugs for Tam—her debts were mounting.

"Thought you'd rather have the blood in than out," Rook said as he wrapped the strip of peacock blue around her arm, where it looked like a badge of war. Sound was returning now, and with it the realization that her upper arm was throbbing. Her mouth tasted of dust and hot metal. "Be glad this didn't hit higher," he said, and he showed her a bloody bit of sharp thing that might have made her feel faint, except she had the funny feeling that she didn't want to feel faint in front of him.

"The trolley," Helen said, remembering. "I was standing here, and then—Tam. Where's Tam. And Jane?"

"They're all right. I took them to my quarters," Rook said. "Up we go. You can manage on your own now, can't you?"

"I can," she said, and a horrible dark thing opened up inside her, an echo, a voice. It was Morse's offhand spiteful comment. *Are you going to help him blow up the slums?*

It couldn't be. She refused to believe it. Rook could not possibly be that cold inside.

He was watching her, wavering there, and he did not put out hands to steady her.

"What are you doing then?" she said.

"Going in to help," Rook said.

"I'm going, too," Helen said. She did not know what possessed her to say it. And yet she thought she saw his hazel eyes glimmer with respect.

"Let's go then," he said, and with a trace of his usual levity added, "You can make a fine number of bandages with that skirt."

"Not as many as you're thinking," she shot back, and the wit and raillery lay like a bright warm thing over the cold gulf that separated them.

They plunged into the destruction. It was dark and snowing and utter chaos. Frightened men and women ran through the rubble calling the names of friends, lovers, children—answered by terrible sounds of pain from those that had been hit. A woman was trying to move a smoking piece of metal off of someone with her bare hands. Several men were working to safely move the downed wires from the tracks. Ahead of her, in the shadow cast by the destruction, lay a tiny woman in a brightly flowered skirt like Helen's mother used to wear.

Helen made a beeline to her, moving with a purpose and energy she had not felt in a long time. A metal bar lay half on top of the *dwarvven* woman, pinning her down. She was moaning.

Helen bent down. "Are you all right?"

The woman grunted. "Just my leg," she managed, trying to sit up.

Helen wrapped her gloved hands in the knit skirt and shoved the twisted beam the few inches off of the woman. She saw the torn flesh and shuddered. The woman must be in too much shock to fully register the pain. "Lean on me," Helen said, and, hoping she wasn't making things worse, she helped the woman hobble the short distance to where a makeshift field hospital had arisen. Helen helped the woman sit down, patiently waiting her turn in the line, and thought,

This is what I could do to help. She had done it before, so long ago, when she couldn't raise a shovel herself and head onto the field. . . .

"Wait," Helen promised the woman, and went to where several *dwarvven* were ferrying in supplies from their nearby home.

"Just get them patched so they can get home," one was saying rapidly as he unloaded buckets of supplies from a makeshift wagon. "Fimn's running the stretchers back and forth."

"Broken bones are one thing," said another. "But some are going to need the city hospital."

"If they'll take us," muttered a third. "If they're not overjoyed to hear this."

"I hardly think—," said the first, but then the third noticed Helen and nudged the others.

"Can I help?" said Helen. All three looked up, eyed her with suspicion. "I can clean wounds and apply dressings. I did it in the war. Debride, probe for shrapnel . . . if I can't stop the bleeding or there's a fracture I'll call for a surgeon. I know when I'm in over my head."

The first looked at her carefully. After what seemed like a long time but was in reality probably a very short time due to the speed at which they were working, said, "Over there with Nolle's crew."

"Thank you," said Helen. She could feel them watching her as she walked in the indicated direction, stripping off her gloves.

It was still chaos there, but a controlled chaos. The groans of the wounded mingled with the bangs and thumps of people sifting through the destruction, bringing in supplies. Nolle, a sturdy dark-skinned *dwarvven* woman with long wavy hair, wasted no time letting Helen start working on the people being brought in. She pushed Helen toward a *dwarvven* man who had been struck just above his ear, the skin torn back. Helen swallowed, picked up the carbolic disinfectant, and stepped toward him. This was a thing she could do. "This is going to sting," she said.

Nolle did not slow her own work, but gave a brief nod of approval in Helen's direction. Despite the trouble that Copperhead was stirring up between the races, it was equal opportunity here, Helen was pleased to see, and they patched up *dwarvven* and humans with equal care.

It was full night now. The makeshift work lights had dimmed and been replaced three times by the time the line of people slowed. Helen's fingers were numb as she bent mechanically for a next victim that didn't come.

Nolle left what she was doing and touched Helen's arm. "You should know we saved nearly everybody," she said. "You have done well." And then, as if it was something formal, she said, "I acknowledge our debt to you and take it on. Now sit down."

Helen nodded, and found herself wavering, toddling out from the tented area into the wreckage, which was now quite covered in snow. It was starkly quiet after the time in the tent with the wounded. It was peaceful, almost beautiful, like something that had happened a million years ago to someone else. The people were mostly gone now, either helped in the tent or stumbled on home. It was down to a few figures still searching the wreckage to make sure they hadn't missed anybody. Perhaps it hadn't even really been all that long since the explosion, and yet it seemed a lifetime. A lean shadowy figure came through the snow from the other end of the trolley, a crowbar over his shoulder. The cold and fatigue suddenly got to her and she sat down, hard.

"Helen!" she heard from a distance, and saw him drop the crowbar and hurry toward her, and she thought, so maybe he cares a little if I faint?

The snow fell in white clumps, blotting out him and the smoking wreckage. She didn't see the trolley; she saw the battlefield that she did not enter. She stood there with Mother as Charlie and Jane marched into the field and all they could do was watch and let them go. There were farmers to bandage and wounds to tend and she did that all day and into the night, worked straight through the numb shock while mother wept and Jane keened.

All of this flashed in front of her eyes, superimposed on the twisted struts and billowing blue smoke. Her legs were wet with snow, everything was wet with snow and she was so cold, or perhaps so warm. . . .

Then gentle arms were picking her up and now she was the one being helped along. "Didn't you know you have to take it easy after you have a concussion?"

"No one told me that," murmured Helen.

"I'll have a word with Nolle," Rook promised. "Basic medical training." This and similar nonsense kept her awake, got her through the junk store and down the stairs to the tunnels below the surface. "You need to come see Jane and Tam," he said. "Reassure yourself that they're all right."

She was shivering now as she warmed up. The tunnels were not warm, but the wind had been fierce, she only now realized. "C-c-cold," she managed. They walked along the occasionally lit cement pathways and she studied the different painted symbols marking the tunnels, tried to keep a map in her head. Tunnels were not for her.

"They've commandeered all the blankets but I wouldn't let them touch mine," Rook said. "Jane will share with you. She's been warm and safe—if not sane—the whole time."

"She's still . . . out of it?"

Rook shrugged. "She's not the Jane that Frye told me about," he said. "That Jane sounded on top of things. Frye always spoke of her as if she could rule the world."

Helen drew back from his arm. "Maybe she can," she said to the awe in his voice.

His arm fell away as she moved, as if he was ready for them to walk on their own, apart. "But your sister seems different than I expected," he said carefully. "I know you said there'd been trouble since the warehouse. But . . . frankly, I'm somewhat worried about her motives." They turned into a larger hollowed-out space that had been chopped up into many small chambers, with dividers made of grates and bricks and scraps of tin.

"Her motives?" Helen said wonderingly. "She's dazed from whatever they did to her, but Jane means well."

They stopped outside the very last chamber, a fully walled brick one set farther down the tunnel, a good deal apart from the rest. It made her wonder if he'd managed to obtain a nicer one simply by virtue of being *havlen,* and therefore no one had wanted him as a direct neighbor. "Helen," he said, and stopped so she had to face him. Her eyes were level with his. Quietly he said in her ear, "Some think the trolley was no accident."

"No accident?" She sucked air across her teeth. This was

what Morse had implied, but why was he telling her this? "What are you saying?" she whispered back.

"In the front cabin. There appear to be traces of some sort of bomb."

"And you don't know a thing about it."

"No, I do." Rook looked down at her. "I was the one to pull the driver out of the wreckage. He . . . didn't make it. But he told me he saw a girl in a grey dress come into the cabin and take something out of a large bag."

"What? No."

"I know you thought she was kidnapped," he said. "What if she's actually . . . working with them?" Quickly he added, "I haven't told anyone but you. You need to help me figure out what to do with her."

Instinctively Helen backed away from his words, flattened against the door to his bunk. "Maybe she was lost. She's confused but she's not militant. Not like that. You don't know."

Rook sighed. "I've locked her in my room for now. Go in and talk to her. I'll come right back and meet you. I think there are a couple people that are suspicious, but no one would harm her because of you."

"Me?"

"The way you helped us."

"Anyone would have," Helen demurred.

Rook shook his head silently, then touched her shoulder. "Don't let your love blind you," he said, and then turned and vanished into the dark of the tunnels.

Fingers shaking, Helen turned the doorknob and pressed into the room. What did he think he was saying? How could they possibly suspect Jane? It was Rook who was supposed to attack the *dwarvven*—Morse had said so. Rook had orders from Grimsby. That was the business he'd been doing there, the double-crossing he'd frankly admitted to. Jane was a red herring, an outsider he had seized on to blame.

Helen was adrift. She could not trust any of them, and she had led Jane and Tam into this rats' nest. Besides, what did he mean, they would turn on Jane if not for her help? Her help was nothing, insignificant. The barest of candle-flame breaths and the *dwarvven* would blow the other way, come and roust them from their room into the snow. Or worse.

Helen sat down on a small trunk beside the bed, shrugging her coat off. The wet wool stank of smoke and blood. Tam was snoring peacefully on a cushioned chair in the corner, his explorer hat shading his eyes and his binoculars tight in his hands. Jane lay under the covers, dark hair spread around her pale face with its red lines. Yet her cheeks were pinker than they had been; she breathed.

Helen took Jane's hand in her own, looking around the tiny brick room. The floor was a wood platform, raised off the cement below, and the ceiling was open at the top to the tunnel. A faded brown quilt hung on the wall, and when she flicked aside the edge of it she saw there was a short tunnel there, a back escape hatch. The only things in the room were the bed, chair, and trunk, and it was as neat as a pin. No ornaments or mementos. It was not the room of someone who intended to be there for long; it was not the room of someone who felt at home.

She was suddenly curious what was in the trunk.

She should not look, of course, but if she did everything she was supposed to she wouldn't be here in the first place. She released Jane's fingers and rose, swiftly knelt and pushed the lid back. She had a sudden thought that perhaps this wasn't even Rook's room at all, despite what he had said.

But there was a thin black jacket folded on top, and she thought that perhaps it was Rook's after all. Carefully she lifted it off. A few more items of clothing, all dark. A knife. A stack of books. She lifted the top one out, curious.

Jane stirred and instantly Helen was there, seizing her hand, crushing it. "You're back," Helen said. She shoved the jacket back into the trunk and sat down.

Jane smiled and she was there in her eyes. "I am," she said.

Helen squeezed her hand tighter. "What's been happening to you, Jane? Do you know how strange you've been?" The tactless words tumbled out.

Jane sobered. "I have felt so strange, Helen," she said. "I remember you finding me at the warehouse and leading me around. But large gaps are missing. It's like a dream, that fades when you awake, and you only see snatches."

"But you're back now, really back," said Helen, as if repeating it enough could keep Jane with her. She thought of what Rook had said and cast it aside. Jane could not hurt a fly, even *if* Grimsby's machine had damaged her mind. Sleepwalking did not change who you were. She stared into her older sister's face, reassuring herself over and over that Jane was Jane was Jane.

Jane seemed not to notice. "What are you reading?" she said, nodding at the book Helen still held.

"It's Rook's," said Helen. She turned it over in her hands. It was a crackled black book, quite weathered.

"Is he the man who brought me here? I almost wonder if he's part *dwarvven*."

"He is," said Helen, and read off the spine, "*Lady Adelaide's*

Secret. I have heard of it, but I never did read all those books I was supposed to in school—did you?"

Jane raised amused eyebrows at the title. "Yes, but it's not a school assignment book. It's a scandalous thing about a man who accidentally marries two women. You'd probably like it. The man tries to do the right thing and leave the second wife, the one he really loves, but . . ."

"But?" said Helen.

"But the first wife is actually a murderess, and the second one is a detective tracking her down. And then it turns out the husband's really been dead since about halfway through the book, and you don't even know it even though he's been telling you the whole story." Jane put a hand to mouth. "I might have ruined it for you."

"Thus marking the first time *I* tell *you* to think before you speak," said Helen. She sighed and carefully replaced it in the trunk. Not a clue then, except to the fact that he really was half-*dwarvven,* as they had notoriously lurid taste in fiction. "Jane," she said. "I'm worried that Rook was involved in the accident."

"The trolley?" said Jane. "But the detonation happened at a *dwarvven* stop. And he went in to save people."

"Oh, but I haven't had a chance to tell you everything," Helen said in a low voice. "Alistair told me Rook was working for Grimsby, and Rook confirmed it. That he was like a double agent or something. And then, tonight, Morse said something about how Rook was going to blow up this compound."

"Was he very drunk?" said Jane.

"As always," Helen admitted.

Jane shook her head. "There has to be another explanation.

The *dwarvven* I know are not like that. They're strict. They're fair. They love scandalous books and dancing."

"Rook said they were having one tonight," said Helen. She smiled ruefully. "I put a dress in your carpetbag just so I could go."

"You should go meet him there and feel out his motives."

"Nonsense," said Helen. "They couldn't possibly be dancing now. Not after the trolley."

"Funny people, the *dwarvven,*" said Jane. "Nothing stops a celebration when they've decided to have one. Not hell, not high water. You'd like them."

"They wouldn't want me," Helen demurred. She felt suddenly shy. Rook had said she was on their good side, she was the offset for Jane. These people liked her.

It could only go downhill from here.

"It's not a date, it's sleuthing," Jane said with some asperity. She rummaged a thin hand through her carpetbag and produced Helen's go-to dress, none the worse for being shoved in a bag and going through an explosion.

Helen glanced over at the sleeping boy, then quickly stepped out of the ruined peacock blue knit and into the clean apple green voile Jane held, turning so Jane could hook up the side. She felt better already. "If you're sure you're all right in here."

Jane's fingers moved nimbly up the hooks. "I feel much better," she said. "I have a lot of thinking to do. Have you made progress with getting the women together?"

"Yes," said Helen. "Well, I've done some, and Frye's working on it right now. We'll get them to the waterfront like you said."

"I did?" said Jane. She looked concerned, then flashed a brilliant smile from that fey-enhanced face. "I must have had a good reason," she said.

A cold knot began to form in Helen's belly. Getting the women together was something Jane had ordered them to do when she was supposedly sane. Helen threw out another lead. "Grimsby's taken Millicent somewhere, but I don't know where."

"I'm sure it's someplace safe," said Jane.

The cold knot tightened. "But she was going to run away from Grimsby."

Again confusion flashed across Jane's face and vanished. "Yes, but he would hardly get rid of her in this state," she said. "Everyone knows. It would be a scandal."

"Perhaps you're right," Helen said. Her forehead creased as she stared at Jane and flipped the problem over and over in her mind. "Will you be safe here with Tam? Will he be all right if he wakes up?"

"You're stalling," Jane said.

"Perhaps," said Helen. She wadded the torn and smoky dress into a ball. She hated to just leave it in Rook's tidy room.

"Put it in here," Jane said, waving those thin hands at her carpetbag. "And hurry back and tell me everything."

"All right," said Helen. She stuffed the dress into Jane's carpetbag, and then stopped, her eye caught by something in the bottom.

"What is it?" said Jane.

"Oh, just wondering how I'll ever make it up to Frye," said Helen. Her fingers shook as she closed the bag, but she tried to keep them steady in front of her sister. "I'll see you later. Don't wait up."

"Not a chance," promised Jane.

Helen backed out of the door and into the darkness of the tunnel, where she closed her eyes against what she had just seen. Hot tears pricked her eyes, stress and memory shook her bones as she saw again and again what she had seen in Jane's carpetbag.

Traces of blue and shrapnel.

Just like the fey bomb that had killed her brother, so many years ago.

Chapter 12

OUT PAST CURFEW

Helen found herself hurrying through the tunnels, desperate to get away. Up the stairs to the bookstore, past the woman who actually smiled at her and worriedly said, "Remember curfew—," but Helen just kept on going, out into the dark and the cold and the whirling snow.

How could Jane be responsible for this? For this ruthless destruction?

The trolley lay there just outside the slums, a twisted pile of metal. Everyone was gone now, but the signs of the tragedy remained. The area around where the trolley had derailed had been stamped and packed into hard, dark-stained snow. The snow had lessened but still it fell, erasing the disaster, sifting a fine layer of clean white over the ice.

The icy air whipped around her bare arms, and then she was walking toward the warehouse. All these things were there, the warehouse, the wreck, the slums, all had converged on this point in time. Whatever else happened, it would be down here, she felt, down near where the statue of Queen Maud held open arms to the river to embrace her people. All people: humans and her beloved *dwarvven.*

Jane could not have done any such thing.

Unless she had been made to.

Once Helen thought it, she couldn't unthink it. The thought unfurled in her mind and she knew that, deep inside, it was what she had feared all along and not acknowledged. She was out of ways to explain away Jane's behavior.

Jane had been taken over.

It was a strange case, clearly. Jane had been protected, back when she had had iron in her face. A fey couldn't get around that—but a human could. Boarham, she supposed, had stripped Jane of her protection when they kidnapped her.

But more, usually when a fey took someone over—that someone was gone. Vanished. Helen herself did not remember any of the few seconds that a fey had been inside her, except for a horrible erasing feeling. She certainly had not been able to communicate with anyone. Her body was no longer hers.

But Jane seemed to come and go. Sometimes she was rational. She was Jane.

Or a very good imitation? . . .

Helen pushed that thought down. The Jane she had talked to just now was definitely her sister, fighting for control of her body. She did not know how that was possible, but it was the only thing that made sense with her behavior.

Helen's eyes filled with grief. Her sister. Her only family. Helen had fought, and she had tried, and Jane was still going to disappear on her in the end.

A black motorcar drove down the road ahead, yellow searchlight sweeping the sides of the street. Curfew. Helen pressed herself into the side of the buildings, into the sheltering shadow. Across from her a new sort of poster caught her eye—this time bloodred, with CURFEW on it in big black letters, and below it, a raft of rules in smaller type. She did not have to move closer to tell that it was signed the same way as the notice in the paper: BY ORDER OF PARLIAMENT AND COPPERHEAD.

She did not want to go back to the *dwarvven* slums, where Jane was. She did not want to go home, where Alistair was. Not that that really seemed like home anymore. Perhaps it never had been hers; it had only ever been his. Despite her best intentions to find herself a home, she had come adrift, and now there was not one place she could call her own.

She reached for a handkerchief that was not there and her fingers brushed the copper hydra that hung around her throat.

Her necklace. Her hand closed on it and the copper warmed in response. One picture glanced across her vision, a memory of the warehouse. She was inside, hand on Grimsby's copper box, and she was looking down at a pale still figure on a white daybed. . . .

Helen walked along the shadowed line of the buildings, walked fast and sure to the warehouse.

The windows were lit blue, as they had been before. Helen crept around to the window above the slag, looking to see if there was still a way to make it up the snow-covered piles of junk. The high energy was wearing off and she was freezing, but at least the warehouse blocked the sharp wind. She clambered up in her ruffled voile and looked in the smeary window. Her vision was obscured this time. A pile of boxes and bars was pushed in front of the window, where the table had been. But through the clutter she saw figures moving around.

She could not easily get in, but perhaps they would not notice if she cracked the window, not with those boxes in front of her.

Carefully Helen pushed the window open, and was treated to a gust of warm air from a vent just above. And there, there below her was the scene she had imagined on the street. Millicent lay on the white daybed, there in the warehouse. Helen's hand closed on the necklace. Something was strange about that necklace, the back of her brain suddenly told her. Something that she had been unable to see. It almost hurt to think about it.

She made her fingers let go, arched her shoulders so the copper fell away from her skin. Then looked more carefully at the scene in front of her.

Grimsby, one of the snaky funnels in hand, was bending over Millicent.

Helen swallowed hard as she watched him attach the funnel to Millicent's fey face, her perfect face. It looped behind the head, held on with rubber clips. She remembered Jane standing there in the warehouse, holding the funnel to her face as if breathing in fumes, and she breathed fast, faster. When Grimsby was satisfied he strode back to the copper box in the center of the room and plunged his hands through the bars, grasping the coiling snakes.

Helen's necklace warmed in response, grew hot. It felt like a smaller, more focused version of when she had touched the box herself and seen all the glimpses of the city.

She did not know what Grimsby was doing, but she knew that it clearly was not good for Millicent. Helen could think the best of Grimsby and wish it was something to roust Millicent from her coma—but she knew it was not. And all that remained to Helen was to shove her manicured nails into the glass window, trying to prise it all the way open and get in to *stop it.*

But before she could get the window all the way open, the sounds and sights of the box doubled, expanded, grew sudden and violent, raging over her with such force that she could only cling to the window, staring at things that were not real.

She was plunged into a waking dream, a feverish world where the city flickered behind her eyes in shades of blue and white and black. There were so many sights and sounds she could not make sense of it. Until one sound, one pair of sounds, seemed closer than the rest, and she let everything go, let it all float away, until she could pick out the echo of those two talking, like a scratchy gramophone.

<<You'll let your hatred of *dwarvven* destroy us all.>>

<<I'm finishing the task I've taken up. I am the only one who can do what needs to be done.>>

<<You're mad.>>

<<Aren't we all?>>

They were like the not-voice she had heard three nights ago at Grimsby's meeting. They didn't even seem to be words, really, though she heard them as words. More like feelings, colors, intuition.

<<How far can you get? Can you find all of *you*?>>

<<Not yet. Need more juice.>>

<<There's ten lined up for tomorrow.>>

<<Need more now.>>

In the warehouse, there in her half-waking state, Helen suddenly knew what that meant. She willed her feet forward, but as in dreams they would not go. <<Millicent,>> she shouted, and somehow it seemed to break and fall into that ocean of sound and hue that was all around them. She was part of it as she called <<Millicent! No, no, no! . . . >>

There was a horrible sucking feeling. That horrible copper machine was using fey to power it, just as Grimsby had said at the meeting. And right now the fey it was using was the fey in Millicent's face. It was pulling it right out of her—and with it her life. She could not sustain it—Millicent had already wasted away so much in the three days of fey-induced coma that there was hardly anything left to her at all. She had nothing with which to fight.

And Helen said to the sound, <<I'll fight for her then.>>

But she was small, far too small, and far too late. The main voices could not even hear her tiny words as she forced her frozen feet up the wall one centimeter at a time. She could feel the machine reaching into the bit of fey in Millicent, and spreading out across the city. For a moment Helen saw the city like a grid, with a few random little bits extra lit up here and there, few and far between. There was a strange pressurized feeling, as if those few random bits were struggling to coalesce somehow. But Millicent was too weak. <<I'll fight for her. I will.>>

And then the storm of movement finally took the last drop it could from Millicent, and imploded in a spot of grey light. The bits did not coalesce. The city faded out.

<<Never mind,>> came one of the voices as the grey light vanished, <<it will all work when we have more power.>>

Everything faded and then Helen was looking at Grimsby in the center of the room, tall and stoic, examining Millicent as if she were merely a failed experiment.

Helen clutched her necklace, willing him not to see her.

As if in response he looked over to where she was. But all that happened is the air seemed to suddenly go out of him, like a popped balloon. He sagged, a ventriloquist's dummy gone slack, limp in every joint.

"Millicent," he said, softly, brokenly. "This is all my fault. . . ."

He reached down and gently unclasped the rubber funnel. Helen saw Millicent's face then, blue-white as if all the air had gone out of her. The funnel and black rubber tube fell to the ground, one in a sea of tubes. Her eye traced the tubes back to their cages, where the funnels hung on the outside of the iron bars. With dawning horror she realized what the oval mountings actually were. She looked around—yes. There was one without the funnel.

Rows and rows and rows of them, that's what Jane had said, *looking at you with their black blank eyes.*

It was a woman's face. The original face of someone who was now startlingly beautiful, like all of them.

Calendula Smith.

The masks were placeholders for where the women were to go. This was his machine, this is why it had a hundred tubes leading to a hundred cages. *It will all work when we have more power.*

What will work?

With great effort Helen tore her gaze away from that oval mask, that caricatured skin, as ugly as the current Calendula was beautiful. She remembered Jane telling her how the rows and rows of masks looked when they still hung in Mr. Rochart's house, their skin sagging and wrinkled from drying on the wall.

Helen's eyes were tight as she watched Grimsby delicately close the eyelids of his wife. She did not know what to do. Did he care? Was this an accident? What was he?

He sank to his knees and buried his head in the long trail of dress that hung over the side of the bed like a torn banner, fraying in the wind.

Helen stood up, her eyes stinging, and pushed herself away from the window.

She pushed herself through the numb cold and black night, back through the shadows toward the *dwarvven* underground. There near the bookstore she stood out of sight, and waited for the next black car to drive down the block. They were circling. They knew where the *dwarvven* were. She did not know what they were waiting for, but she knew if she went down to the underground, she would be found with them.

She went.

She went through the bookstore and down the stairs. She had seen Millicent go and so she went through the underground tunnels to the dance to find Rook. She did not fully think through why being miserable and lost meant she wanted to find Rook, she just went and stood in that gay mad atmosphere of *dwarvven* who were going to damn well enjoy the dance of the last night on earth and she saw Rook dancing.

He was dancing with a girl and Helen's heart thudded to her knees.

He was dancing with a girl, slim and lovely and so petite that Helen felt like a big oaf, even though she and Rook were of a height, and she was slim herself.

She was there and he was dancing with another and that

was the way it was going to be forever and ever, all because Helen had once told herself that the true things inside didn't matter, and that you could tell your heart what to do and it would obey.

She knew how wildly wrong she had been and she was stuck.

The music pressed in on her as they danced, laughing. Helen turned to a *dwarvven* man next to her and said things, all manner of things, let them tumble out of her mouth, and she had no idea what any of them were a second after she said them, because her heart was breaking. She was witty, she was bright, she was a whirl of apple green ruffled voile. She made the man laugh, head thrown wildly back, and another *dwarvven* man brought her a bathtub gin, and Helen made him laugh, too. She let this one lead her into the dance, and she whirled around and around with the skills she had from a lifetime of tenpence dances, dances with Alistair, dances from every moment of her existence. The city could burst into blue flames and still Helen could dance.

The dance ended and Helen drew back, waving her gin glass as an excuse. "It's not empty," the man said, and she tossed it back and laughed, and escaped. She did not know what she had said or saw; all she knew was the skirts whisking around her, triumphant laughter belling the air as Rook danced with somebody else.

She bumped into a gentleman—said something delightfully saucy, who knew what? Admiring eyes followed her. She tried to lean into their approval, but she had been doing that for half her life and tonight it was flat and hollow. Millicent was gone and Rook was gone and when would Helen be gone? Not soon enough. It was all noise, so much noise that she could no longer hear any particular words, so much sight that she let it blur in a wash of color across her path.

The next man she bumped into did not move.

She tilted her head to let her mouth chatter wildly and found herself looking into bright hazel eyes, a face that she had surely pieced together herself out of the chaos of color and spectacle around her.

"Dance with me," Rook said.

"I am getting gin," Helen said, because in the merry-go-round around her ears it was the one thing she could make sense of. The words were crisp and staccato. The clever chatter left her, and all that was there was something like truth, which was that she definitely wanted a gin.

He took the glass from her hand, dropped it into the bemused hand of a fat *dwarvven* man standing by the wall. Next her hand, fingers lacing through hers, and Rook drew her in. Their eyes met, level, equal. He was light and lithe and deft in the dance. A touch here, there, and they were moving in time together around the floor, his fingers subtly guiding, hers subtly suggesting.

The detachment was leaving her now. She was suddenly very there, very present in his arms, very there for his uncharacteristic silence. He looked at her thoughtfully, and Helen looked back as if she had nothing to hide, because she could no longer think how to hide it.

"Funny us meeting like this," she said. It was meant to be a joke, and yet it slipped out without breath, and he let it hang there too many seconds to still sound like a joke.

Music, the sort that lifted you around and around, violins and piano, a heartbeat rhythm pounding faster, stair-stepping higher. A familiar refrain worked into the melody, repeating itself, and her fingers beat it out upon his shoulder as it came round again.

It did not matter how many dancers were in the room, they were alone as the melody went round and round, climbing to a finish that was heartbreaking in the way it triumphed and broke apart, fading away like dying applause, everything wonderful has just happened and now it is over, over, over.

Her heart pounded the echo of the finished music, racing without a song to follow.

"Helen," he said, and took her hand tightly, so very tightly. Everything was a blur of color around her. She only saw him, and beyond him, like an afterimage, a mirage, a girl in a white dress with a grass green sash.

"Helen," he said, again, seeking for more words, but she knew the future of all the words he would say.

"Don't," she said, and she freed her hand from his grasp. She pressed one finger, two to his lips.

Rook caught her hand before she could pull away, slip away like the tale of the girl who has to flee the dance at midnight, leaving behind one fey-blue shoe. "Isn't there something I can do," he said in a low voice. "I must be able to . . . to free you."

"No one can help me," she said. She tugged against his grip. "I must go."

"But."

"No," she said, and turned on him. "You must never speak this. Not even think it to yourself. That is how you can help me."

She saw him see the fire in her eyes, and think of something, and not say it. But then he opened his mouth again.

"You will not speak," she said, and the words came out too

fast, too fierce, in an attempt to stop him from saying anything that could crush her fragile will. "I am a grown woman who has made rational choices and you dishonor me by suggesting that I have made poor ones." Let him wriggle out of that.

He opened and shut his mouth. Then: "Mrs. Huntingdon, I will do as you tell me. I had sooner destroy my left hand than disobey."

A smile flickered at the corner of her mouth. "Only left?"

"*Dwarvven* are generally left-handed. Didn't you know?"

"Perhaps I should have guessed from the backward way they dance."

"Come, not fair."

"No, not."

The music stopped completely then, and there was a great banging of spoons on glasses. The crowded room grew silent. Helen turned to see the source. A woman stood at the front of the room—clearly an official, a leader. She had a coronet of grey-black braids and the air of someone who was used to being listened to. "Friends," she said softly, and they all grew stone-still.

Her manner was calm, her posture straight. She looked around at everyone as she spoke, meeting the eyes of her people. "The *dwarvven* have had a rough road to travel in recent years. Tonight was a hard event to have happen, here on the doorstep of our home. The careful work of Nolle and her team, working under the most adverse conditions, helped to ameliorate this terrible accident." She did not call it an attack, Helen noticed, and there were murmurs from those in the crowd who disagreed with her. The woman raised her hands. "Now is not the time for argument. Now is the time to honor the two men we lost tonight." She named them—the trolley driver and a passenger—offering a couple sentences about the kind of men they were, biographies that sounded truthfully funny about the men's strengths and weakness, rather than grandiose overstatements of their worth.

There was silence for a moment, remembering.

"And now," she said, "I ask that you take your places, as I have reports from Tumn that policemen are advancing on the bookshop. To . . . *investigate* the accident."

"Where were they *during* it?" shouted a young man from the crowd.

"We will meet them calmly," said the woman, "and only if they cannot be turned away with words will we fight. The *dwarvven* are always ready."

Helen looked around and saw what she meant. Men and women were rolling back sleeves or unbuttoning dress shirts to reveal the ever-present chain mail that *dwarvven* always wore. She did not know much about *dwarvven* custom, but this she did, as it was nominally fashion. The *dwarvven* always wore chain mail. It tended to be symbolic—just a touch here or there. The unrolled sleeves and unbuttoned shirts were equally symbolic, exposing their chain mail wristlets or chokers. They were ready to fight, just like their ancestors.

Across from her a hardened-looking man had removed his whole shirt to show he was in chain mail from head to toe. He casually held a knife in his hands. Her heart thumped into her throat at the sight of it. It didn't matter one whit that he was shorter than Helen—she knew she wouldn't stand a chance against someone like that.

She looked around again and thought, how could I have possibly dismissed the *dwarvven* as symbolic a moment ago?

She was as insensitive as Copperhead. She saw warriors, saw hard glints in their eyes, off their mail. She backed up a step into Rook, whirled to face him.

"I must go. Go get Jane. Get her out of here," she said.

"I will walk you there."

She nodded and did not protest that he had agreed to leave her, for she did not like the way that angry eyes met hers, as if all her work tending the wounded was nothing, set against her race. Perhaps it wasn't.

They hurried out of the dance room, among the sea of *dwarvven* going to their places to be ready against whatever might come. It was dark in the halls and they were jostled, and he took her hand to pull her along the route he had memorized.

She winced as he seized the bandage. "I'm sorry," he said, letting go. "I didn't realize your hand was hurt in the accident."

"I wasn't—it's nothing," she said, pulling away, but he stopped and gently took her hand and she did not pull away again.

"How did it happen?" he said in a low voice. His fingers ran gently over her palm in the dark. There were shouts and clanks as the *dwarvven* hurried around them.

"It was nothing," she said. "Just a broken glass. It wasn't intentional."

"Was he drunk?"

"Yes," Helen had to admit, and they did not need to say who *he* was.

Rook's fingers tightened on hers, not painfully but completely, so that she felt every bit of the palm of his hand wrapping hers, covering it. "I said before that you wouldn't fit in in *dwarvven* society," he said. "That they are closed to outsiders. But at the same time, we don't care about certain things the humans find important. The conventions of human society are meaningless."

She tried to say it simply, frivolously, but the blood pounded her ears and her mouth ran dry. "Such as?"

"Marriage," he said.

"You can't pull the wool over my eyes," Helen said, and even managed a light laugh. "I know married *dwarvven*."

"Certainly we marry," he said. "But we also unmarry. No *dwarvven* woman would stand that behavior for a minute."

Helen pulled away, set off down what she thought was the right path, so he would have to follow. "So now I am weak-willed and cowardly?"

Rook caught up with her, and in a low voice, though in truth none of the men and women hurrying past were listening, he said, "I think divorce is difficult to attain for humans, and any sensitive person would shrink from the public scrutiny it would entail. I am saying, among the *dwarvven,* no one would particularly care what paper you had or didn't have that said in what state some human courts found you to be."

It was true. Divorce was a nasty process. She would have to go before men in wigs and convince them that Alistair was drunk and brutish. And they would be friends of Alistair, and they would laugh at him for not being able to control his wife, which would make him worse-tempered and not change anything for the better. And then, if the best happened and they granted her her plea (out of some moment where they were sympathetic to Alistair for having to put up with her), then, *then,* she would have nowhere to live, would be ever after unhirable to work with children and would have no way to support herself. The rest of her life would be squalid and short, and would probably involve mooching off of Jane, who was in little better situation. Helen didn't even have a cow to barter for room and board.

But what if Rook was suggesting what she thought he might be suggesting? (No, he hadn't said it. But imagine for a moment.) Her heart beat that yes, then, she could just run off, but her brain, that sad pathetic lump of organ that she continually tried to coax into working better . . . well. It said what then, Helen? *What then.* You go to live with Rook. You think you love him. You think he (might, might) love you. Just as you thought Alistair loved you. And if he changed, what then? Now you can't get any job, not just not one working with children, but no job at all, for you have been living in sin, and they would see you as little better than a prostitute, and all society would be barred to you. Well. Perhaps you could live in Frye's garret for a couple weeks. But then she, too, would kick you out, like Alberta said she did when she grew tired of having company.

They left you. The people you loved always left you.

"I would have nowhere to go," she said, and in that space he said:

"You would have me."

They were near his quarters then; she recognized the brick wall in the dim glow of his flashlight. And she dropped his hand and pulled back and said, "You do not mean it."

"I do."

"You think you do. But I would be a burden to you. And besides. You promised you would obey my wishes. What happened to all the business a few minutes ago about your left hand?"

"Difficult to stick to," Rook said with a faint laugh.

But Helen rose up, her thoughts ballooning out as large as the room, encompassing everything, and she said in a way that would roar and echo, "You don't even know me. You don't know what you're asking."

He opened his mouth, but she went past him like an ocean.

"I changed my husband," she said. "I manipulated him. I took the power of my face and I changed him. Now what do you think of me?"

"What do you mean, changed him?"

Helen touched the chin of her perfect face and said, "With this I changed him."

"You mean the fey allure?" said Rook. "It makes people be drawn to you, want to like you, sure. But it isn't your fault beyond that. You didn't change him."

"Yes, I did," she said, and she told him exactly what she had done to Alistair.

A strange light came into his eye. She recognized it as the same way she had looked at him after the trolley crash. Diffidence. Suspicion. Trying to pull back, trying to let go. She saw all those things, and she saw, too, that she could change him as easily as she had changed Alistair and the thought of it made her gasp, miss a beat.

"What else?" Rook said.

"You," Helen said, and it came out all strangled-sounding. Was she worried that he would leave her? Well then. She could make it so he never could. And she looked at his dear bright hazel eyes in the light of the flashlight, dimmed now with worry, with concern, with trying to let her go and failing and trying to understand what she was saying. "I could change you," she said. "I could make it so you thought I was the most wonderful woman in the world."

"I do," he murmured, and she gasped, and laughed, and steamrollered over that:

"The most sensible woman, then. I could change you and you would not know you had been changed. I could fix you."

He shook his head at her. "But you wouldn't."

"No," she said wildly, and clutched his shoulders, startling them both. "You don't understand. I could have already done it. You wouldn't know. What if I made you follow me. What if I made you protect me that night on the trolley. What if I spotted you at the Grimsbys' the night this all started and said, you, *you* will do this thing for me and turned you then."

"But you wouldn't," Rook said. "You didn't."

She looked at him. "Help me," she said, echoing what she had said to him three nights ago when she had thought he was Alistair in the confusion after the lights went out. And he *had*.

His hazel eyes looked lost.

"You can't be sure," she said. "You never will be sure. That would poison us even if there could be an us."

"I wouldn't let it," he said.

She laughed at him—a dry, brittle sounding thing—and drew back. "Go, find your *dwarvven* warrior and stand at her side," she said. "I must take Jane to safety before your people turn on her."

"Helen," he said and one hand, two, seized her shoulders, so lightly.

"I fixed him," she said, raising her hands as if to escape. They landed on his chest; she tried to make them obey her, and push him away, but they only lay there. "Don't you see, I fixed Alistair. Everything will be all right." Her voice rose in hysteria, drowning Rook out. "He will be all right, forever and ever, for he can be fixed, he can be like you, I can make him be whatever I want—"

In pure disbelief he said, "Be like *me*?"

She stumbled over her rising hysteria, incoherent babble, "I didn't mean, really—"

Rook pulled her close and kissed her.

It felt like flying, like falling. Like being taken over by the fey. Like dissolving from her own self, which she knew she shouldn't want but oh she did.

And then there were shrieks and shouts, and everything went pure white, white with intense light. Floodlights shrieked through the tunnels. Their moment was torn away.

Rook grabbed her fiercely and quick and intense he said in her ear, "Listen, you don't know. I was supposed to—they wanted me to kill—"

"Who, Grimsby? You'd be doing everyone a favor, almost—"

"Listen, Helen. No. All of them. They wanted me to kill all of them. All the men of Copperhead. *That* was what I was doing as a double agent. Not just spying."

She stared at him in disbelief, her lips forming the single word "Alistair" to his silent, unreadable expression. The floodlights swept over them as humans in black stormed down the stairs, through the halls. Shouting, running, chaos. The barricade had fallen.

Rook shoved her behind him and shouted in her ear, "Behind the quilt!" and then she was through the entrance into his bedroom and the door was closed behind her, and he was gone. Jane and Tam stood there, blinking at her. Tam was bleary-eyed but awake. Jane was vacant.

"Come on," Helen said, and, grabbing their things, flung aside the brown quilt to reveal the hole in the wall. It was very short, and she could see lights just beyond it—a drop-off. "Hopefully not too far down," she muttered, but she was sure Rook wouldn't have sent them through it if they were all going to break legs.

She lifted Tam up, and he slithered through and called back, "It's fine; come on!" and so shortly they were all through and then pounding down an escape tunnel marked by red sigils, splashing down tunnels and ducking under grates. They were met by other *dwarvven* children and elderly at various intervals, caught up in a sea of them running to safety, until at last they reached the point where the old sewer tunnels had poured into the river. The thin water trickled past the grate, out into the cold of the rushing river. There were narrow steps there leading them up to safety, and they scrambled up and tumbled out into the snowy dark at the waterfront, by the statue of Queen Maud.

The freezing air was bracing after the tumble through the tunnels. Helen kept a tight grip on Jane and Tam, searching through the confusion for a way out, a way somewhere.

Helen saw Nolle in the midst of chaos, calmly directing refugees to a line of barges. A small smile warmed her face as she saw Helen. "We'd been planning for this eventuality," Nolle said. "The *dwarvven* are going home. Every last one. Leaving the city for good. But I wanted to thank you."

"I hardly did anything," protested Helen.

"You stood with us," Nolle said, "and I think you will in the future. I will not forget my debt." A short nod and she turned back to her work. "Goodbye."

Helen pulled Jane and Tam through the crowd, out of the way. If everyone was going to insist on believing the best of her, she might have to actually live up to it.

"Where are we going?" said Jane absently.

"Frye's," Helen replied, and they tramped through the snow.

It was only during that cold black walk back to safety that she finally let herself think about the moment that had just happened, ever so briefly before everything ended. Not the moment itself. She couldn't quite think about that; it was too fine, too vivid. But the moment before, the moment when she rattled everything off hysterically, when she had said she could make Alistair be like Rook. Helen closed her eyes against her mouth's foolishness. For then there was the moment *after* to deal with, too, when Rook said what he had been sent to do.

Rook was supposed to bring them all down. Alistair included.

But he hadn't, had he? Was that for his conscience's sake? Or was it for her, all for her? And what did that mean, what *could* that mean—that he cared for her? Or that he didn't? Helen did not want Rook to kill, nor did she want Alistair, despite all his faults, to be killed. But she couldn't make it work out in her head. Rook had come to the meeting planning to bring Alistair down, and then, having met Helen, decided Alistair should live, and thus Helen and Alistair stay happily married for all time. . . .

Her eyes were dry against the black and snow-falling night when they reached Frye's street. Her wet coat smelled like a battle and weighed a ton. Tam was so tired that Helen had resorted to carrying him, and he sagged trustingly in her arms, asleep. She stumbled down the street, half-asleep herself. What was going to happen to Tam after all this was over? She hadn't tried to break the news to him about his stepmamma yet. She couldn't let him go back to his father. His stepmamma had risked her life—*given* her life to try to get him away. And yet his father had all the claim. The courts would never see it any other way, no matter what vague, lunatic-sounding charges Helen could bring to bear.

A bid for Tam would be as bad as a bid for her own freedom. It would all be so messy, so public. So futile.

Yet her day with Tam had been surprisingly nice, hadn't it? Studying at the museum, spying on fashionable young ladies attempting to resist chocolate sundaes. . . . She had never liked children, but Tam seemed to be cut from a different cloth than the rest of them. Yet Alistair would never agree to foster Tam, even if charges *could* be brought against Mr. Grimsby. And the courts would take her even less seriously as a divorcée.

And there she was, thinking about Rook again. He was from a different world, and there was no possibility for the two of them. Besides, Nolle had said: All the *dwarvven* were going home. All of them.

She needed to put Rook from her mind just as she had told him to do for her.

Despite that kiss.

Helen's hands tightened on the small boy as she staggered up the walk to Frye's narrow row house. She hated to always be running from things, but maybe that was her only course left to her. She could just take Tam and run away, far far away. . . .

The door burst open before she could figure out how to ring the doorbell and still hold Tam.

"Helen!" said Frye, and her gap-toothed smile was wide. "Get in here right now." She took Tam from Helen's tired arms and ushered them down the hallway toward the biggish room where the dancing had been. Deftly she divested Helen of her disgusting overcoat, patted a stray copper curl in place. "You, and you, Jane, just go right in here. I have some folks for you to meet."

Frye opened the door to a wave of expensive scent; rose and lilac and geranium billowed out in a fine cloud. An entire room of beautiful women turned to see Helen as she made her tired way through the door. The room lit with the glamour of their smiles.

Chapter 13

WHAT THE HUNDRED DID

Helen moved among them, clasping hands and kissing cheeks. It was like some sort of twisted reunion, and they were all so pleased to see her. Some had been dozing, many were wide awake, but they all greeted Helen happily, with gay chatter or with calm fire. "We're going to do this. We are," she heard over and over. There was Calendula Smith. There was that dancing girl. There was Desirée. Helen could not find Alberta or Betty in the crowd, but there was Frye, presiding over it all in her billowy dragon-embroidered caftan, looking like the cat who swallowed the proverbial canary.

"They're not all here," Frye said, "as I was only one person with one day. But I made a big dent." She gestured at the sea of dazzling beauty.

"Thank you," said Helen. She felt like collapsing, but she straightened her spine, for it was her cue now. She moved into the center of the room, meeting their eyes and giving encouraging nods. There was a little carved bench and she stepped up, her apple green voile falling gracefully around her. She stood, feeling the slick wood under her heels, bracing herself. Her moment onstage.

"Frye brought you all here so we can reverse the damage done to us," Helen said. "So we can all be safe. Safe without iron masks. Safe without being locked in our rooms."

Nods of assent.

"But what we thought a simple procedure that my sister Jane could manage has blossomed into something more," Helen continued. "Mr. Grimsby, the leader of Copperhead and the instigator of this curfew, is playing a dangerous game. Three nights ago he had one of the men of Copperhead kidnap my sister, leaving his wife caught in the fey sleep. We have found Jane, but . . . well. Let's say the experience may have cost her." She pointed to Jane, who was sitting on the floor in her torn and dirty grey dress, tracing the patterns in the carpet.

"*Helen* found her," put in Frye from the sidelines. "She's been putting the clues together. Risking herself."

"Jane said we needed to all gather and change back now," Helen said. "Which seemed reasonable enough, when she first said it. Except changing back now involves Mr. Grimsby, and this warehouse, and his invention that some of you saw a couple nights ago, the one that surged all the power in the house and zapped Jane. And I don't know exactly what his plan is," she said, and took a deep breath. "But he has all of our original faces. All at the warehouse with him."

Gasps, denial. "No!" and "How do you know?"

Through the din, Helen pointed a finger at Calendula. "Because I saw one of them, plain as day," she said.

Calendula went white and red all at once as shock warred with embarrassment. "Me, there," she said. "The original."

"All of us," said Helen, cutting over the voices. "We're all in this together."

"But what's he planning to do?"

Helen swallowed. "Something involving hooking us up to the machine. It drains us through the bit of fey in our faces, feeds some sort of power to the machine. I don't know what he plans to *do* with the machine. But I saw him drain one of us. His wife." One woman let out a sharp cry of sorrow at that, and Helen felt deep regret that she could not have told Millicent's friend in a more measured fashion.

"So he has our faces as what, bait?"

"Perhaps," said Helen. "Regardless, Jane said that all of us are supposed to gather there—tomorrow at noon."

"You trust that?" someone said, pointing at carpet-tracing Jane.

"Clearly not," Helen said, to both gasps and laughter. "No, it's a trap," she said. "And we have to spring it."

Another wave of riot. "That actress didn't say anything about danger," said someone.

Another: "Thought this was making us *safer*."

"We have to," Helen shouted through the crowd, and the hold she had on them started to slip. "He's got ten of us lined up for tomorrow. I heard him. They may be bait, but we have to rescue them."

"And you think they'd do the same for us?"

"I came through curfew for this?"

The voices swelled, rose up loud and ugly. Underneath, another sound from the hall—thumps, bangs, and the loud clack of heels as Alberta burst into the room, disheveled and splattered with mud. "They got Betty," she said. Silence fell as heads turned to look. "We were leaving her flat—and I had my eyes peeled for cops, you know—but this joe nobody on the street corner said, 'Don't you birds know not to break curfew,' and then he turned and he had the copperhead pin on, and suddenly there was a black car pulling up and they grabbed Betty. And they got my scarf, but I twisted out and dodged them. I had to lose one of them on the way here." She glanced behind her as if to double-check that they were still alone.

A low voice said into the shocked silence: "The first to fall."

Across the room Helen caught Alberta's eye. The one woman with more reason to keep her new face than anyone, and here they were at the moment of truth, and Helen didn't know how Alberta would decide. Alberta nodded at Helen and came forward into the room, straightening out torn fabric and brushing off mud under everyone's gaze. Helen said calmly to the room, "I want you to hear a little story first. Then you can decide if you want to stay or go home."

In simple, plain language, Alberta told them of the husband she had fled. How her new face that made her vulnerable to the fey was the only thing that kept her safe from him. "But I'm tired of letting him win," Alberta said. "And you're all tired, too. Every day we go around with these new faces we're in danger of our lives, and those lives aren't even our own. They're borrowed. Well, I've had it. I want my own life. I want my own face, my own city, and my own freedom. I want to walk around after dark whenever the hell I want. And I don't want the fey, or Copperhead, or some damn husband telling me what I can and can't do. I'm going to get my own face back and then I'm going to see my husband divorced and put behind bars. And then I'm going to go out after midnight and paint the town red. *That's* what I'm going to do."

They didn't all nod, but many of them did, because the

ones that were here were the ones who were brave enough to come through the night, break the curfew, come to Frye's. Helen scanned the room, seeking out who was being swayed, who needed more convincing. She could do that. But not from a distance.

"We need your help," said Helen, and she took center stage once more. "Frye did a lot, but there's only one Frye. We've thirty-five of us here. Six have been done. The seventh . . . well. That means fifty-seven left to go—minus the ten he already has, but we don't know who they are, so we can't cross them off. Then a few people are listed by first name only. How many of those are there, Frye?"

"Five," Frye answered immediately. "Women, think who of your acquaintances is spectacularly beautiful and answers to one of these: James, Marlys, Phyllis, Ulrich, Yvette."

"Yvette Aubin!" shouted several women at once.

"James and Ulrich?" questioned another. "Do we want to get men involved?"

"Perhaps not," said Helen. "There were only three of them, if I remember correctly. At least, if you do try to take the men on, feel them out cautiously before telling them what's going on. If you see a hydra pin, run the other way." Helen looked at Frye. "So what does that leave us, fifty-four?"

"Monica Preston-Smythe was taken by a fey last week," someone said. "Her family hushed it up."

"Fifty-three then," said Helen, not missing a beat. Gallows humor. "All right, everyone. Go to Frye and collect one or two names."

"I know Louisa Mayfew," shouted one. "She isn't here."

"I know Agatha Flintwhistle. She'll come if I have to threaten to uninvite her to next week's dance."

"Come to that, where's my invitation?" joked Helen, and the woman shot back, "In the mail with everyone else's," which made everyone laugh and things grow a hair less tense.

"Good, good," said Helen. "Between us we should know practically everyone on that list. Maybe we can figure out the rest of the cryptic notations. As soon as it's light and curfew lifts, go. Convince your women they have to come meet us. We're all in this together. And everyone bring iron. A knife or a hatpin or what-have-you."

"Something sharp and poky," shouted Frye.

"Right," said Helen. "Together we're a lot stronger than those men would believe. We'll meet at the warehouse at noon."

She stepped down, turned away from the center of the room, making way for the women to move to Frye and the journal. Some did. Some did not.

Helen drifted back toward the wall, watching the roomful of color ebb and flow. She was so tired, and they were not even all moving to Frye. And this wasn't even half the women. If they could not even convince all these, how could they possibly convince all one hundred?

Over the shoulders of the crowd she saw a blond woman pushing her way to the door. Alberta was following her, trying to reason with her, but the blonde was agitated. Behind the blonde pushed a dark-skinned brunette, and then a pale redhead. . . .

Everything they had done. Helen could not bear to make more mistakes, and the huge rushing hollow in her heart could not tell her if it was worse to let them go or to make them stay.

But what was the point of power if you didn't use it for

good? She had been willing to change Alistair. She would have been willing to change Grimsby. She was losing Rook because she couldn't trust herself *not* to change him, and if she was going to pay the penalty for the power, she should use what she was buying.

Helen pushed through them all until she blocked their frantic exit. They stared at her with their inherent fey glamour, but Helen had her own, and she was the one with practice wielding it, she was the one who knew what Frye had said. That you could convince.

One by one.

Helen touched soft hands, squeezed silk-clad shoulders. Looked into their eyes and, with the help of the fey intuition, saw what they were made of, told them what they needed to hear. For some, that was enough. For the rest, she gripped her copper necklace until they fell to her charm, blindly agreeing to go, to bring everyone here, to save them all. She was on her last wind, but every woman who fell to her power boosted her, bore her up. Perhaps I shouldn't, Helen told herself each time, but I am and I will. She was setting all of her pieces in play to win.

Helen did not stop until she was looking around for another woman to convince and found they had all been done; that they all sat in clumps, little knots of color eagerly discussing plans and strategies for the morning. Alberta caught her as she stubbed her toe on a chair and fell, staggering.

"When did you last sleep?" Alberta said.

"A very long time ago," said Helen.

"You can't leave till dawn anyway," said Alberta, and she pulled Helen through the throng and made her go into Frye's guest room and lie down.

"But Jane, and Tam—," said Helen.

"Asleep in the kitchen and under the piano, respectively," said Alberta.

"And Mr. Grimsby, and the warehouse—" Helen's mouth felt full of marbles. She was so tired now that she actually was on the bed, and lying down. Had Rook gotten away? Had they all? Helen could not think who had been trying to get away to where. Some people who were dear to her, all going home to the mountains, for good and always. So tired, and her eyes were shutting, shutting. . . .

"Ssh," said Alberta, and turned out the light, and Helen slept.

They let her sleep too long. The house was eerily silent when she woke, and the slanting sunlight betrayed the hour of the morning. Helen shook out the skirts of the apple green voile she had not taken off. It was well-creased from sleep and she said to it, "You can withstand a trolley explosion but even you have limits." She looked around, thinking that she would perhaps stretch Alberta's kindness too far by borrowing—and then likely destroying, the way things had been going—one of her dresses, and her eye fell on a neat pile of clothes by the door. Someone had cleaned and pressed—and apparently, even mended—her herringbone suit from the day before.

She picked up the jacket, and the blouse, and the skirt you could not really climb in, and below that was one more neatly folded item, and she shook it out and found it was a pair of trousers. "Well, then," she said, and took off the apple green voile and put them on. They had not been Frye's, for they were only a little big, and she belted them with the accompanying belt, and put on the blouse and herringbone jacket, and put her hands on her hips, contemplating.

She strode out into the rest of the house before she could think too hard about it. Jane and Tam were in the kitchen, frying bacon with one of the piano players—Stephen—for company. Everyone else appeared to be gone on their tasks. Jane looked lost and Tam looked as though he had a hangover. Brilliant sun streamed through the narrow windows, erasing the usual November fog.

"I think you're loony," Stephen said in a chummy gossipy voice, not turning around from his bacon. "A hundred of you girls against those fey? Against that awful Grimsby person who runs Copperhead? You know he's attempting to have the Prime Minister tried for treason, don't you?"

"Not girls," said Jane. "Women."

"Semantics," Stephen said cheerfully. "Here, eat up before you go into battle."

"It's not battle," said Helen. "We're just going to show up and take our faces back. Oh, and take apart his weapon, whatever the heck it is. Then leave." She began to repin her hair, using a small round mirror hanging between the show posters. It was funny, but she felt as though she moved differently in the slacks. They were just clothes, weren't they? And yet she of anyone should know the difference that clothes made.

"Bacon, bacon, bacon," said Stephen, dropping it onto plates. "And what's to stop him from making another weapon?"

"Well, he won't have us to do it with," Helen said to the reflection. "There's that."

"He didn't exactly have his wife's permission, did he?" said Stephen.

"How did you know about that? I didn't think you were here last night."

Stephen shrugged. "Jane's been telling us the whole story. How you went to look in the warehouse window last night and saw him there. Oh, and talking to someone in a sort of fey trance. Did she make it all up?"

Helen sat down at the table, straddling the back of the chair because she could, and looked hard at Jane. "You know things," she said. "I didn't mention those details."

"I know things," Jane said dreamily.

"Listen, Jane," Helen said. "There's a fey inside you. I know it."

Tam raised his head from his hands, looking wide-eyed at Jane.

Jane suddenly backed up from the table, skittering away, and Helen cursed herself for a fool. "He's not, he's not," she said, eyes wide. "He's not."

"What do you mean, *he's* not?"

Jane closed her eyes. "He comes and goes," she said. "Sometimes I vanish. Sometimes I see everything. I saw you in the warehouse. I saw Millicent. I saw her go out into everything, searching into all the blue. And then . . . go."

Stephen looked from one to the other, eyes wide.

"Tell me," Helen said urgently, and she gripped the back of the chair. "Are you Jane now? Can you tell?" She did not know what this *sometimes* business was and yet it fit with everything she'd seen so far. She had thought Jane was warring with a fey that lived inside her. But how could the fey come in and out? Jane herself had said several months ago that the fey could not do that. Once they went into a person they were there until death—their death, or the body's.

Jane's eyes darted around. She seemed unable to speak.

"Tell me," Helen pressed. Subconsciously her hand closed on the copper necklace. "Tell me."

Jane's mouth opened. "That's him," she said, pointing at the necklace. "That's him too."

They all looked at the copper hydra. The necklace that had been clinging around Helen's neck like a snake itself ever since Alistair had given it to her. The necklace that did not want to come off. Helen started to pull it off and said, "That's silly, Jane. How could a necklace be a fey?" She let it fall again.

"Copper's not poison to fey," said Stephen. "Back when we had all the bluepacks—bits of fey I guess they were—you put them in copper casings to run things."

"I think my lapel pin's hollow," said Tam. "Maybe they all are." He rubbed bleary eyes, peering at Helen's hydra charm as if he were much older.

"It seems so silly to want to take it off," said Helen. "And now that's making me feel very disturbed. Why don't I want to take it off?"

"You should keep it on," Jane said dreamily.

"I think not," said Helen. But her hands did not move.

"I'm not touching it," said Stephen.

"I'll do it," said Tam. He scrambled off his chair and clambered up on the one next to Helen, binoculars waving. Carefully he stood and reached for the necklace. "It feels . . . funny," he said. "Like a friend."

"Don't trust it," said Helen.

Tam grasped the chain and carefully lifted it from around Helen's neck. Instantly Helen felt the compulsion to keep it on lessen. She could see it as just a pretty necklace. "It likes me," Tam said. He stroked the copper heads. "It likes Jane. Mostly it just wants to go home."

"What are you, the fey whisperer?" said Stephen. He looked at Helen with disgust. "Did you know you'd been walking around with that on?"

"Of course not," said Helen. Although she should have known. She had been able to do more with it, hadn't she? "Give it here," she said suddenly to Tam.

Obediently he handed it to her, and she cradled the little piece of copper in her hand. It was hard to believe it had a piece of fey captured inside. And yet . . . "It likes Jane, you say?" Helen looked at Jane. "Like should call to like, I think," she murmured.

"What are you—*oh,*" said Jane. She put her hands to her face.

"Come here," Helen crooned. "Come here."

Jane's face lit up a strange fey-blue for a moment, then faded away.

"Did you see that?" Helen said.

Tam put a hand to Jane's face. "It wants to come," he said. "It wants to join the one in the necklace."

Helen cupped her hands around the necklace and tried again. "Come here," she said. "Come here."

Again the blue rose to the surface. It started to spin out toward Helen, blue smoke tendrils curling through the air.

"Come here," Helen told it, and she could see it trying.

"Stop it," Stephen said suddenly. "You're hurting Jane."

Helen looked and saw that Jane's face was dead white where the blue had left it, pink around the edges like a curling ribbon. Like her face was lifting away.

"Her face," Helen said.

"Don't they all have fey in their faces?" said Stephen. "The Hundred?"

"Oh no, oh no," said Helen, and she tried to reverse the command, tell the bit of fey to return to Jane. "It's the bit of fey that animates the clay on her face," she said. "Without it it wouldn't act like skin."

"She wouldn't have a face," said Tam.

"Or anything," said Stephen, for Jane was having trouble breathing now. She gasped for air, her skin dead white.

"Go back, go back," crooned Helen as fervently as she had bid it come to her. But the fey in Jane's face had tasted freedom, felt its bit of fellow fey in the necklace. Helen grasped the necklace tightly, enclosed the fey in her hand. "Go back to Jane."

Tam reached over and grabbed Helen's fist in his two little hands. "Go back," he told the fey, along with Helen. "Go back."

Slowly, slowly, the blue returned to Jane. It sank in and disappeared, and as it did, pink life returned to her cheeks, and she started to breathe normally again.

Helen seized Jane in her arms and hugged her close, patting the dark hair. "Well, that didn't work," Helen said, with a touch of hysteria at the understatement.

"What were you trying to do?" said Stephen.

"I thought there was fey in her. Like a whole fey. I thought I could make it come out. But I guess all the fey is only that little bit it's always been. How can that be a problem? We all have that, and Jane knows how to deal with it."

Under her arms, Jane stirred. "Because it's the same fey that's in your necklace," she croaked. "It belongs to the same entity."

"Jane!" shouted Helen. She seized her sister's hands and sank down next to her. "It's you! It is. Tell me what just happened."

Jane shook her head, and her green eyes held all the intelligence and fire they once had. "I feel as though you wiped the fey clean for a moment," she said. "It may not have done what you wanted, but it shook it up. It's just a little piece again. And I'm me." She shook her head, seeming to remember all the times she'd made similar claims over the last day and a half. "Me for real. I promise."

Helen narrowed her eyes. "Do you remember coming in and out before? And the memory gaps, and the confusion, and telling us things like go to the warehouse?"

Jane grimaced. "Yes. It has been very strange—and by strange I mean terrifying. Like a dream where you are half-asleep, and sometimes you can make the right words come out, and sometimes you can't."

"So what do you mean about a fey that's the same as the fey in the necklace? And why would that matter?"

Jane swallowed, felt around her forehead delicately, as if seeing if her face was still attached. "I've been thinking, very slowly, way in the back of my mind. A fey needs a piece of fey to attach to to enter somebody," she said. "And we always thought if a fey took someone over, they were stuck there."

"Unless they're killed with iron, or the host dies," said Helen.

"I think this fey has found a loophole," said Jane. She looked directly at Helen, who knew her next words, a sad blow to the heart. "I *was* taken over by a fey."

Stephen gasped. Tam looked on somberly.

"He calls himself the Fey King," said Jane. "He's very

strong—as strong as the Fey Queen was. Maybe that's part of it. But he's able to come and go. Sometimes I have no control, other times I have a little, but I'm dazed. It's not like when the Fey Queen tried to take me. She was ready to wipe me clean. He—it's almost like he wants me to be able to use my body. But he wants to use it, too." She shuddered. "Sometimes I would be cut out completely, and then I felt lost in the back of my own mind, trying to fight my way out. He's been going in and out since the night in the garret, but he always had a toehold in my mind. Watching. You shook him out for a moment."

"But why—?" said Helen. "How? How can he do this?"

"Do you remember that I told you that I suspected the Fey Queen took over Edward occasionally?" Jane looked sideways at Stephen, a little embarrassment showing at talking about the delicate situation of her fiancé. "I've often wondered how she could. I think it was because the fey in his hands was a part of *her*. Not just some random fey, but part of the Fey Queen specifically. Somehow that made it possible for her to slip in and out without getting stuck in the host body."

"And this?" said Helen.

"I think the fey in my mask once belonged to the Fey King," Jane said.

"And the fey in your necklace, too," said Tam.

They all looked at Helen's necklace, dangling gently from her fingers, swaying in the still air.

"Get rid of it," said Stephen.

"Does it make you do things?" said Jane.

"I don't think so," said Helen. "*I* can do things with it. It's given my power a boost."

"You think. But maybe he's making you. You don't know."

Helen's fingers closed around the necklace. "You," she told Jane firmly, "have been in and out of it the last few days. Loopy as a crocheted curtain. I've had to do everything."

"But listen, Helen."

"No, *you* listen," Helen said. "I'm the one who's been here. I'm the one who's been putting all of this together while everyone is drunk and off their heads around me. *I know what I'm doing.*"

Jane raised her eyebrows. It was completely infuriating, and it made Helen close her hand tightly on the necklace. It was warm and comforting in her hand—a tangible source of the power she'd never had. She had made Alistair change, she had made The Hundred change, and she would win this war yet.

Small fingers tugged her fist open, took the copper snake away. Tam looked apologetically up at Helen, but said, "You don't really want this." He threw it down on the table, and with a strange, set expression, ripped off his lapel pin and put it there, too. "It can see us," he said in a voice that rose high. "He sees out of them." He looked around—saw the iron skillet. He kneeled up on his chair, hefted it with both hands, and dumped it with all its bacon grease on top of the two copper-covered bits of fey. "I always wondered how my father knew everything I was up to."

"Oh, Tam—"

"He's not my father," he shouted, and his voice broke.

"Oh, Tam—," Helen repeated helplessly. She pulled him into a hug.

"You might have cleaned out the pan first," said Stephen. Helen glared at him. "Oh, sure, blame me for saying what we all were thinking." He pushed his chair back from the table, throwing his napkin onto the rivulets of bacon grease oozing out from under the pan. "Well, I'm off. Another day in the salt mines."

"I thought your *Saucy Whatnot* wasn't going forward," said Helen. She reluctantly let go of Tam as he sat up, rubbing his face.

"Men in drag," said Stephen. He took his coat from his chair and headed down the hall, saying over his shoulder, "Only one man has quit in solidarity with the women so far—the rest are all 'The show must go on.'" He shrugged. "Besides, I rather like the music. Cheerio."

Stephen opened the front door, and from down the hall they could hear another voice saying, "Pardon me, is Miss Eliot within?"

"Edward!" said Jane. "Dorie!" She rose to run to them, and, turning white with the effort, hurriedly sat back down. The man entering broke into a run at the sight of her, seized her close.

Helen felt a funny shock of pain at the sight of their happiness. She firmly swallowed it and looked down the hall to where a small figure was standing by the door. "Dorie," she said. She seemed to remember that Dorie was not much for being touched, so she merely went down the hall, and beckoned her to come in and join them at the table.

Like her father, Dorie was neatly dressed, but the seams of her dress betrayed where they had been let out, and both outfits had places that had been carefully mended. At the clothes the resemblance ended, for Dorie looked like a china doll, with blond ringlets, blue eyes, and a rosebud mouth, whereas Edward Rochart tended to gauntness and was not conventionally handsome. One of his hands had two stiffened fingers; the other was ruined, the fingers stiff and curled in—he usually kept that hand in his pocket.

Mr. Rochart stood, clasping Jane's hand with his mostly good one. "You're holding up well," he said to Helen, his eyes traveling over the face that he had created. He sighed and turned to Jane. "I wish I could help you restore all the faces, but—" He gestured with his crippled hands.

Jane laid a good hand on his ruined ones. "No," she said. "I'll be able to finish this task."

"Not until you rest," he said. "And more than that, we need to get the fey out of you."

"We tried—but it looked as though it would make things worse," said Helen.

"Let me consult," Mr. Rochart said. "Dorie?" He turned to see Dorie and Tam sitting cross-legged on the floor together, both apparently entertained by something; Helen couldn't think what.

Tam turned, and for the first time that morning a hint of a smile crossed his face. "Look what she can do!" he said.

Helen's eyes widened as she saw that the little girl's hand had disappeared, replaced by a hand of fey blue.

"Dorie," said Mr. Rochart with some asperity. "Not now. Come and look at Miss Eliot. Can you lend your talents to study her? She's not strong enough to resist the Fey King from coming back. We need to keep him out."

Dorie obediently crossed to Jane, who smiled and hugged her close. Dorie's hand of misty blue touched Jane, and Jane very obviously tried not to flinch, even as she kept her tight hug on the girl. Dorie shook her head. "Can't get it out," she said. "Give her a mask."

"Is there damage? Is she all right?"

Dorie nodded. "Sure."

"Please make your hand back into a human hand now," Jane said patiently. Dorie sighed and obeyed.

Mr. Rochart sighed, an echo of his stubborn little girl. "This is part of what we were doing in the woods," he said. "Dorie has fey heritage. She's determined to find out more about what it's going to mean for her future. We have a fey guide. . . ."

"And I still say there are safer ways to 'explore heritage' than go into that forest," Jane put in, spots of color rising to her cheeks. "It's not a good idea for either of you." It was clear this was an old argument, and Helen briefly wondered if that was part of the reason Jane had refused to talk about Edward lately.

"Fey are dangerous," said Mr. Rochart. "Capricious, even. But they're not vicious. Not the mass of them—and most of them aren't in the forest now, regardless."

"No, they're all in the city," said Helen.

"Without a leader, they prefer just drifting around," said Mr. Rochart. "The Fey Queen ruled for a thousand years. She molded them into shape. She started the trade with the humans. And she instigated the fey punishment of forcing them to split into pieces whenever they were being punished—the trade literally consisted of bits of fey, you know. Without her, they'd be more like the copperhead hydra—deadly if it strikes, but you can avoid it, or avoid provoking it. It wouldn't come seek you out."

"Bad analogy," murmured Helen irrepressibly. She rose and started cleaning up the bacon grease for something to do. "Mr. Grimsby is very fond of seeking The Hundred out. He'd like to strike us all down."

"And the fey," said Jane.

"And the *dwarvven,*" said Helen.

"And all women really, and . . . ," said Jane.

"Wait, Mr. Grimsby?" said Mr. Rochart, interrupting this litany. "I don't understand why he'd be so set against fey faces. He has one himself."

Helen looked at him in dead shock.

"If it's the same Mr. Grimsby," said Mr. Rochart. "It was quite a while ago, but it was a very different case. Not like most of the clients. He had an unusual given name—Uriah or Ulysses, something like that."

"There was a name like that in the journal," Helen said slowly.

"Ulrich," Jane said quietly. To Rochart she said, "It was only in your notes by the first name."

"He was a very private man," Mr. Rochart agreed. "I'm trying to recall the details. There'd been an accident of some sort. . . ."

"The motorcar accident," Helen said. She felt all trembly and she sat down hard. "That's what Mary said. He was in an accident with his wife. He went through the windshield. He . . . he must have been cut up all over his face. You can still see the scars in his hair, but they stop, just over his ears—" She looked at Mr. Rochart in horror.

"That's correct," said Mr. Rochart. "He wanted to look the same again. Not handsome."

"And then no one ever suspected him of having fey in his face," said Helen. "Because he's—"

"Hideous," said Jane.

"Mary said he changed because he hit a *dwarvven,*" Helen said. "That he went mad from guilt." She shook her head.

"But that wasn't it at all." She remembered the moment in the attic when he had seemed genuinely sad about Millicent. "It's just like Jane," she said. "Sometimes the old Mr. Grimsby comes out. But mostly—"

"He's been taken over by the Fey King," Jane finished. She looked quite ill. "The same one who controlled me. But why start Copperhead? They hate the fey."

But Helen knew these kind of social mind games. You turned on whoever was necessary to rally your circle together, make you come out on top in the end. "It was the best way to get power," she said. "And it explains so clearly why Copperhead has that weird bent against the *dwarvven* as well."

"But you said he destroyed a fey. In front of everyone."

"What better way to demonstrate his loyalty?" said Mr. Rochart.

Helen nodded. "To get into closed circles, you turn on your dearest, most unfashionable friend, and you destroy her." She thought back to the warehouse. "But his machine then, the one that your friend Niklas made. Grimsby can't be planning to destroy all the fey with it. That would be too far."

"Niklas has gotten quite fanatical," Jane admitted. "But he wouldn't have made something to harm humans."

"No," said Helen. "But Grimsby's been making 'improvements' to it—so who knows what its real purpose is? Well. Not the real Grimsby, of course. That horrible Fey King, making Mr. Grimsby destroy his own wife. Just like he made you . . ." The sentence trailed off as Helen saw Jane *realize* what she had done on the trolley.

Jane went ashen. The horror penetrated her bones, followed a split-second later by the mind-numbing, irrevocable guilt, and Helen felt it all along with her, because of her fey empathy and because it was her *sister* and she could not bear it.

A bewildered Mr. Rochart was reaching out to comfort Jane, but Helen seized her sister and helped her cry. With wet eyes she looked at Jane's fiancé and said, "Even if you two wanted to come help us stop Grimsby, you can't. Jane must stay here. You must stay with Jane."

"Of course," said Mr. Rochart. And Helen carefully helped Jane to sit up, and brought her more tea, and watched her looking at nothing as if she was taken by the fey all over again, and felt her heart crack even as she was glad to be the strong one, the one who was there for her sister.

Jane shook her head, trying to turn her thoughts away from what she had been made to do, trying to bear up under the combination of starvation, brainwiping, and anguish. "So long," she whispered to Helen, and her face was white and red as her empathy for others poured out. "He's been taken over for so long. His poor son." Jane looked at Tam, who was playing on the floor with Dorie. Softly said, "His mother gone. His stepmother. And his father—?"

"Has long been dead," said Helen softly in response. She remembered that moment when Grimsby had wept at Millicent's side and amended her statement. "Or at least, there's only a sliver of him left inside. I don't know if it can come back out."

Chapter 14

WHAT ALISTAIR DID

The Hundred met on the cobblestoned alley by the warehouse. Well, not quite a hundred. Despite all their best efforts, some of the women simply couldn't be convinced—and then, of course, there were those who could not be found. Still, there were a lot of them, and they spilled out around the building in hues of violet and buttercup and rose. They were beautiful. They were delicate. They were mad.

Helen went among the newest ones, shaking hands and turning on her fey-enhanced charm to make sure they were fully rallied to the cause. She talked to them face-to-face, and then she had them pull their iron masks on and buckle them securely. By the time she had made the entire rounds, everyone except for her had on their full iron mask.

Now they looked grim. Even in their sea of beautiful dresses they were frightening with their identical iron grey faces. Helen smiled to herself at how delightfully awful they looked in the shining silks and glinting metal. The world was bathed in sunlight; the snow of last night was melting rapidly, and Helen found she was not particularly missing her wool coat. The slacks were a good deal warmer than the voile, or for that matter, than the skirt that usually went with the jacket. Helen took a deep breath of the crisp and river-stenched air as she made her way to Frye, identifiable as always by her trousers.

"The doors aren't even locked," said Frye. "It can't be this easy, can it? That we just walk in?"

Helen grimaced. "I doubt it. But what else can we do? How else do you spring the trap?"

Frye shook her head, then grinned. "That's why you're the ringleader of this circus," she said. "You get to make the hard decisions."

"Yeah," Helen muttered, and then a flash of movement behind Frye caught her attention. "Tam?"

He crept around Frye, wearing his binoculars and explorer hat and a stubborn look. "I followed you," he said.

"Tam—," she began.

He cut in quickly, "Dorie said you might need this after all." He held out a copper hydra charm, shiny with wiped-off bacon grease.

She took it from him and said, "And now you must go home. We have to face your—"

"It's *not* my father in there," said Tam. "You know it's not. I have to see."

"It's not a good place for you to be," said Helen gently. "Besides, that creature *looks* like your father. That's going to be hard."

He set his lips in a line and she remembered Charlie picking up a staff and saying he was going in to fight.

It was hard no matter where you were. It was hard whether you stayed back, or went in, and though she would have protected him from this with her last breath she also would not stop him now. She looked up at Frye, who looked quite sympathetic to Tam's cause. "You two stay to the rear," she ordered.

"Yes, ma'am," said Frye.

"And if it looks at all as though he's in danger, you take him away."

"Yes, ma'am," said Frye again.

Helen looked down at Tam. "You swear to obey Frye? This isn't a free-for-all. There are rules in war."

He nodded, and Helen shook her head with the tension. Frye clapped her on the back. "Cheer up. You only live once."

Gallows humor again. Helen smiled because there didn't seem to be anything else to do.

It was eerily silent from within the warehouse. She held the shiny necklace in the palm of her hand and concentrated, studying the way the warehouse lit blue when she focused on it. She let go and the light faded. The women milled about, chattering, but she knew the nervous energy, the anticipation, would shortly turn to funk and gloom if they didn't move soon. None of these women had done anything like this, knew what they were up against.

Helen squared her shoulders. *Nobody* knew what they were up against. Nobody had faced down a fey leader except her sister, six months ago.

And what Jane could do, so could she.

"All right, women!" Helen shouted. No need for a surprise attack. Whoever was inside knew the women were here, not least because Grimsby surely knew of Helen's whereabouts through the necklace she held. Well then, let him see. She held it up as she moved through the crowd to the front, and shouted: "Everyone is in charge of finding your own face, first and foremost. As soon as you do that, focus on finding the women they've captured and freeing them. Don't get distracted by whatever the men do. If we take back what we own, they lose control over us." She took a deep breath. "Iron masks secure? Now. In we go!" Helen flung open the warehouse doors.

The room was a thick cloud of fey blue that swirled and blew. Helen could not see her hand in front of her face. She felt her way forward—and then shouts from behind made her turn.

Helen whirled to see the women behind her being pulled to the side of the warehouse as if being sucked under by a wave. In a clear space in the blue fog she saw a large strange machine that whirled and made a loud thrumming sound. The little iron letter opener Frye had lent her slipped through her fingers, slicing them as they went, and flew toward the machine.

"Masks off, everyone!" Helen shouted. "It's magnetic."

So this was part of the trap—they had to advance without protection. Several women helped those who had been caught get unbuckled.

The blue cleared as Helen stepped forward. Inside the cloud she saw them. The men. Twenty or so of the highest-ranking members of Copperhead. Alistair's friends.

Each one stood in front of a supine body. A caged woman, a funnel attached to her perfect face. And in the middle of the room, sucking all their fey power into the copper hydra box—Grimsby.

Helen's heart broke as she saw those women. Some she knew, instinctively, without seeing their faces. She knew the missing ones of The Hundred—and some of them had the misfortune to be the wives and girlfriends of Alistair's friends. Without a doubt she knew that Morse, for example, was standing next to the body of his very own wife. And there, next to Hattersley—poor Betty, who had been supposedly taken by the police for curfew violation.

Heart beating rapidly, she looked for Alistair, but she could not find him. She almost laughed in relief, but then he advanced out of the shadows and said, "Grimsby wishes me to tell you your presence is requested."

"What are you doing here?" she said.

"I am appointed emissary," he said dreamily. "Ambassador. Go-between. We men understand that sacrifices must be made in war. Today, we will annihilate the fey. We would like you to assist in the glorious cause."

"You men understand very little," said Helen sharply. "We do not choose to lay down our lives for some fey's nefarious plot."

There was movement then, and she heard some of the men shifting in concern at her words, but whether at the "lay down our lives" or "fey" she did not know.

Alistair turned wide dreamy eyes on her. "Our leader has assured us that none of you will be permanently harmed," he said. "If anything, you may come out of it more docile and sweet-tempered, which surely you would rejoice to hear."

Helen smiled then, with all her teeth. "You may tell Grimsby—or rather, that fey living in him—that our presence is neither necessary nor required. Except that we will get what we came for."

"You think so?" he said with curiosity.

The blue sharpened and the men stood straighter.

Helen set her jaw. "To your faces!" she shouted to The

Hundred, and they all poured in. Their iron letter openers and scissors and kitchen knives had been taken by the magnets, but they came with fingernails. They came with copper hatpins. They came with the golden pins of diamond brooches. They came, and they came, pouring into that cold warehouse.

It is almost like a dream, how she stands above them all and sees the wave of women break and flow around the jutting rocks of men. She sees potato-faced Boarham rub his hands together and say, They really did all come, Grimsby, how clever of you—before falling under a sea of sherbet silk. Yes, that is Lady Dalrymple, leading that charge. And there, Agatha Flintwhistle, unhooking faces one by one, handing them carefully to Louisa Mayhew. Tam clambers up the crates like a monkey to throw random junk at the men's unprotected heads, and Frye whoops and hollers whenever he scores a shot. Alberta stands near them all, whacking men with a wooden bat when they get too close. How clever of Alberta to prepare for the human enemy instead of fey, Helen thinks, for the men did not have a plan to ward off bats.

She sees Calendula Smith, leading a battalion of women in an organized attack into the heart of the room, where Morse and the others are attempting to keep their women tied to their beds. Hattersley has pushed Betty's bed away from the others—she can't tell if it's to keep Betty safe or to deliver her to Grimsby for some even more nefarious purpose. Calendula barks orders like a lieutenant, and the women work together to loosen wrists and ankles, to push and shove and kneecap the men. Calendula herself overpowers scrawny Morse and pushes him with all her sturdy bulk onto the bed, holds him down while another woman ties him up. A lewd comment falls from his lips—another women stuffs rags in his mouth and then nobody has to hear him.

The men are strong, but there are more of the women. And the men are not really expecting a battle. Helen sees that again and again, sees the surprise in their eyes when a pack of beautiful ladies plows into them and bites.

But surprise only works for so long. The men remember that they know how to box and hit, that they have a warehouse full of scrap wood and metal they can pick up and swing. The fighting wears on and she sees the Prime Minister's wife crumple under a powerful blow from Boarham. Helen herself has been methodically going where she is needed, where she sees a woman alone and outnumbered. It has all been very numb and she is surprised to find she has tears in her eyes when she looks down and sees Calendula Smith's old face crumpled on the floor, the forehead twisted and smashed from a vicious twist of a heel.

In the blurriness she stands, and there is a man bearing down on her with a lead pipe. There is no time, and suddenly a copper knife flashes out and into the man's arm, and he stumbles, and drops the pipe. "Iron allergy," Desirée says to Helen with satisfaction. "Magnets didn't catch *me*." Desirée picks up her copper knife and grins fiendishly at the bleeding man, and he turns and runs out of the warehouse.

He's not the only one who has run, Helen notices. There are fewer men than there were when they charged in, and some of the ones left are tied up or otherwise indisposed. Backlit by the open warehouse doors she sees Hattersley helping Betty pick her stilettoed way over machine parts and fallen bodies. They flee out the door and Helen watches them go with a mixture of pride and disappointment. They are not the only couple to leave together, and though she is glad that some of these Copperhead husbands are still open to being persuaded to reason, she also wishes more men had turned to fight against their old party as soon as it was clear that not all was as Grimsby said. She remembers again how Alistair spoke of avoiding the Great War five years ago—he paid a poor soldier to take his place. The men of her generation, the ones that are left, are cowards.

Helen wades back to help free the remaining women and faces, to unhook, uncouple, release that machine. She turns and there is Rook, working alongside her and suddenly everything snaps clearly back into focus and they are alone in the midst of a battle.

Like in the dance.

Like in the trolley.

He was there, helping them. He had been there all along.

"You missed your boat," was all she could think to say.

"I stayed," he said. "I had to see finished what I started."

"But how will you get home?" She did not want him to leave and yet the words kept coming out.

His mouth set and he shrugged. "Take a passenger boat. Or go overland. I can't crew a ship but I do know how to walk."

"You can't possibly walk all that way," she said. "I'll give you money for the train if you need it."

"Alistair's money?" he said, and she reddened.

She matched the intentional rudeness with coldness of her own, retreated into ice. "I suppose *my husband* can spare it."

His lips twisted, and he said, "There's always a husband."

She wanted to break then, to let the floodgates open but here they were in a battle, and she was too tired to see anything but the future she had already laid out, that she would go one way and he another.

The silence lengthened until his moment of levity fell away, and he said softly, bitterness tracing his tongue, "I suppose you can make him be how you want," he said. "Keep him so he's never himself again." He turned away and she heard the last words called back, "He'll never have to know how he's failed you."

She stood there, heart beating. *Keep him so he's never himself again.* What had she done to Alistair?

She was no better than the Fey King, changing Grimsby to suit himself. She remembered Grimsby in that moment of kneeling at Millicent's side, crushed and heartbroken. A moment when he was free from the Fey King's spell. When he could be his own person, make his own mistakes.

What had she done to The Hundred?

When did the end stop justifying the means?

Helen moved out into the remains of the melee, moved among the women as if in a daze, undoing what she had done. They fought hand to hand for control of their faces, themselves, and she reached out and touched them, and told them silently to make their own mistakes, live without her command.

She expected a rout. That the battle would suddenly swing back the other way, even with fewer men left to fight.

But she had misjudged them.

There were women who had been afraid. There were women who had been brave. There were women who had been weak and strong and sharp and tough and feeble and clever. Helen could not tell who was who as they wrestled for themselves, to win the day.

The battle was dying down now. The women were winning—had won. At what point did you declare, *won*? she wondered. At what point were you no longer afraid?

The women found their faces and she and Frye told them to take them and go. Go back to Frye's. Find Jane. Become yourself again. And many did, and many stayed, helping the others, for there was still much left to do.

Through it all Helen moved, until she found Alistair, dreamily helping a woman over a pile of rubble and out the door to safety. He smiled kindly at her, and she thought, perhaps I have misjudged him, too. Perhaps he is who I always thought he was, and he stands apart from Grimsby because he is something better, something finer.

And even if he isn't, he deserves his own chance to make mistakes.

She touched him on the arm and took all her changes back. One by one she took them away until he was wholly himself again. He shook himself, blinking, and she smiled up at him and said, "Thank you for helping us."

Alistair looked around, getting his bearings. Then his eyes narrowed and he seized her arms. "What have you done?" he said in a broken voice. "What have *I* done?"

Helen swallowed. And then said calmly, firmly, "I changed you. I shouldn't have. But you were helping us win." More quietly: "*Aren't* you helping us?"

"Out in public?" Alistair dropped his head to his hands. "Grimsby will never forgive me now. Oh, it's hopeless. I tried to help you, I really did. But you've been nothing but trouble to me."

"Really," Helen said coldly. She was not going to stay for this. She turned away to help the others.

"I was going along fine as a bachelor. Thought I needed a wife. More fool I. I should have run the other direction when Hattersley told me about you. . . ."

Helen swung around. Her heart seemed to be beating preternaturally still, as though she was a hawk in the instant before it swoops. *Hattersley.* That single dropped sentence last night about Betty being a consolation prize for Helen. Everything in her fell to the tip of her tongue, into one swift, dangerous question. "What do you mean, *told me about you*?"

Alistair did not have the grace to stumble or look abashed. Glumly he said, "About your bargain with the doctor, of course. Hattersley boasted about how he'd found the perfect girl; all he had to do was rescue her from a doctor friend of his. He couldn't believe the doctor would try to get balloon payments out of you when a variety of obvious answers were staring him in the face. Hattersley's a family man at heart, though—he wanted a wife. He was thrilled by the lady-in-distress routine, talked of being your white knight." Alistair laughed ruefully. "That was his undoing. Of course we all had to troop down to the tenpence dance hall and see you for ourselves." He looked up at her now, as if seeing her then, a girl in a white dress with a green sash. "Well, perhaps it can be okay again," he mused. "Served old Hattersley right I got to you first, I always thought."

"Got to me first," Helen said. He didn't see the hawk's claws closing on him, didn't know he was only a mouse and she blazed with pure predation.

Alistair sighed. "This is why I didn't tell you," he said reasonably. "I knew you would take it the wrong way."

So many years of splitting herself into private Helen and public Helen left her unable to speak. Unable to say the deep thoughts that came roiling up. She could smile and joke with him and laugh it off as a misunderstanding, except she couldn't. She did not have the words, only she knew like a gut punch that there was something pathologically inequitable about seeking her out when he already knew she was blindly grasping for any lifeline.

No, she could not speak. All her cleverness had deserted her.

But she could be the hawk, all muscle instinct and focused fury.

"Come on," Alistair said. "We can still reclaim our place. Just let's go on home before anyone sees. We'll meet up with Grimsby later. He'll make it out okay; he's like a fox."

"I am not going home with you," she said, carefully, precisely. "I am not going to your home ever again."

The color faded from his face as he saw that she meant it. She registered that in the back of her mind, that she had chosen a life of trouble and chaos and public ordeal . . . and freedom. It blossomed in her mind that if she made it out of here alive, she would have freedom.

And then, because there seemed only one thing left to do, she moved to the center of the room and picked up the last remaining funnel. She would not be like poor Millicent—she hoped. Because she would be both the source and the wielder of the power.

And she moved to the copper hydra that ran it all, and placed one hand on it, even as she placed the funnel on her face.

She was plunged into that waking dream again. But this time she was moving among it herself. She wondered if poor Millicent had felt that before she vanished, that she was a figure on this alien landscape, as she touched every corner of the city at once and they all fed to her eyes and ears and mind.

She could see the fey that controlled Mr. Grimsby in this maelstrom. The self-styled Fey King. He was out there, and he had pieces of himself all over the city, not just in Mr. Grimsby's face and her necklace. He was in other fey faces. As Tam said, he was in every single one of those hydra pins and necklaces. Before the advent of the iron masks, he had been able to dip in and out of a handful of well-placed people—and now with the copper pins there were another few hundred he could use as eyepieces to the whole city. It was how he had gained so much power so quickly. How he had risen to prominence and caught the ear of the Prime Minister. He must have planned long ago for this, seeding the clay given to Rochart with bits of himself. He was everywhere.

Helen felt it all, and her thoughts ranged across the city. It was something. But it was not enough. She could not reach out to stop the Fey King, who was moving rapidly, connecting pieces of fey out there into nets that pulled and tensed. She felt what she had before in the warehouse, that sense of the bits of fey trying to coalesce, and as the tension grew stronger and stronger she felt the power growing behind it, a sense of stored energy as the grid of fey that lay all over the city crackled alive, joining together in one massive grid of power.

He was definitely not combining all the fey to destroy them.

She saw all those images as she had before, and she tried to focus to where a particular part of the city was becoming strongly blue.

<<Almost have it,>> she heard, and then the other voice, <<Almost do,>> and it seemed to her now that both voices were the Fey King himself, split apart into so many pieces that he had become schizophrenic with it.

She could see the blue in that part of the city, lying along grass and sidewalk and embankment, and the air around it hummed with electricity, hummed like she was able to hear and see a downed wire from the trolley. A bird flew too close and was zapped, fell to the ground with singed feathers.

Helen froze as she saw what he was doing. What he had been planning to do all along, since he had forced the fey six months ago to split and begin settling over the city, lying in wait until he would be ready to use them all at once. He was pulling all the fey into one massive grid of power that would trap the entire city in a single charge.

He would kill all the humans. Once the net was finished. He had gained enough power from the women he had drained to go everywhere. They would reach out and electrify everyone.

But the women were detached now, and the Fey King hadn't gotten the entire hundred he wanted, and he was slowing down. Helen saw that, and she saw that he would have to make choices.

And she just needed a little boost.

She dropped the funnel to the floor, because she saw she didn't need it. It had helped her figure out how to focus, but she was her own power no matter how it came. With her now-free hand she pulled the necklace from her slacks pocket, that had the little bit of the Fey King in it, and touched it to the copper.

The blue wriggled free of the copper hydra. Then melted in.

In the maelstrom, Helen seized the bit of fey before it could find the rest of the Fey King, and rode its tail as it zoomed to him, bouncing around his multiplicity. He was frightening and dense in the imaginary world, strung out across the city, bloated and gathering blue.

But it was only a little boost, and it was not enough. She had control over the machine, but not over him.

Electrified blue she said to the warehouse at large, *I need more power.*

And they came.

Of their own free will they came, those few of The Hundred who were left. Frye and Calendula and Alberta and Louisa Mayfew and Agatha Flintwhistle, they all came and put their trust in her, put funnels to their faces, and fed her their power.

Helen pulled on them, pulled just a little, pulled not too much, pulled on them until she was stronger than the Fey King, because each of the little pieces of fey in the women tenuously connected to their own larger selves out there in the grid, and those fey did not like the Fey King either. Those larger bits of fey came, tunneling through to Frye and Calendula and Desirée, six of them, ten, twelve. They came and came and together, together, they were all stronger than the Fey King, and Helen could put out her hand and crush him.

He gathered all his strength, but it was not enough.

Because as the rest of the fey saw Helen's group massing, they flocked to her, away from the Fey King's grasp. <<We want to go home,>> she heard, over and over. <<He kept us apart. We want to be whole again.>>

<<You will,>> she promised, and her hand that was not a hand closed on the Fey King.

He whimpered.

He cried, there in the blue, and in the warehouse Mr. Grimsby curled into a ball and sobbed.

Helen stopped, and everything she had ever *not done* flashed before her eyes.

If I had gone into battle to save Charlie, perhaps, I, too, would be someone who had killed, she thought. Jane is someone who has killed, and I am the one who stayed with Mother and tended to her while she let herself slip away. No matter how much there needs to be *one who stays,* the one who stays will always regret not going, and perhaps it takes a particular kind of strength to both stay and bear up under having stayed.

I am still not going to be one that kills. I am never going to be one who has killed.

Directly to the Fey King, so they all could hear, she said: "If I let you go, will you promise to go back to your homes in the forest and never fight us again?"

It flung itself around inside her mental grasp, screaming.

She waited, patiently, waiting for the tantrum to wear itself out. I can and will choose not to kill, she thought, and the heady rope of power thrummed around her. She felt a new kind of power settling in place somewhere in the back of her skull, the feeling that she could make and own her decisions, and that people could decide for themselves whether or not they liked them. It didn't matter to her anymore. When you ended up with great power you had the responsibility to not abuse it, but you also had the responsibility to *use* it, if that was necessary. When Queen Maud turned back the Armada, did she worry about what the Armada would think? And now Helen had the power, and even though she had a lifetime of bad judgments behind her, still, perhaps it was time to trust that she had learned something from them.

But perhaps she didn't mind threatening death, for a good cause. The Fey King had quieted down and so Helen said, "If you do not promise, I will kill you all now." The large mass of blue on her side thrummed in dismay.

It grew cunning. "I am only one leader. What if they break their promises after I am gone?"

"Fey live a long time," she said, as if bored by the whole discussion, though her heart pattered through her chest. "Make them all swear, for all their lifetimes."

It raged again, but then it quieted down. There was a thrumming, and she felt the question go out, through her, through all the women, into the fey that carpeted the city. There were no words, but they said in the way that bits of fey said it, <<I swear,>> <<I swear,>> <<I swear,>> and she heard in that how glad they were to be going home.

"Then go," she said, eager for all of this to be done, and through her the word went out and they all picked up. She sent her vision out to the ends of their reach and she could see the whole city, the blue lifting, peeling back from stone and step, lifting, going, going. They joined up with each other as they flew, bits of fey finding their counterparts in mad joyful rushes, and she could feel through that extension of power how glad they were to be back with themselves. The fey leader had a lot of power, she realized, to make them split like that and keep them that way. She remembered Jane telling her how in the old days the fey that ran all the bluepacks were little bits of fey, a punishment system. Is that how the self-styled Fey King had made his order stick? Presented making them split up and cover the city as punishment for not winning the war?

As the blue joined together the blue aura dimmed, because it was made up of them, and they were leaving. She suddenly worried whether the command would extend to the bits of fey in The Hundred's faces, but the women were detaching themselves one by one now from the funnels, and they looked fine, and Helen herself felt fine. Perhaps it was because those bits were solidly embedded in the humans; perhaps it was because their punishments dated from the time of the Fey Queen, and therefore some unknown quantity of time had not yet been served. She did not know, but she was not ready for those bits to be gone quite yet.

The fey were at the edge of her range now, ecstatic, flying home to the forest. Helen thought that perhaps humans did not really need to worry about the run-of-the-mill fey, as long as there was not a leader hell-bent on making them do something it was not in their nature to do.

She thought, too, that the real thing was that you had to both try to do right, and then deal with the fallout, whatever it was. Strength was not something that happened in a moment, but a sustained note that you held over time. She gestured to the rest of the dozen to detach, which they eagerly did, leaving the warehouse at last, going home.

Helen herself let go of the copper hydra and stood quietly in the warehouse, feeling the power go, feeling herself become only and wholly herself.

She was feeling pretty good about the decision to bargain with the Fey King rather than obliterate him.

And then Grimsby attacked.

Chapter 15

BLOOD AND COPPER

Helen was flung back against the wall with the force of the Fey King's power. Everything splintered, fractured. She was pushed aside and soon she would be no more.

And then as quickly as the attack had come it was gone and her mind was clean and clear. Rook was standing over Grimsby with a steel dagger, its point poking the soft flesh of his neck.

The tall man with the snake eyes cowered, blubbering. She saw the man he had once been: a weak drunkard, now pitiful and crying. Inside him raged the fey, sharp and cunning, choosing to let the human take control for the sake of those tears.

Rook's knifepoint did not waver.

"No," Helen said. "He's not worth it."

"He would have destroyed the city," shouted Rook. "Sometimes things are worth it."

She thought he might be right, but at the same time, she had seen his face when he told her about his past, his present, about the indentured servitude of spying that went on and on and on, all for the mistake of being born *havlen*. It was not right that this man should bear any more guilt. "No," she said, and slammed Grimsby back, hard, into the wall away from Rook. He was hooked into the machine still, and so she still had access to the little power he had left, in addition to her own. He could never be stronger than her.

"You lied," she said, and she was vast and blue. "I thought your kind had to keep promises."

"You heard what you wanted to hear," sneered the Fey King, and oh misery perhaps that was true. All the fey had promised except this one. But she was not going to waste time in self-recrimination. If she had to have a blot on her soul, so be it. Sometimes you had to bear up under things.

The fey from the city were all gone, but she seized all the power from Grimsby himself, sucking it through the machine and into her until he was nothing, an ordinary man with a bit of fey remnant, cowering in the warehouse.

"You can't hold me forever," he said weakly. "You have to let go or keep me inside you."

Helen could feel the power of the Fey King thrumming inside and realized he was right, and that further, she knew how strong the Fey King was. He would wear her down and take her over if she was foolish enough to think she could hold him.

But there were not only two choices. She could contain him in iron, she thought. Forever. "Rook, get that iron cage. We'll put him in there for now and then get handcuffs." She pointed at Grimsby, motioning him toward one of the hundred cages. "Push him in the minute I say go."

Snarling, Grimsby backed up. At the mouth of it he stood, and she had to leave the door open to let the fey completely back into him. "Watch him," she said, and then she let the power unspool, going back, back, back, until Grimsby was starting to stand, whole and healthy and hale.

He started to lunge, and she shoved the last bit back into him with all her might, shouting, "Go!" but he leapt at her.

He leapt at her with a sharpened copper pipe in his hand and she hadn't thought to counter for anything like that, and it was coming at her, and Rook was still turning, still hurrying, but it would be too late, too late.

Then a heavy bright shape flashed in front of her, an iron stake held high. It bore Grimsby down to the ground, and she saw then that the iron stake was held in two canary yellow gloves. The copper and the iron flashed; the bodies rolled over and over in a tangle before Helen could fully register that the dark shape was Grimsby, and the bright one was Alistair.

"Let him go," Helen shouted, and Rook, who had no weapon, plunged in to try to pull Alistair free. Long after, she remembered that.

Rook shouted in pain and her rapidly beating heart threatened to break, a bright hot thing that would shatter at any minute.

But this was not the battle in her hometown. And that was not Charlie.

And then Alistair shouted, a shout of victory, and as Rook pulled him out of harm's way she saw the sharp iron spike lodged in Grimsby's ribs, heard the shriek, felt the universe expand and collapse as the self-styled Fey King inside shredded out and dissolved, obliterated.

He was safe. They were safe. She looked down at Grimsby's body and wondered how it had felt to be Grimsby, to be slowly eradicated over time. To know, like Jane, what was happening. To not be able to fight your way out. To lose your wife, your son. To vanish.

"Helen," Rook said quietly.

She turned, heart willing him to be okay. But he was. He was kneeling, and his hands rested quietly on Alistair's shoulder.

"Alistair," she said brokenly, and she dropped to her knees on the hard cement beside him, as Rook backed away, one silent shake of his head signaling everything that was already obvious.

The sharpened copper pipe had sliced through his gut. She knew, she remembered from that battle, about belly wounds, and even if she didn't, only a fool could stand and look and smell and expect something besides what was going to happen.

Alistair breathed faintly, his eyes closed.

Helen took his left hand in her own. Her fingers trembled as she closed around it.

"Rook," she said then, and looked up at him with anguished eyes.

Rook looked somberly at her for the space of a heartbeat. Then in a low voice, jagged and slow, said, "I will leave you," and turned, and walked down the long echoing warehouse toward the door. All that work of splitting herself with the blue fire and yet now was when she felt split in two. A piece of her walked out the warehouse door with Rook, into the icy November night, and somehow she knew it wasn't coming back.

Gently she held her husband's hand, and listened for his breath.

His eyes flickered, opened halfway. "Did she get out of

harm's way?" said Alistair. His voice was so thin, like wind shaking the dry leaves.

"Who?" said Helen. He was so white, so clammy-pale.

"Jane," he said. With pauses between the words that grew longer and longer, he said, "I sent her. A warning."

Helen couldn't figure out what he meant, but his eyes held hers, pleading for her to understand without further words. The cold damp of the warehouse floor seeped into her knees. Then realization. "The death threat." Cut from liquor labels.

"To save her," Alistair said.

Helen crushed his hand between hers, as if by doing so she could keep him from dying before help arrived. "You sent it," she said.

A little smile. "Not a coward," he said. "Tried?"

There was a great rushing void of grief inside for this man who had tried to break away from his friends, his vices, after all. Too little, too secretly. But he had done one thing. He had tried to keep Jane from playing into the hands of Grimsby, and starting down this terrible path. A foolish, ridiculous thing.

"You tried," she said to that taut body, but there was no air in it and he could not hear her. She could see him, past all his vices and depravities, him, Alistair, living on the map of his face. His skin was a hundred years old, but the last bit of life in his body lived right there on it, waiting for Helen to tell him he tried, that it was okay, that he could depart from this world in some sort of peace.

She couldn't make it okay. Couldn't make everything he had done or failed to do vanish, like clouds parting in the sky. But she could tell him he tried, for it was true, though sad and touching that at this moment all he could think of for proof was a frightening torn-paper note.

But there was more to credit to his account. Alistair had saved her from her own foolishness once. No matter how he found her, that he might have thought she was easy prey—still. In this moment she could give him the benefit of the doubt and go by the bare cold facts of the matter, which were that he had paid her debt then—and just now he had saved her life.

He had been a terrible husband, would have been a terrible father. But these things he had done.

"You tried," she said, carefully and clearly, because that much she could say.

He breathed then, and relaxed, as if everything had been waiting for that one benediction. The wrinkles on the map of his face smoothed out, relaxed.

Then he was gone.

Helen released his hand and laid it gently on his body. His wedding ring was tarnished, but still there, on his finger. Gently she tugged her own off and placed it between his fingers.

Perhaps he had loved her after all, in his fashion.

Helen knelt beside the still body and wept for them both.

Epilogue

It was a fine May morning, crisp yet sunny. Helen kneeled on the wooden pine floor, pinning hems in place on a pair of slim-fitting trousers. "A little more ankle," she said. "Don't you think?"

The model—Alberta—grinned. "As long as you let me wear this to my gig for the evening. Will I turn heads!"

"Midcalf then," said Helen. "As long as you're going to wear slacks, you might as well go whole hog."

The door jingled and Helen called over her shoulder, "Just a minute!" She bent back to her hem. "Bring it back first thing in the morning and report word for word on what the audience said. I'm thinking this might be a summer hit, for the brave. Of course I'll have to source more of this twill. . . ." Helen looked up at Alberta, who was staring over Helen's shoulder with a peculiar expression. "What?"

Helen turned around and saw, silhouetted against the bright spring light flooding her shop, a lithe man in close-fitting black.

She dropped all the pins.

"I'll just be off then," said Alberta, and she vanished behind the curtains that led to the shop's back door.

Helen hastily bent to pick up the silver pins. "So what brings you here today?" she said over her shoulder. "Looking for something custom?"

"You could say that," the man said. He moved silently toward her until he passed beyond the sunlight and his face resolved into Rook. Or it would have, had she been looking at him, and not resolutely at the pins, which required a lot of concentration to pick up. "No pleasant greeting for an old friend?"

"I always appreciate it when my old friends come to see me," Helen said. Her heart pounded, but she would match him coolly, using dry words like *pleasant* and *friend*. "Some of them didn't like it that I opened a shop. Some of them didn't like it that I went back to my old name."

"But they weren't really your friends anyway," Rook said.

"No. No, I suppose they weren't." She smiled up at him then, a smile that threatened to turn warm. "And really they are very few anyway. The Hundred all come, and what The Hundred do, everyone does. And that includes Frye, and *she* wears my designs onstage, and then they all come. They all have to come, to keep up." She dropped her pins into a box. "We're setting fashion here, whether they like it or not. They don't shape trends anymore. We do. Frye does. The Hundred do, and so many of The Hundred are *doing things,* you know."

"I know."

He was so still in the middle of the room and she could not think what he was doing there. If he wanted to see her, why hadn't he come six months ago? Why was he here now, to break her routine, her newfound sense of self? But perhaps he had a new girl; he always did, didn't he? And perhaps that new girl wanted the designs that the fashion-forward were wearing. Helen had seen many men from the old days. Even Hattersley had slunk in here, not meeting her eyes, to purchase a bias-cut slip skirt for Betty.

Helen adjusted the folds of a sundress on a mannequin. "Did you want to see some clothes?" she said. "Something for someone in particular?"

"No," Rook said, and she almost smiled, but then he said, "Yes. Show me your favorites."

"Well," said Helen. She pulled a somber navy dress from a rack and said, "This is what I wear when I want to convince Tam's school that his foster mother is serious and appropriate."

"I had heard that," he said, though he did not say how. Frye, perhaps, and that made her upset that someone she knew had seen him, shared details about her life with him, and still he had not come. "I'm glad."

"So are we," she said, and added, "I've gotten quite the education on magical snakes."

He fingered a beaded belt hanging from a hook, not saying anything.

Helen did not know how to respond to silence. She pulled a bright green sundress from a hanger and held it in front of her, smoothing down the pleats. "This is all mine. People need something a little frivolous these days, you know? Spring's here—almost summer. No more curfew. No more fear." She knew the green offset her copper curls, and she looked for his reaction.

He made a noncommittal noise and turned away.

Frustrated, she tried a more direct approach. She moved to a mannequin in the shop window and directed his attention to it. "I'm rather fond of this one, with all the seed pearls. But it fits very tiny. Some of the *dwarvven* have stopped in, now that they've trickled back to the city, but it's out of their budgets I suppose. I really need to cut one of them a deal on it—Nolle, perhaps—she repaid her debt by bringing me customers, you know. Is she *dwarvven*?"

"Who, Nolle?"

"The girl you're picking this out for."

Rook looked moody. "No. She's not." He pointed at the seed pearls. "Isn't that one expensive?"

"Yes," Helen admitted. "I sank rather a lot into it. And then accidentally made it so small that everyone who can afford it looks at it and feels guilty about the second high tea they had, but that doesn't do anything for the dress. It doesn't get sold."

He glowered around the room, his hazel eyes dark. "I suppose it's not just that dress. You've sunk a fortune into this place."

"Perhaps," Helen said, "but in fact it's very calculated costs, this dress notwithstanding. Turns out I have a head for such things."

"I'm not surprised," Rook said. "I always thought you could move mountains."

"I expect to recoup the initial investment within two years," Helen said, "but even if I don't—" She stopped and looked at him sharply. "Is that what this is? Are you in here worrying about how wealthy I am now?"

His hazel eyes were sharp with misery. "I knew this was a mistake," Rook said. "I need to be going."

"Look," Helen said. "I may have inherited a fortune so large you could fill all your bathtubs with large bills and roll around in a scandalous fashion. But that doesn't change *me*."

The joke did not make him laugh. "You're just being kind to me," he said, sounding grumpy. "You can't help it, I suppose. The fey glamour."

She had never seen him like this. Her heart beat faster. "Fey glamour?" she said.

"Yes, whatever you do I'll interpret as nice, because I'm bewitched. If I get too uppity, then as you said before, you could change me so I'll leave you alone." He glowered. "You already told me to leave town with the rest of the *dwarvven*. Practically threw your purse at me to get me to go. And here I am looking for another excuse to be under your fey spell." He turned. "I suppose I'd better leave now, before I embarrass myself further."

Helen swallowed hard and did not move. In a voice a little too high she said, "I suppose you object to my freckles, is that it?"

He was at the doorjamb, the iron-free doorjamb, and then he stopped. Slowly he pivoted on his heel. "Your freckles?" he said. Something sharp and alive crackled all through him, a hint of his former self.

"And the bump on my nose," she said.

"What bump?" He took one step back to her. Two.

"Jane's been doing us one by one. Freeing the little bits of fey. Didn't you know? They deserve their chance to go home."

"Doesn't everyone?" he said. The spring sun slanted through the window, the dust motes sparkled in the air.

"You know, I find it highly unflattering that one viewing of Miss Eglantine Frye in a performance could make you rush all up and down the street buying flowers, but for someone you've actually shared a highly inappropriate dance of the Shadow with, you don't even check in to see if she's recovered from a murderous fey attack."

"Dear Miss Eliot," Rook said. He was near enough now for her to smell that faint hint of sandalwood. "I believe you told me I do many things badly."

"Such as?"

"Dancing, for starters."

"And?"

"And maybe this." He kissed her.

When she came up for air she said, "No, perhaps not that."

"Not that? Well, apologizing then. Probably that."

"And being late for things," Helen said. "And willfully misinterpreting my concern over your getting home as evidence that I wanted you to go there."

"That was very badly done," he conceded. "But not this?" He kissed her again.

A little bit later she said, "Well. I suppose that might need some practice."

"But you'll teach me?"

"I might," she said.

Rook's eyes were level with hers and the old gleam was in them. She smiled, mischievously, and turned him around till she was behind him, one hand on his waist, one hand grasping his, looking past his dear face through the open door into the clear sweet sunshine.

"Dearest Rook," Helen said. "May I have this dance?"

Acknowledgments

The grandparents:

I got pretty lucky in grandparents, but I would especially like to dedicate this to the memory of my grandmother. She was whip-smart, an autodidact, chic, feminist, witty, political, a lover of theatre and the arts. She loved traveling, and she took me to the Children's Theater Company in Minneapolis (*Raggedy Ann & Andy!*), to the Shelburne Museum in Vermont (circus toys!), to a Wayne Thiebaud retrospective in Kansas City (all those delicious painted cakes). At their house I first read *The Annotated Alice,* Saki, and Ogden Nash. I miss her dearly—I wish I would have traveled with her more, after college—and I like to think she would have liked many of the moments in this book, particularly when The Hundred pour in with hatpins.

The thank-yous:

The wise and insightful K. Bird Lincoln and Katherine Sparrow for reading the first draft; Cassie Alexander and Anatoly Belilovsky for heroically answering medical questions (any oddities remaining are thoroughly my own); my dad for asking a lot of tactful questions about discrepancies in the third draft; my mom and Eric for taking the toddler every time I needed to finish yet . . . another . . . draft; Anne Brontë, whose work I so greatly admire; Kij Johnson and the CSSF novel workshop for invaluable advice for future novels; my agent, Ginger Clark, for all her wisdom and excellence; everyone at Curtis Brown for theirs; my editor, Melissa Frain, for her keen eye and general fantabulousness; Alexis Nixon, Susannah Noel, Irene Gallo, Larry Rostant, and everyone else on the Tor side for their support, attention to detail, and many et ceteras; all the bloggers, reviewers, podcasters, interviewers, and every single person out there who helped me share *Ironskin;* the incomparable Tinatsu Wallace for sculpting me a miniature half-mask in silver to be my lucky charm on tour; my dear friends at the St. Helens Book Shop; the wonderful librarians and booksellers who welcomed me at PNBA; and especially a tremendous thank-you to the bookstores who so graciously hosted me on the *Ironskin* tour—the Raven in my hometown of Lawrence, Barnes & Noble in Oak Park, Mysterious Galaxy in Redondo Beach, the University Bookstore in Seattle, and, of course, my beloved Powell's Cedar Hills right here in Oregon.

April 2013
Portland, Ore.

Read on for a sneak peek at the
next book in the Ironskin series

Silverblind

Available October 2014

Chapter 1

INTERVIEW

Adora Rochart had not called on her fey side for nearly a decade, except for the merest gloss of power that helped keep her unnoticeable: allowed her to slip onto trolleys without paying, to slip under the radar, and incidentally to keep breathing. When the fey had showed her how to extract the blue from her system, they advised her to keep the tiniest film of fey dust about her. There was no other creature such as she: no other half-human, half-fey, and on many things the fey could not advise her.

But the Monday morning she went to her job interviews—that morning, for the first time in seven years, she unlocked the copper box of concentrated blue, and dipped her fingers in it. More than the dusting she had had. Far, far less than her whole self.

The blue must have sparkled on her fingers before being absorbed. Surely it must have tingled. But mostly, we may never know—why that particular morning, did she decide to bring the fey back into her life? Was it for luck? Was there fey intuition at stake, telling her she was about to need it? Or was it somehow the fey themselves, desperate about all that was about to come, slipping their blue poison in her ear, telling her that she must side with them in the final war?

—Thomas Lane Grimsby, *Silverblind: The Story of Adora Rochart*

* * *

Dorie sat neatly on one side of the desk, hands folded on top of the dirt smudge on her best skirt, heart in throat. This was the last of the three interviews she'd managed to obtain—and the most important.

The desk was sleek and silver—like the whole building, shiny and new with the funds suddenly pouring into the Queen's Lab. The ultra-modern concrete and steel space had opened a scant year ago, but the small office was already crammed with the books, papers, and randomnesses of some overworked underling. On a well-thumbed book she could make out the chapter heading: "Wyverns and Basilisks: A Paralyzing Paradox." A narrow, barred window was half-covered by a towering stack of papers, but there was some blue summer sky beyond it. Perhaps if you stood on that chair and peered around it you could see the nurses marching at the City Hospital. Not that she was going to do anything so improper as stand on chairs today. This was her last chance.

The door buzzed as the underling scanned his ID medallion and walked in. Late, of course. He was probably a grad student from the University, thin and already stooped, in a rumpled blue suit, with a brown tie that had seen better days. Dorie refused to let her heart sink to her feet. There was always the chance that this boy was better than the two men she'd interviewed with that day, even if they had been higher on the ladder.

The underling sat down in his chair and moved stacks of papers with a dramatic groan for his overworkedness. Took out a pencil and began adding up a column of figures on a small notebook he carried. He didn't even bother to look up at her. "Let's get this farce over with, shall we?"

No. It was not going to go better at all.

Dorie pulled her papers from her satchel and passed them over. "I'm Dorie Rochart," she said, "and I'm interviewing for the field work position."

He dropped the papers on top of another stack without a glance and continued adding. "Look," he said to the notebook, "it's none of my doing. I'm sure you had very good marks and all."

"I did," Dorie interjected. She found his name on a placard half-buried in the remains of lunch. "Mr. . . . John Simons, is it? Pleased to meet you. Yes, I was top of the class." She had worked hard for that, after all. Firmly squashed all her differences and really buckled down. "I have a lot of fantastic ideas for ways this lab could help people that I'd really like to share with you."

"I'm sure, I'm sure," said Simons. "But be sensible, miss. You must realize they're never going to hire a girl for a field work position."

And there it was. He was willing to say what the first two men this morning had only danced around, mindful of keeping up the appearance that their labs were modern and forward-thinking and sensitive to the current picketings going on around Parliament. She could almost like him for being so blunt.

"I'm very qualified," Dorie said evenly. Of course she could not tell him exactly why she was so qualified. Being half-fey was the sort of thing where they might just throw you in an iron box for the rest of your life. If they didn't hang you first. "I grew up in the country, and I—"

"I know, I know. You always dreamed of hunting copperhead hydras and silvertail wyverns like your brothers."

"I don't have any—"

"Or cousins, or whatnot." Simons sighed and finally put his pencil down. "Look, I don't want to be rude, but can we call it a day? I still have all this data to sort through." Finally, finally he deigned to look up at her, and his mouth hung open on whatever he was going to say.

This was the look Dorie knew.

This is what she had encountered twice before today—and more to the point, in general, always. The curse of her fey mother: beauty.

He stammered through something incoherent, in which she caught the words "girl" and "blonde." Finally he settled on, "I am very sorry. Terrible policy, terrible policy. Should be hiring girls right and left. You're not going to cry, are you?"

"Of course not," she said flatly. Dorie Rochart did not cry. She might, however, cause all those papers behind Simons to dump themselves on his head. It would be very satisfying. The fey in her fingertips tingled with mischief. She tucked her hands under her legs and sat on them.

He brightened. "Oh good. I wouldn't know what to do." The mental wheels behind his eyes turned and Dorie braced herself, for now was the moment when they all propositioned her, and she didn't know what she would do then. The other two men that morning had done that . . . and her fey side had reacted.

Dorie had locked away her fey half for seven years. She couldn't trust herself with it. This morning, for the first time, she had retrieved just a trace. Just a smidge. It had felt so good, so *real.* Like she could face the day. Like she could sail through these interviews. A drop of blue, just to bring her luck.

But in seven years she had forgotten all her habits to control that part of her.

Her fingers had twitched, flicked, and had made a hot cup of tea "accidentally" spill on the first interviewer's lap. The second one, she had dropped a nearby spider down his collar. Simons had the misfortune to be third in line, and papers dumped on his head would be just the tip of the iceberg.

But to her surprise, he said, "Look, are you good at sums? There aren't any indoors research jobs right now, but I believe they're hiring more ladies to work the calculating machines. There's some girls in the physics wing crunching data."

Her fingers relaxed with this minor reprieve as she stood. He was safe for the moment. "I'm afraid not. Thank you for your—"

The door buzzed again. It swung open and a young eager face poked his head in. "Wyvern's hatching! Wyvern's hatching! Ooh, girl!" He blushed and left.

Perhaps Simons saw the light on her face, for he bended enough to say, "Look, I know you're disappointed, miss, uh, Miss Dorie." He blushed as he said her name. "I could . . . I could sneak you in to see the hatching before you go? As a, uh, personal favor?"

Dorie nodded eagerly. This was by far the most tolerable suggestive remark of the day, since it had the decency to come with a wyvern hatching.

"Stay behind me then and keep a low profile." His thin chest puffed out. "Top secret, you know? But they won't get too fussed about a girl if they see you—Pearcey brings in his latest bird all the time. I'll show you out when it's over."

Dorie followed Simons down the concrete hall to a lab room crammed with all the boys and men of the lab. He scanned his medallion and pulled her through behind him as the door opened. She caught a glimpse of the copper circle and saw a thin oval design there, its lines a faint silver glow. The same symbol was visible hanging on the lanyards of a few other men as well—some sort of new technology. Using electricity, she supposed. And a magnet, in that lock? She had not seen this sort of security before, but then she had been consumed with finishing her University studies this year.

She stood behind him, out of the way. She did not need to be told to stay to the back, as she felt conspicuous enough being the only girl. It was a clean, cold room, with metal tables and more rows of those narrow barred windows. The overhead lights were faintly tinged blue, and a smell of disinfectant hung in the air.

There was a small incubator in the middle of the room, made of glass and copper and lined with straw on the bottom. Inside was a grey egg speckled in silver. The top was thoroughly cracked and it was rocking back and forth. More chips from the egg tooth and a large piece broke off.

A man in a lab coat was making sure everyone was at their assigned station—from that and the murmurs she pieced bits together: one man was fetching a mouse for the new hatchling, another man was readying to seize the eggshell at the precise moment the wyvern was done with it and rush it to something called the extraction machine.

What was so important about the eggshell? Dorie wondered. In her childhood, she had made note of the elusive wyverns whenever she stumbled across a pair, crept in day after day in half-fey state to that bit of the forest and stared in awe. No one had been interested in them then, or their eggshells. But she was not supposed to call attention to the fact that she was here, and she did not want to be thrown out, so she did not ask.

Across the concrete room she saw someone in a canvas field hat and her heart suddenly skipped a beat. Tam had always worn a hat like that—he called it his explorer hat. She hadn't seen her cousin for seven years, not since they were both fifteen and in the fey-ridden forest and—well. She wouldn't think about that now. Dorie peered around shoulders, wondering if it could possibly be Tam. He would have liked this job, she thought. But the man turned toward her and she could see that it definitely wasn't Tam, not even Tam-a-decade-later. Of course, Tam had too much class to be wearing a hat inside.

Another crack, and the wyvern's wet triangular head came poking out. She heard an audible "awww" from someone. The man assigned to the task stood at the ready, gloved hands out and ready to scoop up the apparently precious pieces of eggshell.

The egg broke all the way open and the little wyvern chick came wiggling out. Dorie barely noticed the process with the eggshell, as her attention was taken with the wriggly wet chick. They were bright silver at this age, and the sheen of liquid left from its hatching made it shine like a mirror under the laboratory lights. It stalked along, screeching for food. A short man swung a cage up onto the table, reached in with gloved hands to grab a white mouse by the tail. Dropped it into the incubator.

The little wyvern stalked along, its tiny claws clicking on the metal, its feet splaying out as it tried to learn balance. A man moved in front of her and by the time Dorie could see again the wyvern was comfortably gnawing on the mouse.

"Bloody minded, aren't they?" said someone.

The short man brought a shallow bowl of water to set on the table and the wyvern chick stopped eating long enough to flap its wings and hiss, causing much laughter as the short man jumped back, spilling the water. A tall man in a finely cut suit said, "Doesn't like you much, does it?"

"Nasty little things don't like anyone," retorted the short man.

"And here I thought it was showing good taste," said the tall man in a pretend-nice way. The other scientists laughed sycophantically and Dorie thought this must be someone with power. She dropped her eyes as she realized he was looking back at her, and turned to Simons.

"What now?" Dorie whispered to her interviewer. "Will they return the chick to its parents?"

"Oh, no," Simons said. "We sell the hissy little things—to zoos and other research facilities, mostly. We're only interested in the eggs here, and they don't breed in captivity. Every so often someone makes arrangements with Pearce to purchase one as a pet—don't ask me why people want them. They don't like anybody. All they do is spit and scream at you, and when they're older, steam, too."

"Who's that man?" said Dorie, for Simons seemed to be in a question-answering mood. "The one looking at us."

Simons stiffened. Hurriedly he stepped in front of her as if to block the man's view. "Come on, come on, let me show you out," he said. "That's the lab director, and if he's cross about me showing you this I just don't even know. Hurry, miss."

Dorie started to the door, but stopped, Simons running into her. That boy, all the way in the corner, getting the wyvern chick more water. Wasn't that Tam after all? Or was her mind playing tricks on her now? She had not seen him for seven years, but surely—

"Dr. Pearce," said Simons, swallowing.

"Yes, this must be the one o'clock, correct?" The tall man was there, beaming down upon them in more of that faux-friendly way. "Showing her around a little bit?"

"Well, I—"

"Good, good. Miss Rochart, isn't it? If you'll come this way? I'd like to continue your interview in more comfortable quarters."

Simons looked as startled as Dorie felt, as the lab director escorted her to his office.

In stark contrast to the underling's office, this office was expansive and tidy. You could make seven or eight of Simons's office from it, and everyone knew that guys like Simons were the ones who did the real work. The omnipresent barred windows were replaced with a large plate-glass window. The new security building was across the street—a twin of this one, in blocky concrete and steel. And here was that clear view of the old hospital—and yes, the women with their placards attempting to unionize: FAIR PAY FOR FAIR WORK. A VICTORY FOR ONE IS A VICTORY FOR ALL. Dorie strained to see if she could see her stepmother, Jane, who was not a nurse, but liked a good lost cause when she saw one.

The other significant object in the room was a large glass terrarium. Its sides were made of several glass panels set into copper, including a pair of doors fastened with a copper bolt. The top was vented with mesh, and the ceiling above the whole shebang was reinforced with anti-flammable panels of aluminum. Inside this massive display was an adolescent wyvern chick, about the size of a young cat. It was curled up in a silver ball on a nest of wool scraps and looked very comfortable.

Dorie wondered how secure the copper bolt was.

Dr. Pearce pulled out the chair for her, and leaned down to shake her hand. She realized now who he was—she had heard all the stories of his tailored suits, suave manner, and ice-chip eyes. Her hope bounded upward—talking to the lab director himself was an excellent sign. She had not gotten this far with the other two interviews.

Dr. Pearce had her sheaf of papers with him—her stellar academic record, her carefully acquired letters of recommendation. He smiled at Dorie—they always did—and sat down across from her. "The lovely Miss Rochart, I presume? So pleased to finally meet you."

Dorie tightened her fingers together at the mention of her looks, but she did not stop smiling. *The Queen's Lab. Focus on the goal. With this position you could really start to make a difference. Don't drop spiders on the lab director.*

She knew what she looked like—the curse of her beauty-obsessed fey mother. Blond ringlets, even, delicate features, rosebud lips. She could put the ringlets in a bun—which she had—and put on severe black spectacles—which she hadn't; she couldn't afford such nonsense—and still she would look like a porcelain doll. She had several times tried to tease the ringlets apart in hopes they would turn into a wild mop, which she always thought would suit her better. But no matter what she tried, she woke up every morning with her hair in careful, silken curls. Even now they were intent on escaping the bun, falling down to form softening ringlets around her face.

"And I you," said Dorie. Her normal voice was high and

dulcet, but through long practice she had trained herself to speak an octave lower than she should.

He steepled his fingers. "Let's cut right to the chase, Miss Rochart—Adora. May I call you Adora? Such a lovely name."

"I go by Dorie or Ms. Rochart," she said, still smiling.

"Ah yes, the diminutive. I understand—after all, I don't make my friends call me *Dr.* Pearce *all* the time." He smiled at his joke. "Well, then, Dorie, let's have at it. I understand this is your third interview today?"

"Yes," she said. The laced fingers weren't working as well as she had hoped. She sat firmly on one hand and gripped the leg of her chair with the other. It would be terribly bad form to make that porcelain cup of tea with the gold rim levitate off the desk and dump itself down his front. "I understood that information to be private?"

"Oh, there are so few of us in this business, you understand. We are all old friends, all interested in what the new crop of graduates is doing." He smiled paternally at her. "And your name came up several times over lunch today."

"Yes?"

"Again, Adora—Dorie—let's cut to the chase. My colleagues were most amused to tell me of the pretty young girl who thought she could slay basilisks."

"I see," said Dorie. "Thank you for your time, then." She began to rise before her hands would do something that would betray her fey heritage and have her thrown in jail—or worse.

"No no, you misunderstand," he said, and he came to take her shoulders and gently guide her back to the chair. "My colleagues are living in the past. They didn't understand what an opportunity they had in front of them. But I understand."

"Yes?" Her heartbeat quickened. Was he on her side after

all? A rosy future opened up once more. The Queen's Lab—a stepping-stone to really do some good. So much knowledge had been lost since the Great War two decades ago, since people started staying away from the forest. Simple things like what to do with feywort and goldmoths and yellowbonnet. She could continue her research into the wild, fey-touched plants and animals of the forest—species were disappearing at an alarming rate, and that couldn't be good for the fey *or* humans. And then, the last several times she'd been home, she'd hardly been able to *find* the fey in the woods behind her home. When she did, they were only thin drifts of blue.

But Dorie could help the humans. She could help the fey.

She was the perfect person to be the synthesis—and this was the perfect spot to do it. The Queen's Lab was the most prominent research facility in the city. If she could get in here, she could solve things from the inside.

Surely even Jane would approve of that.

Dr. Pearce smiled, one hand still on her shoulder. "If you've met any of the young men who do field work for us, you know they grew up dreaming of facing down mythical monsters." He gestured expansively, illustrating the young boys' fervent imaginations. "Squaring off against the legendary basilisk, armed with only a mirror! Luring a copperhead hydra out of its lair, seizing it by the tail before it can twist around to bite you with its seven heads! Sneaking past a pair of steam-blowing silvertail wyverns, capturing their eggs and returning to tell the tale!"

"Yes," breathed Dorie. She put her hands firmly in her pockets.

"Those boys grow up," Dr. Pearce said. "Some of them still want to fight basilisks. But many of them settle down and realize that the work we do right here in the lab is just as important as risking your neck in the field." He perched on his desk and looked right at her. "Our country is mired in the dark ages of myth and superstition, Dorie. When we lost our fey trade three decades ago, we lost all of our easy, clean energy—all of our pride. We've been clawing our way back to bring our country in line with the technology of the rest of the world. We need some bold strokes to align us once more among the great nations of the world. And we can only do that with smart men—and women—like you."

She heard the ringing echo of a well-rehearsed speech, and still, she was carried away, for this *was* what she wanted, and more. "And think of all the good we could do with the knowledge we acquire in the field!" she jumped in, even though she had not planned to tip her hand till she was hired. "Sharing the benefits of all we achieve with everyone who truly needs them. Why, the good that can be accomplished from one pair of goldmoth wings! From a tincture of copperhead hydra venom! Do you remember the outbreak of spotted hallucinations last summer? My stepmother was the one who realized that the city hospitals no longer knew the country remedy of a mash of goldmoths and yellowbonnet. We worked together—she educating hospital staff, me in the field collecting. With the backing of someone like the Queen's Lab, I could continue this kind of work. We could make a difference. Together." She was ordinarily not good with words, but she had recited her plans to her roommate over and over, waiting for the key moment to tell someone who could really help her.

"Ah, a social redeemer," Dr. Pearce said, and a fatherly smile smeared his face at her youthful enthusiasms.

This was not the key moment.

"But more seriously, Dorie," he went on, and his voice deepened. "I would like to create a special position in the Queen's

Lab, just for you. A smart, clever, lady scientist like you is an asset that my colleagues were foolish enough to overlook." He fanned out her credentials. "Your grades and letters of recommendation are exemplary." He wagged a finger at her. "You know, if you had been born a boy we would never have had this meeting. You would have been snapped up this morning at your very first interview."

"The Queen's Lab has always been my first choice," said Dorie, because it seemed to be expected, and because it was true.

He smiled kindly, secure in his position as leader of the foremost biological research institution in the country. "Dorie, I would like you to be our special liaison to our donors. It is not false praise to assert how important you would be to our cause. The lab cannot exist without funding. Science cannot prosper. We need people like you, people who can stand on the bridge between the bookish boy scientist with a pencil behind his ear and the wealthy citizens that can be convinced to part with their family money; someone, in fact, exactly like you."

Her hands rose up, went back down. A profusion of thoughts pressed on her throat—with effort she focused to make a clear sentence come out. "And I would be doing what, exactly? Attending luncheons, giving teas?" He nodded. "Greasing palms at special late-night functions for very *select* donors?"

"You have it exactly."

"A figurehead, of sorts," said Dorie. Figurehead was a substitute for the real word she felt.

"If you like."

"*Not* doing field work," she said flatly.

"You must see that we couldn't risk you. I am perfectly serious when I say the work done here in the lab is as important—*more* important—than the work done by the hotheads out gathering hydras. You would be a key member of the team right here, away from the dust and mud and silver-tail burns."

"I applied for the field work position," said Dorie, even though her hopes were fading fast. In the terrarium behind him, the adolescent wyvern was awake now, pacing back and forth and warbling. The large terrarium was overkill—their steam was more like mist at this age. It could as easily be pacing around Dr. Pearce's desk, or enjoying the windowsill. All it would take was a little flicker of the fingers, a little mental nudge on that bolt. . . .

Dr. Pearce brought his chair right next to hers and put a fatherly arm on her shoulder. She watched the wyvern and did not shove the arm away, still hoping against hope that the position she wanted was in her grasp. "Let me tell you about Wilberforce Browne," Dr. Pearce said. "Big strapping guy, big as three of you probably—one of our top field scientists. He was out last week trying to bring in a wyvern egg—very important to the Crown, wyvern eggs."

Dorie looked up at that. "Wyvern eggs?" she said, trying to look innocent. This is what she had just seen. But she could not think what would be so important about the eggs—except to the wyvern chick itself, of course.

Dr. Pearce wagged a finger at her. "You see what secrets you would be privy to if you came to work for us. Well, Wilberforce. He stumbled into a nest of the fey."

"But the fey don't attack unless provoked—"

"I wish I had your misplaced confidence," Dr. Pearce said. "The fey attacked, and in his escape Wilberforce stumbled into the clearing where his target nest lay. Alerted, the mated pair of wyverns attacked with steam and claws. He lost a significant amount of blood, part of his ear—and one eye."

"Goodness," murmured Dorie, because it seemed to be expected. "He must have been an idiot," which was not.

Dr. Pearce harrumphed and carried on. "So you see, your pretty blue eyes are far too valuable to risk in the field. Not that one cares to mention something as sordid as money"—and he took a piece of paper from his breast pocket and laid it on the desk so he could slide it over to her—"but as it happens, I think that you'll find that sum to be very adequate, and in fact, well more than the field work position would have paid."

Dorie barely glanced at the paper. Her tongue could not find any more pretty words; she could stare at him mutely or say the ones that beat against her lips. "*As it happens,* I have personal information on what your male field scientists get paid, and it is *more* than that number." It was a lie—but one she was certain was true.

Shock crossed his face—either that she would dare to question him, or that she would dare talk about money, she didn't know which.

Dorie stood, the violent movement knocking her chair backward. Her fey-infused hands were out and moving, helping the words, the wrong words, come pouring out of her mouth. "*As it happens,* I do not care to have my time wasted in this fashion. Look, if you did give me the field job and it didn't work out, you could always fire me. And what would you have wasted? A couple weeks."

Dr. Pearce stood, too, retrieving her chair. "And our reputation, for risking the safety of the fairer sex in such dangerous operations. No, I could not think of such a thing. You would need a guard with you wherever you went, and that would double the cost. Besides, I couldn't possibly ask one of our male scientists to be with you in the field, unchaperoned. . . ." His eyebrows rose significantly. "The Queen's Lab is above such scandal."

"Is that your final word on the subject?" Her long fingers made delicate turning motions; behind him the copper bolt on the glass cage wiggled free. The silver wyvern put one foot toward the door, then another.

"It is, sweetheart."

The triangular head poked through the opening as the glass door swung wide. Step by step . . .

"Thank you for your time then," Dorie said crisply. "Oh, and you might want to look into the safety equipment on your cages." She pointed behind him.

The expression on his face as he turned was priceless. Paternal condescension melted into shock as a yodeling teenage wyvern launched itself at his head. Dorie was not worried for his safety—the worst that could happen was a complete loss of dignity, and that was happening now.

"I'll see myself out, shall I?" said Dorie. She strolled to the office door and through, leaving it wide open for all to see Dr. Pearce squealing and batting at his hair as he ran around the wide, beautiful office.